THORN

SHAWN McLAIN

HELLBENDER BOOKS

an imprint of Sunbury Press, Inc.
Mechanicsburg, PA USA

an imprint of Sunbury Press, Inc.
Mechanicsburg, PA USA

NOTE: This is a work of fiction. Names, characters, places and incidents are the product of the author's imagination or are used fictitiously, and any resemblance to actual persons, living or dead, business establishments, events or locales is entirely coincidental.

For information about special discounts for bulk purchases, please contact Sunbury Press Orders Dept. at (855) 338-8359 or orders@sunburypress.com.

To request one of our authors for speaking engagements or book signings, please contact Sunbury Press Publicity Dept. at publicity@sunburypress.com.

FIRST HELLBENDER BOOKS EDITION: October 2023

Set in Adobe Garamond | Interior design by Crystal Devine | Cover art by Colin Richards, cover design by Lawrence Knorr | Edited by Sarah Peachey.

Publisher's Cataloging-in-Publication Data
Names: McLain, Shawn, author.
Title: Thorn / Shawn McLain.
Description: First Trade paperback edition. | Mechanicsburg, PA : Hellbender Books, 2023.
Summary: Henry is a poor elf living on the outskirts of a human town. He dreams of adventure and being someone. One day he meets a half-elf girl. Together they find adventure, terror, friendship, and loyalty as they attempt to save the world.
Identifiers: ISBN : 979-8-88819-158-3 (softcover) | ISBN : 979-8-88819-159-0 (ePub).
Subjects: FICTION / Fantasy / Action & Adventure | FICTION / Friendship | FICTION / Fantasy / Dragons & Mythical Creatures.

Product of the United States of America
0 1 1 2 3 5 8 13 21 34 55

Continue the Enlightenment!

To Kathy and Carol, thanks for your support.

PROLOGUE

The Southern Kingdom of Elro was large yet sparsely inhabited. It had a few major cities, but mostly it was an agrarian society. The land was made up of rolling hills and large fertile plains. To the north was the Kingdom of Notelek.

Notelek had large cities surrounded by great defensive walls. Many of these cities were great centers of trade and commerce. While crisscrossed with rivers, the land also held vast forests and tall mountains. The woods and mountains were home to all manner of creatures, from elves and fairies to ogres and goblins. Further into the mountains and deep within caves dwelled the dark creatures, feared by many and understood by few.

The cities of Notelek surrounded themselves with high walls to separate the good people of the cities and those who were less desirable—non-humans.

The arrangement lasted for centuries until circumstances forced a change. The once powerful and plentiful elves began to die. The race of elves had lived many hundreds of years. They were rarely known to become ill, as many were powerful healers. Those who did not practice recovery Magic wielded powers that rivaled the mages. But they were no match for the coming plague.

The epidemic grew to where many forest villages and great elven cities built up and into the trees were abandoned. Many began to camp outside the human cities hoping to find work or food. While the elves had never cared much for humans, humans had other ideas about the elves.

Elves were creatures to be wary of. They had magical powers and were stronger than regular men. Many nobles even sought help from the elves in times of turmoil due to their abilities and the fact that all elves could be fierce warriors. There was one duke who had twelve elf maidens as his personal guard. Their ferocity in battle was only outmatched by their beauty and grace.

Elves were tall and lean. Their hair, while mostly pitch black, could be found in many colors depending on their use of Magic. They were masters of architecture and music and skilled craftsmen. Elven swords and armor were always sought after.

Many humans secretly rejoiced when the Elven Plague hit, for they had lived in constant fear that the elves would enslave them. So the elves became ostracized and marginalized. Finally, only villages scattered deep in the forest and settlements of ragged poor on the outskirts of cities were left. Without the elves' protection, many creatures disappeared further into the forests and mountains, avoiding the humans who despised them. This, of course, was almost their undoing.

The Elro Kingdom in the south had long envied Notelek in the north but feared their elven allies. However, once the plague decimated many of the elves, Elro thought the time had come to claim some of the wealth and prosperity of their northern neighbors. So, through the winter, the lords of Elro planned and plotted. Hiding their movements along the now empty forests, they continued encroaching further and further into their neighbor's territory.

In late spring, the armies of Elro invaded. The main forces crossed the border. Moving quickly, they joined the forces that had arrived during winter. Suddenly, armies were taking many smaller towns with little or no struggle.

As soon as Elro took over, what little diversity these armies found was swiftly and cruelly destroyed. Unfortunately, this action was not unwelcome by the residents of many of these border settlements.

Emboldened by these quick and easy victories, Elro proceeded on a steady, deadly march toward the Capital. However, a stalemate settled in by summer after a fast and victorious advance in spring.

The front lines moved back and forth along the same bloody few miles for the next three years, with no end in sight. Even after thousands of dead and multiple ineffectual generals, things in the Capital became dire. Notelek's army could not launch a counter-offensive that could stall the enemy. Finally, in desperation, the king called upon the elves and many other persecuted creatures to join the fight with promises of equality and fairness. Promises they would not receive if the Kingdom of Elro won.

With guarantees and treaties in hand, the non-humans joined the fight. In four months, the fortunes of war turned. Facing an army with Magic, numbers, and strength superior to their own, the Elro Army was forced into retreat.

Finally, after years of war, the towns and villages liberated by the demi-humans celebrated their arrival. Notelek was on the verge of victory. Elro had retreated behind their ancestral borders, and a peace treaty was nearly agreed upon.

The Elro Kingdom had invaded with the promise of an all-human world. They decried the demi-humans and renounced them as equals. Little did they realize the mantel of their fight would be taken up against them. A new threat appeared as Notelek celebrated its victory, and the Kingdom of Elro began healing.

An elven witch appeared during the peace summit. She was welcomed by Notelek as she was an ally. When it came time to sign the treaty to end the war, the witch rose up to speak, and her words stunned all in attendance as she called for the death of all humans. Then she proceeded to decimate those at the summit. From there, her army spread out to conquer the war-weary nations.

The new war raged for another two years. The Elro Kingdom now became an ally. Even though the witch called for a world devoid of humans, many demi-humans fought on the side of Notelek. They had their treaties and promises of equality. They did not want to rule the world, just to live in peace in it. Finally, the armies of Elro, Notelek, and the demi-humans overwhelmed the witch. Although rumors surrounded her capture, the mage who heroically stopped her and her disappearance continue to this day.

The end of this war left the Elro Kingdom decimated and annexed by Notelek. However, since many demi-humans rose up to join the witch's cause, all treaties and guarantees of equality were nullified. As a result, the elves, a once proud people, were left broken and hated, while many other demi-humans disappeared back into the forests and mountains. Their oaths of revenge and hatred for humans struck fear in the hearts of people who had seen war nearly devastate their world.

This is the world Henry Dreamweaver was born to, a world of uncertainty and secrets, where the shadow of an elven witch threatens to reopen the past.

CHAPTER 1

My dad has always been soft-spoken. He's known as capable of negotiating arguments and finding solutions to problems. My mom, on the other hand, is known to be firey. That's what my dad says, anyway. She has very little time for people like Mrs. Heraldry. Mr. Heraldry and my mom get along very well—too well if you ask my dad.

Mom is well known as a talented healer. Even the humans would come see her for help. But, of course, they'd never admit to it. She's also rumored to be a witch. I remember Scratch asking Mom about it once. Before she could answer, my dad said someone had mispronounced the word. As soon as he said it, I remember him running from the house, followed by Mr. Heraldry, who couldn't stop laughing. Then, a swarm of bees appeared out of nowhere to chase them around the house. Both men apologized every time they ran by the open window where Mom sat, humming to herself. Finally, on their third lap, the bees disappeared.

Scratch has been my only friend and the biggest problem in my life for as long as I can remember. His name is actually Sebastian Heraldry. No one calls him that. He's what Mom calls "an enabler." If we get into trouble, you can bet it was his idea. At least, that's the way I remember it. So, naturally, he'll claim it was my idea in the first place. I argue that I may have come up with the idea, but he would be the one to act on it. That's how it was when we were younger. After age ten, I think we can agree that whatever hijinks we got into, it was his fault, which is, of course, best all-around since, as an elf, the trouble would be far worse if it had been me alone.

Growing up, there was always something going on, always some trouble to get into. But, alas, all good things, as they say, must end. To everyone's surprise, the end came when Scratch was accepted as a cadet in the Lord of Dayok's

Guard. He was sent to the regional barracks to begin his training. Scratch left the day after my fifteenth birthday. As my father put it, this left me with not much to do and no partner in crime to help do it.

Our fathers have known each other forever. To say we are unique in our community is an understatement since humans and elves don't exactly live in harmony. The human town sits on a hill surrounded by a high wall. This border used to be where the settlement ended when they needed to defend it against invading non-humans. Those wars are long over. Now, humans have started to build houses outside the walls, expanding the city ever further.

The city lay in Notelek far from the Capital and is named Dayok, after some chief or leader (ask Scratch—he would know). I live in the elf town of Non-dayok. Creative, I know. Things were pretty simple: We rarely went into town, and they never came to our village. But now that humans have expanded past the walls, they need more land for their houses and fields. The easiest field to till is the one that has already been worked, and those are the ones held by my people.

Last summer, the old arguments about elf lands, elf rights, and human superiority, whatever that is, kept my parents up at night. Small fights between some humans and elves led to official arrests, followed by broken windows and destroyed crops. The unofficial retribution for stepping out of line. The lesson being, one elf causes trouble and all elves suffer. I've heard of other places where elves have been run out of their villages. They've had crops and homes burned and their property was taken. Some have even been killed outright, their bodies left as a warning. We're told that humans and elves aren't meant to live close to each other. So naturally, no one seems to completely trust either of our fathers. Pretty stupid if you ask me.

About a week after Scratch left, I thought I would lose my mind from boredom. Scratch and I had already explored almost every inch of the North Woods, the East Woods, and the Western Marsh. My finger lazily outlined the places I knew on an old map. I'd been to these places so often, I felt I knew them almost as well as my house. It was then that a thought hit me. Why had we never ventured into the Southern Forest? That's when I realized no one did. None of the people from the elven village or the human town ever went into those woods. I lived right next to the forest and had never thought to go in. Whenever Scratch and I left on one of our adventures, we always turned right, heading *away* from the forest.

Looking up from my map, I looked out my window toward the woods. A shock ran through me. I saw something I had never noticed before—a path leading into the forest. I didn't remember a path, just trees and brush. My internal debate lasted a breath. It was early in the day, and I had nothing better to do. I was down the stairs and out the door in an instant. My feet seemed to carry me of their own free will. As soon as I was out of the house, I felt like there was somewhere else I needed to be. Growing up with Scratch, I learned to ignore this feeling. So I headed toward where I had seen the trailhead.

Instead of a path, I found confusion. The trail I saw from my window was nowhere to be found. I retraced my steps as my annoyance grew. I knew what the problem was. I just wasn't sure of the best way around it. *Someone was hiding the path.*

However, it was not hidden well enough. One of the first spells I learned was to obscure things. This skill was necessary when doing things that might not meet parental approval. I also knew how to defeat the spell. Truthfully, I read how to do it. How hard could it be? Anyway, I channeled my thoughts and recited the incantation. Nothing happened. I tried again. This time I was pretty sure the vegetation only got denser.

On my fifth—and if this didn't work, *final*—try, the path was finally revealed. It appeared sparsely traveled yet recently used. I stood there thinking there was no way my parents didn't know about it. I wondered if they were the ones who obscured it in the first place. I shook away the thought. However, my legs that had rushed to get me here now hesitated. I had to force myself to advance. As soon as my foot hit the path, the entire environment changed. The warm sun I had been enjoying disappeared, and all sound was hushed.

"Nice try!" I shouted, hoping it was just another illusion. I steeled my nerves and took a few more steps. Finally, the day's sun and sounds returned about ten feet into the woods. After traveling for about half an hour, my excitement at finding the path waned quickly. I found nothing of interest and no evidence of either danger or magic. My great adventure had turned into a pleasant yet uneventful walk in the woods.

I had just begun contemplating returning home when I felt that I was no longer alone. Instead, I was being watched—no, not watched, *observed*. Some-one or something was curious about me. I didn't feel threatened, not really. However, I didn't like not knowing who or what was watching me. So I tried again to use the incantation to reverse an obscuring spell. Either I failed to do it right again or nothing was obscured. So next, I tried a location spell. I was successful for a moment. However, whatever was watching me moved too fast once it was detected. I searched the catalog in my mind for something to help me. Finally, I remembered the reverse view spell. This would allow me to see back to whoever was watching me.

I performed the spell perfectly on the first try. I saw myself for a second. Then I was zooming through the trees. I glimpsed something light purple and pale blue before I instantly snapped back to my current surroundings.

"Don't do that again!" a female voice commanded. The voice sounded as though it came from everywhere.

I spun on the spot, trying to locate the owner. Then, turning back to the path my vision had taken, I tried again to spy on my new companion. "Show yourself!" I ordered.

"No," came the reply.

"Why are you following me?" I demanded. Whatever little game she was playing was starting to get annoying.

This time the answer surprised me. "Because you aren't supposed to be here." She was laughing, and I saw movement off to my left. Then there was a rustling of leaves behind me. "No one ever gets this far." Her voice held amusement and perhaps a little interest. "Are you an elf?"

Her question was odd. There was no denying my elfness, as Scratch would say. "I am," I replied. "Haven't you seen an elf before?"

"My mother was an elf." Her reply no longer held amusement. "Elves are cruel, spiteful, and mean."

I rolled my eyes. I was talking to someone I couldn't see, and now they were insulting me. My patience was being tested. "How can you say that if you didn't even know if I was an elf?"

"I had to make sure." Then, as leaves fell off one tree and then another, she called, "My mother was an elf, and she hated me."

"I'm sorry to hear that," I said, then muttered, "I can see why."

"You don't sound sorry," she accused as she leaped from tree to tree.

I couldn't see her clearly, only traced her path through the disruptions. She moved in a circle, making me turn on the spot to follow her voice. I felt like I was being messed with, and I was tired of playing. So, ignoring the movement above me, I turned to head back down the path toward home.

"Where are you going?" she called.

"Home!"

"Why?"

I didn't answer. A sudden shower of twigs had me throw my arms over my head.

She was directly above me. "Hey, do we know each other?"

Her strange question set off my anger. "Hmm, I'm not sure," I shouted at her. "I'm acquainted with so many disembodied forest voices. How the hell could I tell you from the others?" There was another shower of leaves, twigs, and acorns, followed by a soft thump. Something had just landed behind me.

Slowly I turned around. I'm not sure what I expected to see, but it certainly wasn't what met my eyes. Even though she was bent over slightly with her hands on her hips, I could tell this girl was shorter than me. Your average elf, mind you, is about six feet tall. I was still growing, so I was only about five foot six. She seemed barely five feet tall, if even that. Her ears were pointed and very elf-like, while her face was more human with hints of elf. Her hair, however, was neither human nor elf. It was a light purple that lay just below her shoulders. It somehow matched and contrasted her pale blue tunic nicely. Then there were her eyes. They held the almond shape similar to my elf eyes, yet one was the brightest intense blue I had ever seen. Her hair fell across her face, generally hiding the other eye. However, I had glimpsed it a couple of times. It was the same blue at one moment and almost amber the next. She was the most unique creature I had ever encountered, yet she was somehow familiar. It was as if we had met in a dream or another life.

"What's your name?" she asked. Her smile was friendly and carefree. But nevertheless, it annoyed me for some reason.

"Greetings, my name is Henry Dreamweaver." I bowed. "And whom do I have the pleasure of gaining an acquaintance?" I asked, using my most formal tone and manner.

"Well met, Mr. Dreamweaver." She returned my bow. Then standing straight with her hands behind her back, she explained. "When I was born, my father brought my mother a rose from our garden." She paused, blinking expectantly at me. Then, when I did not reply, she continued. "When my father handed her the gift, my mother pricked her finger on it, so she named me . . . ?" She stared at me expectantly.

I shrugged. "Rose?" I asked as though it was the most obvious thing in the world.

"No!" she shouted, her smile vanishing in an instant. "No!" She stamped her foot in anger. "No, she named me Thorn!" She glared at me as if I had given her this name. "You know why she named me that?" she demanded as she advanced on me.

I found myself backing away fearfully.

"Because I was ugly and brought pain to her beautiful life. That is what that elf woman told me."

She had stopped moving. However, her glare still pierced me. Her blue eye froze me like ice while a flame seemed to burn in the amber eye. Finally, she rolled her shoulders, closed her eyes, and took a calming breath. Then, bringing herself to her full height, which was not very impressive, she exclaimed, "Yes, I am Thorn Caterous." She stood there proudly, waiting for my reaction.

"Um, congratulations?" I offered.

"Daughter of High Mage Caterous?" she explained hopefully.

I shrugged.

Her shoulders slumped. "He's really famous."

"Sure, right," I mumbled as I started walking away again, "Well, anyway, it was nice to meet you,"—I emphasized my next word—"Thorn," as she really was a pain in my side. I followed the path, thinking maybe this was why no one came here. No one wanted to be accosted by a crazy half-elf. It took me a moment to realize she was following me. I increased my pace. Suddenly she was walking right beside me.

"Whatcha doing?" she asked. She walked with her hands behind her head, not looking at me.

"Walking away—what does it look like?"

"Huh, oh, it looks boring. No, it *is* boring." She hopped in front of me, matching my pace as she walked backward. "Come on, Henry Dreamweaver, let's do something exciting, dangerous."

"And fun," I finished for her. It was the same words Scratch and I used every time we were about to do something we shouldn't.

"All right!" Thorn shouted, leaping into the air with one first raised. It was the silliest yet most endearing thing I could remember seeing. I couldn't help but grin at her enthusiasm. Her smile was bright and warm, the sunlight on her purple hair highlighting her pretty face.

There it was again, Scratch's voice in my head: *Don't bother. It won't work.*

The smile that had formed on my face slid back off. Scratch's reminder referred to the many times I had misread a woman.

"It was only twice," I grumbled.

"Huh, what?" Thorn asked. However, she didn't wait for an answer before grabbing my hand to pull me along after her. Her hand was soft, yet her grip was firm. Again, I heard Scratch's warning. He had been correct, of course. The human girl who was *interested* in me was actually just being nice. She felt bad for the poor, uneducated elf, who couldn't be productive without the firm guiding hand of the humans in town. Never mind the fact that our fields out-produced with better yield than a human's, our understanding of agriculture far outstripped theirs, and we could use *Magic*.

I had been so caught up in my thoughts that I hadn't noticed that Thorn had taken me off the path. Then, of course, the memory of the second time I made that mistake jumped into my mind. This time it led to Scratch and me not speaking for a week.

An elf maiden in my village began coming around my house. I enjoyed her company and thought we were getting close. I should have seen the signs, but I was too taken with her at the time. It was during one of her visits that it became clear. Scratch had just left for home, and she was leaving too. I realized she always left when he did, so I asked her. I found out she only came around because she had a crush on Scratch. I knew it wasn't his fault, but I was still angry with him all the same. I know it was stupid.

"Ow! What are you thinking about? You're crushing my hand," Thorn complained as she suddenly stopped.

"Nothing, sorry," I muttered as I let go of her hand. I imagined a look of disappointment when I did. However, that thought was erased as I exclaimed, "Whoa," when I saw the cave entrance she led me to. It was like something I had seen in some of my father's books. Crumbling statues of great elves stood on either side of the entrance. Old Elvish and symbols were carved across the archway. I could feel the Ancient Magic radiate from the darkness.

"I'm not supposed to go in there," Thorn explained, her voice excited yet hesitant as she glanced at me. "I probably shouldn't go in alone." She took a step away. "Especially not with a perverted elf."

"What the hell? This was your idea!" I shouted. "And I am not perverted!"

"It's okay. You can't help it." Thorn waved away my outrage. "Everyone knows all elves are. So you try to seduce humans whenever you can."

"What?" I stammered. I had never heard such a thing, even among all the other lies humans spread about us.

"I guess it will be okay," she reassured herself. "I'm only half-human, so don't bother. Your spells won't work on me." Then, without a backward glance, she disappeared into the cave.

Outraged, I followed her. "We don't try to seduce ugly ass humans!" I spat, then found myself uttering, "Whoa," for the second time in ten minutes. We stood in a cavernous room.

Thorn held up her hand, supporting an orb of light. She splayed her fingers, sending the light toward the ceiling as it brightened. I forced myself not to say "whoa" again. Clearly, her Magic skills were higher than I thought.

All along the walls were intricately carved elven pictograms and Old Elvish I couldn't read. The figures were so beautifully carved and exact that they seemed to move in Thorn's light. As I approached, I recognized the story.

It told of the migration of men of the South to the great forest. It portrayed the elves bringing civilization and agriculture to the barbaric humans. Hidden in our house was a book of Old Elvish tales, the *Ancient and Complete Record of the High Elindi,* that told this story. So naturally, it was a forbidden item to own as it portrayed a different narrative than what humans wished us to believe. Although this was far older than what was written, I was intrigued. Finally, I came across some arcane Elvish that I could barely read. From what I could make out, it told the story of the humans' betrayal and attempted enslavement of the elves. However, the wording was confusing. I thought it read, *from the enslavers to the enslaved,* but that couldn't be correct. I re-read the line, trying to remember the meaning of a word. I sounded it out to see if I could make sense of it by saying the word differently.

"It means forced conscription," Thorn explained, her face too close to mine.

"Isn't all conscription forced?" I asked, backing away, hoping the heat emanating from my face was not noticeable.

"This line here," Thorn brushed past me. She smelled faintly of flowers and sunshine. "This is why I say forced. What are you staring at?" She glared at me as I realized I was staring at her and not looking at the wall.

"Sorry, what?" I asked, trying to focus my attention.

Then, frowning at me, she shook her head in disappointment. "I told you that wouldn't work on me."

"Now, wait just a second," I complained. "I didn't do anything. You were the one who did something. How do I know you're not the one trying to seduce me?" I took a step away from her.

"Ugh, no." Her reply stung. "I'm simply trying to educate you." Her attention returned to the writing. "You see right here?" She turned quickly as if trying to catch me at something. Slowly she returned to point out a few words. "The elves were forced to fight their cousins, the goblins."

She had finally pushed too far.

"That's it!" I shouted, my voice booming against the domed ceiling. "You continually insult elves even though you know nothing about us." I stormed away, stumbling over my feet, nearly blind with anger. "We are not related to goblins!" Frustrated, I tried to locate the exit. Light in the distance told me I found the path. I rushed through it without looking back at her. Then, I burst out of the darkness into the sunshine. Now I was blindly blundering in the general direction of home. I ignored Thorn shouting my name.

I heard her coming but pretended not to. She caught up quickly and placed herself in my path. I tried to go left, then right, and she blocked me until I finally stopped. I did my best to stare daggers at her. I hoped I was even the slightest bit intimidating, but I doubt it. It didn't matter, though. She kept her eyes on the ground with her head bowed, so all I could see was the top of her head. My fingernails bit into my palms. I unballed my fists as I spat, "There she is, the human is trying again to keep the elf in his place."

"I'm sorry." Her voice was barely a whisper. "I don't really know how to talk to people."

"That's not obvious at all," I hissed sarcastically.

"That's not the way back to the path." Her quiet voice quivered slightly. She reached out tentatively. When I didn't recoil, she slowly grabbed my sleeve, pulling me in a different direction. I wasn't sure I trusted her, but we were back on the path in less than ten minutes, and she released my shirt.

"I'd like to learn more about you," she said so quietly I almost didn't hear her as her back was to me. Not only that, but her head was bowed again. She kicked at a tuft of grass. "I was just teasing about the seduction thing. I thought it would be funny. It wasn't. I'm sorry."

"Um, well, okay." I tried to stay mad, but I felt bad for being angry. Mustering my righteous indignation, I finished strong. "Just don't do it again." What I intended for her to understand was to not say things like that to elves. But unfortunately, that was not how she took it. She jumped in the air and spun to face me, an excited smile plastered across her face.

"I won't!" she exclaimed, bouncing excitedly. "When will you come back?" Her wonderfully mismatched eyes dazzled me with anticipation.

"I, well, I, um, you see," I stuttered. The smile slowly slipped from Thorn's face, and the brilliance dimmed in her eyes. My heart suddenly ached.

"Oh," she mouthed, a blush chasing the last vestiges of her smile. "You meant in general, not just with you."

"No, I mean, um, it's cool."

"Feels warm to me."

"No, I mean, I can come visit again."

"That's okay. You don't have to," Thorn said, but her tone held hope.

"No, I'd like to. I can come see you tomorrow." I couldn't believe I was saying this.

"You will? YAY!" she shouted.

Then something happened that I had never experienced before. I received a hug from a girl.

"So tomorrow then." She jumped away from me. She bent over to look up at me with a grin and bounded away laughing. I watched as she used several tree trunks to bounce between, gaining height. Finally, she reached some thin branches. She ran along the limbs, looked down at me, laughed, did a flip, then disappeared into the leaves.

I stood there smiling like an idiot for several minutes until I realized, "Wait! What time tomorrow?" I didn't receive an answer.

My thoughts spun as I thought back to the entire encounter. I was so lost in thought that I didn't even realize I had left the forest until I opened my front door. Then, thinking it might not be the best idea to venture back there to a crazy half-elf that seemed quite powerful with Magic, I decided to stay home the next day.

My feet had their own plans and to my surprise, I found myself on the path into the woods the next day. By mid-morning, I was already past where I first met Thorn. I decided to double back to see if she was waiting there. It took a bit of investigating, but I found what I thought to be the spot. I spent several minutes convincing myself that the scattering of twigs and leaves was where she jumped down.

After about an hour, I sat on the ground, playing a made-up game. It was a simple enough game with a small stick and some acorns. The goal was to hit an acorn into a hole at the base of a tree. I was starting to get pretty good at it too. I only missed every fourth or fifth time. I was trying a particularly difficult bank shot off a rock. I lined up my stick and the acorn. I judged the distance and decided how much power to put into the swing. I aimed at the portion of the rock that would deflect my shot at the correct angle, making a couple of practice swings to ensure my calculations were correct. I breathed deeply and let it out slowly as I took my swing.

The stick made contact with a resounding clack. The acorn struck the rock with a satisfying twang. It hit at the perfect velocity and precise angle. The acorn flew toward the tree, hit the ground, bounced once, then rolled the last few feet into the hole.

"Woo hoo! That was so cool!" Thorn shouted from behind me. "You're really good at this game!"

After I recovered from the scare and my heart finally returned to a normal pace, I asked her how long she'd been watching.

She was doing that bowed thing while digging her heel into the dirt. "Oh, about forty-five minutes." Then, she stood up and moved too close to me. "Show me how to play."

Forty-five minutes? I couldn't believe this girl. I had been bored out of my mind waiting for her, and she had been here almost the entire time. "Why didn't you let me know you were here?" I growled.

If she noticed my annoyance, she didn't show it. Instead, she selected a stick and gathered a handful of acorns. Then to my horror, she knelt down in the dirt. Her richly embroidered suede pants got dirty, and the fine linen tunic brushed the ground. The tunic, I noticed, had an intricate ivy pattern running along the sleeves. It matched the pattern on her trousers and continued all the way to her extremely well-made boots. Her outfit was finer than the richest person in Dayok could afford. One of her boots was probably worth more than my family's house. Yet, here she was, grinding dirt into the knees and tips of the boots as if they were nothing special.

After standing straight and dusting herself off, Thorn slapped me on the arm. Brought back from wondering how rich she must be, I was overcome by her smile. How her pale skin held a bluish tint contrasting with her purple hair. Her intense blue eyes flashed with excitement. *But wait, I thought they were mismatched.*

"Hey," she said, waving a hand in front of my face. "Come on, teach me how to play."

"Well . . ." I shrugged. "I just made it up while I was waiting for you."

"That's so cool!" she exclaimed as she jumped up and grabbed my hand, pulling me along to sit on a log. "Let's make some rules and assign point values." Her excitement was infectious. So we sat together, making and agreeing on some rules and points for shots. Then it was time to play Sticky Bat. We laughed every time we said it, especially since one rule was your points didn't count unless you shouted "Sticky Bat!" at the end of your turn.

In our first few games, I won easily. By the time I realized I hadn't eaten all day and it was getting close to dinner time, Thorn and I were pretty well matched. So, when I told her I had to go home, the look on her face made me feel like I had just told her I was taking away her new puppy. She only brightened when I promised to meet her again tomorrow.

Thorn walked me back to the edge of the woods. When we arrived at the point where we could see my house, I asked, "You want to come have dinner with us?" I could see a yearning in her eyes. "I'm sure my parents wouldn't mind."

"I can't," Thorn whispered fearfully. Then, she took a step back into the shadows. "I shouldn't be this close." She continued to backtrack. "Don't tell anyone you met me." She froze, her eyes wide with fear. "You didn't already tell someone, did you?" Her hand caught my upper arm in a death grip as she pulled me behind a tree. "Please, please, tell me you haven't told anyone about me," she pleaded as she pinned me to the tree. Tears welled up in her eyes. She tried to hide them by resting the top of her head against my chest.

I thought hard and couldn't remember seeing anyone yesterday or this morning. So I couldn't have told anyone about the mystery girl I met in the woods. When I told her this, she nearly collapsed with relief.

Thorn held my arms for support as she laughed nervously. "Thank you—thanks—gods." Her relief was fleeting. Her eyes met mine with hard intensity. Her face tightened, as did her grip. "You can't tell anyone about me."

Her grip was starting to hurt. Nevermind her small stature—this girl was strong. Trying to shrug off her vice-like grasp, I asked, "Why not, and ow!"

"Sorry." She loosened her grip but didn't let me go. "If you tell, we'll both be in big trouble." Finally, she released my arms, letting her hands fall to her sides. I saw that doubt in her eyes again. "Maybe you shouldn't come back tomorrow," she mumbled as she resumed a stance I would come to hate. Her head was down with her shoulders slumped in defeat.

"Well, that's too bad." The words came out quietly. I cleared the reservation from my throat and continued. "I still want to win *every* game of Sticky Bat. But since you're my only opponent, you'll just have to play me again tomorrow."

I shrugged as if this was obvious, and *there* was the prize I was looking for. Her infectious smile and the sparkle in her—wait—green and blue eyes. I'd have to ask her about that sometime.

"Really? Yay!" she jumped up with her fist in the air again. Weird but cute. Then cute was replaced with that scary intensity. "But you can't tell anyone about me."

"Okay, okay," I assured her, "I won't tell a soul."

Thorn grabbed my hand, giving it a squeeze before she jogged back into the woods. I was about to step out when she called to me.

"Make sure no one sees you coming or going." She did that strange bending over with her hands on her hips and smiling at me thing. Then, without waiting for a response, she did a kind of turn, jump, skip thing, and then ran off out of sight.

Smiling, I checked my surroundings carefully and exited the woods. Then, I saw my first test around the corner of my house.

My mother was just walking up to our front door. "You seem awfully happy," she called out.

"It's just a really nice day." Of course, I tried to make up a better reason. Fortunately, my mother was distracted by her own thoughts and didn't press me for information.

Nevertheless, Thorn's concern that I should not tell anyone about her weighed on my mind through dinner. I tried to follow the conversation my parents were having. They were discussing some rumored new restrictions on elf travel. My mother was saying something about not taking something for some time or something.

"Is there another town to the south of here?" I asked as I pushed my food around my plate. I didn't mean to say it out loud, nor did I expect it to cause the bizarre reaction it did. I looked up to see the concern on my parents' faces. They blinked at me, then exchanged some non-verbal conversation that told me I needed to explain.

"I just was thinking we never go south." I pretended to be only slightly interested. "The Empire's Capital of Notelek is north, and Ebensburg is east. There was that place you took me to once in the West." I acted like I was trying to remember the name. "Warrentston, that was it. I just thought, what's south of here?"

"As you already know, we're close to the border here," Dad explained. "There are some towns, but they weren't originally part of our country. And they aren't friendly to our kind, so we don't interact with them."

"What are the elves like there?" I asked in what I hoped was an innocent tone.

"What few live there are the same as us. Why do you ask?" My mother's tone was as innocent as mine, but I could tell I had pushed too far.

"No reason. May I be excused?" I decided to end the conversation, as I regretted even starting it. I also remembered a book in our library on the different clans of elves. But, of course, I had just made it more difficult to grab that book without raising suspicion.

"If you're interested in other elves, why not read that book we have?" My mother suddenly suggested. The warning look she received from my father was waved away. Something was going on. Something that made it less suspicious for them but far more for me. I just opened up a box of some kind of trouble.

As I left the table, I heard the urgent whispers of my parents. "Something happened. He saw or heard something," my father hissed.

"More likely, it was something deeper. I never agreed to what was done," my mom countered.

"It was for the best." Dad's voice was firm as if that was all to be said.

"Was it?" my mother asked before she noticed I was hovering. "*Deu Noch ser num*," she quickly proclaimed in Old Elvish. It meant, *we'll discuss this later*. I had long ago learned the language when I got tired of them having discussions I couldn't understand. Unfortunately, this skill was discovered. Now they had their private discussions in a closed room. My mother placed a charm on the door to keep them from being heard.

I retreated to the library, as we called it. The room contained maybe fifty books. In an elf household, that was extraordinary. Nevertheless, I quickly found the old tome I was looking for. It was the largest book we owned, other than the one hidden deep in a closet in my parents' room.

I loved this book. The cover was faded leather, the embossed lettering nearly completely warn away. The pages smelled of old tobacco smoke and lost knowledge. When I was younger, my mom read to me about her people far to the north. I remember thinking that all the history of the elves was contained here. The hidden book held the fairytales. So I began searching for references about half-elves and their powers and characteristics. I also wanted to know about the mages. I assumed they were humans or elves that were gifted in Magic. Maybe they weren't what I thought. I pictured Thorn in my mind, the odd hair color, her changing eyes, or even the faint bluish tint to her skin I noticed when we played Sticky Bat.

I barely noticed when Dad lit a lantern for me. When I nodded off, I realized how late it was. I had been reading for a few hours. Finally, tired and frustrated, I closed the book and set off for bed. There was no reference to anything about mages and elves having children. The only real mention of mages was they were not to be trusted. "Magical beings that wielded incredible power." That was helpful, but not.

I spent a restless night thinking about my parents' whispered conversation and Thorn's claim she was a half-elf, half-human. From what I read, there were obvious signs of a human-elf union, the mix of her human and elf features. However, that did not explain so many of the traits that were neither elf nor human. A terrible thought gnawed at my stomach. I wondered if she might be something else entirely. A shapeshifter would be bad news. It would, however, explain a lot, like why there was an enchantment on the Southern Forest. It was a warning to stay out. Then there was her short stature and unfamiliarity with elves. She might have only seen them from afar. I would have to test her when we met up in the morning. Judging by the sky, the morning wasn't too far away.

I had just closed my eyes for what felt like a second when I heard my mom calling me. "Henry, get up! It's mid-morning, and I'm leaving for the Wetherlys," she yelled up the stairs to me. "I left some muffins for you. See you tonight."

I heard the front door shut. My bed did not want to let me get out of it. After realizing I had fallen asleep the second time, I finally managed to exit my covers. After a quick wash, I dressed and searched through my desk drawers for the silver pendant my grandmother had left me. I remembered her telling me it would uncover the truth of many creatures who choose to hide their identity.

I grabbed a muffin and some fruit for lunch and headed into the woods to meet with Thorn. I would just casually show her the pendant and see how she reacted. The silver would burn her if she were something other than what she said she was. I know that sounds mean, but shapeshifters are dangerous. They're known to lure people into hazardous situations or abduct them to take over their lives. I'm not really sure, but I heard they were bad news. It was better for her to have a small burn and for me to be safe than for her to eat me. But, on the other hand, if she really was an elf, the silver would sing.

After a brief trek into the forest, I spotted her. "Been waiting long?" I asked with a wave.

She smiled as she waved back. "Only just got here. I think I'm supposed to say, 'been waiting an hour, actually.'" She laughed.

"Hey, want to see something cool?" I asked. Might as well get this out of the way, especially since I was still somewhat close to home. My dagger suddenly felt heavy on my hip. "I found this talisman my grandmother gave me years ago."

Thorn was immediately interested. "My father has tons of talismans. He said there were several to keep my mother away."

I forced a chuckle as I handed her the pendant. Thorn looked at it sitting in the palm of her hand for a second, then covered it with her other hand and began screaming as if in agony. I jumped away in terror.

Guilt constricted my heart. "I'm so sorry," I cried. "I didn't think it would hurt you that much."

Her cries of pain turned to whimpers that morphed into giggles, then into full-blow laughter. Wiping tears of mirth from her eyes, she held the pendant between her thumb and forefinger. It hummed in a calming way. It was singing. Her emotions changed from humor to what I could only describe as disappointment. "You really thought I was a shapeshifter?" She tossed the charm back to me.

I caught it and kept my head down, looking at it.

"As I said, Father collects them."

"I'm sorry, it's just I . . ." I mumbled, embarrassed.

"You've never seen anyone like me before."

I knew she glared at me with her hands on her hips, bowed slightly. I didn't even have to look up.

"I have weird hair, and sometimes my eyes act weird when I do Magic."

I chanced a glance at her. Thorn's back was to me. She was starting to pace.

"Just another *gift*." There was spite in the word. "From my mother." She kicked at the dirt, sending it flying over my already dirty and worn boots.

I did not protest. I deserved Thorn's ire.

Thorn grabbed a handful of her hair. "She used a potion or spell. Father explained it once."

I rushed to stop her from hurting herself. "I like it," I yelled.

"Just another way she could make sure I was different, shunned and alone," she raged. "Whatever she could do to keep my life miserable." Thorn let loose a growl that turned into a scream. "I didn't ask to be born. It wasn't my fault. Wait, what?" She was staring intently at me.

"I said I like it," I replied, not meeting her gaze.

Thorn smoothed her hair. "Then why did you test me?"

"You're just so different." I swallowed. "I was researching elves and humans and their children. There was never anyone like you. I guess whatever your mother did is why." I was rambling.

"Yes, my mother did this to me." She stopped fidgeting.

"You could have told me." I shrugged.

"You could have asked."

"Would you have told me?" I couldn't hide my disbelief.

"Why wouldn't I?" she asked, confused. "We're friends, and friends tell each other everything, don't they?"

Her words hit my stomach like lead. "You're correct," I agreed. "I'm not a very good friend. I'm sorry."

She looked at me critically. "Well, you're the only one I have, so . . ." A slight smile appeared. "Try to do better. I don't want to have to find a new one."

I had never been anyone's only friend. Of course, Scratch was my best friend, but I knew he had human friends. I knew how Thorn felt as I had only one friend up until that moment. It was weird to have two. I wondered if they would get along.

"I'll do better," I promised. "What do you want to do today?"

Then, I remembered the elf girl and decided I didn't want to know if Thorn and Scratch would get along.

CHAPTER 2

Seventeen years earlier

T he mage must be stopped!" a demi-human with raccoon markings shouted.

"If it were not for the mage, we never would have taken the western territories."

"But at what price?"

Surrounded by his advisors, a military general sat listening to the debate as more fights broke out. The man shook his head slightly in frustration. Slowly a bear-woman leaned over to whisper in the general's ear. She was one of his most trusted soldiers. But unfortunately, the news she delivered wasn't what he'd hoped. As soon as he stood, the hall became quiet.

"I am afraid negotiations have failed." At his words, a murmur rippled through the crowd. "Althea will not stop the purge." He sighed heavily.

"What can we do? We can't go up against the witch!" someone shouted.

Agreement to his words echoed.

"Where has Caterous gone? He could help."

Anger grew among the crowd. "Where are they? They should stop her!"

The bear-woman rose. "We have a secondary plan in place. The mission is already underway."

"What is it?"

"How will this help end the wars?"

"Will we finally have a homeland?"

"Please, please," she shouted over the soldiers' questions. "We will know by dawn if the plan has succeeded." Then, her tone returned to the familiar one of the commander. "If it has failed, we will advance on the fortress." A large map was brought in and laid on the table before her. On it were a representation of mountains and a castle on the far east of Notelek. On the plains before the castle, represented by several small flags, were the unified armies of Notelek. "I need the commanders to gather. The rest of your fighters, recover your strength and ready your weapons. For tomorrow may be the hardest fought of the war."

Far from the meeting, three shadows advanced up the sheer rock face. Their goal was a small window, barely large enough to be a vent. It was still at least fifty feet up, while the drop below was at least a hundred. Thanks to an anti-gravity spell, they moved with great speed and stealth. While it wouldn't keep them from falling, it did help them from tiring. When they reached the window, they paused to listen. No sound met their ears. One by one, they slipped into the fortress of the enemy.

———✧———

Dawn broke. Horns blared to announce the advance. An army of elves, demi-humans, goblins, men, and orcs began their march. Their last-ditch attempt to avoid this battle had failed. The ranks were quiet, knowing that today would likely be the last for many of them. The fortress stood ominously, staring down at the advancing army.

The general and his second rode in the lead. "Ursula." He held out his hand to the bear-woman. "When this is over, if we win the day, there's something I must ask you."

She squeezed his hand tightly. "When this is over, then."

Tension mounted in the soldiers as their pace increased. Any moment the black gates would open. The enemy forces would pour out, and the fighting would begin.

Then, finally, it was time. The herald brought the horn to his lips, prepared to signal the charge. Hesitating at first, he took in an extensive breath.

"Hold! Hold!" the general and his commanders shouted. Two soldiers emerged from the shadows, each helping the other toward the troops. Then, limping behind them, a third man emerged. Murmurs of fear and excitement met the trio. Curious fingers pointed at the figure that floated in front of the third man. A body was bound in a huge bag and wrapped in glowing chains. All three men were covered in blood and wounds.

"It is done." One of the soldiers said as the three fell to their knees. From above, chaos erupted. The black gates did indeed open. Instead of an army advancing to battle, it was a panic flight. Some attempted to organize to fight.

Arrows rained down. The fighting that followed was short yet costly. None left in the citadel survived the day.

For the winning army, the victory was marred as with any battle by those who were lost. The great general sat alone in his quarters. He did not get to ask Ursula his question.

Memories of that day swirled in the minds of two elves and a human who sat drinking at an elf pub.

CHAPTER 3

I snuck out of the forest that night, tired, a little dirty, and grinning from ear to ear. Thorn and I had explored all day. We found a cave behind a waterfall where we told each other stories of how the cave might have been used. We sat under a huge weeping willow, eating lunch and discussing the Magic we knew. She was far more knowledgeable than I was. We talked about our families. It was really only me telling her about mine. She got along with her father, but other than some words of disgust, she would not speak about her mother. Then, without thinking, I mentioned Scratch. That memory chased the smile away with a nervous twinge in my chest.

Thorn had been excited to hear about my human friend. When I told her he was training with the Lord of Dayok's Guard, I didn't miss the wistful look in her eyes. They were back to that electric blue I could stare at forever.

I wasn't stupid. I knew Scratch's appeal—strong, tall, and apparently handsome for a human. Fortunately, the conversation didn't last long. That was one of the great things about Thorn. At this point, she was easily distracted. So I turned the conversation to Old Elvish, which took us to the end of our day together.

I hopefully refrained from anything suspicious at dinner. I asked about my parents' day and lied about mine. I said I was out in the East Woods, reading and doing some exploring. A raised eyebrow from my dad was all I got in response. Inwardly I cursed myself. Dad and I knew there wasn't an inch of the East Woods Scratch and I didn't know by heart. Fortunately, he didn't press the issue.

I was worried about how I'd keep coming up with stories to tell them. However, this became less of a problem. Apparently, trouble was brewing in Nondayok. My parents began spending a lot of time in the village, coming home late, too tired to hold much of a conversation. I decided it was best not to ask too many questions. We'd had trouble before, and my parents always worked it out.

As time went by, Thorn and I spent almost every day together. We'd make up games, or she'd teach me new spells. She'd bring books from her father's library. We'd read about Magic, history, and even some fiction about heroes and adventure. We'd make up stories about adventures we would have. We also became braver—or more foolish, depending on your point of view.

One rainy sort of day, we snuck into my house. Thorn stood in our tiny, unimpressive living room library in awe. "I have never been in anyone else's house. This is wonderful." She picked up some trinkets Dad had collected. "Are all elf houses like yours?"

"No, we're a little better off," I muttered. I knew many of our neighbors had much less than we did. Add to that Dad's friendship with Mr. Heraldry; we weren't the most trusted of families. I decided not to mention that.

After that, we snuck into other places. I took Thorn to the East Woods to show her all the places Scratch and I found. We hid at the edge of town so she could watch the humans doing business. I remember explaining why some women had blue or bright red hair. "You mean they do that on purpose?" She gawked.

"They would rather have wild-colored hair instead of letting anyone know they're getting older."

"That's wild?" Thorn looked at her light purple locks, then at me. "Would you like it better if mine was brown or black?"

I told her no, then later, I took her to watch the elf farmers. Everything was new and exciting to her. I loved being able to bring so much to her life.

Then I got a letter from Scratch's father. Scratch would be home for a few days. Of course I was excited to see him, and I accidentally told Thorn. She was even more excited. That was when the thought of sharing her with Scratch or the rest of the world became something I wasn't ready to do. Selfishly I decided she wasn't ready to meet more people. So, every time she brought up meeting Scratch, I'd change the subject. Finally, after several tries, she stopped asking about meeting him. Then, the day before Scratch arrived, Thorn asked if I would come to visit her.

So I lied to Thorn about having to help Mom in town, and I went to visit my only other friend. I felt terrible about the lie. However, things didn't improve when I met with my old pal. I wasn't really lying to him so much as omitting Thorn. I was sick to my stomach. Scratch could tell something was bothering me. Thankfully, he didn't press the issue.

"Hey, Dreamweaver," he said, "I'm sorry I split for the guard this summer."

I could see he meant it. "Naw, it's cool—don't sweat it." I tried to play it off like it was no big deal. I loved hanging out with Thorn, but I would be lying if I said I hadn't missed my partner in crime. I was hoping he had some new adventure in mind that would take my mind off the guilty feelings I had. But, unfortunately, this was one of the days Scratch didn't feel like leaving town, and the reason was obvious. The giggle of human girls was unmistakable. I rolled my eyes and accepted that today would not be very interesting.

Scratch was sitting on top of the wall surrounding his garden. I envied his apparent lack of caring about what others thought of him. But I remained out of sight for his sake and my own. Elves were not exactly welcome in Dayok, a fact Scratch and his father never seemed to notice or take seriously enough.

His mother was another story—I was happy she was out running errands. Scratch's mother and mine couldn't be any more different. Mrs. Heraldry rarely left Dayok. Even after all these years of knowing my mom and dad first, and now me, she still feared elves. When we visited, she'd generally stay out of the way. One visit, I guess she thought we'd left. We walked in as she counted the silverware and other knick-knacks. I had never heard Mr. Heraldry raise his voice until that day. I always thought he was easygoing and smiling and that nothing seemed to upset him. He was scary, possessing a violence and strength I had never seen before. Scratch's mother had cowered under his gaze before he even raised his voice.

"I will not stand for this kind of ignorance in my home! You dare insult my friend?"

I swear the room shook. Even though my father was also angry, he placed a hand on Mr. Heraldry's arm, an action I had never seen an elf do. My dad whispered something in Elvish to Mr. Heraldry as he made a quick gesture toward Scratch and me. Whatever was said calmed the man. I asked Scratch about it later. He'd never seen his father lose control like that either. His mother left the village for a while to visit her mother, but I think she was sent away by Mr. Heraldry. When we came home and told my mom what happened, I saw a fire ignite in her eyes. Again, dad said something in Old Elvish I could not understand. However, it calmed my mother. Then my dad said something to my mom about mistakes and ale. I didn't catch all of it. It defused the situation almost immediately, leaving my mom laughing.

"Yo, Henry, come check this out."

Scratch's voice pulled me back to the present, and I released the poor blades of grass I had unconsciously been mangling.

I knew, without even looking, that girls had caught Scratch's attention. Why he thought I would be interested, or more to the point, they would be interested in me, was a mystery. Like I said—Elf. Knowing my presence would not improve his slim-to-none chance of impressing a girl, I didn't move from the shadow at the foot of the wall. I liked being unseen. It's harder to hit a target that you're unaware is there. Even better if the side of the stone partition I was leaning on wasn't facing the road.

"Henry, dude, you have to see this!" Scratch insisted. He started pushing my head with the toe of his boot. I seriously thought about shoving him over the wall. *That* would impress this girl. The thought of Scratch falling into some horse manure made me smile, but I stayed my hand at the idea of causing him injury. He was goofy, unaware, and kind of a screw-up, but he was my friend. Grudgingly I got to my feet. As I expected, several girls gathered around some stalls set up in the middle of town.

I sighed. "I told you, human girls are not going to be interested in me." I frowned at him. "Or you, for that matter, if they see you with me." I ground my teeth in anger. He wasn't even listening to me. But then, I noticed he wasn't looking at the same girls I was. Instead, his attention was on a lone figure meandering toward the square.

Scratch slapped my chest with the back of his hand. "Look, look, look. Is that an elf?"

I slapped his hand away as I glared at him. Then, I looked at the approaching person. They were definitely female, but not exactly an elf and not entirely human. "Oh drat," I breathed as my stomach disappeared to be replaced with hot, boiling terror.

"Is she a halfling?" he asked.

I cringed at the term. It was better than "pointy-eared freak" or "stinking half-breed," but still unpleasant. The girls at the stalls had not noticed her yet. As soon as they did, we were in trouble.

"Dude, wait, hey, where are you going?" I heard Scratch call as I ran to the half-elf.

Why in the world was Thorn here and walking around like it was totally normal? Here in Dayok, an elf, even half-elf, wandering around with exposed ears, was forbidden. Top it off with the fact that her pale skin was offset by light purple hair, one shining ice-blue eye, and one green as a spring field. Why did she have to have mismatched eyes today of all days? Blue eyes are not unusual for elves—most of us had blue eyes—but they always matched. To top it all off, she was also wearing more refined clothing than the rich daughters of Dayok. This could only mean trouble.

She waved as I ran toward her then pulled her into an alcove. "What the hell! Elf boy, you better re-think what you're doing!" She pushed me hard against the wall as I pulled off my cloak.

"What the hell are you doing here?" I demanded. "You have to cover your ears." I thrust the cloak to her. "And you never look humans in the eye."

"What? Why? Oh, and you lied to me," she explained grumpily. "What's wrong with my ears, and why can't I look them in the eye?" Confusion crossed her face.

I kept a lookout. Thankfully, the town girls still hadn't noticed anything. If I could get her back to the safety of Scratch's garden, we'd be safe. Then, I could borrow something from him, and our dads could sneak her back out of town.

"My father told me it shows you acknowledge their superiority," I explained. She looked outraged. "I'm not saying they are." I threw my hands up. "It isn't right, but that's the way of things for now." I couldn't believe this girl.

She looked me up and down. Her face held skepticism.

"Hey, as a matter of fact, an elf was nearly beaten to death on the road outside of town. It was said he wouldn't cover his ears or avert his eyes to a group of humans."

Still looking doubtful, she pulled on the cloak. To my horror, she sniffed it, and her nose scrunched up in disgust. "This stinks."

I couldn't help but glare at her.

"Um, thank you," she said sheepishly.

"What happened to, '*You can't tell anyone about me*?'" I fought to keep from shaking her. "We always kept out of sight. What made you want to walk right into town?"

I realized Thorn stood out far more than I did. We might have been able to keep her ears from poking out of her hair, but there was no hiding that color. So I pulled the hood further up.

"What are you doing?"

I almost laughed at the look of disgust on her face. "You need to hide your hair as well as your ears," I said, looking out to the street. I didn't see anyone. When I looked back, Thorn adjusted the hood and stuffed her disheveled hair under it.

"I didn't think my hair would be a big deal after we saw the human women," she offered apologetically.

Without thinking, I reached up to push some hair she had missed back into the hood. You would have thought I smacked her in the face from the way she jumped backward. I was stunned by her reaction and how soft her hair was. The way she was looking at me was like something stuck to the bottom of her shoe. Her eyes felt like they were trying to burn a hole through my face. So, I said the only thing I could.

"Why are you so angry?" I hissed.

My question refueled her anger. "You lied and said you had to do something with your mother." Her voice was calm, barely a whisper, yet I felt in big trouble. "I saw her leaving your house alone."

I couldn't think of anything to say, and unfortunately, I didn't get a chance.

"You there! Elf, what are you doing skulking back there?"

I turned to face the gruff voice, trying to hide Thorn from view. I was trying to push her further back. I thought she understood until—

"Stop that! What are you trying to do?" she demanded. My heart froze.

A leather-clad hand grabbed me painfully by my ear, pulling me out into the street. A small crowd was already gathering, including the town girls, pointing and laughing behind their hands. My knees collided with the cobbled street.

"This disgusting elf was trying to molest a young maiden."

My blood froze in my veins, yet pounded loudly in my ears. A town inspector towered over me. I recognized him as one of the commanders. His job was to keep order—in other words, to keep the elves in line. I could see the disgust and hatred in his eyes. Panic churned in my stomach, making it hard to breathe.

"How dare you parade your deformed ears in front of good people," he roared, his gloved hand connecting painfully with my face. "Come out, child— it's okay. We'll keep you safe from this repulsive creature."

She had to escape. I prayed she would just run. *Run to where?* I couldn't think of a safe place. We were too far from the Southern Forest. Maybe if I made a diversion? What tiny glimmer of hope I had evaporated when she didn't run. Instead, Thorn stepped out with her head bowed. She kept glancing at me, her face unreadable. I tried to tell her to run, but the inspector's foot collided with my back, sending me sprawling.

The breath was knocked out of me. I threw out my hands to keep from going face-first onto the cobblestones. The thick heel of the inspector's boot rested on the back of my head, pushing me down. Mud smeared onto my face. Blood coated my tongue when I tried to tell her to run. The blood mixed with the filth from the road garbled my words. I mouthed it, I motioned with my eyes—everything. Then she did what I prayed she wouldn't. She dropped her hood.

"Why?" She was looking down at me. Then she turned her eyes to the stunned inspector.

His mouth fell open, recovering quickly. His warm tone and demeanor dropped faster than Thorn's hood. Suddenly the pressure on my back eased as the man stepped away. Many in the crowd recoiled.

"Disgusting," I heard him murmur before I cried out. His boot crashed into my ribs.

"You see!" the man cried. "Like rats, they find a dark hole, and there, even in public, they're trying to breed."

"That's disgusting!" Thorn yelled as several in the crowd agreed. "How dare you say that." She pointed accusingly at him. Her look was defiant even though he towered over her. His thick leather and steel armor creaked as he took in her appearance.

The fact that she was female and young made little difference to this man. The inspector grabbed Thorn by the hair, lifting her off her feet. Thorn's scream hurt me more than the injuries I had already sustained. She cried out as she dangled in his hand, clawing at his leather glove. He snarled and threw her on top of me, and my ribs, already hurt from the kick, cracked.

"This creature is even less human than that elf!"

I couldn't move my head. All I could see was the inspector's boots moving slowly toward us, and I knew he would beat us. I wanted to cover my ears. I didn't want to hear Thorn's pain. I didn't think I could move my arms, so I closed my eyes tight.

Thorn began squirming and painfully shifted off my back. I could breathe again. I tried to call out to her to run. All I could muster was a whimper. Curling into a ball of pain, I saw Thorn on her feet again. Her fists balled at her sides. I closed my eyes against the agony.

"How dare you!" Her voice was a growl.

The crowd gasped and cried as heat pulsed over me. I opened one eye. I watched the feet of our tormentor stumbling back. The whole area had turned red. Thorn's angry voice thundered for a second, "I demand you . . ."

Then everything changed.

Something thudded next to me. Thorn was on her knees.

A sniff of contempt turned to a bark of laughter. "Not so tough now, half-breed," the guard sneered.

Thorn braced herself with her hands while my broken ribs screamed in protest as I tried to crawl to her. As I got closer, I could see more of her; what I saw was horrifying. Blood ran down her face from above her left eye, and a deep wound gaped on her forehead. Her already pale face lost what little color it once had. The guard's shadow told me he had used his mace on her. I watched in horror through the shadow as he raised the weapon again to deliver a fatal blow.

With all the strength I had left, I threw myself over her. I knew I couldn't let him kill her. I braced for the blow that didn't come.

"Stop!" A voice reverberated against the stone walls. Although it wasn't loud, it carried a power that commanded. I took a chance to glance up. A man in a dark, thickly embroidered purple robe stood alone on the road holding a long staff with a wolf's head carved on the end. People hurried away in terror. "What gives you the right to beat children?" the man demanded, slowly advancing on the obviously nervous inspector. Our savior's staff struck the cobblestones with each step, sending sparks into the air. I cradled Thorn the best I could, trying to keep her out of sight as the robed man finally stopped a few feet from the now cowering inspector.

The man who, seconds before, was ready to kill us was now reduced to unintelligible muttering. Then, I realized several voices whispered the same question as the robed man. Even though the people were now questioning his actions, our attacker kept looking to the crowd for support. Straightening his posture and smoothing his clothing, the inspector attempted to regain his composure. Now, he stood straight and tall. His face contorted in arrogance and defiance, although sweat formed on his forehead. Finally, he found his voice, even though it cracked at first. Defiantly, he explained, "They're elves. Disgusting creatures that breed like rabbits. I was doing my duty to keep the vermin in check."

"Are they not subjects of the empire?" the robed man questioned. His tone made me shiver, filled with a quiet fury that pulsed with malice.

"Well, yes, but—"

"They are children *and* subjects of the empire!" The staff hit the stones, sending up another shower of sparks. The inspector stepped back. "The only disgusting creatures are the ones who attacked the innocent." Now the robed man turned to address the crowd. "And those who did nothing to stop it." An uncomfortable murmur spread through the spectators as they quickly shuffled away.

Even though I felt we were no longer in danger, I still held Thorn close, but I also became aware she was talking. Not out loud, though. I don't know how, but I heard the conversation in my head. I heard her begging the robed man, "Please, Father, don't hurt anyone. This is my fault—please."

My breathing, which was already difficult, caught in my chest. The man in the elegant robes was Thorn's father, meaning this man was a powerful mage! To my shock, she was also begging him not to kill the man about to kill her. I hazarded a look at the man—Caterous. His eyes blazed with power and fury. I swear I saw death in his gaze. Then, for a second, he glanced at me. I saw surprise and recognition. If I had blinked, I would have missed it.

Then I heard his voice in my head. "Enough, Daughter! You will be silent. You will claim to be a cousin of this . . ." He paused as his eyes flicked back to me. If his anger was intense, it was equally matched by his look of annoyance. "Of all the elves, Henry Dreamweaver? Thorn, you will say you're a Dreamweaver from Norslandia." If the shock of being known to a mage wasn't enough, for him to address me in my mind was double that shock. "Dreamweaver, you will also go along with this charade."

Our mental conversation was interrupted verbally by the inspector. I had almost forgotten he was here. "I am an official of Dayok and a soldier of the empire. I must do my duty to enforce the laws of decency."

"Decency!" Caterous roared. "What can children of this age do that is indecent?" As the mage advanced on the now shaking and whimpering official, Caterous's staff was sparking again, leaving small craters with each step he took. "Your mind is what is indecent here. You are sick!" The few townsfolk who still supported the inspector quickly melted into the background.

"I have a right and a duty to keep good people free from vermin," the guard spat, trying to save what little dignity remained.

"Your actions shall be reported," Caterous spoke over the guard's quivering protest.

I heard someone running toward us. Next, I heard Scratch's mother's panicked breathing. "Oh dear, oh dear," she whispered. "I, I can't help—they're too badly hurt." She was fussing over Thorn and me. Her worry and kindness toward me was another shock in a day filled with them. I thought I must be dying.

Then came one more surprise when I heard Mr. Heraldry's voice. "Caterous!" he skidded to a halt. "What? How?" Finally, he noticed me. "Oh no, Henry," he groaned.

"If this filth is in your charge, you will do well to mind them better," the inspector addressed Scratch's mother as he tried not to acknowledge her husband.

"Oh, blow it out your ass, Melvin," Mr. Heraldry called at the man's retreating back.

Melvin, the inspector, took the opportunity to kick away several packages Mrs. Heraldry had dropped as he roughly pushed past her.

"That's why she wasn't home," I muttered. "She'd picked up things at the market."

It's odd what you say when you think you're about to die.

"My Lord Mage, I am so . . ." Mrs. Heraldry began to apologize.

Caterous and Mr. Heraldry stared daggers at each other.

I don't know what else was said because Thorn was poking me in the back. "You can let go now," she whispered.

I pushed myself off her. Half her face was swollen and covered in blood. She tried to smile at me. I remember saying, "I'm glad you're okay." Then I coughed, sending blood to cover the other half of her face. I don't know what happened after that.

It took a while for me to understand what was happening. First, I was lying on the floor, staring up at a familiar ceiling. Then, as consciousness regained full control of my brain, I realized I was home. Then the pain hit. My mother was softly chanting a healing spell over my chest. Unfortunately, I couldn't hear the incantation because angry, raised voices filled the room.

"How could you let this happen!" Mr. Heraldry demanded.

"Me?" Mage Caterous roared. "Can't you see what your kind did to my daughter?"

I followed his gesture to my friend sitting in our living room. Thorn was pale and shaking. I tried to sit up, but my mother held me down with slight pressure on my shoulder. My father was carefully cleaning the deep wound on Thorn's forehead. I was about to say something until I noticed the fire flashing in my mother's eyes as she treated me. I wasn't sure if her anger was directed at the bickering adults or me.

"I'm so sorry." Thorn's voice was weak and barely audible over the shouted accusations. Still, it brought silence to the room. Thorn held my father's hand as he finished bandaging her head. "Mr. Dreamweaver, thank you for attending to me. I'm sorry I've caused you so much trouble."

"You're no trouble," my father replied kindly.

"I am, though." Thorn sniffled. "Mr. and Mrs. Dreamweaver"—a sob wracked her small frame—"I am so, so, sorry Henry got hurt." She looked imploringly from my mother to my father. "I-I thought the humans would ignore me like they did the last time we were around them." The instant the words left her mouth, I saw the horror in her eyes.

I groaned inwardly. This was the worst time to admit it.

Caterous sputtered as he spun to glare at his daughter. "Y-y-you've been around humans before? With *him*?" Sparks shot from the finger he pointed at me.

My father flew to stand between me and the angry mage. "Now you listen here, Caterous," he began before he was interrupted.

"Like that would ever happen. When was the last time Caterous listened to anyone but himself?" Mr. Heraldry was the one who interrupted. He glared at the mage.

Returning the glare with a vengeance, Caterous advanced on the two men. "Martin, I'll have you know," he began, his voice filled with suppressed rage. The air in the room seemed to freeze and burn simultaneously.

Thorn tried to move to block her father. But, when she did, what little color she had faded, and she was forced to remain seated.

"Okay. That's enough," Mom exclaimed calmly, yet with finality. The three men immediately looked like young boys who were caught being naughty.

"He started it," Dad said as he pointed at Caterous.

"Did not," Caterous defended.

"Yeah, you did," Heraldry retorted, re-entering the fray.

"I said *enough*," Mom repeated more forcefully. She stood with her hands on her hips, giving them a look she usually reserved for me when I was in trouble. The effect was instantaneous.

"Sorry, Dear."

"So sorry, Ames."

"Apologies, Amelia."

My mother surveyed the men. "I have two injured children to attend to," she explained. "After that, I will deal with you three. Now out!" She pointed to the front door.

"Do we have to?" Martin Heraldry whined.

"But, she's *my* child," Caterous protested.

"What did *I* do?" Dad cried.

Mom didn't reply to their words. Instead, she kept pointing to the door. Finally, when they received no reply to their protests, they shuffled outside. As they left, looking like puppies that had been yelled at, they complained to each other about how unfair it was. The three men's familiarity left me confused, but it felt warm and correct.

Despite my pain, a smile spread across my face, but it vanished when my mother turned her attention back to me. I, however, noticed Thorn slowly slipping off of her chair. I tried to reach out to her, but the pain in my ribs was blinding. Once the dark tunnels receded and I could see again, I saw my mother wrapping bandages tightly around my chest. Thorn lay on our couch, sleeping or passed out. I didn't know.

"She's asleep," Mom explained, and I sighed in relief. "She's had a rather traumatic day as well." Mom looked at me, her eyes filled with pain and concern.

I felt guilty for causing her any worry. I was about to apologize when she shook her head.

"I have to straighten out three old fools." She smiled as she headed to the door.

"I wish I had a mother like you," Thorn whispered, then fell asleep again.

A look of sorrow and pain shot over my mom's face before she smiled at Thorn. "Henry, you don't move, and you keep that girl from moving around too much if she wakes."

Light spilled in through the opened door. As my eyes adjusted, I saw three men waiting. My father, Mr. Heraldry, and Mage Caterous were pointing at each other as they spoke over one another to explain something to my mother. Finally, the door shut, blocking out the sound and the scene.

"Henry."

I turned to see Thorn watching me from the couch. Her eyes were that sapphire blue I could easily get lost in.

"I'm sorry about today."

I swallowed my guilt. I found I couldn't look her in the eye. "I should never have lied. This is my fault."

"As far as I can tell, you're both idiots." Scratch wandered into my field of vision. "I heard rumors of a mage. Remember that, Henry? A mage that lived in the woods? The thing is, we searched everywhere and couldn't find him."

"We never searched the Southern Forest," I corrected.

"Huh, damn." Scratch grunted. "If I had known there were such pretty creatures in those woods, I might have gone there."

"Henry." Thorn tried to sit up but couldn't. Finally, she settled for a look of disdain as she lay back down. "Who is this annoying human?"

"Thorn Caterous, I present Scratch Heraldry," I explained. "He's a huge pain in the ass."

Scratch walked closer to Thorn and bowed. "The pleasure is all mine."

Thorn rolled a little to look up at the ceiling. "You're correct. It's *all* yours."

Scratch found her statement extremely humorous. "Oh, Dreamweaver, you have met your match in this one."

The front door opened, and everyone calmly returned to the living room. Caterous and my father began assisting my mother in healing.

Mr. Heraldry saw Scratch leaning against the wall. "My son goes off to be a soldier yet comes home with abilities closer to a burglar or spy."

"Oh, Father," Scratch smiled. "I had these skills long before joining the guard." He knelt to squeeze my shoulder. "I'll check in on you and your lady friend soon." He either didn't see or ignored the glare he received from Thorn.

"Heraldry, you may as well follow your military son. Neither his nor your prolific skills are needed here," Caterous stated, not looking up from Thorn.

"Sorry, but I think he's right." Mom patted Mr. Heraldry on the arm.

"Hey, Dad, what skills is he talking about?" Scratch called as he followed his father out of the house.

Other questions tugged at my mind as I slowly let sleep take me away from my pain. The biggest of all was, how did Caterous know my family?

More importantly, how did my parents know *him*?

CHAPTER 4

I t had been three days since I had the crap beat out of me. The fallout of the event was still being evaluated. Scratch sat at my desk in my upstairs room.

"These are pretty good," he said, looking through some of my drawings. "Looks a lot like her."

To my embarrassment, I realized I had left drawings of Thorn out on the desk. I tried to grab the pictures. That was a huge mistake. My ribs reminded me emphatically that I was still in no condition for fast movements. Groaning, I lay back and let him shuffle through the pictures. My chest was tightly bound in bandages, and I could finally smell the herbs my mother used to help with healing.

"I think it was cool as hell what you did," Scratch explained, "but not sure your old man thinks the same." He stood to inspect the bookshelves. Not sure why. He didn't read much. On top of that, he gave me over half the books sitting there. "My pops thinks *it's time for them to take action*." He mimicked his father's voice, then turned back to shrug at me. "You guys, elves, need to take a stand. Whatever that means."

"Yeah, I get what he means," I laughed, then wished I hadn't. "Your dad is an advisor to the magistrate, and mine leads the elf council." I moved into a slightly more seated position. "That has always helped our popularity."

"Yeah, not to mention our friendship." He shrugged. "Our fathers have always acted like elf and human friendships are normal. This incident isn't going to help matters." Scratch picked out a book and began flipping through it. "I'm still a little pissed at you, by the way." He put the book back and continued his previous thought. "They say it's time for action, yet they both do absolutely nothing." Scratch frowned at me. "In fact, I don't think relations between elves and humans have been worse in a long time."

I knew he hated the way people treated the elves and how they treated him and his family for being friends with us.

"Especially when the elf in question leaves out important facts about his new girlfriend."

I groaned, knowing this was going to come up sooner or later. "New—that term would assume I had a previous girlfriend." I lay back to stare at the ceiling. "And she's not my girlfriend. She is a girl and my friend, but not my girlfriend. I mean, I'm not sure if we're even friends now."

Scratch raised an eyebrow at that.

"Well, I doubt I will ever be allowed to see her again after what happened." I frowned at the thought.

"I don't think you'd take a beating like that for me," Scratch teased.

"Listen, I'm sorry I—"

"Wanted to keep her all to yourself?" Scratch smirked. "She is cute." He must have gotten the reaction he wanted from me because he burst out laughing. Then, his mood soured. "All they ever do is talk." He kicked the edge of my shelf. "Not like the Lord Mage Caterous, man. That guy was scary." He returned to the desk chair. "I've met him before."

I sat up a little straighter. "Did you know it was his daughter that was being attacked?"

By the look on his face, he clearly didn't. "I don't think my dad knew Caterous had a daughter." Scratch leaned forward to shuffle through the pictures again. "She looks to be about our age."

I was silent for a moment as jealousy chewed at my stomach. Then, finally, I forced it away. "It was weird. I heard them talking in my head."

"Well, you've always been a little weird and got hit pretty hard. I'm sure you heard a lot of things." He laughed, dodging my feeble swipe. "Dude, you were more worried about my mom's packages than you were about the fact that you were drooling blood like crazy." Again, he laughed. "I wish I would have been here when the mage brought you back."

"No, I don't think you would have," I muttered. I tried to remember the details. Although it was fuzzy, I could piece a few images together. Thorn floating beside me into our living room, looking deathly pale and lifeless. My mom nearly panicking, yet taking control immediately.

Now that I thought about it, it was odd. Neither of my parents seemed even remotely intimidated by the Mage Caterous. In fact, I remembered the argument that broke out between my dad and Caterous almost immediately. My mom put an end to that one pretty quick. I wasn't wholly conscious, so I don't know what had caused the first altercation. It seemed like my dad accused Caterous of hiding something or not well enough. I guess I passed out before finding out what he had hidden. "Thorn!"

"No, dude—sorry, still me," Scratch teased.

"No, I think she was what my dad accused Caterous of hiding. But, no, that doesn't seem right." I closed my eye, concentrating on the memories. "No, he accused Caterous of failing to keep her hidden."

"Your dad knew about her? Mine sure didn't," Scratch mused.

I kept thinking back to what I overheard. "When I woke up next, I was lying on our table. I was cold." I rubbed my arms as if I was still cold. "There were some . . . strange smells," I closed my eyes trying to remember the details, "that accosted my nose. I knew Mom was boiling herbs and mixing potions. . . ." I looked around the room in my memory. "Dad and Caterous seemed to have put aside their dispute." Tilting my head, I tried to recall the conversations around me. "Caterous was cleaning the blood from Thorn's face. . . . Her face twitched, but she remained unconscious. . . . I remember I tried to sit up. It hurt . . . a lot. The next thing I knew, I was looking into the crystal blue eyes of Mage Caterous. . . . He held two fingers against my forehead. . . ." I realized I was shaking and still holding my shoulders. I forced myself to relax. I glanced at Scratch, my face burned with embarrassment.

He was on the edge of his seat, listening. "Well?" he demanded when I guess I was quiet for too long. "What happened next?"

"Thorn whimpered as my mom bandaged her head. A flood of relief washed over me." I didn't look at Scratch. I could feel my face still burning. "I tried to roll over again but couldn't move."

I didn't tell him what happened next. I saved that memory only for myself. My hand inched across the table until I found Thorn's. I squeezed her hand lightly. With a moan, she turned her head slightly, her eyes barely open. She didn't seem to understand where she was or what was happening. She smiled at me. "You're a strange elf," she laughed. The next second she passed out again. I wanted to shake her.

I continued. "So she was out of it again, and Caterous was chanting something under his breath. At the same time, my dad, speaking in Old Elvish, held his hands on either side of Thorn's head. Blue light emanated from his hands."

"Yeah, I got there right about that time." Then, Scratch whistled. "He was doing the same thing to you after that."

"I remember. It was weird." I could feel it now. "Warmth spread from the mage's fingers through my body. I was relaxed and comfortable until I saw my mom approaching with this large bandage that stank of herbs." I laughed.

"It doesn't smell that great right now." Scratch laughed, holding his nose. "Although that could just be you."

I ignored him and continued to relive the memory. "I felt myself being pulled gently into a seated position. When Mom applied the bandage to my skin, it burned." I recalled hearing myself scream in pain before darkness took me. I blew out my frustration. "After that, it's just a confused group of images and sounds. Angry voices of men. My mom's admonishments to Dad, Caterous, and your dad." I didn't tell him about someone squeezing my hand. I knew it was Thorn, but I kept that for myself, so I told him, "The wooden table was replaced by a soft mattress and the warm comfort of my room."

"Well, you slept for two days after that," Scratch replied.

I knew he had been by every day. I think less to see how I was and more because my mom and our dads were constantly in a conference. Something had them furious, frightened, and, if possible, impressed, and it wasn't just my injuries. Caterous had done something they did not like. I still couldn't get my head around how they spoke to a mage. Where were the reverence and respect I thought a mage would demand?

"Hey, Scratch." Dad nodded as he entered my room. "I made you boys something to eat."

I looked at the turkey sandwich he handed Scratch. Once he accepted it, Dad helped me sit up. I assured him I could eat the soup on my own.

"Dad," I asked before he could leave. "Have you heard if Thorn is okay?"

Scratch was chewing as he stared at my dad, who paused at my door.

"Caterous's daughter is recovering well."

I watched his anger fight with his reassurance that everything was okay. "Why don't you like Thorn?"

"She seems like a nice young lady," Dad frowned. "It isn't her that I have an issue with."

I wanted to ask more questions, but I could tell my dad was not ready to answer. "We'll talk more about this when you recover."

I again tried to speak.

"And when you do," Dad interrupted, "you are to never interact with that girl again."

"Why?" I felt my anger rise. "It wasn't her fault! That bastard human—"

"She is responsible!" my dad shouted. He took a breath to calm himself. "She should not exist. If Caterous had not—" He ran a hand through his long black hair. "This wouldn't—Just stay away from her. She's bad news."

I doubt Dad was three stairs down before Scratch asked, "So when do we go see her?"

"We don't know where she lives." I sighed. "Oh, and sorry about that human comment." I did feel bad about that.

Scratch waved away my apology. "Looks like we have another wood to explore." I saw that same old mischievous gleam in his eye.

I agreed. I really wanted to see her again. To make sure she was okay at the very least. Scratch was now on the move like a man on a mission. He began gathering paper and quills. "We need to make a plan," he stated in his best soldier voice. I smiled to myself. I had missed that look that said, *Adventure awaits*.

"Here's what we know," Scratch explained. He flipped over the parchment I had used to draw a picture of Thorn. "She's the daughter of Caterous, the mage. She walked to town, so they can't live far."

"She told me she lives in a manor," I remembered excitedly.

"A manor?" Rubbing his chin, Scratch jumped up and began to pace. "It couldn't be. No, Dad told me it was abandoned and haunted."

"Dude, what the hell are you talking about?"

"There is this huge house out in the woods." Scratch took a seat at the desk. "The path to it is overgrown, but you can still follow it."

"Yeah, I've been on the path. But, unfortunately, the entrance is hidden by a spell. You can see it from the window, though."

Scratch jumped up again, rushing to the window. "Have you been there?"

"Yeah, I found the path. That's where I met Thorn." I told him the whole story.

Scratch paced again. "How do you get onto the path?"

I explained it to him.

"All right, Dreamweaver, you stay here," he said with a laugh as he bounded down the stairs.

I lay impatiently on my bed, staring at the walls. I hated being stuck in bed, especially when Scratch was out on an adventure, and worst of all, what if he met up with Thorn?

Scratch was gone for a couple of hours. During that time, I positioned myself to see out the window. Then, finally, I saw him sneaking back into our yard. I swear, he took more time than was really necessary to return to my room. When he finally did return, he was unreadable.

"Did you find her house?" I hissed, not wanting anyone to overhear.

"Well, no." He shrugged. "Maybe, I found it—I think. I found a wall. It was like twenty feet tall, and there was no door."

"Probably concealed by Magic," I muttered.

"How do we get in then?" The gleam of adventure hadn't left his eyes.

"Well, we have to use Magic to fight Magic."

"Cool—when you're better, you can find it." Scratch beamed at me.

I did not feel as confident. "I think you're overestimating my abilities." I eased myself down. My ribs were really starting to ache.

"Dude, you found one hidden entrance. What makes you think this one will be different?"

"I told you, it took me several tries to find that path." I took several short breaths to fill my screaming lungs. Once I felt I could speak without coughing, I continued talking. "I had only used that spell to find stuff Mom and Dad hid, but they didn't put much effort into their concealments."

"Still, it's so cool you can use Magic." He smiled. He had always been enamored with my family's abilities even though they were generally forbidden. We were given a little leeway because Mom was a healer. "In a couple of days, why don't we see what you can do?"

"Scratch, we're leaving," his dad called from downstairs. I could tell an agreement hadn't been reached by the edge in his voice.

"When you're better." Scratch gathered up his jacket. "We'll go find your girlfriend."

"Go home, dork." I threw my napkin at him. The pain it caused me made me wish I hadn't.

CHAPTER 5

Scratch had been by a couple of times over the next week, when one day, he brought an old map of the woods. "Where did you get this?" I asked, astonished at its age.

"Dad has all kinds of maps and stuff in his study." Scratch laughed. "He thinks they're really well hidden." He smirked. "Well, at least from my mother." He shrugged before showing me where the path to a large house drawn on the map began. "So this is your place right here on the edge of the woods, and this is the place I found." He frowned at me as he pointed out the two sections.

"What?" I demanded. I knew I was defensive even as I tried to quell a cough.

"Our adventure will have to wait, though. Heavy rain is moving in for the next three days. But when you can walk more than ten feet and not sound like my grandfather trying to make it up the stairs, I say we find the way into this place." His finger tapped the picture.

I growled at him.

I had sustained more damage than we first thought. However, my ribs barely hurt anymore and I was feeling much better now—physically, anyway. I could get around pretty well, even with my mother hovering and constantly asking if I was okay. It was great having Scratch around so much, but I was really starting to miss Thorn. I began to realize how much I enjoyed being around her.

The rain, mixed with not being allowed to do anything, was becoming overbearing. My desire to see Thorn was compounded by being cooped up in my room, which made me a bit irritable. Scratch told me so as he left around dusk.

I had been lying around for so long that I needed to get out of the house. It felt like a month since I had been outside. I looked at the map, and the image of

Thorn's smile played in my mind. The large drawing of a house and wall seemed to call to me. However, looking closely at the drawing, the only thing remotely resembling a manor house was the governor's mansion on the top of the hill in Dayok. Rubbing my eyes, I decided to get some sleep.

The rain appeared to have stopped, so I lay down, thinking maybe tomorrow I could follow the path. Then I could see Thorn. Memories of her face swam into my mind as sleep tempted my consciousness.

I dozed for a while, but the thought of finally leaving my room kept waking me. After tossing and turning for a while, as much as someone in my condition could do those things, I decided to test my legs. I happily made it silently halfway down the stairs before stumbling. I didn't think it was loud, but my mom has the hearing of a bat. She was beside me before I could straighten up, asking if I was okay, if I was hurting, did I need something? I tried to tell her I was fine, but Mom insisted on re-wrapping my chest.

I decided not to complain, at least not when she attended to my still-mending ribs. Then Mom insisted on giving me something for the pain and to help me sleep.

I was dreaming about the inspector looming over me, about to deliver the killing blow. As I watched in horror, he transformed into Mage Caterous. The mage glared at me with fire in his eyes, angrily striking his sparking staff near my feet. Suddenly I awoke, confused and terrified. There was no way I would get back to sleep. I lay there staring at the ceiling, trying not to fear every shadow. I calmed my mind by thinking about Thorn. My breath caught as my body froze. The sound of Caterous's staff striking the ground echoed through my room.

My chest, already bound, tightened even more. My fingers ached from gripping the blanket. Again, I heard the tapping, not as loud this time. I relaxed slightly as I determined it was coming from one of my windows.

I thought this was weird as my room is on the second floor, and there are no tree branches near my window. I waited, but the sound did not return. I relaxed further. I decided I had imagined it. I assured myself my mom had been so flustered when she made my medicine that she overdid an ingredient or something.

My hands relaxed, as did my shoulders. I began getting comfortable until the tapping returned. I slid my hands over my ears. I told myself it was only my imagination as I tried to ignore the sound. Determined to show my imagination that I was in charge, I announced, "You know I don't hear you."

That turned out to be a big mistake. The tapping became a knocking, then a pounding. There was no way I could ignore it. I was also terrified of what my mom would say if I woke her twice. I eased off the bed, cautiously approaching the window.

I moved slowly for two reasons. First, it hurt, and second, I was absolutely terrified. Some strange thoughts ran through my brain. The city guards had come to get me, or the other elves had come to drive us out of town. Worse yet, maybe Mage Caterous had returned to take revenge. When I finally reached the window, what I saw was even more frightening.

A young girl about my age was staring at me through the glass. I knew instantly she wasn't human or elf. Instead, she was one of the creatures we refer to as a blood demon—what humans call a vampire. I had never met one before, and I couldn't think what I could have done to upset one. They didn't generally bother elves unless there was an insult or trespass of some kind. In fact, these creatures rarely interacted with the other beings in our world. So, I didn't know much about them other than that they are extremely powerful and deadly. They are fierce warriors, which I could understand because I heard they could rip an elf apart without trying.

I stood there staring at her. I knew she was an incredibly dangerous creature—I could feel her power emanating through the glass—yet I couldn't look away. She was beautiful. She had the kind of presence and appearance that made you want to take care of her. You would see her and think you needed to protect her. I knew this was part of their danger. For some reason, they could only enter a home if invited. So I knew I couldn't allow her in.

She knew it too and glared venom at me. "Open the window," she hissed, her fangs showing as she did. "I'm not going to hurt you. Open the damn window." When I didn't move, she rolled her eyes and explained, "I'm a friend of Thorn's."

For some reason, this information unstuck my feet. Before I knew it, I had the window open, and my head was out of it. I couldn't believe what I was doing. Giving her access to my neck was not an intelligent thing to do. However, there I was, my head sticking out of my house while a vampire sat on my roof. She looked grumpy. Her arms encircled her knees, pulling them up to her chest. We looked at the rose garden until I couldn't stand the silence.

"You came to see me, Vampire," I stated, but it came out much harsher than I meant. I couldn't help it. Vampires have a terrible reputation, and I was afraid of her.

"You're a really stupid elf, aren't you?" she growled.

"What? Why?"

"I could rip your throat out with ease and drain you dry." She lurched at me with fangs bared and fingernails sharp as claws. My terrified screech turned into a moan as my head collided with the window and my chest hit the sill. A look of concern passed over the girl's face but was gone in a breath.

"You know," she said, moving away from me, "only a few of my kind actually drink blood." An evil grin spread over her lips, and her clawed fingers moved strangely as she told me, "Most of us can control the blood of our victims." The devilish smile disappeared. "Most of us just have the adverse effect of siphoning off the life force of others. Because of this, vampires tend to spend time alone. Most people don't want us around since we tend to deplete the vitality of everyone around us. Many can't control it—simply being around them tends to drain the person."

I could feel my energy and patience slowly ebbing away. "I didn't ask."

"My name is Serina," she explained, moving a little further away from me, and the sapping of my energy lessened. "And you're an ass," she grumbled. "Stupid elf."

I found that I didn't particularly care for her. She was a little too straightforward and vocal with her opinions. Also, being around her was draining. Even though her actions were similar to Thorn's, she lacked fun and innocence. She seemed to sense my discomfort, frowning at me as she shuffled further away.

"I'm straining your life force," she sighed. "I expend more energy than I absorb. Mortals have a challenging time being close to me." Her annoyance held a hint of bitterness. "A stupid hurt elf will probably pass out soon."

Offended, I replied, "What the hell?"

She glared at me.

I glared back. "You came to my house, and *you* are calling *me* names."

"You called me 'Vampire.' How about I just call you stupid elf?"

"I didn't know your name!" I countered, my anger flaring.

"You didn't ask," she stated matter-of-factly.

"Well, I'm sorry." My sarcasm could not be hidden, but I did feel a little bad at referring to her as her species. That was rude. "You did come to see me. Why?" I decided to try to make amends. "Serina." Using her name seemed to assuage her.

"I don't think I like you," she said. "You tried to help Thorn, though." She shrugged but then pointed accusingly at me. "You haven't tried to find out how she is." Serina was searching my face for some reaction. What she saw she didn't like. "I thought you two were friends." Her gaze filled with disgust. "I bet you don't even intend to see her again." Serina stood up slowly and as she did, what I thought was a shawl around her shoulders unfurled.

My mouth dropped open. "Wings?"

Serina's disgust deepened as she spread her black, bat-like wings. A gasp escaped my throat. She turned to glare at me. Then, she began flapping her wings. Her feet had already left the roof when I panicked. I tried to grab Serina before she could fly off.

I had to ask, "Did she say something about me?" Even in the dark, I was sure my blush was visible. "Wait, please, I *have* asked! My dad said she was recuperating. Scratch says he knows where she lives, and when I'm better, we're going to find a way into the wall around the manor." I said all of this really fast. It was like I was trying to make excuses.

"She says you're a friend." The announcement shocked me. "If she's wrong, I won't be happy with you." She pulled what appeared to be a magnifying glass from a pouch at her waist. "It might be nice if she has a friend who could spend time with her in the daytime." She held out the glass to me. I thanked her. She gave me a grudging smile, then, without another word, Serina flew off into the darkness. She left me exhausted and confused yet excited. Finally, I would see Thorn again. I looked at the magnifying glass. It looked ordinary, and that's when I realized I had no idea what to do with it.

"Wait," I called. "How do I use this? What about her father?"

Serina did not seem to have heard me.

CHAPTER 6

Serina allowed herself to feel jealous. Finally, Thorn had found a new friend, one she didn't have to hide from her father. The elf might be an idiot, but he obviously cared for Thorn. Serina's thoughts traveled to the past as she flew through the darkness.

Vampire Kingdom council meeting
Ninety years ago

The council consisted of representatives of the five vampire clans. Four families, or clans, separated themselves along the points of the compass. They used this as a way to choose their adversaries and allies: North against South, East against West. Then there was the fifth family, the Varatos, who claimed to be the orginators of all vampires. This claim made them the outcast of the four points of the compass and a common enemy for the others.

"The Southern Clans will not tolerate this . . ." Crandle, leader of the southern vampires, cast around for the most effective words. ". . . tyranny." His fist smashed against the table as he stood and pointed an accusing finger at the newly elected King Nicodemus and Queen Asha.

"War with the humans is inevitable," the king argued. "It's only a matter of time." His statement was met with jeers and cynical laughs. "It may be a century or next week, but war is coming," Nicodemus continued, ignoring the barbs. "We should decide now if we should join one side or the other."

"Our choices are between two lower groups? The humans or the rabble?" someone shouted. "I choose neither. We are now and always should be neutral!"

"You all know this is more than the humans and the others!" Mylissa, the trusted advisor to the royal family shouted. "There is another at work here, and I do not believe they are on our side."

"We all know of your great prophetic powers," Crandle rolled his eyes as he spoke. "I, for one, have not seen the signs."

"I doubt someone of your perception could even read." Mylissa's lip curled as she spoke. "I do not believe the humans are trustworthy." She chose her next words carefully. "Nor do I believe we should side with our less fortunate cousins."

"Then who?" Crandle leaned forward, his hands planted firmly on the table.

"The elves," Mylissa replied calmly. Shouts of *weaklings!, traitors!,* and *cowards!* filled the room.

Crandle looked aghast. "The Southern Clans will not ally with elves. They betrayed us all to humans centuries ago. They have made themselves sheep, slaves to the ones they chose!" Crandle slammed the table again. "Chose over us!"

"I do not debate that the elves' transgressions against us are vast. However," Mylissa held up a hand for patience, "they are our closest cousins in this world."

Her words were again met with a storm of protests and jeers.

"You have always shown a weakness for the elves and other lower castes," Crandle sneered when the shouting subsided. "The elves are not of vampire blood. So you may feel it is appropriate to mingle bloodlines. Yet I, as I am sure the rest of our kin will agree, shall remain pure."

"Yes, continued inbreeding should be maintained," the queen sneered sarcastically. "See what it has done for your ally." A delegate from the Varato Clan hissed his hatred at her. Serina, a newly appointed Queen's Guard, grasped the hilt of her sword.

The Varato ignored her as he stood, extending his arms toward the rest of the group. "You would not exist if not for us. We are the originators of our race. You owe us your allegiance."

"That has never been proven!" someone shouted.

Other jeers and accusations flew. "We all know you are hiding the fact that you are nothing more than vampiric orcs."

The insult was an old one, but it had the desired effect. Hands pounded on the table along with some of the most vile slanders of inbreeding and beastiality. Serina moved closer to the king and queen, her sword a quarter of the way drawn. She didn't see the first punch thrown, only the the chaos that followed.

Screams for the head of one family while the head of another tried to reach over an advisor to pummel the opposition. As Serina's group began shuffling the royals away from the melee, Serina was jostled, pushed, and knocked into. She fought the urge to cut down the fools around her. A sudden surge of combatants lurched toward the royals. A mace struck Serina's helmet, leaving a deep dent in the thick metal and knocking her off her feet. When she managed to stand, she slid her sword from its scabbard. Silent tension filled the room as the tip of her blade drew a fine bead of blood from the Varato representative's throat. With her free hand, Serina pulled off her dented helmet. Her red hair became a darker crimson as blood flowed freely from her wound.

Crandle stepped forward in an attempt to grab Serina by her armor. "Control your welp," he growled. But before his hand touched Serina, an unseen force threw Crandle across the room.

"You dare insult the royal family's daughter." Serina's eyes were fathomless black pools of hate. The Varato at the end of her sword drew a sharp breath. The tip of Serina's weapon dug deeper into his flesh.

"Asha, control your daughter!" the king roared.

Serina slowly pulled her blade away from the representative's neck and the entire room seemed to exhale their tension. Suddenly Serina's sword flashed and impaled the chest of the Varato. She lifted his screaming body off his feet. Shouts filled the room as the lifeless corpse was flung from Serina's weapon. His body lay broken against the wall. Serina stared wide-eyed at Crandle, who stood next to the body.

Holding his hands in surrender, Crandle began begging. "Please don't kill me!"

Serina, sword still held out, swung around to face her parents as members of the meeting yelled in terror.

"Mother, I didn't," Serina stuttered.

"Princess, behind you!" someone shouted.

Serina turned just in time to avoid a fatal wound. Crandle's dagger dug deep into her shoulder between the plate armor. Her scream of pain turned into a roar of fury. Crandle sneered his hate into her eyes. In an instant, she threw him off. Crandle drew his sword to attack her again.

To ensure all eyes were on them, Crandle began speaking. "She murdered the representative of the Varato," he shouted as he pressed his attack. Serina, ignoring the searing pain in her shoulder, defended against the first slash of Crandle's sword.

"I didn't mean to, I—" Serina tried to look at her mother. The glimpse she caught was one of disappointment. Crandle took advantage of Serina's break in concentration. Fortunately, his aim was poor. His sword banged harmlessly off Serina's chest armor, and anger flared again in her heart. Their blades crashed against each other. The wound in her shoulder screamed for her to stop while the wound in her heart from her mother's doubt hurt far worse. Crandle had her struggling to push him back. Finally, they were face to face, glaring at each other through crossed steel. The room was a cacophany of jeers, shouts, and clashing blades.

"You're not the only one who can push others with magic," Crandle whispered, unheard by the others. His smirk at Serina's shock turned sour. Serina's fangs elongated as her eyes changed to black pools of fathomless hate. If he had hoped to overwhelm her, he was fatally mistaken. Serina pushed and spun into her attack, then Crandle's head rolled across the table. The room fell into a stunned silence.

Cries of "Murderer!" fought with calls for Serina's execution and those of war threats until the room exploded in violence. The floor, walls, and table were covered in blood and bodies when it was over. Then, the remaining Southern and Varato delegations members declared promises of vengeance and violence.

The king and queen had been ushered out when the melee became too chaotic. Serina had been separated and now waited in a room in the guard tower. She could hear the other soldiers returning from the meeting hall. Horrified, they spoke in hushed tones, disgusted by the brutality and carnage.

"I can't believe the princess would do that."

"She has led us into war."

"What do you expect from a union of those two?"

"Guarding other vampires should never have been a child's duty."

"You will show respect to Princess Serina!" The voice of Serina's captain admonished the soldiers. "While you may consider her a child, she is one hundred and eighteen. An adult in our world." The intensity of the captain's glare caused the seasoned veterans to recoil. "She has been one of our more trusted and capable fighters. Until we know what occurred," the captain drew herself up to her full height, "we will not engage in rumor or speculation."

The sound of metal on stone told Serina the guards were kneeling. "My daughter has seen battle," Asha snapped. "She has valiantly dispatched our enemies." The queen's anger flashed, sending a tremor through the soldiers. "I seem to remember you were quite happy with her saving your life."

"Y-yes, My Queen." Serina recognized the voice of Martock. It was true. She had saved him from a nasty troll.

"Serina! Where is my daughter?" Asha demanded. A moment later, the door to Serina's room opened. The queen stared at her daughter, holding out her hand expectantly. The captain hesitated, then placed Serina's blade in the queen's hand.

Asha presented it to Serina, who took it and, with a flourish, returned the sword to its sheath.

"Come, daughter, there is much to discuss."

As her mother passed, Serina attempted an apologetic smile for the captain, then she followed Asha.

When they left the tower, Serina tried to explain what happened. "Mother, it was Crandle. He used magic to push my hand. He killed the Varato."

"That may be true," Asha sighed, pain lacing her voice, "but since he is also dead, we have no proof." She turned on her heels, heading at a quick pace toward the main hall of their home. Serina saw her father pacing and giving orders while her younger brother, Jamie, watched as she was ushered into a small room.

Three vampires she knew knelt as she and the queen entered. "I believe you are all familiar with my daughter," the queen stated. "I believe you were . . . friendly . . . during training."

One of the three raised his head to smile at Serina, who returned it quickly.

"I have an important mission for you," the queen continued. "Serina is to be exiled." The word caught in Asha's throat. "And I would ask you to please accompany her."

CHAPTER 7

Serina's visit had done a number on me. It was mid-morning when I finally woke up. My ribs felt better, and I made it down the stairs without faltering. I found my mom reading in the living room.

"You seem to be feeling better," she greeted.

"Is Dad home?" I asked.

Her smile faltered a little. "No, your father and Mr. Heraldry had some business to take care of in town." She frowned.

"You still mad at them?" I asked.

"It's nothing," she sighed. "They're just so caught up in what happened. I mean, it's too late now. The damage is done. It's not like it can be undone." Mom shook her head and smiled. "Never mind my rambling."

I figured she wasn't talking about what had happened to me.

"Oh, um, okay." My hand found the magnifying glass in my pocket. I considered asking Mom how to use it. I quickly disregarded this thought as I would then have to explain where I got it. I doubt she'd be too happy about her son getting late-night visits from vampires. "I think I'm going to go see Scratch." I tried to sound casual while heading to the door.

"He isn't in town today. Didn't he tell you?"

"What? Oh, right, he returned to his army training." I had forgotten Scratch had left before I was well enough to head out on our adventure. I felt a little guilty, but I was happy I wouldn't have share time with Thorn. "Well, that's okay. I, um . . ."

My mom's eyes felt like they were boring into my soul.

"I just want to get out of the house for a while."

Her look of distrust deepened.

"You know, some sunshine and time in nature. You know how we elves love nature." I was blowing this, and we both knew it.

"Don't go too far, and don't overdo it. Remember, you're still healing."

"Right, right. You know me." I laughed unconvincingly. "I'm all about safety."

"I remember you saying something like—" She imitated my voice. "*Mom, if it's worth doing, it's worth overdoing.*"

"I'll take it easy. I promise."

She raised an eyebrow but nodded.

I kissed her on the cheek quickly before hurrying out the door before she could change her mind.

Finally free from the house, I felt energized. The day was bright and comfortable. The air was fresh and clean after the rains. It took me a while to get onto the path. I was anxious to get going, but I was paranoid my mom was watching. Finally, I decided I had been boring enough that Mom must have stopped spying. However, it took a while before I could find the beginning of the path again. Acting casually but most likely not looking like it, I slipped through the familiar illusions, a smile spreading across my face as I strolled along the now familiar path. I checked many of the places where Thorn and I had spent time. Unfortunately, I didn't see any evidence she'd been there. Finally, I spotted some footprints on the trail deeper along the path. They were small, so I could only assume they belonged to Thorn. I felt a sharp pain in my chest. Coincidentally, it happened just as I thought of her. It must have been my chest healing. At least, that's what I told myself.

My promise to my mother was sorely tested. The trip to the woods was, by definition, overdoing it. I sat on a stump, trying not to breathe heavily because each breath reminded me that my ribs hadn't completely healed. I contemplated at what point I should turn back and try another day. I had just decided to go ahead for another half hour when something rustled the bushes nearby. I waited for Thorn to pop out. When she didn't, I concluded it was just an animal.

I continued down the path for another five or ten minutes. My ears caught every snap of a twig and crunch of a leaf. With every step, I became more certain I was being stalked. Even though the animal was quiet, I felt its gaze. Whatever was following me was not small.

My brain listed all the creatures of the forest. Nothing native to this area would come after an elf or man. *Trolls, or maybe an orc*, my brain was kind enough to offer. *Oooh, maybe a dragon*, it added unhelpfully.

"There hasn't been a dragon here in years," I hissed, "more likely elf hunters." Now I was worried about being killed, killed and eaten, or enslaved. I was desperate to run away, but I tried not to let my fear overwhelm me. Whatever was following me was an animal, I decided. I would already be killed or captured by now if it wasn't. If the thing following me were a bear or a wolf, it would outpace me in a second. So, I decided to confront the beast. Stopping in the middle of the path, I turned to stare into the tall bushes about six feet behind me. As I did, I saw something staring back. I saw the eyes first. Then I saw the pointed triangle ears poking out from the top of the bush. They were too tall for a normal wolf.

It might have been a minute or a second—I don't know. When my heart finally started, my feet took their cue. While I could never claim that the scream I expelled was masculine, it seemed to scare the beast as much as it scared me. I heard it crashing away as I hurried in the other direction. A good thing, too—I didn't make it far before I was on my hands and knees, coughing while trying not to pass out.

"Oh gods, Henry, you scared the hell out of me."

I swear my heart stopped again when I heard Thorn's voice.

"What was that noise you made? I've never heard a cry like that before. It was terrifying."

I kept my head down. My face burned with embarrassment. Thorn kept talking, completely unaware of my discomfort. All I wanted to do was sink into the ground.

"I think you took a few years off the life of the minareta I was training." Then, finally, Thorn's boots came into view.

Trying to collect my thoughts was difficult. I was still shaking from the adrenaline and embarrassment. "What the hell are you trying to do to me?" I demanded. "I came looking for you, and you send your familiar after me?" I was still bent over with my hands on my knees. I couldn't bring myself to meet her eyes, so I studied her boots instead. They were made of lovely soft tan leather with an embossed intricate ivy pattern.

"Hey, you okay?" Her voice was edged with concern. I waved off her question as I stood straight. But, unfortunately, my assurance that I was fine was somewhat hampered by a coughing fit, and I won't lie—it hurt.

Her hand touched my arm tentatively. Again I felt the Magic. Her power was extreme.

It was several seconds before I remembered I was mad at her. "Seriously! A wolf? That's what you chose?" I stared at her, astounded.

"Father said a minareta, or a familiar, as you put it, should be strong," Thorn argued.

"Well, sure," I agreed. "But if you sent a wolf into a town . . ."

She cocked her head at me in confusion.

I shook my head and continued. "The people would either panic or kill it, or both." Now I had to keep from laughing at her.

Thorn's mouth comically formed the shape of an O. "Yeah, I guess that would be a problem."

"What were you going to do with it?" I asked, exasperated. How could she not think this through? Where did she think she could send such a creature?

"I was going to use it to talk to you," she replied, a blush creeping up her neck.

"You were going to send a wolf to my house?" I demanded.

Thorn drew circles in the dirt with the toe of her boot.

"How did you think that would go?"

"I thought you would like it," she replied meekly.

I couldn't believe her. But then again, "Well, yeah, that would be pretty cool. Terrifying—I mean, they're like twice the size of a normal wolf—but cool." I pictured a huge wolf coming up to the house to deliver a message from Thorn. I couldn't keep the smile from my face. Mom and Dad would freak out—literally

"I know. How awesome would that be?" She hopped a little with excitement. Then her demeanor changed again. She kept her head down, averting her eye. "What are you doing here?"

"You left without saying goodbye," I said stupidly.

She kicked at some leaves. "Well, I caused enough trouble."

I searched for something to say. "I'm glad you're okay."

"Yeah, you doing okay?"

I cringed. I had so many conversations with Thorn in my head as I lay recuperating. In every imagined scenario, I was cool and witty. Yet, here I was, out of breath, wheezing after running and screaming from her wolf familiar. "A bunny would not attract attention, and they're swift." It was then that the thought came to me. "Um, Thorn, where's the wolf now?" I nervously scanned the woods around us.

Thorn giggled a little as she dug into the soft grass with the toe of her boot. She held a finger curled at her mouth, a smile playing on her lips. "You have to promise never to tell anyone," she whispered.

I nodded stupidly. Thorn looked all around as if someone might be listening behind the trees. I waited as she decided it was clear. She giggled slightly, took a deep breath, then shook her head vigorously while exhaling. I nearly fell over again.

Thorn stood before me, looking exactly the same, except her elf ears were gone. Instead, the top of her head now sported the same triangular wolf ears I saw in the bush. Her eyes, too, seemed more beastlike.

"Well, what do you think?" she asked.

"Um, you have wolf ears." I cringed as she frowned at me. I couldn't stop staring. Thorn's wolf ears were perfect. I had never seen or read anything like this. Trance-like, I moved closer to her. I started to reach up. "Can I touch them?"

"I, uh, I guess." She frowned. "I've never had anyone touch my ears, so, um, just be careful."

I stood with my hand out.

"Are you going to do it?"

Jolted out of my stupor, I moved closer. My hand passed right through the wolf ears touching nothing.

Thorn had her eyes closed like she was enjoying a joke. Fur had sprouted over her whole face.

I tripped over a log as I stumbled back. "What the—you're a lycanthrope?" I backed away as she came toward me.

"No, I'm sorry." She stopped trying to approach. Shaking her head again, Thorn returned to normal. However, she was smiling mischievously.

"Wait—*you* were the wolf?" I shouted.

"Shh!"

"Why were we talking about familiars then?"

Thorn shrugged. "You brought it up, and it was funny."

"Wait, wait, wait." I began to pace. "You let me think you were training a wolf as your familiar."

She nodded. "Correct."

"But there was no wolf."

She nodded again. "You're a bright elf."

"Instead, it was you." I spun to meet her eyes. Her face still held that smirk. "So what? You transformed yourself, but I couldn't touch your ears."

Thorn looked at me as if waiting for me to work it out.

I returned to my pacing. "It was just a projection of a wolf—a magical disguise!" I concluded. "Elves don't have that ability. Is it because your father is a mage?"

Her face held genuine excitement. "I learned it from my father. He wanted me to use it to be unseen when I was younger."

"That's a very rare talent." I couldn't help but be impressed.

"You can't tell anyone about it, though." She thought for a second. "Not even Sebastian, okay?"

When Thorn mentioned Scratch, my stomach burned. I didn't like how she said his name. "You're swearing me to a lot of secrecy. How do you know you can trust me?" I blurted out, instantly feeling bad as she looked at me seriously.

"I trust you because we're friends." Her statement was clear and final. She cocked her head to look at me as if just realizing something. "Why are you all the way out here, running around with obviously still hurt ribs?" Her anger flared, and her glare pierced me. "We're going to see my father for something to help with the pain. Then you're going straight home to bed." She was shorter than me, but standing in front of me, with her hands on her hips and browbeating me, I cringed.

How did this become about me? Suddenly all her words registered in my brain. "Whoa, wait a second! I don't think your father would be too pleased to see me."

"Well, no. In fact, Father will be unhappy with both of us." But then, she took my hand and smiled. "I'm never supposed to see you again."

I squeezed her hand. "I heard the same thing from my father." I regrettably dropped her hand at the sound of a rustle in the brush. Now it was my turn to look for eavesdroppers. "I think our dads know each other, and I don't think they like each other," I whispered.

She matched my hushed tone. "That was the feeling I got as well. My father has been grumbling about your father and Sebastian's."

"Scratch, but yeah."

"Huh?"

"Sebastian goes by Scratch. No one calls him Sebastian," I explained.

She nodded, although she didn't seem convinced. "Why Scratch?"

"It's because . . ." Now I had to think. "You know, I have no idea." I realized she was leading me further along the path. I was about to protest when we came to the wall Scratch told me about.

CHAPTER 8

s Thorn led me along the imposing wall, I realized Scratch hadn't exaggerated. The structure stood at least twenty feet tall. Ivy grew thick into the masonry. However, that only made it look less inviting. We walked about halfway down the length, with Thorn looking at me expectantly. "What?" I finally asked, unable to stand her scrutiny. She huffed but didn't explain. I continued walking and realized she'd stopped. She must have been near the opening I couldn't see. I already hated these little tests she gave me.

Annoyed, I walked back and forth past Thorn. I tried to ignore the raised eyebrows and the hands on her hips as she waited for me to figure out how to get in. I looked left and right along the wall but couldn't determine an opening. Then, taking a step forward, I studied the stone. I ran my hands over the rough surface. I even pressed my face sideways to see if there was any noticeable bump or depression.

Frustration permeated the air from both Thorn and me. Each time I took a new direction to discover what I assumed would be the entrance, Thorn huffed in annoyance.

Finally, my fumbling caused her impatience to spill out. "Think back. Did you receive anything unusual recently?"

I stared at her momentarily, trying to make sense of her statement. Finally, the pieces locked into place in my mind, and I slapped myself on the forehead. How could I have forgotten Serina's visit? Grumbling, I pulled the magnifying glass from my pocket and inspected the wall directly before me. Listening to Thorn's exasperations, I played a kind of blind man's bluff until I stood several feet from the wall. Then, looking through the glass, the door began to materialize. It was imposing, with dark thick wood set back into the gray stone. It was held in place by huge, carved, black iron hinges. Below the handle was a nasty-looking gargoyle face for the keyhole. As offputting as the door was, I looked at Thorn triumphantly as I marched to the portal. My victory was short-lived, though. Smirking at Thorn, I tried the handle. It didn't budge.

"Oh," came an embarrassed yelp from behind me, "forgot I locked it."

Now it was my turn to be exasperated.

She sheepishly pulled out an old key. "Force of habit." She shrugged, inserting the key into the protesting mouth of the gargoyle.

"I thought you were worried about my chest," I grumbled, following her into the enclosure, "yet you made me run through that exercise. Then you forget you locked the door?"

"Huh? What? Oh, right, follow me." Thorn kept glancing at me as we passed the threshold. Once we were through, she must have seen what she had hoped for on my face.

It was like walking into another world. A canopy of leaves muted the sunlight that only a moment before seemed to shine down uninhibited. Even though the tree cover didn't change, at least at first glance, I looked closer. The trees were different, as were many of the plants. Then, to my shock, I saw the animals. Creatures from fairy tales flitted about, unafraid of Thorn or me. I was in a sanctuary of Magic. I felt its energy around me as well as in me, filling me.

Thorn, who had been leading, stopped, noticing that I had paused. A grin spread across her face as she let loose a happy yelp, rushing to me and taking my hands in hers. "I knew it. I felt it in you!" She hopped around, pulling me with her in a circle.

I realized the warm glow around me wasn't simply the sunlight. Instead, I was being charged with Magic.

"Your inner power is awakening." She let go of my hands, smiling and dancing around in a circle. "Come on—I want to show Father." My hand was back in hers, and she pulled me hurriedly in her wake. My chest began to hurt again. Then the sight emerging from the trees stole all thoughts of asking Thorn to slow down.

The house was huge. More extensive than any place I had seen in Dayok, more like half of the homes put together might be the same size. Dozens of chimneys protruded from the roofs. An east and west wing boasted leaded glass windows. Great granite blocks made up the exterior. Thorn led me to the massive oak double doors. I was surprised to see the giant iron knockers and embellishments. Being close to the fae, elves tended not to enjoy the touch of iron. It wasn't deadly, as it could be to fairies, but it wasn't something we liked to endure.

Thorn pulled me up the few steps to the door before turning to me with a frown. "We have to be careful when we speak to Father." She shifted uncomfortably. "You see, Father had to cut an important trip short to come save me. He had to go through the fae lands." She could see my shock.

I didn't even know one could pass through their lands.

"He traveled through the land of the faerie folks without permission. Naturally, that doesn't sit well with their queen, Titania. So Father has to do all kinds of acts of contrition and things to make amends."

"Don't forget, my dad and yours are not on the best of terms right now either," I reminded her.

"Yeah, that too," she sighed, reaching for the latch only to have the door pulled open out of her grasp.

"I thought I said further contact with this elf was forbidden." Caterous stood glaring imperiously down at us.

I was surprised she didn't step back as something like murder flashed in his eyes. I retreated by two steps.

"Father—" Thorn began until Caterous held up a hand, ending her protests instantly.

"Sir, this is my fault," I tried to explain. However, when he turned his eyes on me, the glare he fixed on me froze my words in my throat. My heart pounded against my chest, and I wasn't sure what hurt more—my ribs or the panicked beating.

"House—now!" At the command, Thorn glanced at me fearfully. "Now!"

She squeaked and hurried into the house.

Next, the mage addressed me. "You as well. Now!" He pointed in the direction Thorn had just disappeared.

My heart, beating a mile a minute when Caterous opened the door, seemed to stop. I glanced inside. I saw Thorn several feet away, staring back at me, holding out her hand. I ran to her, grabbing her outstretched hand. Terrified as I was, her Magic mixed with the house overwhelmed me instantly. I felt her start to let go, so I grabbed her hand tighter while we stood in the hall.

The door swung shut with an ominous boom. Thorn dropped my hand the instant her father joined us. Mage Caterous brushed past me, and Thorn followed in his wake with her head down. The hall was dark and cold. I could see her outline beckoning me to follow. As I did, she disappeared through a door. As soon as I entered the room, I found myself in an extensive library. The area was larger than the entire ground floor of my house. There were no windows and only a few small lamps for light, except the room was bright. The smell of leather and ancient paper filled me with a sense of great knowledge locked away in all those pages just out of reach. If I were here under any other circumstances, I would have been elated at the number of books surrounding me. As it was, the fact that we followed an angry wizard into the room dampened the mood.

Thorn was already sitting on an oversized leather couch. She was staring down at her boots, tracing the intricate ivy pattern on them with the toe of the other. I swore the ivy was moving. Then, I became painfully aware of a presence behind me. I didn't need to see his face to note his displeasure.

"Sit," Caterous's stern voice commanded.

I took a seat on the other side of the couch from Thorn. Caterous swept around us to a massive desk and sat in a high-back leather chair. I kept my head down but stole glances as he observed us over steepled fingers. His eyes burned into mine. I tried to look past him. However, the large horned skull mounted behind the mage was equally disturbing. Over his other shoulder hung a painting that could only be described as the depths of hell, and the inhabitants were moving. I imagined I could hear the screams of the damned. I worried I was about to join them.

"Sume," Caterous sighed, "what am I going to do with you?" His voice was surprisingly gentle and calm.

"Sume?" I muttered.

"Pet name," Thorn explained with a blush. "Father, I—" She faltered under his piercing gaze.

"Sir—Lord Mage," I began until his eyes turned to me. "I came to see Thorn. I, um . . ." My mouth had gone so dry I could barely speak. "I was worried about her after we met the inspector in town." The words finally tumbled free. I realized I was holding something in, and now it was going to come out whether I wanted it to or not. "I am so sorry—I never wanted her to get hurt."

"She would not have been in town if she had listened to her father." His power and his anger emanated in waves from across the room.

"I'm sorry, sir—I wasn't thinking, sir. I just wanted to help her out. I saw her heading to the market. She seemed so excited. She just forgot she needed to be careful and hidden." Then, out of the corner of my eye, I saw Thorn's shoulders rise. "I'm not blaming you," I said, reaching out to her.

She recoiled, so I withdrew.

"No," the mage growled, "she should not have to hide who she is." Caterous's fury was terrifying. Unconsciously I had forced myself deeper into the couch cushion, trying not to cry. Finally, Caterous blew out some of his anger.

Then he inhaled deeply and explained, "She did not forget. She simply has no idea how your world works." He rose slowly. "That's my fault. I should have instilled the correct amount of . . ." He seemed to search for the right word. ". . . disgust, she should have for your kind. Not to mention the violence of the human world."

Both Thorn and I began to protest.

Caterous sighed and shook his head at me. "Still, you did risk your own life in a vain attempt to keep her safe." He frowned. "Foolish elf—he would have destroyed you and still took her life." His exasperation was evident through his mutterings. He rounded the desk to stand in front of us. "All my power, all my influence, and I can't control my own daughter."

"Father, I'm sorry, I just—"

His raised hand halted her speech again. "It was my mistake to think I could keep you isolated and safe forever here." He fixed me with an evaluating stare. Something about me caused his eyebrows to rise infinitesimally in surprise.

"Father." Thorn pulled his attention from me briefly. "Henry has the spark."

Caterous stepped closer to me, his gaze piercing me. Muttering an incantation and moving his hands with measured ease, I felt the energy flow into me. Again, I glowed. A slight smirk creased the mage's lips.

"You appear to be correct, Sume."

"Shouldn't we try to cultivate that Magic?" she asked, rising to her feet. "I'll do what I must to assist him in learning the arts." She stood, looking up expectantly at her father, a defiant gleam in her eyes.

Caterous looked down at her with an intensity that made me want to crawl away and hide. The stand-off stretched on. Then suddenly, her defiance faltered under his gaze. However, so did his resolve.

He sighed as if he had resigned himself to something unpleasant. "Since it appears I cannot keep you two restrained or from causing trouble nor seeking each other out, I can at least train you to take care of yourselves."

Thorn's smile was infectious as she beamed at his words, and her excitement was evident in how she bounced on the balls of her feet.

"Really, Father?" She slapped me repeatedly on the arm. It hurt, actually. "Father is going to teach us defense and Magic." She bounded to him, grabbing her father in a tight hug.

It was the first time I saw anything even remotely resembling a smile from him.

Then, just as suddenly, Thorn let go, bowing her head. "Sorry, Father."

His face returned to stone.

Her embarrassment turned to concern. "Won't you need to travel again and . . ." she swallowed nervously, ". . . will *she* be back to watch over me?"

I wasn't sure who "she" was, but Thorn didn't seem to care for her.

Caterous patted Thorn kindly on her head. Judging by her reaction, this must have been an unusual act of affection. "No, the silver lady has refused, saying she has business elsewhere." He stopped in the doorway. "I think, perhaps, you have caused her too much trouble. No, I have someone else in mind."

The way he said it made me think Thorn would not be pleased with this chaperone either.

Next, he addressed me. "Young Elf."

I sat up straight.

"Enjoy this day of play. Tomorrow you begin training to be a healer." I began to protest that my parents were already teaching me to be a healer when he finished, "*and* a defender."

I was as stunned as Thorn seemed upset.

Before he disappeared, he spoke again. "Don't be discouraged, Sume. You will train as a loach."

Her mouth hung open, then turned into the happiest smile I have ever seen. "You better learn to defend yourself!" She slapped my arm again. It really hurt.

"I'm training to fight!" I sat stunned. What had I gotten myself into?

CHAPTER 9

When the door closed, the grand mage leaned wearily against it. A small smile played at the corners of his mouth. His daughter's excitement was infectious. He remembered his friends and how similar the situation was. One bubbling over with excitement and another, a little unsure but willing to follow her anywhere.

———⚬—⚬⚬———

On the campus of Fluxx Academy in the Western Realm
Twenty-five years earlier

"Where is Caterous now?" Micha Dreamweaver asked as he searched the crowd of teenage humans, elves, and other creatures, all dressed in similar uniforms.

"Where do you think?" Martin Heraldry laughed. Instantly his attention was lost on several young females. They giggled as he tried to get their attention.

"Oh, Martin, you're so dreamy," Amelia Gareth swooned before collapsing in Micha's arms. "Oh, Dreamweaver, I'm afraid I must leave you for this round-eared devil."

As he faced Martin, Micha let Amelia drop to the ground. "You'll pay for stealing my future spouse's heart."

"Haven't you three tired of this act?" Althea Shadefall rolled her eyes as she watched Micha help Amelia to her feet. Hurrying to join the group was Lawerence Caterous.

"Althea, you left your scrolls behind." Caterous breathlessly handed them over.

"Thank you, Lawerence—you're so sweet." Althea smiled, ignoring the pantomime of being sick that was being displayed behind the young mage. "I'll see you at dinner." Althea waved as she hurried off.

"You're all very immature," Caterous stated haughtily.

"You, however, are a lovesick puppy chasing after Althea all the time," Amelia replied, not unkindly. "She only sees you as a friend."

"That, and she's aloof and arrogant," Micha added.

"And more than a little pretentious," Martin offered.

Amelia glared at the two men. "Ignore the creepy little boys. They don't understand women."

Caterous still looked ready to fight.

"Come on, Lawrence, we're just trying to look out for you." Martin smiled. His humor faltered as he saw the anger in Caterous's eyes.

Micha walked up and threw an arm over the mage's shoulder. "Come on, Caterous, you know Martin's an idiot."

"Hey!"

"Shush—he's right, though. We're trying to look after you," Micha said as he steered Caterous away from the library. Amelia took Micha's free hand as Martin followed, grumbling.

"Althea is pretty and talented," Micha continued, ignoring Amelia's grumpy sideglance and Martin's mutterings. "She may see that you're a great guy."

Martin made a noise between a laugh and a cough. "She thinks she's far superior to our magician friend."

"I'll be a great mage one day!" Caterous broke free of Micha's grip. Advancing on Martin, electricity crackled in his hands.

Martin pulled his sword to easily deflect the lightning sent his way. "Too predictable, Lawerence." Martin's sword crackled with blue light. He swung toward Caterous, unleashing his own spell back at him.

"Come on, boys, stop it. You'll get into trouble again," Amelia called, although she sounded defeated and tired. Then, sitting on a bench nearby, she gestured to Micha.

"Who's predictable now?" Caterous laughed, catching the spell. He swirled it around, making it larger and more powerful. Martin took a stance as if to hit the spell back as soon as it was released. Instead, Caterous fed more and more energy into the ball of lightning. Martin tensed. A smirk played at the corner of his mouth.

Caterous pulled back his arm to cast. Instead, the ball of energy flew forward and fell directly to the ground. Martin, in anticipation, swung his sword. Unfortunately, Martin also ended up in the dirt without the resistance to stop his swing. Both men stared at each other briefly before turning their eyes to Micha.

Raising his hands in surrender, Micha called, "Hey, it wasn't me!"

All three turned to see Amelia slowly rising to her feet. "You boys done playing yet?"

"One day, I'll be the strongest mage alive," Caterous grumbled as he offered a hand to Martin.

Taking the offered hand, Martin muttered, "One day, she won't be able to best me in battle."

"One day, that elf will be my wife," Micha smiled as Amelia walked into a building. Then, too late, he realized he had turned his back on his two best friends. A thump of a sword on a spell made him spin. Martin and Caterous were both looking up. Micha had a second to swear before he was covered in slime. Martin and Caterous high-fived as they ran away from Micha as he pulled slime from his clothes to fling at them.

———◦\◦———

In the present day, Lawerence Caterous, one of the strongest mages alive, was surprised by the tear he wiped from his cheek. He swore as he swept down the empty hall.

CHAPTER 10

With breathless excitement, Thorn explained what my life was about to become. At the time, it sounded exciting. She was to become a loach, a warrior mage who learned to handle weapons and offensive magic. I would become proficient in one weapon aside from a dagger and become her defender. I would learn defensive magic: shields, barriers, disillusionments, and all sorts of ways to hide our presence. Before I knew it, late afternoon was upon us. With a borrowed beginner's spellbook and promises of being back tomorrow, I left Thorn at the entrance to the wall.

My walk home took an instant, my head still swirling with all the things Thorn had told me. I was so excited that my ribs didn't even hurt from the walk. My euphoria continued. It was like I was in the clouds all through dinner. Mom watched me suspiciously while Dad asked if she got the pain-relieving concoction right for me. I went to bed that night smiling and woke excited for the day. Dressing quickly, I bounded down the stairs and hurried to the kitchen. I was just outside the door when my excitement turned to dread. My heart froze as I heard the familiar rasping voice. I couldn't understand why Thorn's father was in my kitchen. Tension pulsed from the room.

Listening at the door, I heard my mom explaining many of her healing herbs and potions. The mage seemed impressed with her ability. They spoke warmly to each other as I hid. I swallowed nervously as Caterous mentioned my name. It was then that I noticed I was being watched.

I recognized those eyes. They were the ones I'd been thinking about since I first saw them, the eyes I thought about when I was alone or when I was going to sleep. The ones that were peering at me from the corner.

"How long have you been there?" I hissed.

"Your father is very unhappy with you," she explained, emerging from the shadow. A smile fought to gain control of her face. In a flash, she was at my side, listening to the conversation in the kitchen. She was warm and uncomfortably close, her shoulder and arm pressed against mine. Her hair smelled faintly of flowers. I noticed some darker strands of purple in her hair I hadn't before. She moved some of that hair behind her long ear. Against her pale skin, I noticed delicate pink earrings that resembled flowers made of jewels. It took me a few moments to notice she was frowning and waving her hand at me.

"Hey, pay attention," she hissed as she got closer. Then, to my horror, Thorn sniffed at me. I felt my blush coming back. I hadn't bathed. "You stink." I started to protest, but she laughed and covered my mouth with her small hand. I loved how her touch filled me with warmth and power as her Magic mixed with mine.

Every time it happened, it felt as if a whole new world revealed itself. Colors became more vibrant, and I could see Magic swirl around some of our plants, not to mention several faeries who were surprised when our eyes met. I would have to tell Mom she was right about the fae being in our house. I was amazed at how much more I could see of the other world. I also realized I could again hear much clearer.

My mom was about to explain a complex mixture of herbs and oils when my dad interrupted. "Caterous, this is totally unacceptable! How the hell did you let this happen?" I could imagine my dad's hands pounding the table.

Suddenly the front door flew open. Bright light in the room concealed the features of a human at the door. Thorn recoiled in fear from the silhouette. Her hand grabbed my arm for support. I pulled her close, terrified. The inspector had finally come to finish us off. Then Thorn exhaled her relief. My confusion only grew. Scratch's father entered our house. Before I met Thorn, I think I could have counted the times he visited us on one hand. Now he was here almost daily. Mr. Heraldry stumbled to a stop to greet me. He turned toward the kitchen and Dad's raised voice before entering the door. He stopped, finally noticing Thorn.

"Oh gods," Mr. Heradley muttered, stepping toward her.

Thorn, still clutching my arm, moved behind me. I moved further to keep myself between her and my friend's father.

"You look so much like her." He frowned as she pulled me further away. Then, addressing me, he gave a pained smile. "Lucky for her, right?" He caught her peeking over my shoulder. "Lawerence isn't much of a looker," he joked.

Someone swore, and something shattered in the kitchen. "Shit—sounds like I'm needed." He pushed through the door.

Thorn and I saw our dads glaring at each other. My mother's arms were outstretched. A blue glow around her hands kept them from flying at each other. Thorn gasped, catching their attention.

"Thorn, you and Henry wait outside," Caterous yelled.

She began to protest when my dad interrupted.

"Listen to your father and take Henry outside!"

Suddenly every adult in the house was staring at us. Then, as if they were of one mind, they all pointed to the door. We did as we were told, although as slowly as possible, trying to hear anything more being discussed.

"You didn't tell me he wasn't allowed to go see her!" my mom shouted. "He was worried about her, and so was I, for that matter!"

"That isn't the point!" my dad yelled in response.

Thorn and I shuffled quickly to the front door as the door to the kitchen banged open. Caterous stood there glaring, with Scratch's father and mine behind him.

"OUT!" the three of them shouted. Hurriedly, we did as we were told.

"Your mother didn't know you weren't allowed to see me?" Thorn hissed. She seemed exasperated with a hint of something. Conspiratorial approval, maybe.

"I'm not sure what you're talking about."

She shushed me as she pulled me toward the side of the house. We crouched low so as not to be seen. She smiled, pointing to the open kitchen window. Returning the smile, I gave her the thumbs up.

The first person we heard was Thorn's father. "I believe I owe you an apology, Amelia."

"How does your dad know my mom's name?" I was confused, and I could see Thorn was as well. She stared at me wide-eyed and shrugged. Sitting side by side, we listened as Caterous continued talking.

"It seems I made an agreement with your husband. Unfortunately, I didn't include you in the discussions." There was a pause as Caterous hesitated. "That was unfair. You had just as much right to know and to be involved in the decision."

My mom's voice held more than a hint of irritation. "You know what we sacrificed. What we all sacrificed and what we all agreed upon."

"What are they talking about?" Thorn hissed. It was my turn to shrug in confusion.

"I assure you, Caterous," my dad's voice cracked venomously. "It will be made clear to our son not to bother you or your daughter."

"That's not why I am here," Caterous interrupted, frustrated, as he tried to explain.

"You made a promise." Scratch's dad joined the conversation.

"And I have fulfilled that promise, haven't I?"

"Yes, but how did you let this happen?" My dad's voice was right above us. "How could you make such a mistake?"

The breakfast dishes rattled in the sink. "Oh no," Thorn muttered, grabbing my sleeve pulling the material tight. "I don't think your dad said the right thing." Her eyes narrowed while her grip pulled my sleeve so tight it started to hurt.

"How dare you!"

Thorn jumped up. Grabbing the bottom of the window, she pulled herself up. "Father! Please, be calm—oh!"

Her surprise became my fear. I jumped up to join her. What I saw was so unexpected, so surreal. In my kitchen stood my mom with her hands held out. Both of our fathers were suspended above the floor. Mr. Heraldy was casting a shield charm between them. Energy crackled in Caterous's hands while flame danced on the blade of a sword held by my dad. My jaw dropped. Suddenly a blue light filled the room, knocking Caterous back. He stumbled slightly but remained on his feet. Thorn screamed at her father. I was too shocked to understand what had happened. My dad was lying flat on his back, stunned but otherwise unharmed.

Caterous wasn't looking at my dad. Rather he was staring at my mom. Her hands started to shake. No, not shake. They were actually moving rhythmically. Energy hovered between Caterous, Mr. Heraldry, and my dad.

My mother dropped her hands and fell back. Then, using the counter for support, she glanced at Caterous. "I'm sorry, I-I panicked."

Caterous's lips turned into a slight smile. "Amelia, you've been hiding your skill for far too long." He shrugged his robes straight, holding his arms wide. He bowed to her. "I promise I was not going to hurt your family." He held out a hand to my dad. To my surprise, Dad took it. "It has been a while since you cast?" Caterous asked my mom, a hint of concern in his voice.

"Nothing this large in a while, no, not since—" She didn't finish her thought, instead turning her attention from him to address us. "I think you two need to take a nice, long walk." She threw a glance over her shoulder. It was a look I had seen cast my way many times. It was the look of being in deep trouble. I was astonished to see its effect on three grown men, one of whom was a powerful mage. "We have things to discuss." She gave everyone a significant nod. "Calmly."

I dropped to the ground, pulling Thorn with me. Above us, we heard three voices.

"Yes, dear."

"Sorry, Amelia."

"What did *I* do wrong?"

I had to laugh at Scratch's father. It seemed the father could be just as clueless as his son. Thorn and I waited.

"I said take a walk!" my mom called from the window before it was shut with a snap. I heard a hum, then nothing from inside.

"She blocked us from hearing," Thorn stated, impressed. "You didn't tell me your mom was an elf witch."

"Hey, don't call her that." I held my hand out to help her step over the lilies growing under the window.

"What? It's not a bad thing."

"I had no idea she was a Magic wielder." I paused. "I don't know where my dad got that sword and I didn't know Mr. Heraldry could do shield charms." I stopped. Grabbing Thorn by the shoulders, I spun her around to face me. "What the hell is going on?" I demanded.

Her eyes narrowed in anger. I released her shoulders. Once I stepped back from her, she answered.

"I have no idea." She growled at me. Then, the fire died behind her eyes, replaced by thought. "There's something they aren't telling us."

CHAPTER 11

Thorn and I walked away from the house in silence. We were lost in our thoughts as we tried to understand what we'd heard. Something kept bothering me. Actually, there were many things that bothered me. "Did you notice anything weird about today?"

Thorn laughed. "You mean aside from, I don't know, everything?" She bounced with infectious energy as she walked backward to face me.

"No—well, yeah—but with our dads. We've known the Heraldry family forever, although . . ." I was chewing on the inside of my cheek. "This the first time I remember him ever barging into the house. You know, on his own. I assume Dad summoned him, but why and how?"

Yet another conundrum to add to the list of mysteries.

Thorn shrugged. "No one ever comes to our house." She had turned back around. Her hands were behind her head as she raised her face to enjoy the sun's warmth.

"That's the thing, though," I said, watching her. It took Thorn a moment to notice I had stopped walking. "I didn't even know a mage lived this close to us."

Her brows knitted together.

"Listen, I'm pretty sure no one knew. But Scratch's dad called him by name, and your dad knew my mom's name. I swear everyone in the house today knew each other." I thought for a moment. "It was the same when we were brought back from town."

"Yeah, now that you mention it, that was the feeling I got too. A little less angry this time, though." She rubbed her head where she'd been hit. "I don't think your names ever come up at home."

"How do you think they know each other?" I asked. "I think Mr. Heraldry knew your mom." I didn't think Thorn had heard me as she looked over my shoulder. I heard voices and laughter but couldn't tell if they were elf or human. Either way, I didn't wish to engage with them. I was nervously trying to locate the encroachers when Thorn surprised me.

"You'll have to catch me to find out." She sprang away.

I was stunned at her speed as she headed into the woods. I had to sprint to keep her in sight. I lost her the instant she was enveloped in the forest. I paused momentarily, listening to the trees as the world's sounds changed in the woods. I closed my eyes to hear better. To my left, a squirrel scurried through the leaves while birds chirped as they winged overhead. Then, focusing, I found what I wanted to hear: a young woman's laugh.

I hopped up into the limbs of a nearby tree. I had to listen again. "Got you," I whispered. Staying light and quiet, I leaped from branch to branch. Arriving at a clearing, I was sure I could sense my quarry on the other side. Dropping from the branches, I hid in the long grass. Moving slowly to keep from alerting Thorn, I crept closer to the hollowed trunk I knew she was hiding in. I had forgotten her eyes and hearing were better than mine. I was only a few yards from my goal when she pounced. The wind was knocked from me.

"Wow, you're bad at this," Thorn laughed. She had disguised herself as a wolf again.

"Be careful, daughter. His ribs are still not entirely recovered." Her father glared at us from the edge of the woods. "Resume your normal form. What if someone saw you?"

Thorn and I leaped apart. I caught a glimpse before her wolf ears disappeared from the top of her head.

"What else does he know?" The mage was angry but also exasperated.

"I was just playing, Father."

Caterous's voice rose. "Children make mistakes." He beckoned us to follow him into the shade. "Since you insist I not treat you like a child, there's no excuse for what I just witnessed." He turned to ensure I noted his frustration. "You have to be careful. You both have to be careful." He was addressing me now. "What happened to my daughter in town is not your fault." He shook his head wearily. "But there are those who would hurt her. Or use her." Caterous glanced at Thorn, then cut himself off. "You tried to protect her with your life." His attention was back on me. "As I have said, that was foolish but commendable." His gaze returned to his daughter. "You don't want him to have to do that again before you are both ready?"

Thorn kept her eyes on the ground, shaking her head slowly.

Caterous huffed. "Your parents have agreed to let you be trained."

Thorn and I grinned like fools at each other.

"However," he held up a hand in warning. "You will not continue with this type of foolishness!"

"Yes sir," we replied.

"Sume, go to the house and prepare the practice room, please." Thorn and I exchanged a smile before she hurried away. We watched until she was out of sight before Caterous turned his attention back on me. "I suggest you go home. Spend an evening with your family. Then, get a good night's rest." I turned to head home when his hand found my shoulder. "You have questions. I don't know if your parents will tell you what you wish to know." He smiled sadly. "I have promised I will not."

I nodded and watched his midnight-blue cloak disappear into the forest.

On the walk home, I realized I had missed an entire day of training. My chest ached at the thought. I also realized there seemed to be many things my parents weren't telling me. I entered the house, anxious about what would greet me. Oddly, Mom seemed perfectly at ease with me learning Magic. Dad would only grunt at its mention. Needless to say, dinner was a subdued affair.

The sun had barely risen the next morning when I looked through the magnifying glass to find the gate. I entered and immediately found myself facing the Lord Mage himself. We walked in silence for a bit. I was getting uncomfortable.

"I've never met a mage before." Knowing this was obvious, I shrugged off my embarassment and said, "My parents would tell me stories about them." There was no reaction. "They said you're powerful beings that travel the countryside."

A frown creased his lips.

Foolishly I kept rambling. "They said you never knew when a mage arrived if it was a blessing or a curse."

He grunted. "You should have been taught to fear a mage."

I was screwing things up. I decided to change the subject. "So yesterday, uh, sir, Thorn had run away, so I, uh, chased after her."

He paused, eyebrow arched.

My brain was screaming, *shit shit shit, shut up.* "So, um, you've met my family before, huh?" I stammered.

"Yes, I know your father is Micha Dreamweaver, and your mother is Amelia." He sighed heavily.

"Yessir, how are they known to you?" I knew I was pushing his patience.

"I'm familiar with your family. How I've come to know them is a story for another time."

We walked in silence the rest of the way.

Reaching the enormous doors, he told me to wait. Thorn and her father had a loudly hissed conversation. It ended when she stomped up and hit me rather hard on the arm.

"You made it sound like you were trying to hurt me or something yesterday." She sighed. "You have to be the stupidest boy I've ever met." Then she frowned. "I hope not since you're the only boy I've ever met." She grabbed my sleeve. "Are all boys as dumb as you?"

"They can be," Caterous sighed.

I soon discovered he did that a lot around me.

Thorn pulled me into the library. Being pulled somewhere by Thorn was an action I would also come to understand was a frequent occurrence. I swear she never stopped. Once seated, Caterous arrived to stare at us imperiously from behind his massive desk.

"He knows he already intimidates me, right?" I whispered to Thorn out of the corner of my mouth. I dared a glance at her. She either hadn't heard me or was ignoring me. I looked past her to a portrait I hadn't noticed before. An elf woman stared down at me from the ornate frame. Even as paint on canvas, I could see the power radiating from her. I found myself transfixed by her beauty. I could tell she was also a mage but an even rarer elf mage. There was something familiar about the face. I could see hints of Thorn there.

"That is my wife, Thorn's mother," Caterous informed me. "Now that you know who that is, could you kindly pay attention?"

I couldn't find any words to speak. I had annoyed everyone in the room. I nodded my apology while trying to listen. I swear I felt the portrait's eyes boring into me along with Thorn's. Neither were friendly.

Caterous got up. He turned around twice. Both times he returned to face us, two enormous piles of books thudded heavily onto the desk. "This is for you," he said to Thorn, pointing to a slightly shorter stack. "That makes these . . . ?"

"Mine, sir," I almost moaned. It wasn't that I didn't like reading. I just thought there would be more Magic and practical instruction.

"Once you're done with these . . ." Caterous motioned to several more stacks of leather-bound tomes. "You will study these."

This time, I did moan.

As he swept past me, he paused in front of Thorn. "I will teach you and Henry. Do you understand?" He glared at his daughter.

My stomach joined with the unease in the room.

"I do not want her here," he stated with finality.

Thorn looked up at her father, her face a mask of innocence and slight confusion.

"Oh, don't give me that look. I know about the vampire. When I find her, I will evict her."

"Serina?" I breathed, regretting it immediately.

Caterous pounced on my words. "Did you say something, Henry?"

Behind the mage, Thorn held her hands together in a silent plea for me to be quiet.

"Nothing, sir, just—you know . . ." I made a *sheesh* noise. "A lot of books to get through."

He did not believe me. Frowning at one, then the other of us, he walked to the door. "I'll be watching."

"I don't know what Father's problem with Serina is." Thorn stamped her foot as tears formed in her eyes. They didn't seem like the tears of fear, more like anger. "She can't hurt me. He knows she can't."

"What do you mean?" I asked, thinking about how drained I felt in Serina's presence.

Thorn chewed on the side of her bottom lip. "I don't know," she said after a moment. "She just doesn't seem to have any effect on me." Thorn smiled. "Other than being fun to be around. She took me flying once." The library doorknob clicked as it turned. Thorn held her breath.

A shadow, followed by a huff of disgust, fell between the door and the frame. Then came a voice that I can only describe as filled with the most profound loathing and contempt I had ever encountered.

"Oh, it is here." A sniff of revulsion followed. "And it has an elf. Where is the mage?"

Thorn stood in a bow, her head down, arms and hands tight to her sides. "Father is not here."

"I can see that, stupid girl." I felt the cold of the woman's insult seep into my bones.

"I believe he—" I began.

"Vile creature, do not dare to address me," she shouted with such hate.

I fell back a step. Thorn was still bowed. I saw a tear drip off the end of her nose.

"You are so useless. Your tears only prove your pitiful lack of strength." The door snapped shut.

Thorn's knees gave out. I tried to catch her as she sank to the floor. Instead, she pushed me away, swiping angrily at her tears.

"I'm fine, I'm fine," she growled.

"Who was that horrid person?" I stared at the door in wonder.

"That was a Debkohr," Thorn nearly spat the name. "She was my mother's servant. She keeps reminding me of my mother's ideas and thoughts about me."

"Why doesn't your father get rid of her?" I asked. I couldn't understand why anyone would allow such a person to insult their child.

"Because she isn't here," Thorn sighed.

"I don't understand. I saw her."

"You saw an impression of her—not exactly a ghost but a memory." Thorn sat on her knees. She was closely examining her fingers. "She's a curse. She randomly shows up to remind me I'm a disappointment."

"How can anyone be so cruel?" I was aghast.

"When I was born . . ." Thorn's voice was quiet. I couldn't see her eyes. She had moved up to the couch. She was still looking down at her hands, and I watched as she pressed her thumbs into her forefingers. I was entranced by how small and pale her hands looked. Finally, Thorn spoke again, her voice diminished. "My father told me he brought my mother a rose." She smiled for a moment. "He said it was to repay the beauty she had just given him." Then, Thorn's expression soured. "When he handed it to her, she pricked her finger on one of the thorns." Thorn looked at her thumb. "Father said that's when she looked at the blood and then at me." She wrung her hands as if trying to wipe something grotesque away. "He told me she said, I have a name for the girl. So my father says he smiled, looked at me, and said, 'Hello, Rose.'" Thorn's hands dropped to her lap in defeat. "My mother laughed at him. She said, 'Her name is Thorn.'"

"I told her, as I tell you." Caterous's voice caused me to jump. It was soothing but edged with anger. He walked to his daughter. Kneeling before her, he took her hands. "The name is because she is a beauty that can defend herself." He spared a glare at me before warning me. "This is something you would do well to remember." His hands moved to Thorn's shoulders.

I thought he was about to pull her into a hug. I wanted to pretend not to notice.

He didn't embrace her, as she didn't face him.

"If you say so." She shrugged.

He stood, letting his hands fall to his sides. Caterous turned, opened his mouth, then shook his head. He walked to the door, hesitated, then disappeared through it. Again the door was shut, and we were alone.

All I could do was open a book. I had no idea what to do next. "I don't think you're useless," I muttered.

"Says the elf who had to save me from getting killed," she huffed.

"Um, if you want to talk about useless, here's a prime example." I tried to laugh.

"Yeah, that's true." She laughed a little. "At least we're equal in that respect."

"You and me," I held out my hand to her, "let's be useless together." I immediately pulled back my hand. I could feel the blush burning already. "I mean, friends—just friends. I mean, you're pretty, um, pretty awesome, um . . ."

"Shut up and read your book." Thorn laughed. We sat reading for a while, occasionally sharing a smile and a laugh. Then, when it was time for me to leave, Thorn walked me to the gate. "I'm glad you want to be a friend of someone with such a wonderful mother."

I tried to sound mature. "I don't judge someone by their parents."

I wasn't sure what I had hoped for, but Thorn's smile and happy "see you tomorrow" were enough. The walk home was giddy excitement.

CHAPTER 12

My good mood was tempered by the cool reception I received when I returned home. Thankfully there were very few questions from my family at dinner that night. Mom seemed happy, while Dad seemed resigned. After a few attempts at conversation, I let the matter drop. When I asked Mom about it later, she told me Dad was excited for me. "You know he's always wanted to teach you about Magic, and . . ." She seemed to catch herself. ". . . and other things." She played it off by getting me to help with the dishes. Then, after a few moments, she explained, "He's proud of you. He just isn't too happy with who is instructing you."

I asked why, but she wouldn't elaborate.

As the weeks proceeded, I began showing off some of my abilities. When I did, Dad began making inquiries. He'd ask me to show him more and more of what I could do. Sometimes he and Mom commented on my technique. They'd laugh and say something along the lines of, "Yeah, he still favors the old way." Then they'd show me the same spell but in a way that made it easier for an elf. I'd take this back to Caterous. He'd frown and grumble about laziness but would never correct my casting. It was awesome but frustrating as neither side would explain the relationship to me.

Caterous gave me a day of rest once a week. I didn't want to take the time away from the training or Thorn, but I found I needed to recuperate. The spell work took a lot of concentration that left my mind and body drained. However, on this day, I felt refreshed. We'd been studying swordwork. Unfortunately, Caterous wasn't a weapons master, so we had no choice but to learn from examples in a book. I wished Scratch were on leave to help us. I never felt my stances and grips were quite right.

I was practicing in the garden one day. I had borrowed a wooden practice sword and was swinging at an imaginary enemy. After about four swings, Dad called out to me, "Henry, please tell me Caterous didn't show you that?" He pointed at my stance, sword held out before me.

"Um, no." I shrugged. "Thorn and I learn from books."

Dad swore, pinched the bridge of his nose, and shook his head. "Wait here," he commanded grumpily. I did a few practice swings while I waited. When he returned to the yard, he carried a wooden sword similar to mine along with the real thing. He pulled the shining blade from the rich leather scabbard and handed it to me. I nearly dropped it. The heft was much more than I anticipated, especially after seeing how easily Dad handled it.

"It takes some time to get used to the weight," he explained, then corrected my stance. Next, we worked on my grip and swing.

From the different muscles I was straining, I knew I'd been doing this wrong from the start. So when my technique got sloppy from fatigue, we took a break. Mom came outside with some water for us. I was thankful for the drink. I hadn't realized how thirsty I'd become. While I drank, I watched my mom warily. Then, deciding to make some assurances, I put my drink aside. "Listen, Mom. I'm learning tons of spells. Thorn and I have started practicing with swords."

Mom made a noise.

"Wooden swords, Mom—don't worry."

She turned to face me, a strange look on her face. I decided not to tell her too much more.

The sip I was taking fell out of my mouth in astonishment as several things happened at once. First, Mom approached one of the wooden swords lying on the ground. As she leaned down to retrieve it, Dad smoothly reached over to retrieve the sword closest to him. Next, Mom stood up and hooked a toe under the sword, flipping it into her hand. Then, a swish through the air forced Dad to roll backward and jump to his feet. A crack of wood on wood sounded like a thunderclap.

I sat transfixed, staring at my parents. These two elves I'd known my whole life were doing something I never would have expected. They moved around each other like dancers, each thrust and slice countered and blocked. Yet, no matter the move or strike, their faces held concentration and unadulterated joy. Suddenly the dance stopped. My mom's blade was at my dad's throat. However, his sword was pointed at her heart. "We stay together in death, my captain." My father smiled.

My mom stepped back, also smiling. "Together now and always, Lieutenant."

"Wow," I gasped. My parents jumped in surprise. It appeared they'd forgotten they had an audience. "When the hell did you two learn to do that?"

"Language, Henry," Mom chastised. She then gave Dad the kind of kiss that embarrassed me, and returned to the house. She tossed me the wooden sword as she passed. The way Dad watched her go made me want to be anywhere but there.

"Right, well." Dad composed himself. "You see how fast actual combat can be." He cleared his throat. "Now, let us go over the basics."

"Good, now block," Dad instructed.

I swung up to meet his blow.

"Parry!"

I tried to knock his sword aside, thrusting. Dad easily blocked.

"Okay, again."

I did a nice move, almost catching Dad off guard. He had me on the defensive immediately. I pushed him away to gain some distance and tried to catch my breath.

Dad was annoyingly at ease. "So how is the old magician?"

"Caterous? He tries to be mysterious, but his mood is often annoyed." I came at Dad with a quick three-part attack.

"Not bad, but you left yourself open. What have you been studying? Obviously not swordplay." Dad countered every move with ease.

"Most of the spell work is just reading at the moment." I tried a feint, but he didn't fall for it. "So, how long have you known Caterous?"

"You need to sell that move better. How's Thorn doing? How's her spell work?" Dad blocked my attack and my question.

"She's doing mostly combat spells."

"Really? Interesting."

"Why?"

"Promise me, if she ever does anything—nice move—that makes you uncomfortable or scared, you'll tell me." Dad was earnest. Still, it was also a break in his concentration.

I went for it.

"Why would—" I swung like I was going in low, spun, and went for an overhead strike. Unfortunately, my legs left the ground, and my sword clattered several feet away. The point of Dad's sword was at my neck.

"Just promise me."

I had no choice but to surrender and promise. "You know, Dad, Thorn would never hurt me."

Dad didn't say anything at first. As he retrieved my sword, I heard him mumble about it not being the first time. "Her mother wasn't a good person."

"But she *is*." I reminded him. "Who is her mother? I've never seen her other than an old painting."

"It's for the best."

"Why don't you and Mom tell me what happened?" I demanded. Dad looked conflicted. He opened his mouth, seemed to think better of it, frowned, and stared past me at the slowly setting sun. Then, Mom appeared at the back door to call us in for dinner. A broad smile broke out on Dad's face. "She saves me again."

It was an uncomfortable meal due to the way my parents kept flirting. It was also somewhat frustrating, as they wouldn't tell me how they came by the skills they showed.

When my next rest day came, I woke to find Dad waiting for me. "Grab some breakfast and meet me out back."

He had the practice swords ready. He threw one to me and attacked as soon as I grasped the hilt. I did pretty well, in my opinion, at defending the surprise attack. However, it was only a few minutes before I was on the ground, looking up the length of a sword. Finally, Dad removed the point from my throat and grabbed my hand to pull me to my feet. "Remember, your enemy will rarely warn you of an attack."

As soon as I was on my feet, I spun into an attack of my own. I was on my back again quite quickly, my dad laughing. "Good try, good try." He smiled as he helped me to my feet. "You announced each move, though."

"How?" I was annoyed. I thought he wouldn't see it coming. "And how do you know so much about swordplay?"

"Henry, remember this if nothing else." He grasped my shoulder. "This isn't playing. This is a great skill. I'm not teaching you to duel or show off flashy blade acrobatics." His tone was serious, and his face was stern. "Fighting is something to be avoided, but if you can't, it can be deadly." He let go of me to grab the steel blade he'd shown me the other day. "I won't tell you about this blade's history now, but know this. It has taken a life." He returned the blade to its scabbard.

"Were you a soldier?" I asked.

"Not as good a one as your mother." He smirked. "But that's also a tale for when you're ready."

I wasn't sure how I could become any more ready, but I didn't want to push. I didn't want to jeopardize my training and the new bond I was sharing with my dad.

"Oh, stop showing him that boring regimental position," Mom called as she emerged from the house, drying her hands. She tossed the towel through the open door and held out her hand. My father tossed his sword to her. "Here's something he won't teach you."

"Watch out for a left-side attack. She'll then come at you from above. Be ready," my father hissed in my ear.

He was right.

When I blocked it, Mom laughed. "I guess your *old* man can be taught."

"Henry, your sword!" Dad called.

I tossed the practice sword to him.

"If I remember correctly, my love . . ." Their blades cracked and scraped with increasing speed. "Aren't you older than I am, by at least fif—whoa!"

Mom's attack was incredibly swift and strong. Dad was no match, especially since he couldn't stop laughing. Finally, he tossed down his sword and held his hands in surrender.

"I accept your surrender, but you will do the dishes as a prisoner." Mom handed her sword to me with a wink.

"This is what I was saying. If you're defeated, it may lead to a fate worse than death."

"It's just the dishes, you big baby."

Dad and I resumed my training. I knew I had improved, however, Dad was making it easy. His attacks were noncommital, and his defense was weak. I could tell something was bothering him. Finally, it seemed he had come to a conclusion. "Have they told you anything about Thorn's mother?" he asked as casually as he could.

"Um, no." I frowned as I watched his reaction. "I got the impression she's no longer alive."

"I see." He kept his face passive. "I know elf mages are extremely rare. She may just not wish to be seen."

"I don't think that's the case." I proceeded to tell him about the Debkorh, along with how much Thorn hated her mother.

Dad nodded his understanding. "You be careful anyway," he replied, stopping to adjust my grip.

Mom returned to call us in for lunch. "I think it's great that you and Thorn are getting along. Don't you agree?"

"Listen," Dad whispered, "Thorn and Caterous are fine, I guess." He had his back to Mom. "If you ever see Thorn's mother, stay away from that witch."

"Your dad is correct. That woman isn't someone I want you around." Disgust covered her face. "She shouldn't even be allowed to roam free," Mom grumbled so low she thought I couldn't hear it. It surprised me.

"I really think she's dead," I tried to reassure them. "How do you know them?" I asked, unable to fight my curiosity any longer. "You never mentioned them or even that a mage lived near us."

They cast conspiratorial glances at each other.

"If her mother was—or is—so dangerous, why are you letting me go there to learn?"

"No one said she was dangerous," Dad stammered, coughing on his drink.

Mom jumped in. "She just sounds awful from what you've told us about how she treated Thorn."

"Don't forget how she chose the poor girl's name," Dad injected.

"How do you know about that?" I'd finally caught them. I had never told them the story she told me. They had to tell me something—I was sure of it.

"Let's just say we were aware of them long before you were born," Mom said gently.

I was about to argue when someone called my name. Thorn appeared at the kitchen window, waving. We met her in the backyard. As soon as she looked around, her usual energetic smile faltered.

She pointed at the practice swords and shouted, "No fair, no fair!"

What happened next sent my brain reeling. First, Mom grabbed one of our swords and threw the other to Thorn. Then she announced, "I will not have some she-elfling sully my domain with accusations of impropriety!"

"If it is a fight you wish, I shall give you one," Thorn called as she removed her travel cloak.

"What are you doing here?" I asked, rushing to Thorn's side.

"This welp was summoned for lunch. However, it seems young Thorn needs a thrashing beforehand."

If Thorn was upset by my mom's words, her smile surely didn't show it. Instead, Thorn took a stance I hadn't seen in the books we read. However, when Mom took a different stance going from a two-handed hold to a single one, Thorn smiled and adjusted to a single hand. The two women circled, changing and adapting to each other's movements.

"I thought you were learning from a book," Dad whispered. I shrugged in response.

Mom was the first to attack. Then, after a flurry of clicks and cracks, they were back to circling.

"Interesting," Mom smirked. "Not a style I would have expected. Blood-moon, I would guess."

The words caused the briefest moment of surprise on Thorn's face. But then, it was gone in a blink. Thorn now came in for an attack.

Mom easily defended. "Very good, young one. However, you need to stay on the balls of your feet. Your attack was flat."

"Thank you." Thorn beamed, then came in for another assault.

"Are you watching this?" Dad demanded. The man was almost salivating as he ogled my mother.

"Gross," I replied. However, as I watched Thorn's fluid movements, I understood what my dad saw.

The result of the fight was as Dad expected. Thorn was disarmed, and Mom was the victor. A second after Thorn yielded, Mom was hugging her around the shoulder. "That was excellent, really excellent."

Thorn smiled as if she had had the best day ever.

"You lost," I hissed to Thorn.

"Yes, but to lose to such a master is amazing." Her smile flattened a little. "You never told me your parents were soldiers."

"I didn't know until last week that they even knew which was the pointy end of a sword."

"Funny, Henry," Mom called. "Thorn, we have your favorite dessert—strawberry tarts."

I grabbed Thorn's arm before she could follow my parents into the house. "When did you tell her that?"

Thorn frowned in thought as she placed a finger to her chin. "I don't think I told her."

"Then how did she know? How do they know so much about your mother? How can they be this skilled in fighting? What the hell is going on?" I was breathing heavily now.

Thorn ran her hands down my arms in a calming motion. "I don't know, but when I told my father about your training session, he smiled and nodded like it was the most obvious thing in the world."

"There's so much they're hiding from us."

Before we could discuss it further, my mother appeared in the doorway. After that, lunch was pleasant enough, even though Thorn and I were thwarted every time we tried to find out how our parents knew each other. Thorn and

I continued to practice through the afternoon. So I was surprised when she stayed for dinner.

"Thank you so much. I never get to eat with other people. There's so much talking, but it makes the food taste even better." Thorn beamed.

Night was falling when Thorn headed to the door. My parents were being weird again, flirting with each other. I decided to walk Thorn home—at least part of the way. A full moon lit the path as we walked in silence. I felt the urge to say something, to take her hand, I don't know. I just felt I needed to do *something*. If I moved my hand just a few more centimeters, I'd be touching hers. Would she take it?

"Don't you think it's weird?" Thorn stopped abruptly. I pulled my hand back quickly. She didn't seem to notice. "A couple of weeks ago, our parents were opposed to us even talking." She clasped her hands behind her back and started walking again.

I wondered if she did this because she saw I tried to hold her hand.

Finally, Thorn's voice broke through my panic. "I mean, tonight my father encouraged me to have dinner with you." She stopped. I could see her frowning in the moonlight. "In fact, he kind of insisted."

Suddenly she was running.

"Hey, wait for me!" I shouted. I had lost sight of her.

"Something isn't right. Go ahead and go home. I'll be fine." Thorn shouted from a growing distance. I hadn't been running for more than a few moments in my attempt to follow her. I stopped as ever-thickening clouds obscured the moon.

I stood still, listening to the woods as I realized I wasn't on the path. Elves see better than humans in the dark, but I could barely see a foot in front of me. The night had turned that dark. With the blackness came silence. I had no way of telling which direction I had come from. Then, suddenly, something flew over my head so close I had to duck. I heard the rustle of feathers and hoped it was an owl. I began backing away when I heard movement in the brush.

"Thorn?" I whispered hopefully.

There was no answer. The forest was quiet except for something moving on my other side.

I got a feeling in the pit of my stomach, the one that begins as discomfort before it twists into fear and panic. I screamed as another enormous bird flew over my head. I had enough. There were still things in these woods that could be dangerous to an elf, even with some sword training, especially when that elf didn't have a sword. I'm not proud of it, but I ran. I was off the path and crashing through the trees. Everywhere I turned, it felt like something was coming toward me.

The moon broke through the clouds momentarily to reveal an owl and a hawk circling above me. I swear they were screeching out my location to a much larger creature. I could hear it advancing. Diving into the bushes, I rolled into a dip in the earth. I pulled whatever I could over myself, praying the pine and other plants would mask my scent.

As I lay there, I knew it was useless as those damn birds still circled. They kept screeching and calling out to the other beast as it was closing in. I could see their torch through the leaves. Wait, *torches*? Someone was calling my name.

"Henry, where are you?"

"I'm over here," I called out. Two men appeared from different directions.

"What do you think you're doing out here?" they both demanded. Then, finally, the circling owl landed on my dad's shoulder. Caterous held out his arm for the hawk to land.

The two men approached each other. "Thank you for helping find my idiot son."

"I wouldn't have come, but my daughter seems quite fond of him." Caterous shrugged. "I guess this might be as good a time as any," he continued. "Henry's studies will become more . . ." He grimaced. "Strenuous soon. It may be a good idea for him to stay at the manor some nights."

"I assumed so," Dad replied, scratching the owl's head. "I need a guarantee first."

"A guarantee?" Caterous raised an eyebrow. "Ah, yes, right." He rubbed his chin thoughtfully. "Our children's safety is extremely important to both of us." Again Caterous sighed. "And as you are the better swordsman—"

"Superior," my dad said.

"Slightly better than I am." Caterous grimaced. "I would take it as a great personal favor if you continued to help train Thorn." He thought for a second before he reached out to touch my dad's arm. "Micha, be careful if you're seen by the wrong sort."

Dad patted Caterous's hand in understanding. They stared at each other for several moments. Then, something passed between them that I couldn't understand. It was like they debated and laid out rules without saying a word. Then, finally, my dad agreed.

"When you return to the manor tomorrow, you'll bring some items along. If there's a need for you to stay overnight, you should be prepared."

"I'll send Steve to let you know if the lessons go long." Caterous motioned to the hawk. My dad nodded his understanding.

"Did Thorn make it home safe?" I asked as Dad steered me toward home.

"She's safe and overly inquisitive," Caterous replied. However, it sounded like a warning to my dad, who seemed to understand as he nodded without looking back at the mage.

The walk home was a mostly quiet one. Dad seemed lost in thought. Even when he chastised me for leaving the house. It was almost like an afterthought. "You should never go into the forest at night, especially without a torch or letting us know you're leaving."

I almost tried to argue, but he seemed so distracted I simply agreed. I started to ask about Caterous and my parents, but Dad shut that conversation down quickly.

That night I went to bed annoyed. I was just trying to give my parents some alone time. Scratch and I had been out at night a ton of times. So why were they suddenly worried? Caterous's warning to my dad was not lost on me. If the humans found out there were warrior elves nearby, and worse yet, they were practicing and training other elves . . . I shuddered at what would happen.

Shaking that thought away, I decided to piece the big question together. Mom said they'd known Caterous long before I was born. However, I'd never met or even heard about him. Scratch and I knew each other because of our fathers. We grew up together as they said they had.

I knew we weren't originally from Dayok. Mom and Dad moved here before I was born to be close to Mr. Heraldry. The story was that they'd been refugees and became good friends during the war. I realized now that couldn't be true. My parents were obviously soldiers. Was Scratch aware of this? Was his father also in the army? I thought about writing to Scratch but discounted it. He was busy with his training, and a letter from an elf wouldn't help his standing with the guard. Also, hadn't the war been between the empire and Elro? Were elves allowed to fight? If so, who did they fight for? It had to be Notelek. The people of Elro hated us more.

I remember when Scratch and I used to ask them about their time on the road. They'd never tell us. Mom said it was still too painful to talk about it. She'd been there too. Scratch's mother had met his dad after they moved here. I never thought much about that time, but now I wanted to know. Did they meet Caterous before or after they decided to live here? I decided to ask my parents the next day.

Rolling over, I tried to clear my head and get some sleep. I was on the very cusp, where you know rest is almost there. In a second, you'll be asleep. Then, of course, that was when the tapping started. I knew right away what it was.

"Serina, is everything okay?" I asked as soon as I opened the window.

She replied by slapping me on the side of the head. "That was stupid."

I rubbed the spot where she hit me. "What the hell was that for?"

"You made Thorn worry," she growled. It wasn't the first time I saw her fangs. "Your father sent an owl to the house asking if you were there."

I jumped back into my room in fear when she hissed at me.

"Caterous was upset too," she grumbled. "Thorn overheard them talking."

"Who, my dad and hers?" Then, I remembered. "Hey, she ran off and left me there!"

"No, dummy," Serina moved to slap me again, completely ignoring that Thorn had left me. I ducked out of the way. "Caterous and the owl. He sent his hawk to tell your father he was going to look for you with the help of his owl."

"Why didn't he send the owl back?" I asked

"Ugh." The disgust was evident. "Because his hawk doesn't know you. The owl does."

I was confused. "I didn't even know my dad could control an owl."

"There are a lot of things you don't know." But, then, she growled, "I don't know why Caterous is even putting up with you."

"You're one to talk," I defended. "It's not as if he wants *you* around." I regretted saying it right away. The hurt in her eyes made my heart ache.

"I know that," she whispered, "but I have nowhere else to go, and Thorn is my friend."

"What about your family?" I asked.

She frowned. "I left home a long time ago. And I'm not going back," she replied fiercely, then the fire went out in her eyes. "Not like they'd take me back anyway."

I reached out a hand to comfort her.

"Hey, wait, no! Don't!" she yelled as she tried to slap my hand off her arm. Then the room was spinning. I was falling backward. Instinctively I grabbed at Serina's hands. Everything went black as soon as I felt her ice-cold flesh touch mine.

CHAPTER 13

Ninety years ago

"Mother," Serina cried, shocked at what she had just heard.

"This is not up for discussion!" the king boomed. "You have brought us to the brink of civil war!" Then, he began pacing. "The other clans are calling for your public execution!" Finally, he turned, pointing an accusing finger at Serina. "This is your fault!"

Serina realized he wasn't pointing at her but at her mother.

"You encouraged her to be ruthless!"

"If you continue to act this way, you will find out how ruthless I can be," Asha growled as her fangs elongated. The king cowered at her tone.

"Right, we will talk of that later," he muttered before returning to Serina.

She now saw anger and pain in his eyes.

"I only hope your exile will be enough to restore order." He turned his back on Serina and stormed out of the hall. Asha's glare followed him as he left.

Serina was on the road out of the kingdom in less than an hour. "Where is Glacious?" she asked, looking for the friend she had shared the smile with. But instead, her two remaining companions glanced at each other.

"He was, um, called away on urgent business."

"More important than a request from the queen?" Serina mumbled, confused and a little hurt. The reality of her exile still had not set in. Neither of her companions offered any more explanation.

"Do you know where we are going?" Serina called after they had been traveling for a couple of hours.

Asha told Serina she would stay just outside a vampire village. Serina had a distant relative, a cousin, that lived there. The path they traveled wasn't one she was familiar with. Serina's concern began to grow when she heard whispering between her companions.

"The Varatos have insulted us and caused bloodshed on neutral ground," Marcus said. He was a couple of years older than Serina. She wouldn't call him a friend but thought he was likable enough.

Vitoria was someone Serina had been good friends with when they were young. She replied, "They have declared war." Her voice was rising to match her venom. "This insult must not go unpunished." She reigned in her temper.

"I want to avenge our fallen," Marcus answered, drawing a deep breath. "All we have to do is fan the flames of war."

Serina felt more than heard the sword slowly being removed from its scabbard. She could sense a bowstring going taunt. In a flash of steel, Serina deflected the arrow shot by Vitoria and parried the swing from Marcus's blade. Marcus's head lay at his horse's feet in less than ten seconds. His body slowly slid from the saddle to join it. Serina almost lazily deflected Vitoria's arrows until she was close enough to cleave her former friend in two.

Still astride her horse, Serina looked at the blood-soaked path. Anger fought with fear as she took her dead companions' supplies and set their horses free. Her mother had picked these two to accompany her. Had she sent them to kill her? Did her father, in the hopes of assuaging the other clans? What would they do when the horses returned without their riders? Would they know Serina was still alive? Was that the plan? Would they come after her?

All these questions chased Serina further and further from her home. She spent the next few months hiding in caves, abandoned houses, and empty barns. Finally, after a couple of years, with no other vampire sightings, Serina finally felt she wasn't being pursued. She'd been frugal with the little money she had with her, selling off any jewelry or weapons she didn't need, but her funds were dangerously low.

Even though she was over one hundred, Serina still looked like a young maiden, a trait she'd exploited in the past. As she walked alone in the town, she waited for the inevitable, for the unsavory sort that would look to take advantage of a lonely young woman out late at night.

As if she possessed her mother's ability at foresight, along came two of the type she was expecting.

"A pretty young woman like you, all alone at night, should be cautious." One of the brutes explained with a wheezy laugh.

"You never know what kind of people you might encounter," his companion chimed in.

Serina became aware of the third man lurking in the shadows. His voice held none of the smarminess of the other two. "I think it would be in your best interest to let that small rabbit go," called the hidden man, "or maybe, rabbit, you should consider if the attention is worth the ten gold you may retrieve."

The two thugs looked at each other, obviously confused. Serina, however, looked into the shadows, seeing a ranger casually watching her.

"You seem to know something about me," Serina called in a firm voice. Her appearance as a cowering child was thrown off as she spoke. "You have me at a disadvantage, sir."

"You *are* at a distance vintage," the first thug called. "Both of you."

"*Disadvantage*, you dope," the other thug growled. "Why are you such a moron?" He pulled his sword, and his partner matched his actions.

"That is a mistake," the ranger called, although he didn't move from leaning against the alley wall. The fight was over before the thugs even realized it had begun. Blood dripped from Serina's fingers as her claws retracted. Both men lay staring lifelessly up at the sky. One had his throat torn out, while the other had been eviscerated. "Should have listened," the ranger calmly shrugged as he stepped into the low torchlight.

Serina's fangs were still visible as she gave the man an evil smile. "Not friends of yours, I hope," she hissed.

"Them? Heavens no." He waved away her statement. "I must thank you," he explained as he pulled some papers and a ring from the smarter of the two thugs. "You saved me several minutes of work."

"So you were going to kill them as well?" Serina watched as the ranger emptied the dead men's pockets.

"That is what I was hired to do." He tossed a bag of coins in his hand a few times, then threw it to Serina. "A woman of your talents could make quite a profit in this trade."

"What trade is that?" Serina eyed him suspiciously, weighing the coin purse.

"Assassin, mercenary, bounty hunter, any of that sound good?" he asked as he pocketed the papers. "I guarantee the pay is much better than a few coins from back alley thugs."

Serina nodded her agreement. Thus began their partnership.

Serina looked no older than when Conrad, the ranger, first met her. However, it had been thirty years, and he was tired. They were well known for their work, Conrad's team. Five mercenaries with skills and talents that never failed them. Of course, the most feared was the one they called The Rabbit. It was the only name Serina had gone by since she joined.

———ᦙᦙ———

Serina looked around the table at the four scared and worn faces. Her friends, her allies, the men and women she trusted. Then there were the two young attendees. They had been with the group for only a short time. Serina didn't like them. They were undisciplined and brutal, two attributes that had landed her here.

Something else about the two reminded her of Marcus and Vitoria. She always felt they were plotting, which always seemed about her. They'd watch her. She was sure they'd gone through her things. Serina had nothing to hide other than being a vampire princess. She didn't think that mattered, as news from the vampire kingdom had resolved the tension she'd caused. "Likely because they think I am dead," Serina muttered.

Conrad was looking at Serina, a question in his eyes. She shook her head to assure him all was well. Before he could press the issue, the host of the meeting arrived. He was tall, thin, and very pale. Serina sensed he wasn't human—a vampire, or not entirely. Even so, she didn't meet his eyes when he spoke.

"I want you to destroy the village of Tranmonia." The man's voice was soft yet full of malice.

"Why?" Conrad leaned forward. The answer he received was a simple shrug of the shoulders.

"That isn't far from here," Wagner, the young human woman who joined the group a year ago, grinned. "You think the princess would be up for killing some Varatos?"

Serina still flinched internally when she heard the term princess. Wagner and her counterpart Arka had started using the title as a slight. Serina was sure they had no idea who she'd been. Then, Serina caught Conrad's eye. She knew he was uncomfortable with the meeting with an almost imperceptible shake of his head. But it wasn't only Conrad's discomfort that bothered Serina. There was something that tickled a memory deep in her brain. The village of Tranmonia was familiar, but she couldn't place it.

"This may not be something your group wishes to do," their host explained in a bored voice. "I don't blame humans for not wishing to assist the vampire royal family." He now had Serina's full attention. "This village of—what did you call them, Veratos?" Again, he shrugged as if none of this interested him. "They are harboring rebels who wish to destabilize the royal leadership."

Before Serina could ask, Conrad leaned back in his chair, meeting their host's icy gaze. "And why, if this matters so little to you, are you asking us to help those creatures?" The quick glance Conrad spared for Serina was his apology. Conrad was the only one who knew what she was, if not who she was.

The thin pale face became pinched and unhappy. "My reasons to support the royals are my own. Suffice it to say, I want to stop violence before it spills out across the clans and into your world."

The front legs of Conrad's chair connected loudly with the stone tile. He leaned forward on the table. "Why should we help a vampire or try to stop your kind from killing each other?"

"You are mistaken," the man sneered. "I am not a vampire. However," he forced his shoulders to relax, "my business is with the vampires. I do not wish to have it disrupted."

"Blood merchant," Horace, one of the team's old members, grunted.

"We'll take the job," Conrad explained to gasps and grumbles from the others, "on one condition." Conrad held up a hand for quiet. "I need proof the village is a threat." He headed off the interruption he saw coming. "And we will confirm it ourselves."

"As you wish."

The meeting ended. However, the arguments had just begun. Serina was of two minds. She didn't trust their employer and didn't wish to take the job. However, she wanted to keep her family safe. There was also the fact Serina hated the Varatos. If the Varatos were planning on harming her family, she'd stop them. At dusk the next night, they set out for Tranmonia.

No one in their band was ever required to take on a job if they did not wish to. It was a rare occasion when a member didn't agree or participate. However, this particular job had been contentious among Serina's companions. So it came as little surprise that only Conrad and the two new members rode with her to their objective. The closer they came, the more Serina's stomach clenched. She hadn't been this close to home in decades. However, something else was bothering her as well. Something Serina's grandmother had told her about Tranmonia. Unfortunately, Serina couldn't remember if it was something good or bad.

"The Vantos show no mercy to their enemies in combat," Arka growled. "We will show them none in return. *We* show no mercy to anyone."

To answer his statement, Wagner shouted, "Then to Glory!" Her fist pumped into the air to the ecstatic cry of Arka. Conrad glanced at Serina with a warning look on his face. She knew at once he also felt something wasn't adding up. On the outskirts of the village, Conrad called them to a stop.

"You three, wait here. I'm going to do a quick recon of the village," Conrad explained.

Serina nodded. She knew the procedure well. First, Conrad would check the perimeter and note any defenses. Then, when he returned, they'd form a strategy for the attack. While Serina took the time to relax and focus on the job ahead, her companions became increasingly restless.

Serina felt them coming up on either side of her horse. Wagner smiled at Serina. "What do you think, Princess? Ready to kill some Varatos?"

Arka grabbed Serina's arm tightly, "Or should we say kill *more* Varatos?" His wicked smile and firm grip told Serina she was in trouble.

"I don't know what you are talking about," Serina growled, trying to pull free from him. Fear gripped her heart. To her surprise, she couldn't break his hold. Her strength should have been far more than any human.

Arka laughed at her struggle.

"Oh, princess, you are not in control here," Wagner laughed. Her glare turned ugly. "And don't expect help from Conrad. He is already dead."

"Did you think we would forget what you did?" Arka demanded, shaking Serina painfully. "Did you think we would ever stop hunting you?" His fury rose with every question. "Did you think you could get away with killing the Representative and Lord Crandle? You nearly started a war!"

"I didn't kill the Varatos emissary. Crandle forced me to," Serina tried to explain, knowing they wouldn't believe her.

Wagner placed a hand on Arka's shoulder as she looked directly at Serina. "We are not upset that you killed those filthy cowards." Her gaze was of mocking pity. "No, we are upset that you failed to start a war."

Arka spat as he shook his head in disappointment. "See, Wagner, I told you she didn't have the stomach for this."

Wagner shrugged as if she didn't care.

Arka's anger had melted away to almost glee. "I guess we have to ensure the war happens without the intentional help of the Blood Princess."

Serina was so distracted by Arka that she didn't sense Wagner's betrayal until too late. The sting in Serina's arm turned warm. The warmth spread through her body. Wagner held a small syringe in her hand. She was smiling at Serina again, but there was no kindness in that smile.

Serina's heart lept with hope at the sound of approaching hooves. Unfortunately, her optimism was short-lived. A lone rider approached. It wasn't someone Serina recognized.

"Where are Uthar and Ferraris?" Wagner demanded.

Serina allowed some small satisfaction at the response she heard. "That old guy you said we would have no problem with, he killed them." The voice's owner coughed. "Look what that bastard did to me." Serina heard him let loose another wet cough followed by a heavy thud.

"Damn it," Wagner swore. "Looks like it will just be the three of us. Arka, hand me the royal guard robes."

Serina tried to move, call out a warning, and even transform. In the end, she could do nothing. Wagner noticed Serina's struggle. With an evil grin, Wagner held up the small vial again. "Deadman's blood. An amazing paralyzer to our kind. Yet . . ." She shivered like she was shaking off the cold. "A tiny amount hides us from other vampires. Weird little poison." Wagner and Arka laughed, their fangs fully visible. Serina could feel their presence now.

Arka pulled a cloak over Serina's shoulders. She recognized it as her own cloak back when she was part of the guard. Wagner laughed harshly. "I see you remember you used to be someone important."

"Yeah, before she became a tool of the humans." Arka roughly smashed the clasp of the cloak closed against Serina's throat. "Useless traitor. At least we will make good use of you." His face was too close to Serina's. She was able to lurch forward slightly, her fangs bared. Arka swore, then punched Serina across her cheek.

Wagner laughed at Arka and Serina. "Oh, do not get so upset, Arka, and be nice. You are with the first martyr of the war." Finally, Wagner rode close enough to grab Serina by the throat. "When they see how the Varatos desecrate your corpse, who would not want to kill them?" Then, she turned to Arka. "Do whatever you want to her when we are done. Just make sure her face is recognizable."

Serina couldn't contain the shudder of disgust as she saw the leer on Arka's face.

Serina's horse was led into the town square and tied to a post. "You should have the best view from here." Wagner snickered as she dismounted her own horse. Arka dismounted as well, nodded to Wagner, then pulled his sword. Wagner followed his actions. Then they turned to Serina. "Enjoy the show," Wagner taunted. Then she and Arka moved quickly in different directions.

All Serina could see was the view in front of her as she could only move her eyes. However, she could hear. So Serina sat and listened in horror. A tear of frustration burned down her cheek. At first, there was nothing but the occasional sound of a door being kicked in or a window breaking. Then came the screaming. Finally, Arka and Wagner rushed into the square and called Serina, asking for orders to make it appear she was in charge.

Never in her long life had Serina wished for sunrise. This night, however, she begged for the sun to burn her away. She wanted to turn away as her captors continued their grisly work. They went from house to house, their bloodlust growing with each death they caused.

Arka and Wagner had already killed roughly a third of the inhabitants before the alarms were raised. When the bells finally began to toll, what came to fight was not the resistance Serina had been led to believe was present. A tiny hope burned in her heart that maybe there was some way to stop the carnage.

"I did not know Varatos had children," Arka laughed as he calmly walked up to Serina, wiping blood from his sword. Bright light caught his attention, as his eyes widened in shock. "What has she done?" Wagner's section was in flames. "This should be good," Arka exclaimed, grabbing Serina's horse's reigns.

Arka pulled Serina along from the square. Where Arka was impressed, Serina was horrified. Bodies of women, old men, and children hung impaled along the street. When Wagner came out of a house covered in blood, she sauntered to Arka. Wagner could see Serina was fighting against the poison in her system. Arka laughed and patted Wagner's shoulder as they listened to the screams of people burning alive, trapped in the village meeting house.

Serina gave up trying to move. So, instead, she used any magic she could muster. Her attention was on the meeting house. She poured all her energy in a vain attempt to control the flames.

"I drove many of them in there," Wagner laughed. "They thought they would be safe." Her smile vanished in an instant. She could see Serina starting to affect the fire. "What are you doing?" Wagner demanded. "We are here to exterminate these rodents."

"No, this is wrong!" Serina slurred, finally finding her voice. Wagner advanced on Serina as she pulled a new syringe from her pocket. Serina stopped Wagner's advance with a raise of her hand. Fear flickered over Wagner's face as her hand holding the needle exploded. Her brain barely had time to register the loss of her hand since her head followed a second later. Skull and brain matter flew in every direction as the body crumpled.

Arka had wandered off. His attention was on killing until he saw Wagner fall. Arka cried out as he ran his steel through the body of a young boy, his little sister, and the baby she was carrying. Arka screamed in rage as he raised the three children high up, still skewered on his sword.

"The enemies of the united clans shall die by the sword." He flung the dead children at their wailing mother. "All of them." A thrust of the blade and a twist cracked the mother's head in two. Serina's magic was too weak to stop his rampage.

"Monsters!" someone was screaming.

Arka began hacking through a group of terrified, panicked children. He was trying to charge at Serina. She had fallen painfully from the horse, desperately trying to stop Arka from killing more innocents. Crawling over to the shattered corpse of Wagner, Serina picked up the dead woman's sword. Struggling to her feet, Serina used the weapon to push herself upright. Her clothes, hands, and face were covered in dirt and blood.

Arka held his sword, ready to dispatch anyone who dared to question what he was doing. Serina was stunned to see the person calling them monsters was another vampire. However, this vampire was not alone. One of the Varatos must have run to a neighboring village, a village of vampires.

Vampires like Serina and those killing the Varatos.

"Stop this attack!" someone cried out. The person shouting for an end to the violence could only be the leader of the other village. As several others shepherded the frightened children away, she stepped forward. "These people are our friends!" Then, she shouted, "They are our neighbors!"

"They are Varatos!" Arka replied hatefully. "They are nothing more than beasts who attack and kill without remorse." As the words left his mouth, a look of fear crossed his face. He could feel Serina's magic forcing his grip to loosen. His sword clattered to the ground.

"The Princess," he turned, pointing at Serina. "She has ordered these beasts destroyed!" Shocked, Serina lost control of Arka. Taking advantage of her lapse in concentration, Arka ran to the elder. "Help me. She was controlling me by Magic!" He broke down in tears and explained, "Oh, gods, she forced me to kill those children."

Serina's anger exploded. Arka's weeping changed into strangled yelps before turning into full screams of agony. His body began to expand, blood pouring from his eyes, nose, ears, and mouth. Finally, Arka's skin split under the pressure, and his throat closed, cutting off his cries before he exploded in a cloud of red mist. His skeleton stood for a moment. Then, his organs splattered onto the ground, no longer held in place by flesh. Serina became aware of the fearful looks she received.

The elder stood horrified. Looking past her, Serina could see the forest of impaled families. The screams of the people burning in the meeting hall filled her ears. When she turned back to the village elder, she watched as a line of troops slowed to a stop behind her, Serina's mother in the lead.

Serina stood, the only survivor, drenched in blood, covered in ash and mud. She held her sword limply at her side. The faces of the arriving soldiers held neither pride nor triumph. Instead, it was disgust and fear. She saw the same look on her mother's face when she looked at Serina.

Quickly trying to hide her discomfort, the queen dismounted to approach her daughter. She half-raised her hands to hug Serina. But, seeing this gore-covered person before her, she couldn't bring herself to do it or look her in the eyes. "My Queen." The village elder bowed. "Did you order the princess to destroy this village?"

"What?" Asha asked as she turned to address the elder.

"Princess Serina has attacked the Varatos again!" someone shouted.

"N-no, Mother, I did not. It was hired mercenaries. I-I tried to stop them," Serina stammered.

"Why did you kill Glacious?" A different voice questioned.

"I did not," Serina shouted back. "Mother, you have to believe me."

Asha looked back at her troops, then at Serina. Fear and confusion were etched across the queen's features. "I do."

"If that were true, you would look at me." Serina's blade slapped onto the bloody mud. "You would say it loud enough for the troops to hear." She took a step back. "You think I wanted this."

"No, it is just . . ." Her mother breathed, again trying to compose herself and not betray the horror she felt toward her daughter. "No one is left except you. Where are your witnesses?"

"The others were taking orders from her." A villager pointed accusingly. "When the young man escaped her spell, she killed him."

"I did no such thing. Well, I did kill him, but I did not mean to. No, wait!" Again, Serina was drowned out by the shouts of soldiers and villagers. Again, she heard calls for her immediate execution.

"Serina, you have to know how this looks," Asha tried to calm her daughter. "We will get back to the fortress and figure all of this out."

"The faces of our troops tell me otherwise." Serina looked away from her mother only to look into the dead eyes of the siblings Arka had recently slaughtered. "Children," Serina breathed. "With their death, I do not believe I will be found innocent." Finally, her voice barely audible over the cries for justice, Serina muttered, "Goodbye, Mother." Before anyone could move, Serina's wings unfurled.

The queen blinked away the dust from Serina's departure. The smell of burning flesh mingled with death and blood. She turned to the troops. "The

ones responsible for this were zealots, and all died here." She glared at the commander. "They *all* died here!"

Even though she was flying as fast as her wings would carry her, she heard
and understood what her mother was saying. Serina had to disappear. Something was very wrong in the kingdom. Tears streamed from Serina's eyes. The
way her mother looked at her, the doubt. How could her mother think she was
responsible?

———⌒⌒———

On the Dreamweaver roof
Sixty years later

Serina's hand covered the section of her arm where Henry had grabbed her. She
looked into the room to see him lying on the floor. He was unconscious, still
alive. That was somewhat remarkable. "Must be all the time you spend with
Thorn." Serina smirked. "Stupid elf. Grabbing one of us could kill you." She
glanced back, shaking her head. Then, with a flutter of wings, Serina returned
to the manor.

CHAPTER 14

I woke up to blinding sunlight. Blinking and groaning, I tried to work out the stiffness of sleeping on the floor. My head felt fuzzy as I slowly remembered what had happened. My window was still open. I guessed Serina couldn't have helped me because she hadn't been invited in. "Either that's a weird magical restriction, or vampires are just incredibly courteous," I told my open window as I closed it.

Judging by how high the sun was, it was late morning and I was late for my lessons. I needed to clear my head, clean up, and get to the manor. My stomach informed me I had to get something to eat, so I hurried downstairs. My encounter with Serina had nearly drained me completely. I remembered how upset I had made her, and I tried shaking off the guilt and confusion that still lingered. My hand was on the door to the kitchen when I realized my mom was talking to someone.

"Shit," I mumbled as I attempted to smooth my hair and lessen the disheveled look of having slept in my clothes. I took a deep breath and pushed the door open. It was like something out of a story. At first, the light was blinding, but then Thorn appeared. Her appearance today was the exact opposite of mine. Her light blue tunic and the dark purple streaks of her hair highlighted in a braid nearly took my breath away. It was strange how one simple change to someone you see daily can be so stunning.

Thorn turned as I entered. A glimpse of concern crossed her face, replaced with a smile. When she spoke, her etiquette was excellent. "My, Mrs. Dreamweaver, it truly is magnificent how clean and orderly your home is." Her eyes scanned me slowly. "I cannot say the same for all of its contents." Then, with a sniff of contempt, she continued, "Henry, nice of you to join us. Your wonderful and punctual mother has provided me with this delicious tea and muffin."

I was embarrassed. Mom seemed to be trying not to laugh. Thorn was messing with me for oversleeping, I hoped.

"So, Thorn, apparently, the two men have learned to play nice, so you'll be training with us now." Mom smiled, taking Thorn by the shoulders to look her over. "You definitely have the build for a light shift weapon. I think the single-edged Katnijuri would suit you best."

Thorn and I exchanged a look of shock. A Katnijuri, or serpent fang, was a rare, powerful, Magic-infused blade.

Then Mom moved the fringe off Thorn's forehead. She frowned as she inspected the light scar. "I'm glad that awful human didn't do more damage." Mom returned her hands to Thorn's shoulders, appraising her. "Your complexion is just like your mother's."

Thorn's smile flickered.

Mom gasped as she realized what she had said and immediately turned around, busying herself at the sink. "What are you two learning this week?"

"H-how—how do you know about my mother?" Thorn stammered.

"What?" Mom tried to act surprised. "I guess Henry must have described her."

I searched my memory. I don't believe I told her about the portrait.

Thorn turned to look at me. "I didn't realize you could tell that from a painting," she stated, then whispered to me, "or that you noticed our skin tones." The smirk she gave me told me she didn't believe my mom either.

"Well . . ." Mom grumbled and muttered for a moment. "I met your mother before." Thorn and I gaped at her. "It was years ago when I attended Fluxx Academy with your father."

"The what academy?" I pounced.

"It was an inclusive school for Magic, combat arts, and alchemy." Seeing the excitement this news caused, Mom quickly dispelled any thoughts about the school. "It was a very progressive place. It didn't matter if you were human, elf, or orc. If you had talent, you were allowed to study." Then, sadness engulfed her eyes. "The war between the humans and non-humans ended that idea forever. If you had seen it, oh, the campus was amazing. The shared knowledge and the fact that there was no fighting and no hatred. It was how the world should be." Mom swiped at her eye. "Enough of the past. Thorn came to collect you." Mom gave me a look—the one that told me I was being rude.

"Yeah, sorry, I was up late," I muttered, running my hand through my already messy hair, grimacing at the oily feeling on my fingers. "I have to get cleaned up. Um . . . I'll meet you at your house."

"No problem. I can wait if it's all right with you, Mrs. Dreamweaver?" Thorn smiled. "You can tell me about Henry when he was younger." Thorn's smile turned devilish.

"I'll hurry," I shouted, racing to the bath. "Don't tell her anything!"

I heard Mom laugh. Then with a conspiratorial whisper meant to be heard, "Well, let me tell you about when Henry saw a toad for the first time."

I knew this was only my mother's warm-up story. Ten minutes later, I was clean and dressed, my wet hair still dripping onto my shirt.

"To this day, he still won't pick one up." My mom's laughter mixed with Thorn's. I had to separate them before any other stories from my youth were told.

"Hey, I'm ready to go," I exclaimed as I burst through the door. But unfortunately, my sudden appearance only caused the laughter to increase in volume.

Smiling at Thorn, Mom wiped a tear from her eye. Then, catching her breath, she explained, "I have to visit old Mrs. Wildwings." She gathered a basket from the counter. "Will you be okay on your own for lunch?"

I looked at Thorn for the answer. She shrugged.

"Yeah, we'll be gone by the time you get back," I said, unsure if that were actually true.

As soon as Mom left, Thorn grabbed me by the shoulders. She stared unnervingly into my eyes. She was searching for something, and she found it. But unfortunately, it didn't make her happy.

"You never grab a vampire, especially the kind Serina is." Her tone was accusatory.

"She was upset," I defended. "Then I lost my balance."

"You're lucky you didn't make her angry. With her power . . ." She hugged herself, lost in a memory. "I saw her make a feli-bear explode—just caused its blood to . . ." She threw her hands out with fingers splayed while making a *spleew* sound. "It was so gross." She made a face. "If you touch her, she will pull all your warmth and energy from you."

"Yeah, I got that part. *Spleew?*" I mirrored her hand movements.

"*Spleew,*" she nodded, repeating the movement.

I decided I didn't want to see something go *spleew,* nor did I wish to *spleew.* She shook her head slightly. "Come on, let's go do something."

"Like what? Shouldn't we go to the manor?"

"Let's skip it today." She pulled me to the front door. "Come on. It's so nice outside. Let's explore. Tell you what." She spun around to face me, hopping backward down our walkway. "Let's go catch toads."

"Sounds good," I growled, chasing after her. "Maybe I'll throw you in the pond so you can see their slimy homes." Finally, I caught up to her at the gate. She stood with her face held up to the sun, enjoying the warmth. In the bright sunlight, I could see her clothing better. Her pants were suede, while the long shirt that came almost to her knees was a silky light material. Gold thread designs ran through the shirt. Throwing her in a pond dressed like that would be a terrible idea.

"Let's take a walk." Her smile was tinged with mischief.

I nodded and followed her. "I really think we should head to the manor," I commented, trying to steer her to the woods and the path. Undeterred, she turned away from her home, and I followed her in silence for a while toward Nondayok village.

Before we arrived, I had to ask, "Are you sure about this? I doubt your father's okay with it."

"I'm sure he isn't." Her tone was bitter. "He was up to something last night, and I haven't figured it out. Besides, I've been by myself for so long. I mean, aside from Serina, but as you know, I can't be seen with her." Thorn stretched her arms over her head and spun around. "I just need to be out and about," she explained rapidly as she kicked at a stone.

I cringed as the road dirt covered the toe of her beautiful boot. Up ahead, we saw some young elves playing.

"I never got to do that." She pointed at the children. "Play with others." She paused. "I remember a dream or an imaginary friend, but it's strange," she muttered to herself.

"Yeah." I shrugged. "I never really got to play with other kids either. But, you know, I think I also had an imaginary friend." I inspected my worn and dirty boots. "My only real friend is a human who's a bit odd."

"Really? I hadn't noticed." Thorn laughed, jumping up to grab a low-hanging branch. "I have an idea." She smiled, pulling herself up onto the limb. "Let's go to the forest."

"I don't know. You're not going to stalk me again?" Then I remembered something. "Or run off and leave me?"

She laughed. "No, but I know a game. Come on." Before I could protest, Thorn dropped out of the tree and sprinted toward the woods. Then, finally, she slowed so I could catch up. We walked side by side in silence for a while. Our hands bumped a couple of times. I was about to try again to hold Thorn's hand when she made a weird screechy frustrated noise as she jumped in front of me.

"My father didn't want me to be exposed to others," she explained, mimicking her father's voice. Then, returning to her own, she asked, "What's your reason?"

"None of the kids there wanted to play with me." The statement hung between us. Finally, I muttered, "When your father's the village representative, they all blame him and his family when they don't get what they want."

"I don't think we should be judged by who our parents are or what we're *supposed* to be like," she said loudly as she saw a passing villager's suspicious glare at the new person with the Dreamweaver boy.

Seeing their reaction, I said, "We really should head back to the manor. Remember, you're supposed to be a secret."

"I'm tired of being a secret!" Thorn grumbled. "I'm tired of hiding. I want to hang out with my friends openly. I want to be normal. I'm tired of . . . of . . . all of it." Thorn grabbed my sleeve. "You're my best friend, and we'll have the best times." She glared back at a woman who averted her gaze. "I don't care who your parents are or what my father wants."

We wandered into the woods as Thorn talked a lot about her father, yet she avoided any discussion of her mother. Her only comment was, "My mother was someone to be feared but not respected." Then, without warning, Thorn jumped up onto a tree. She was about ten feet up before I knew it. "Come on!" she shouted down to me.

I hurried up the tree to join her, although I wan't nearly as fast. She balanced along the thin branch. I followed cautiously, unsure if the limb could hold our combined weight. When she turned to face me, a wicked grin played on her lips. She leaped to the next tree. All thoughts about going to the manor and our lessons were forgotten.

Standing precariously on an even thinner strip of wood, she beckoned me to follow. I chased her for twenty terrifying and exhilarating minutes. Finally, I caught up to her. Both of us were breathing heavily and laughing.

"That was amazing." I smiled. "I've never done anything like that before."

We sat in the tree, smiling and catching our breath, when we heard voices not far away.

"Did you see Dreamweaver near the village?"

"Did you see the girl he was with? Who did she think she was fooling?"

"She may have our ears, but you can see she's a half-breed."

"Ew, disgusting, and did you see her clothes? Showed how ratty Dreamweaver looked."

Thorn was looking at my jacket and her own shirt. They were very different. It didn't seem like she had even really noticed before.

"Why are they being so rude?" Thorn asked. "Don't you have enough trouble with the humans? Why wouldn't you all get along?"

"I guess when you're treated badly, you look for someone *you* can treat badly."

"That's dumb," Thorn replied.

Three elves from the village appeared below us. I recognized them. It was a group I tended to avoid, led by Greggor, a mean elf.

"Like he has room to talk about half-breeds," Thorn whispered. I shushed her, not wanting to deal with a confrontation.

"Rumor has it he's a part orc," I explained.

Thorn shook her head. "No, I believe his father was a goblin." She pointed at Greggor. "You can see the goblin in those beady little eyes and the way his ears droop."

"Okay, so why do you think it was his father?"

Thorn seemed to enjoy explaining her thoughts. "Well, since he lives in the village, I assume it wasn't his mother." She laughed.

My stomach knotted, worried they would hear her.

"Although you have to wonder what type of woman would mate with a goblin."

"I didn't think we could," I whispered despite myself.

"I told you already, elves and goblins are distant cousins." She held up a hand to stop my angry retort. "Father has books in the library to prove it."

I yelped. A rock hit me hard in the shoulder. Greggor was staring at us, flanked by his two pals. "Dreamweaver's got a girlfriend," he announced to his goons.

Anger flashed in Thorn's eyes as one turned crimson. "So what if he does? That's no reason to throw rocks at people." As soon as she finished, Thorn cried out in pain. One of Greggor's stones struck her hand. Luckily, she'd just thrown it up to cover her face. Suddenly the air was filled with cries of fear.

Trees all around us twisted and creaked. Greggor's thugs hid behind their terrified leader. "Stop doing that!" Greggor shouted. I coughed as a sharp rock hit my stomach. Thorn grabbed at her leg. A dark red stain bloomed on her suede pants.

"That hurt!" Thorn shouted, and the entire area went absolutely still. Nothing moved. Leaves and twigs that had been falling were suspended in the air. The trees didn't rustle in the wind, and I couldn't move a muscle.

Thorn gasped, grabbing my sleeve to hide behind me. I knew she was as terrified as the three boys below us. "How do I undo this? How do I undo this?" Thorn panicked. I couldn't speak or try to calm her.

Suddenly, Thorn's father appeared in the clearing.

"Father, I can explain," Thorn began. I saw his eyes and knew why she went silent.

"Get down," she hissed, pushing my back. I realized I could move again. I hit the ground lightly. Instinctively, I turned to catch Thorn. Her injured leg gave out as she landed. I fumbled with her, not knowing where it was okay to grab a girl. The look I received from her father told me I'd done it wrong.

Fortunately for me, he turned his attention to the three thugs. He seemed to be explaining something to the boys. They were glassy-eyed and nodding. Slowly they turned around and followed the path toward the village. The further away they got, the less stiff they seemed.

"I have made them forget this little encounter." He turned his attention to us.

I wished he hadn't.

"Daughter." His tone was harsh. "You shouldn't be out here." He waved his hand over Thorn's knee. She flexed it and mumbled thanks. Next, he turned to me. I felt warmth cover me, and all the pain left me. "Did you not want to be trained in the magical arts?" I wasn't sure which of us he was questioning. It turned out it was both of us.

"I'm sorry," I spoke up. "I, uh, overslept." If Caterous knew the reason, it would only fuel his anger. I tried to avoid his intense gaze. I didn't know if he could read my mind. I didn't want to find out, either.

"I went to collect him, and the day was so nice," Thorn explained quickly, "I just couldn't see staying inside reading. So, we did some tree skipping, getting exercise."

"While causing trouble for the locals." He glared at Thorn.

"They started it." She pouted.

"You have more power, therefore more responsibility." He turned to me, eyes flashing. "And *you* are to protect her. That means not allowing her to get into petty squabbles."

"Sorry," Thorn and I responded with heads bowed.

"This was a mistake." Caterous sounded tired now. "Neither of you is ready to learn if all it takes is a bright day to keep you from your studies." He stood, shaking his head in disappointment. My fear was replaced by guilt. Then he said words that turned my stomach. "Go home, Henry." He sighed. "Don't come back until I send for you."

"When will that be?" I ask cautiously.

"When I can trust my daughter," he replied, taking her by the arm. Her protests and tears did nothing to deter his anger.

Walking home, all I did was worry about Thorn. The few words Caterous spoke that I could hear as they walked away scared me.

"I thought this would work. However, if you can't take this seriously . . ."

I walked slowly, trying to hear more

". . . his parents are right to be concerned. You have no idea how hard it is for them to trust us." He turned around. I tried to act like I was heading home and not listening. I don't think I convinced him, though.

I wondered if the accidental spell Thorn created was something I should tell Dad about. Finally, I decided it was best not to mention it. I would be in enough trouble as it was.

CHAPTER 15

Apparently, it was more trouble than I anticipated. Dad met me at the door. I wasn't sure if he was upset or relieved that my training was on hold. I was already distraught when he declared, "Since you would rather run around and play, perhaps we should postpone the sword training as well." I tried to change his mind to no avail. Finally, I turned to Mom, hoping she would be on my side. Especially since I felt she'd encouraged our day of hooky. She seemed disappointed in me. She was also unhappy that my training would be on hold. However, she agreed with Dad.

It was unfair, and I was livid. "This is silly. I swear you were already looking for an excuse. Why don't you trust Thorn or her father?" Which, obviously, wasn't true since they seemed to like Thorn. Also, what about the exchange between Dad and Caterous last night?

"We have our reasons to worry when you're with Thorn," Dad stated cryptically.

"Even though I doubt she would ever consciously hurt you," Mom unnecessarily reassured. Then she sighed and placed her hand over Dad's. "I must admit her actions today were concerning."

"She's been all alone for so long. She just wanted to get out and have some fun," I protested.

"The last time she wanted to get out for a bit, it left you almost dead and her injured. This time you weren't the one to get hurt, but if her father hadn't shown up . . ." Dad didn't need to finish—I understood. They knew what had happened. Dad didn't trust Caterous unless he was tattling on us. It was my turn to admit Thorn wasn't only powerful, she was also naive and socially ignorant. Grudgingly, I gave up trying to convince my parents to persuade Caterous to change his mind.

I went to bed that night, thinking I wouldn't get to see Thorn again for a long time. So, I was surprised when I left my house the next morning to find myself beckoned to the shade of some trees by a cloaked figure.

Thorn was dressed simply. There was no silver or gold threading. Her boots were plain, as were her pants. The cloak was heavy and wool. "It's my winter cloak," Thorn apologized, pulling it off. I sympathized as it was a warm day. "I thought maybe you could show me the human village." She kicked at a rock. "After yesterday and how your kind treated us, I'd rather avoid other elves."

I had to agree. "Yeah, humans and elves suck."

The last thing I wanted to do was meet up with Greggor and his thugs again. I also wasn't in the mood for more broken ribs. "Hold on a second," I instructed, taking her cloak from her. I returned to the house and swapped it for one of my mother's.

Thorn pulled on the lightweight material, thanking me.

"I have an idea." I smiled.

Cocking her head questioningly, she shrugged and followed me toward the forest.

Instead of heading toward her house, we followed a path that skirted the woods to a tree-covered rocky ascent. The trail was one a human couldn't easily follow. However, Thorn's elf half served her well as she quickly outstripped me. Through the thinning trees, she could see where I was taking her. I stopped at one of the taller trees, pointing up. She raised an eyebrow and smiled as she clambered up, stopping near the top.

When I joined Thorn, she grabbed my arm, smiling. We were looking down into Dayok. I pointed out Scratch's house, the lord's keep with its high walls, and the old rich part of town. What caught her eye, though, was the market. Colorful banners hung over the stalls. People bustled around like bees looking for nectar.

"That's where he hurt us," she pointed to the market, "just because of these." Her fingers brushed my ear, causing a shiver to run along my spine.

"Yeah, humans think they're *so* much better than us," I grumbled. I realized too late that I had just insulted her father. "Thorn, I mean, not all of them. I—"

Her eyebrows raised to say, *go on.*

"What?" I asked, a little worried. "That wasn't fair," I sighed, "just like I wouldn't like it if they said all elves are lazy." I rolled my eyes slightly.

Was she teaching me to be tolerant?

"Hey, you're the one who called Greggor a goblin," I protested.

"That's because he's a part goblin." Suddenly she gasped, "Get down!" She was gone. I spotted her light purple hair bounding down the tree. Not sure what we were hiding from, I could only follow. I lost sight of her. My feet hit the ground, but I had no idea where to go. I got one, maybe two steps in before I was yanked into the hollow of a tree. That feeling of the world brightening as her hand covered my mouth and Magic flowed into me filled me again. Above my head, a couple of tiny faeries chattered angrily at us. The second Thorn pulled her hand away, the faeries disappeared from my view, and I could no longer hear them.

Thorn was making the same chittering noise the faeries had made. I got the feeling she was apologizing and asking them to please be quiet. A moment later, I knew why. Thorn drew back as far as she could into the tree while I hid her. A large hawk I recognized landed near the opening. It was definitely searching for something—or some*one*, to be more specific.

Thorn sucked in a hiss, so I reached behind and found her hand. I meant to be reassuring, but the effect was less so. As her Magic spread, I could see one of the faeries glaring at us from the entry. It was pointing while Thorn hissed what I could only assume a plea. The longer they argued, the more I began to understand.

"Get out of our house."

"We'll leave as soon as he leaves."

"I'm going to alert him."

"No, please, just allow us a little more time."

I remembered something my grandmother told me years ago. *Never invade the home of the fae folk. But, if you do, make an offering for forgiveness.* I let go of Thorn's hand and began searching my pockets. I had a handful of dried berries. "Here." I thrust the berries at Thorn. "Offer them this to let us stay." Apparently, this did the trick. I watched the berries fly up away from us. Thorn and I exhaled and smiled at each other. Her smile, however, didn't stray long. I turned to see what had scared her. The hawk was glaring at us with one golden eye.

"Move, move." She pushed me out directly at the loudly screeching bird. Wind buffeted me as the hawk took wing. "I have to go," she shouted, rushing past me. "I'll come see you soon." She was already moving away quickly. "I have a place to take you," she shouted as she disappeared into the trees. I stood staring at the last place I'd seen her. The hawk screeched from a branch nearby. I swear it shrugged its wings in apology and then took to the sky.

A few days later, I found myself sitting at the top of a gorgeous waterfall next to Thorn. We'd been walking along the stream when we came to a quiet pool. Rolling up our pant legs, we splashed together in the cold water. Then we found a large rock to stretch out as our feet dried. The roar of the water and the warm sun made me feel sleepy. My hand brushed Thorn's. I moved mine to cover hers. We were just beginning to move them to be holding hands, and I was having a wonderful day, until the hawk arrived. At its appearance, Thorn rushed away.

Very soon, I came to hate that bird. When it appeared, I knew my time with Thorn was over. Although each time, it seemed to take the bird longer and longer to find us.

After a month had passed, I was up early, eagerly awaiting Thorn's arrival, wondering what adventure we would have today. I was walking to our gate when I was nearly run over by her, heading to our house.

"Sorry, were you waiting long? I thought I would get here early, but it looks like I'm late." She rambled at the speed of a wild stallion. "Oh no, did your mother leave already?"

"No, Thorn, you're right on time," Mom called from the doorway. She held a basket. "Come along, I want you to see something, and I brought snacks." She held up the basket. I was surprised to see Thorn and Mom talking. The last time I mentioned Thorn, my mother had been ominous about being in her company.

"When did you two plan this?" I whispered to Thorn.

"This is completely her idea. She sent your father's owl to me with a message last night," she explained.

"It's a surprise for both of you," Mom called.

We walked together, Thorn and I on either side of my mom. As we passed by some trees or a field, Mom would explain the different herbs or plants we could find and how to use them.

"Your father is quite an accomplished mage." She smiled at Thorn. "But he has never been much of an alchemist. . . . That's what they say, anyway."

"Who says? Your friends at Fluxx?" I demanded.

Ignoring my tone, she smiled. "Must have been there." Mom spread her arms wide. "Here we are. Thorn, help me with this." Mom pulled a blanket from the basket. "Henry, see that yellow flower over there?"

I nodded.

"Gather a few of those for me."

Curious, I did as I was told. Thorn handed me some sweet bread and water while we watched my mom mix the flowers with other ingredients. After a few moments, she gave the mixture to me.

I looked at it, then at her.

"Well, go on. Take a sip."

It wasn't bad tasting but not something I would seek out to drink. However, something odd was happening. I felt like I was blurry around the edges. "Am I supposed to feel like this?"

"Why? What's happening?" Thorn asked, a little fear edging her voice.

Mom laughed as she handed the potion to Thorn. "If you feel—how would I describe it?—blurry, then yes."

"Okay, so other than feeling weird, I mean, thank you, but, um, what does this potion do?"

My mom pushed herself up. Standing, she dusted herself off, smiled, and winked. "It blocks others from tracking your Magic." She motioned for us to collect the blanket. "Something I used to make when I felt like someone was watching me like a hawk." She folded the blanket, putting it in the basket, then laughed at our stunned faces. "Enjoy the day."

Pulling me aside, Mom whispered, "The effects only last about three hours." She looked over at Thorn and lowered her voice even further. "Also, I'm too young to be a grandmother." I was too stunned to react as she kissed my cheek and left the meadow.

CHAPTER 16

Grounds of Fluxx Academy
Twenty-two years ago

Amelia, is it working? I feel all blurry," Micha whispered.

"Of all the times for Caterous to be unavailable," Martin growled. Behind him, a building crumbled to the ground. "How are we going to save everyone without him?"

"We aren't," Amelia stated. Micha and Martin understood. "This is our rendezvous spot. The exfil is the south gate. Micha, you're to search the library and practice hall. Martin, take the north dorm and the alchemy lab. I'll see who's left at administration."

Micha knew this was the most dangerous place on campus to be. The human forces were focusing on destroying the professors. Even though Micha feared for Amelia's safety, he knew no one was more capable of the task.

"We'll meet back here in thirty minutes."

"That isn't enough time," Martin complained. "They can't trace us by magic. That should give us extra time to get the students out."

"I have already factored in the extra time the potion will afford us. Now move, soldier."

Amelia was moving before another word could be said. Martin looked at Micha. "You're going to marry that elf one day."

"Yes, I am. Good luck."

"You too."

Half an hour later, less than half the students and less than a quarter of the faculty were hurried out of the south gate. Micha and Amelia were at the rear, throwing spells and deflecting swords.

"We could only save so few," Micha lamented.

"Yes, but we could have lost them all. Quiet, here he comes." Amelia snapped.

"Now we find out how good Amelia's alchemy is," Martin stated nervously.

The unified army of Notelek entered the room. General Wolf slowly walked along the three present soldiers. "It has come to my attention that an unsanctioned rescue mission was undertaken at Fluxx Academy." He stopped directly in front of Amelia.

Her face was impassive stone.

"The perpetrators hid their Magic perfectly and could not be identified." General Wolf turned his back on his subordinates. "The mission was successful, and the survivors have been relocated." He spun around to glare at Amelia, his face inches from hers. "A medal would be in order if the mission had been sanctioned." The general turned away, heading toward the door. "You three are far too important to the fight. Please don't do something like this again."

General Wolf's voice was soft as he spoke, "Good job." Then, the door snapped shut.

CHAPTER 17

The moment I walked in the front door, I knew my day of ease was over. As soon as the door closed behind me, I heard Dad's exasperation. "How could you do that? Do you have any idea how angry he'll be?"

"Oh, let him rage at the mountains," Mom replied, waving off my dad's concern. "They deserved a quiet afternoon."

"I agreed to the time apart," Dad complained.

"I didn't." I heard the annoyance in Mom's voice. "Not then and not now."

"And when he comes here all angry?"

"He knows not to take me on in my own home!" Mom's exclamation left no room for argument.

Dad turned and grabbed me by the shoulders, surprising me. "Your mother can be challenging," he muttered, patting me on the shoulder.

"Scary, too," I admitted. Dad paused, nodded, then headed out the front door. I knew he'd sit out in the garden to listen to the night. That's what he called it when he knew not to fight with Mom.

I decided it would be best not to get involved. I was exhausted, so I decided to call it an early night. Thankfully, sleep didn't take long to whisk me away to dreams of my peaceful afternoon.

When I woke up, I knew I was in my room. It was still dark, but I knew I wasn't alone. I could hear whispering from the foot of my bed.

"He's awake. I need to go."

Light blossomed from a ball of energy held in Thorn's hand. Someone was with her. The girl sitting next to her had hair the color of the sunset.

"Serina," I gasped. "How can you be here?"

"When you fell over the other night, you pulled me into your room." She gave me a devilish grin. "I can come and go as I please now." To my surprise,

Thorn smacked her arm. Serina acted as if Thorn had seriously injured her. "Okay, okay, I'll wait outside." Serina laughed as she stepped out through my window. "That whole thing about us not being able to enter a house without an invite is total rubbish, by the way."

Thorn shooed her away. I heard Serina's wings, then her landing softly on the roof.

"What are you doing here?" I hissed, pushing myself up on my elbows.

"Father was furious when we got home." Her concern was frightening.

"Dad told my mom he would be." I was about to get up when I remembered I was only wearing my undergarments.

"Yeah, Father was upset about not being able to send the hawk to, as he put it, *chastise us*. But he wasn't as upset about that as I thought he'd be." She chewed on her bottom lip, something I'd often watched her do. I thought it was cute. But then, her voice pulled me out of my reverie. "After he told me off for hiding, he went into the library." She got up to pace my room. "He kept talking to himself, saying, 'What if she found out? What if she learned to do it?'"

"Who?" I asked.

"I don't know, but he might have been talking about my mother."

There was a creaking outside my door. Thorn instantly doused the light in her hands.

With the covers pulled to my chin, I prayed it was just the house settling. Then, finally, after several tense seconds, I felt it was safe. "I thought your mother was dead," I hissed.

"No, I only wish she was." I heard the anger in Thorn's voice.

Serina whistled.

"I have to go," Thorn hissed in the darkness. Her hand squeezed my foot under the blanket.

I whispered my goodbye to her shadow as it passed my window. The sound of Serina's wings told me they'd left. I spent the rest of the night worried. My brain wouldn't let me sleep until almost dawn.

⸻

I was dreaming. I knew I was. When I was ten, the old man in the village, who I called Grandpa Windtalker, had long ago joined the ancients.

"Why do humans hate us?" I heard myself ask. I couldn't have been more than four or five.

I could smell the tobacco smoke on the old man's jacket. "It is because of the war that was fought before you were born." He pulled a pipe from his coat.

I watched him clean and refill it. My favorite part of his smoking ritual was coming up. He looked around to see if anyone was watching, then gave me a conspiratorial wink. A flame bloomed on the end of his finger that he used to light his pipe. Smiling, he extinguished it.

He scratched at his chin as he puffed the pipe. "From my understanding, the war was between humans and the many other creatures they considered to be less than human." I sat next to him, eager to hear the story. I watched Grandpa's eyes as they looked into the past. He shook his head. "Ground was won and lost going back and forth between the sides. It looked like the fighting would go on forever." Then, a frown creased his lips. "That was when a witch took up the cause of the creatures."

"So she was our friend?" I asked.

"No, no." Grandpa shook his head sadly. "The witch was worse than the humans. When the war started, the non-humans wanted equal rights. When the witch got involved, she wanted non-human dominance." His frown deepened. "Then she decided all creatures should bow to her." I knew he was enjoying the scared look on my face. Grandpa straightened slightly. Pride showed in his eyes. "An alliance was reached. Men, elves, demi-humans, and some dark creatures banded together to fight."

"Why?" I was confused. "If we ruled the humans, they would treat us better."

"The alliance was supposed to guarantee what the fighting had been about in the first place—equality." He tapped the pipe against the bottom of his boot. "The alliance was not winning. They had a last-ditch attack to kill the witch."

I felt my heart beat with anticipation.

"Before the battle, a small group of elves, men, and a mage snuck into the witch's fortress."

"Did they kill the witch?" I was bouncing in my seat.

"No." Grandpa frowned. "They could have, but they decided to capture her instead."

"That was good. That ended the war," I announced triumphantly.

Grandpa ruffled my hair. He didn't get to tell me the rest of the story because my dad emerged from the house. I remember the scowl on his face.

"That's enough, Mr. Windtalker." Dad frowned. "You'll give him nightmares."

"The boy should know where he comes from and the great deads," Grandpa argued.

Dad held up a hand to stop him. "He can learn all about it when he's older."

Then someone was approaching. My mom bounded out of the house while my dad and grandpa waved a friendly greeting to the person coming. Then, through the haze of memory, I recognized the figure.

It was Caterous.

I heard my voice call out, "Uncle Lawerence!"

I woke up instantly. "That was weird," I muttered to the darkness.

But was it a memory, or was it just a dream?

CHAPTER 18

When I went down to breakfast, my parents were already gone. I wanted to talk to them about the dream and was slightly annoyed. "Well, they can't stop me from seeing Thorn if they aren't here," I announced to the empty house.

I had half hoped and expected to meet Thorn on the way. Unfortunately, it seemed my day was to be filled with annoyances. So I found myself staring at the high wall surrounding the manor. I used the magnifying glass to find the door but hesitated with my hand on the handle. For good or bad, the door opened, Thorn either forgot to lock it, or she was expecting me. I heard the damn hawk screech above me as soon as I entered the grounds.

I wasn't surprised when Caterous met me at the door.

"Welcome back," he said, without anything resembling welcome in his voice. "Is this another social call, or would you like to start learning?" Unfortunately, his question left me somewhat wrong-footed. Before I could answer or ask any questions, Caterous continued. "I think we need to talk." Not waiting for my answer, he swept into the house. I followed, although I did seriously consider running away.

We walked down the hall in silence. Caterous strode with purpose and confidence while I followed like a condemned man. I glanced up as Thorn thundered down the stairs. When she hit the bottom step, she saw us. Her mouth opened to question what was going on. The look she received from her father stole her voice. She glanced at me, worry and an apology in her eyes. The library door slammed shut with the finality of a cell door locking in the convicted.

The man staring down at me was not a mage. He was a father and a worried man. "My daughter has been sheltered her whole life. That was a mistake." He sighed deeply. "It was also for her safety. As you well know, a half-mage, half-elf."

"Half-breeds are hated," I muttered.

Caterous groaned, running a hand wearily over his face. "It is not only her. Her mother was not a good person. Judging by your lack of reaction, you already knew that." He glanced at the door. I was pretty sure I heard something as well. Shaking his head, he continued. "What you are not aware of is how dangerous a woman she was or how sick."

He sat behind his desk, motioning for me to sit on the hard chair before him. I hoped to sit on the couch, further away, but he wanted me to be uncomfortable. I was.

"She was an extremely powerful mage. Because of her power and illness, she was sent away. However, she still has ways of knowing what is going on within these walls." He got up to pace again. "The stunt you and Thorn pulled yesterday is highly troubling." He rubbed his face, agitated. "Not to mention incredibly suspect."

"We did nothing. We're friends—just friends!" I defended.

Caterous raised an eyebrow in disbelief.

"I swear I'm not interested in anything other than friendship."

This caused his eyebrows to disappear into his gray-streaked hair.

"I mean, she's very pretty, and I mean, who wouldn't be interested, but I'm not—well, I am—as friends." A thud outside the door halted my rambling.

"I'm not sure I want to be friends with you anymore," Thorn's muffled voice called from behind the door.

Caterous let out a groan of exasperation. He made a motion with his hand, then something that sounded like a gate slamming shut came from the door.

"That should give us some privacy," he said as his shoulders rolled with tension. "You two have always been trouble," Caterous muttered, then continued, hoping I hadn't heard. "The Magic you used to conceal yourselves must never be known to my wife." He stood glaring down at me. "Do you understand?" His eyes seemed to bore right through my soul. "You are forbidden to use, discuss, or even think about that spell."

I swallowed nervously.

"If you do," his face drew closer as his voice dropped to a whisper, "no spell will hide you." He drew closer.

I backed away as far as possible without leaning back in the chair.

"More importantly, if you hurt Thorn or try any funny business, there will be no need for a spell to conceal you." His eyes locked onto mine. "I will obliterate you." He waved his hand as he stood up.

There was a click, and Thorn fell into the room. She gazed from her father's stone face to my pale, sweating one. Her annoyance grew. "Father, stop threatening him." She recoiled as Caterous turned his attention to her.

"I was just informing Henry of the consequences of his actions."

I felt guilty yet relieved that his ire was on her, not me, for the moment. Sadly, it didn't last.

Caterous raised his voice to ensure I heard every syllable. "His fate would be most dire if he disobeyed me."

I cowered under his returned scrutiny and nodded my understanding.

"Um, sir," I began. I was surprised at how much my voice squeaked as I spoke. "I was wondering if I could ask you something."

The coldness in his gaze told me this was not the time to ask sensitive questions. Behind the mage, a bell rang. He continued to glare at me for what felt like an eternity, then silently, he swept from the room.

Thorn and I were about to say something when Caterous's face appeared at the door. "Don't leave this room," he commanded and was gone before we could respond.

I opened my mouth to say something to Thorn, but she held up her hand to silence me. My mouth hung open as I recognized the two voices that had just entered the hall.

"Mom, Dad? What are you doing here?" I gasped as they walked in. Mom either didn't hear me or ignored me as she whistled, looking at the books.

"You've been busy," she exclaimed, heading to a shelf to inspect the titles.

Dad stood in the doorway staring daggers at Caterous, who returned the glare in kind.

"Oh, stop it, both of you." Mom stood with hands on her hips as she admonished the two men.

Caterous grumbled something about *my house* but stopped looking at my father all the same. Instead, he held his hand out to the couch. Mom thanked him as she sat.

"Please join me." Caterous nervously gestured to my dad. "I fear we must discuss our children again." Every eye glared at us. "And what was offered and what was requested."

Mom gave my dad a look that said, *I told you so*. After that, Dad became very interested in some dirt under his fingernails.

Caterous sighed, then glanced toward us. "I believe it would be in your best interest if the parents discussed this privately."

Thorn nodded, swallowing her fear as she grabbed my sleeve. I wanted to say something. Instead, however, Thorn pulled me out of the library. The door snapped closed behind us.

Thorn spun to the door, placing her ear against it. "Damn it," she growled. "He put a charm on it so we can't hear." Her annoyance was tinged with trepidation.

I had to admit, I was terrified. "Do you think they'll do something to keep us apart?" I couldn't imagine being without Thorn. We had so much fun exploring and hanging out that I didn't even consider the consequences. We had completely ignored that we weren't supposed to see each other. It had felt like a game, but now here we were with our parents having a meeting. "What if your dad curses us?"

"Don't be stupid." Thorn glared at me. "Father wouldn't curse your family." Then her fingers touched her chin in contemplation. "You, on the other hand . . ." She shrugged as she turned back to the door. Thorn was muttering something and checking the door. "Drat, I still can't hear."

I didn't care if she could hear or not. "What do you mean, just me!" I yelped, grabbing her arm. "He won't turn me into a toad or something?"

"Are all elves as thick as you?" She threw off my hand. "Father will make you forget you know me, or make it painful to be around me, or something that will make it so we can't get together anymore." She looked me up and down appraisingly. "Maybe that wouldn't be a bad thing."

"Hey!" I shouted. "Oh man, I was so looking forward to learning Magic."

"Well, then maybe you shouldn't have lied to your parents!" I heard her frustration. She was worried he would revoke her training as well.

"When did I lie?" I demanded loudly.

"Thorn! Henry! Go outside!" Caterous's voice thundered from everywhere.

Thorn pulled me out to the garden with an *eep* scream and a jump like a scared cat. Then, bursting out of the front door, we sprinted away from the house. We ran to the bench near the front gate, where we stopped, hands on our knees. We glanced at each other. Nervous laughter took control for a moment.

"I guess that charm only worked for *us* not to hear *them*, huh?" I gasped, recovering from the sprint and laughing fit.

"Looks that way." She leaned back on the bench to look up through the flowers to the sky. "I don't know what he'll do." Her hand quickly swiped away a tear. "You're the first friend I've had."

"What about Serina?" Scratch asked. He was leaning against the archway into the garden. Thorn's attention was focused on the newcomer. "Hey," Scratch said with a wave. "Glad to see you're doing okay. You were bleeding from the face the last time I saw you."

"Thank you for helping us that day." Thorn smiled. Scratch returned it. Something ran through me. I didn't like the way they looked at each other. It was too comfortable.

"Yeah, thanks," I muttered. "When did you get back?" Then it struck me, "How did you know we were here?"

"Yesterday." Scratch shrugged. "Serina told me."

"Wait, what?" Thorn stuttered, "You said *Serina*? How do you know about Serina?" Her eyes widened, and what little color she had disappeared. "Don't say another word," Thorn hissed, her lips barely moving. I turned to see what had frightened her.

My knees trembled when I saw her father standing near us. Caterous's stern expression hardened further as he glared at his daughter. For her part, Thorn seemed as surprised as her father was angry.

"He wouldn't be talking about Serina, would he?"

"No, sir," I said immediately. "I met a young human girl, Selina, who said she was friends with Thorn. Well, she said she knew her." I babbled, trying to get Thorn on the same page as me. "She said you talked one day in the woods."

Thorn's eyes told me her father wasn't buying this. "He must be talking about a village girl I saw when gathering berries."

"I told Scratch about visiting your house," I explained.

"Before he left for training?" Caterous raised an eyebrow.

"Yeah, that's right—she overheard us and said she knew the place. Then she mentioned Thorn, but wait." I was spinning out of control now. If he asked Scratch, this whole lie would fall apart. "Um, come to think of it, she never said your name. I did." Then I turned to see Thorn frowning and shaking her head slightly.

"Idiot," she sighed.

"Well, if that is the case, we'll say no more about Serina." Caterous looked directly into my eyes. His face told me he didn't believe a word I was saying. "As my feelings on the vampire are quite clear."

"Vampire," Mom asked, intrigued. Her curiosity landed squarely on me. Her eyes seemed to penetrate me. She knew I was lying. I tried to act like it was the truth. I could see she was trying to decide if she should tell the mage. I tried to plead with her through eye contact, but she wasn't looking at me. Instead, her attention was on Thorn, who seemed to beg her to keep quiet.

"Yes, a vampire that has taken up residence at our home. When I find her, I will evict her. My daughter knows this." The mage was gathering his robes around him. "But since there was a village girl, Thorn needs to be more cautious on her journeys." He then turned to my mother. "Amelia, I am asking you to consider my request."

Mom gave Caterous a non-committal shrug.

I was surprised that Caterous seemed suddenly nervous as he spoke to my mom. "I assure you. This vampire will not be a problem."

"She has a name," I grumbled. I immediately regretted it as the mage turned to glare at me. I tried to play it off like I was talking to Thorn. "I said, you want to play a game?" It was pathetic as she hadn't even looked at me. She glared at her father for a moment. Then, with a stamp of her foot, she grabbed my hand, pulling me further away.

"Yes, she does," Caterous's tone was deadly calm. "I believe this conversation is not over." He had spotted Scratch lurking close to the trees.

I hadn't noticed him wander off. I wondered how much of the lie he heard. Thorn seemed to be holding her breath. Scratch waved, then walked right up to Thorn. To my surprise, she grabbed his arm as he passed. He nodded his understanding, then asked, "Wow, it's true. You are, like, radiating Magic. It's hard to keep my head clear."

Thorn let go of his arm, noticeably upset. Scratch shook his head. Then dared to act as if he had just noticed the presence of a powerful mage.

"I can never touch anyone," Thorn grumbled, moving closer.

"Good morning, Lord Mage," Scratch greeted with a low bow.

"Sebastian," Thorn's father returned the bow. "How is Selina?" he asked, watching for Thorn's reaction.

"Oh, have you met Selina? Quite the imagination on that one. She makes up stories all the time. Henry was telling me about your house." He surveyed the building behind Caterous. "It's beautiful." He whistled.

My mom threw a glance at me. I could see her fighting the smile. Scratch continued even as my dad held a hand over his eyes.

"She claimed to have been here." Scratch shook his head in disappointment. "Silly girl, she always wants to have a story to be part of the conversation."

Caterous and Scratch's eyes met. The mage was calm and searching, while Scratch was relaxed and confident.

Caterous frowned. "You and Martin are the same—impossible to read. Very well, give my best to that crafty old spy and your mother."

"Yessir, always a pleasure to see you, sir." Scratch bowed again.

Caterous returned the bow. "Dreamweavers." He nodded to my parents. Then his attention was back on Thorn and me. "I trust you will stay out of trouble and remember my warning." He looked pointedly at me and then swept into the house. My parents bid us goodbye, and they, too, left. Scratch and I stood several paces from Thorn. She looked back at us as if to thank us, or maybe yell at me. A world of emotions ran across her face.

Then she stalked right up to me and poked her finger at my chest. "You have got to be the biggest fool in this village."

"She really is perceptive." Scratch laughed.

"You're a close second," Thorn growled at him. Her comment only caused Scratch to laugh at her. "How do you even know about the house?"

"Henry and I found a map at my house." Scratch smirked. "When Dad found out, I was sworn to secrecy." Then, said in a manner he thought sounded spooky, "About the mages in the woods." He laughed, looking the house over again. "He never thought anyone would be *dumb enough* to go near the place." Scratch shrugged again. All I could do was stare at him.

I learned a few things that day. My friend Scratch could keep a secret, which you definitely want in a friend. He could also lie without a hint of regret. It was something you both want and don't want in a friend. Then his words finally sunk in. "Dude, you showed me that map at my house. Then you came into the woods to find the wall and told me about it."

Scratch looked confused. "Oh, yeah. I forgot."

"Wait, you've spoken to my father before?" Thorn asked.

"Yeah, the lord of Dayok requested a meeting several times. Since my dad knows your dad, he arranged the meetings."

"Why the hell didn't you tell me about this?" I demanded.

"You know . . ." Scratch rubbed the beginnings of a beard and seemed to be thinking hard. "I just remembered it. Weird." He was staring off into the distance, bemused.

Something clicked in my brain. "Last night, I had this dream," I began, and another thought clicked. "Wait, your mother can see what's going on here?" I pointed at Thorn, whose surprise was undeniable.

"Wait, what?" both Thorn and Scratch asked. I told them what Caterous had said about his wife.

"I haven't seen my mother in years," Thorn explained.

"That's a good thing." Scratch nodded.

My whole world swirled, and I almost fell over as memory flooded my brain. "Your mother is the evil elf witch who fought against the elves and men!"

Thorn fell down on her knees. Scratch held onto a tree for support. It was like the three of us had been simultaneously hit by the same memory.

Thorn looked up at me, tears streaming down her face. "What just happened?"

CHAPTER 19

I think—I think a spell just broke," Scratch replied, trying to catch his breath. I couldn't believe what was happening. Why would someone make us forget each other?

"Do you think it was just us?" I asked, feeling like my mind had been dragged through a dry field. "Do you think that's why my parents are so concerned?"

Scratch and I turned our attention back to Thorn. She was still on her knees, her hands covering her face. I could tell by the shaking of her shoulders that she was crying. I rushed to put my arms around her, but she pushed me away as she jumped up. "Don't come near me!" It felt like she punched me in the stomach.

"Hey, Thorn, Henry didn't mean to call your mother an evil witch," Scratch defended.

"NO!" Thorn shouted at us. "No, he said it, and he's right!" She was pacing. Terror and anger fought for dominance over her face. "I have always hated the woman. I always said she was evil. I just didn't know *how* evil." Then, suddenly, she turned to glare at me.

I backed away, scared of the anger emanating from her.

She pointed accusingly at Scratch and me. "Your fathers were right. I shouldn't exist. I'm the bastard daughter of an evil elf witch. I mean, why wouldn't I be?" Then, she wasn't looking at us anymore. Instead, she looked at her hands. "Of course you are. Why else would you never be allowed out, never allowed to have friends? Why do you have to be hidden away? Because you're evil, the daughter of the most hated elf witch to ever walk the earth."

The more she ranted, the more frantic she became. Heat pulsed from her small frame as the ground rumbled then shook under our feet. Scratch began pulling on my shirt.

"This explains why the Debkohr reminds me how much I'm loathed," Thorn howled.

I broke free from Scratch's grasp. Waves of anger, heat, and energy pulsed from Thorn. I had to fight to stay on my feet as I slowly took one step, then another, and another as I fought to keep moving. Thorn's growing despair pushed me back each time I moved. I called out to her, but my voice was drowned out by the whirlwind of her pain. I glanced back to see Scratch holding onto the tree again, trying desperately to get me to take his hand. I forced another step forward, then another.

Thorn turned. She watched with eyes that had turned a deep crimson as I leaned into each step. I reached out to her, and she recoiled. "Why? Why are you trying to get near the tainted daughter of evil?" she demanded in a voice straight from the bowels of the underworld.

"Because." I fought to take a step and get the words out. "You're . . . my . . ." I stretched out and grabbed her arm, ". . . friend." I panted as I pulled her into a hug. The world went silent as she dissolved into sobs in my arms. I heard Scratch lose his balance and fall over behind me when her waves of despair suddenly stopped.

"Why?" Thorn asked in a voice so small I almost missed it.

"Because you're everything to me," I whispered.

"But you said, in the library—"

"I was talking to your dad," I explained.

"So you'll fight through waves of Magic—and what was that, anger?—to reach a girl, but her dad scares you?" Scratch asked as he got up, brushing himself off.

"Then the elf has his priorities straight," Caterous's voice sounded above me. I continued to hold Thorn as she regained control. "Again, I find myself thanking you for helping my daughter." His eyes were kind yet sad. "It appears this father has much to explain to his beloved child."

He held out his hand to Thorn while her arms held tightly around me. Caterous didn't insist or demand. He just held out his hand. "Sume," he whispered.

Thorn sniffed, then I felt one arm release me. Her hand was in mine as she reached out to her father. Just before she took his hand and released mine, she turned to face me. "You promise?" she asked.

"I promise," I replied.

"You really promise?" She sounded scared.

"I promise with all that I am."

She squeezed my hand at these words and let her father lead her back to the house.

As I watched them go, Scratch moved to stand next to me. I glanced at him and was surprised to see he didn't seem disturbed by anything that had happened. Then a frown creased his face. "What did you just promise?"

I laughed. Thorn hadn't said it, and neither had I. "I promised to be with her. To be her friend and support her for as long as we live." I knew that was my promise, and I was pretty sure she had just made the same promise back to me.

"Well, congratulations—you just got married." Scratch clapped me hard on the shoulder.

"That is *not* what just happened. Thorn's my friend," I argued.

"Dude, whatever you say. But, that sounded like you just promised to love her forever."

I shook my head at Scratch as I threw off his hand. We'd had our memories altered. Thorn had thrown a magical conniption and could have killed us, and Scratch was giving me grief about a perceived declaration of love, no matter how true it was on my part.

I had to put up with his teasing all the way back to my house. I still couldn't believe *that* was his real takeaway from the events. I invited him in, but he pointed out my mom waiting at the door. "I think this is a conversation I don't want to be involved in."

Agreeing, we parted ways. Scratch wished me luck as he turned toward Dayok.

I was angry the moment I stepped through the door. "When did you agree to have my memory messed with?" I demanded. "How could you do that?"

"Caterous has been very generous." Dad spoke as if I hadn't said anything. "He has agreed to resume your training."

"I don't know if I can trust him or you," I shouted. "What other memories have you changed?"

Mom glared at Dad, who pretended not to notice. Then they did that thing again where they had a conversation silently using just their eyes. Mom frowned, then sighed as if she resigned herself to the outcome of their discussion.

Dad, however, seemed to come to a different conclusion. "No, Amelia, you're right. As always," he sighed.

Mom looked shocked.

"It's about time Henry knew the truth." Then, at the warning glance from Mom, he added, "At least how we all know each other."

I sat listening to their story, how Mom and Dad grew up together. How they met Martin Heraldry at Fluxx Academy and befriended Lawerence Caterous and Althea Shadefall. From there, I finally began to understand who my parents really were. They were heroes, some of the fiercest and most victorious warriors to serve in the war against the Southern Kingdom of Elro and then against Althea the Evil.

Nightfall outside of a destroyed village on an unnamed battlefield near the middle of Notelek
Twenty years ago

The third year of the war was drawing to a close. The coalition army suffered heavy losses in their most recent victory over Elro's forces. Snow and ash mingled as they fell on battered troops huddled close to fires or trying to find warmth in blankets and small tents. A larger pavilion reserved for strategic planning was removed from the main staging area.

"Even if we win, do you think they'll keep their promises?" Althea's fist crashed down on the table.

"We have no choice but to trust they will," Amelia sighed as her now husband, Micha Dreamweaver, bandaged her arm.

"We have to believe in the coalition," Micha agreed.

Suddenly Martin appeared through the tent flap. "Caterous's squad captured an Elro messenger."

A moment later, Caterous entered behind Martin.

"You seem troubled." Althea moved closer to rest a comforting hand on Caterous's face.

"Notelek has sent an emissary to the Elro." Caterous's face suddenly contorted in anger. "They are trying to broker a peace treaty."

"They want to make a deal with the humans, you mean." Althea's anger flared again.

"That isn't what he said," Martin interrupted.

"Of course, you would defend the humans. You have nothing to lose. The war ends, and your life returns to how it was before."

"Althea! That isn't fair, and you know it," Amelia defended. Suddenly the two women were poised for battle.

"Calm down, both of you!" Micha shouted.

"Did you forget it wasn't the Elro Army that destroyed Fluxx Academy?" Althea cried.

"Southern sympathizers," Martin tried to interject.

"Lies! They were regular humans. All humans hate us," Althea screamed, casting a spell at Martin. Amelia threw out a shield spell, saving Martin from serious injury.

"Your feeble Magic cannot hurt me," Althea growled. Then, suddenly, she glared at everyone. "You have always been beneath me. You are *nothing*. You deserve the fate you shall receive from the filthy rulers of Notelek. I don't need the coalition or any human to grant me the rights I deserve."

"Althea, please calm yourself," Caterous pleaded.

"Enough with your simpering!" Darkness clouded Althea's eyes as she stared at Caterous. "Join me now. This is your final chance."

Present day

"Caterous had been in love with Althea for as long as we could remember." There was sadness in my dad's voice. "I thought for sure he would follow her."

"He didn't, though," Mom explained, giving Dad a moment to compose himself.

"Okay, great. Yay, love." I was sarcastic, and I didn't care. "That doesn't explain how and when they got together. Nor does it explain why you altered my memory—*our* memories! Why?" I was confused and angry.

Dad glanced at Mom, and Mom nodded, then Dad nodded back. I had to figure out how they communicated like that.

"What did you say to each other!" I shouted. "How can I trust you *or* Caterous?"

"Damn it, Henry!" Dad shouted, leaving me stunned. He took a deep breath, rubbing the bridge of his nose. "There were reasons—reasons I will explain later." He held up a hand, cutting off my protests. "For now, just trust that we had your best interest at heart."

I stood fuming as I stared at my parents. I needed to clear my head. "I'm going for a walk!"

"Henry, please don't go far. Stay close to the house tonight." Mom's urging seemed odd, but I had so many thoughts fighting for dominance. First, I was worried about Thorn. Second, I was angry at my parents and thoroughly disturbed by how Scratch didn't seem bothered by anything.

I walked past the pool of light surrounding my house. That's when I felt someone watching me. Serina slipped out of the darkness, an awkward smile on her face.

"You were really good with Thorn today," she said. Then, before I could thank her, she laughed. "Remember, today's the day your peaceful world began changing." Then, her wings unfurled, and she was off into the night.

"Thanks!" I shouted angrily. "That helps my confidence!"

CHAPTER 20

I walked back into the house with one more person on my list of annoyances. Finally, Dad seemed ready to move forward. "Caterous told me you'll train as a defender when you and Thorn aren't blowing off studies."

I cringed but nodded my assertion.

"He still wants you to train with Mom and me. Thorn as well." He smirked before adding, "Your Mom's all right with swords. Maybe we'll have Thorn train with her."

Mom swatted Dad on the arm. "Which is good, so she'll be better than you. Just as a warrior needs be," she explained, pointing a fork at Dad.

Deciding not to engage, my Dad sighed. "We've only trained you in a few spells and potions. The skills you'll learn from Caterous are far more than your mom or I could teach you."

"Magic will open many opportunities for you," Mom explained. "However, it also comes with consequences." She glanced at Dad. "You will have power. With that power comes fear. There will be those that fear you because they don't have the same abilities. You'll need to be cautious, especially around humans."

Dad quickly added, "And around elves who will try to use your power." The seriousness on his face melted away as he smiled lovingly at Mom. "However, there's another benefit to Magic. The more you use it, the less you seem to age. For instance, your mother is actually over one hundred and—"

"Thank you, dear," Mom interrupted, throwing a dishtowel at him. "Henry, this isn't something to be taken lightly. This is a commitment." Her face turned serious. "Your father's right. Magic will change everything. You must decide if this is the path you wish to take."

I listened to my parents explain that if I began the training, I might have to be away from them for a long time. Yet for all their misgivings about Caterous, they seemed genuinely excited for me.

After dinner, I stepped out into the garden. I stood looking at the home I'd lived in my entire life. I suddenly realized I was just a kid who'd been asked to choose the path for the rest of his life. Most of my time now would be spent learning Magic in a huge house with a mage and his daughter. I looked up at our small house on the outskirts of town. My knees felt like jelly while my stomach churned. I wasn't ready for this, I wasn't going to be good enough for this, I was terrified. I wanted to run away or hide under my bed. But, at the same time, I couldn't wait until morning.

I wandered back inside, lost in my thoughts. How would my life change? When it did, what would I do about it? I would be an elf with Magic and combat training. What would that mean? Elves weren't exactly welcome in human towns, so a warrior elf would be less welcome. Would my abilities end up causing trouble for my parents? They had built a nice quiet life here. No one knew their past. How would they explain my absence?

Then again, something was going on. I could *feel* it. I know Mom and Dad were trying to shield me at first, but now I wondered about the reason they'd been training me and were willing to trust Caterous.

Are my parents training me to fight for an elf revolution? I gripped the garden wall for support, trying to shake the idea away. There was no way my parents would want me to fight. They'd always spoken out against violence.

"But why are they okay with this?" I whispered into the darkness. "They've fought in battles. They told you as much."

"Maybe they think trouble is coming," the darkness answered in Serina's voice.

My cry was muffled by deathly cold hands covering my mouth.

"If you're going to be a warrior, you better learn not to scream like a little child."

My lips and face felt numb when she removed her hand.

"There were some visitors to the manor a few days ago," Serina explained. I watched her move through the shadows. Her presence was blacker than the darkness of the night. "Some travelers . . ." she hesitated, ". . . came to ask for lodging for the night."

"Who were they?" I couldn't help but ask.

"They were a band of goblins."

"Goblins—are you sure?" I couldn't believe what she said. "There haven't been any goblins here in years."

"Are you sure about that?" Her tone was facetious.

I then recalled what Thorn said about Greggor's father. "But you never see them," I stammered.

"They tend to travel at night," she sighed as if I was a small child asking why the sky was blue. "And no. They aren't like me. They can travel in the daylight." Her red eyes appeared inches from my face. "But answer me this—why would they want men and elves to notice them?"

I sputtered as I recoiled from her fiery gaze.

"Your kind reacts with violence whenever you meet something you fear."

"Why shouldn't we fear them?" I demanded. "They've attacked and murdered hundreds of elves."

Serina matched my annoyance. "Defending their lands or retaliating against your attacks."

"My people have lived under the yoke of humans for centuries. Since when have we attacked?!" I shouted.

Her hand clamped over my mouth again. Those blazing eyes bore into mine with anger and a slight hint of fear. "You have no idea what happens outside of your little world. What would happen if your parents found me here?" she hissed.

I pulled her hand away. "Well, they'd be more upset if I was meeting a girl this late at night, first off," I hissed back.

"You are so naive," she spat. "They would try to kill me, or drive me away, or both."

"Why? You're my friend. They wouldn't hurt you," I growled. How could she think such things of my parents? People she had never met.

"We are *not* friends," Serina muttered.

"Why not?" I was confused. "Why would you say that?"

"I . . ." She seemed to struggle with the words. "I don't have friends."

"So what is Thorn?"

"She's different. She understands."

"Well, maybe I would too."

She inhaled deeply through her nose. I recognized her effort to calm herself. "Henry, that's sweet, but you'll never understand. Let's say we're *acquaintances* and leave it at that?"

"No," I replied, watching her darkness travel toward the gate. "You're my friend, just like Scratch and Thorn. Besides, you'll see more of me at the manor, so we should be friends."

"I-I only came by to—as a favor to Thorn." Serina huffed. "She says to tell you . . . ugh." I couldn't see her face. However, I knew by her tone she wore the same one I had when I saw my parents earlier. "She is really looking forward to training with you."

I could almost hear her eyes rolling. "Thank you, *friend*," I smirked.

"I bet Thorn you would blow yourself up in the first week."

Before I could respond, the flutter of her wings told me she was already gone. I stood in the dark, trying to keep my thoughts from colliding into chaos. However, Serina's visits always left me exhausted. So I decided to call it a night and do my best to sort out my thoughts and worries in the morning. Soon I was in a fitful sleep, filled with nightmares of goblin attacks and bloody battles.

CHAPTER 21

Morning came too quickly, with Dad shaking me out of another bloody battle dream. Even though my dreams were terrifying, I was still fighting the effects of Serina's visit and wanted to sleep. Something hit my fuzzy brain. How come her touch didn't knock me out? Dad took my glazed expression as trying to stay in bed, and he was having none of it. "Wake up. It's starting to get late."

Dad's smile didn't entirely make it to his eyes. I could tell he was worried and didn't want me to know. I had so many questions swirling in my brain. I didn't know which one I should ask first. Finally, as I sat up, he sat down on the bed.

"Dad, I was wondering—"

He interrupted me by placing an arm around my shoulder. "I think I know what you're thinking." He sighed. "Your mom is amazing and loves you very much. Then there's me," he exclaimed. "I'm no slouch either. I know you're worried about measuring up. Just do your best. That's all we can ask." He acted like being him was such a burden, then laughed at the look on my face.

I twisted from his grip. "No, Dad—I mean, a little—but . . ." I was confusing myself. "I don't know what I'm trying to live up to. You and Mom have a history with Caterous that you've never mentioned. You apparently are heroes and helped win a war. I don't know how to live up to something I know nothing about. Why didn't you tell me about your past, and why did you mess with our memories?"

Dad sighed. Before he could say anything, Mom appeared in the doorway.

She smiled sadly at Dad, then she shook her head. "Henry, there's too much to tell you and not enough time." She chewed nervously at the inside of her cheek, then explained, "We should have done something sooner." She inhaled

as Dad joined her and touched her reassuringly. She nodded to him and continued. "We can't explain right now, but things have been put into motion that
we thought would never come about."

Dad took her hand and smiled, then looked at me. "It wasn't our intention
to become part of this village. We thought we'd only stay for a little while. Then
a little while turned into a year, then two, and we just stayed." He smiled at me.
"We got more than we expected when you arrived."

It felt like my heart was being pierced.

"No, no, you've made your mother and me extremely happy and proud.
Don't think for a moment that we don't want you around. On the contrary,
we're terrified for you but want you to have a better life. Learning Magic and
how to defend yourself away from prying eyes is the first step toward that life."
He held me by the shoulders to look me straight in the eyes. "We love you and
want you to make the right decision."

"If I don't like it or can't . . ." I fought through my fear. ". . . can't do it. Can
I come home?"

"Always." Dad smiled.

———— ✺ ————

Reassured but still confused and annoyed, I got dressed. My parents were
still keeping things from me. I decided that today wasn't the day to push further. Instead, I ate a quick breakfast and waved goodbye as I left the house. I
noticed the trail into the forest was no longer hidden. I started down the path
to Thorn's house. I thought I would make this trek every day for however long
it took to learn what I needed to know.

That day Caterous worked us relentlessly. Reading, practical spell work,
alchemy, and for some reason, an obstacle course we had to run four times.
Night was falling, and I was exhausted from the training and wasn't paying
attention to the path. It felt like I was almost sleepwalking. Then, as I reached
the edge of the woods, I froze. I wished I was asleep, and this was another
nightmare. I heard horses galloping and angry yells. Something in the air felt
wrong.

Leaving the path, I kept to the woods, remaining out of sight. I was stunned
when my house came into view. It was surrounded by soldiers. I watched, terrified, as they kicked in the back door and swarmed inside. Keeping near the
ground, I made it to the low wall along the edge of the property, hiding behind
a bush. Mom had been after Dad for weeks to cut it down. I silently thanked

him for not getting to it. From my hiding spot, I could hear the soldiers blundering around in my house. I bit back my anger at their intrusion.

"Report," an authoritative voice demanded high above me. The thudding of hooves told me the person was on horseback. Chainmail rattled as someone approached.

"We searched the house, sir. They appear to have been warned. It looks like they left this morning. We found their breakfast abandoned."

"Or they intend to make us think that's when they left," the man on the horse growled. Then, before the soldier could answer, the horse galloped away. I could only assume, based on the sound, they were heading back to Dayok.

"I didn't know we were after such strategic masterminds," I heard the soldier grumble. Someone near him gave a gruff laugh. I waited, hidden in the bush. Darkness quickly overtook the land. I listened closely to the air. It had been a while since I had heard any chainmail moving around. Then, hoping it was safe, I crept slowly out of hiding. A sudden noise halted me. Large wings fluttered through the air, followed by a thump on the roof.

"What the hell was that?"

"It went into the house from a second-floor window."

"Nerkens, Wulruf! Go check it out." Someone was shouting orders. "Smith, cover the back of the house." The air was filled with the sounds of rushing soldiers. I scuttled back to my hiding spot. I waited as it became quiet except for the muffled shouts inside my house. Suddenly, the shouting became screams. Glass shattered, and something heavy hit the ground, causing cries of terror. Slowly I rose just enough to see over the wall. A body lay on the ground, bloody and broken. A soldier burst through the front door.

"Demon! There's a demon!" His knees gave out. He fell forward without even trying to catch himself. Protruding from the back of his head was what looked like one of our table's legs. The dead man's limbs were at horrid angles. Even from where I was, I could see broken bones poking out of the skin. The grotesque sight left the two soldiers in stunned silence, staring at their fallen comrade. Then a scream from behind the house sent them running.

I waited, crouched at the wall. My heart was slamming into my breastbone, and my breath stalled in my lungs in anticipation. Finally, after a few moments, I saw one soldier return. Then from the other direction, the other came around the side of the house. He shrugged as he raised his hands in confusion.

They looked up in unison as what I assumed was the soldier named Smith fell hard onto the roof. He rolled off the shingles to land in a mutilated lump at the remaining men's feet. There was a glance between them. Suddenly they dropped their swords and shields, running away as fast as their heavy armor would allow them.

My fingers clenched the wall. I was terrified. Whatever had attacked and killed these men was incredibly strong. It was also swift and, from what I could see, invisible. I heard the wings again. Something landed softly behind me. Fear gripped my heart and constricted my throat. I tried to swallow as I turned my head in small steps until the creature was in my vision. It was like nothing I had ever seen. The enormous black wings had a white bone spike at the top and bottom points. The creature's head held large curving horns. The beast's upper body was shrouded in a black cloak that reached down to its hairy goatlike legs. The legs ended in cloven hooves. It was something from a story, a demon from legends.

The demon opened its mouth. I cringed, waiting for its howl as it alerted death to my imminent arrival. But instead, a voice I recognized said, "Would you mind turning around? I don't like people watching me change."

"S-S-Serina?" I stammered.

The massive demon glared at me. "Yeah, duh. Now turn around." Shocked, I did as I was told. A moment later, she said I could look. Standing in front of me was the familiar girl with flaming red hair. "I don't know how long those fools will take to return with reinforcements." She looked off toward Dayok. "So you better collect what you can and get back to the manor." She walked up to me when I didn't move, spun me around to face my house, and shoved me.

I took about five steps before I turned to ask, "Do you know what happened to my parents?"

"I think Caterous knows." She was watching for returning soldiers. "I heard him say you might be in trouble."

"Thanks for coming to help me," I replied sincerely, and I admit, a bit frightened.

"You can thank me by moving your ass. Now hurry the hell up," she ordered. I took another two steps before her hand caught my upper arm. Sharp talons dug into my flesh as Serina snarled in my ear, "Also, you will never mention what you saw here. Understood?"

I nodded nervously as her grip relaxed, squeezed my arm again, and finally let go.

I couldn't help but gasp as I entered the house. Our furniture was in tatters. It looked like every dish, bowl, and cup had offended the soldiers. They were destroyed with extreme prejudice. My parent's bedroom had been ransacked. We had nothing of value. That must have been the reason for the absolute destruction of our belongings. Numbly I stumbled into my parents' wrecked bedroom. Even in its disheveled state, I saw something wasn't right. One of the walls was cracked and partially open.

My hands shook as I pryed it the rest of the way open. A banner with a massive Wolf's head and two swords hung on the wall. Dad trained me with one of those swords after we sparred, and the other was the Katnijuri blade Mom said would be perfect for Thorn. On the floor was the book of elf history and folklore. I grabbed everything from the alcove and then rushed to my room.

When I reached the second floor, the gore and smell of violence were overwhelming. Averting my gaze, I rushed into my room. I wasn't sure how I felt. Either the soldiers were tired of destroying things, or my possessions were just that unimportant. Thankfully most things here had avoided destruction. I had grabbed as much as I could and returned to Serina's side before I realized I was crying. I was angry and heartbroken at what the humans did to our home. There was no reason for so much wanton destruction.

Without asking, Serina took my bags. "Hurry to the manor. I'll keep watch from above." She was in the air before I could say a word. I looked at the smashed front door and the dead bodies in the yard, taking grim satisfaction at the men's deaths. Then I immediately hated myself for it. I closed my eyes, remembering my parents waving at me in front of the house. I chose to have that as my memory of the place. I turned around without opening my eyes, then looked straight ahead. I ran and didn't stop until I stood in front of the enormous oak doors of Caterous's home.

Breathing heavily, I stooped over, hands on my knees as I tried to catch my breath. My bags thumped down on either side of me. A moment later, Thorn threw open the doors. She pulled me into a tight hug, and I found myself crying again. I had no idea where my parents were. I just lost everything I thought I knew and understood. My home was left in shambles, and I witnessed the death of three soldiers at the hands of someone I thought I knew.

Caterous appeared behind his daughter. His face was grave. "I understand your parents were able to escape."

"Escape? Where did they go? Did you know about this? Is that why you kept me so long today? When can I see them?" The questions tumbled out. The mage held up a hand for silence. I realized Thorn was holding me around my arm.

"I did not know anything for sure until you had already left," Caterous replied as he led us to the library. "Mr. Heraldry arrived at nightfall. He told me your family had to leave."

I opened my mouth to demand more answers, but Caterous cut me off.

"I don't know where they went. The Heraldrys are meeting up with them and going into hiding."

"Why?" I interrupted.

"That is information I do not have. However, I do know your friend Scratch is safe. He is with the knight's detachment in Lovo. He was able to get a warning to your parents of the coming trouble." Caterous looked sympathetically at me. "Your parents are well-respected elves. The Heraldrys are outspoken supporters of elf rights. The human rulers must have believed that their power was being questioned, so they put on a show of force."

"We've seen that before. Soldiers come in and intimidate us. They break up some stuff and ruin a field or two, but my parents have never run away," I argued. "Why is this different?"

Caterous hesitated as if he didn't want to say something, then inhaled deeply. "I fear I may have helped bring this upon them. Since they started training you and Thorn in swordsmanship, I believe you may have been observed." He didn't look at me as he continued. "Elves with your parents' skills have always terrified humans in power."

I couldn't believe it. "So that's why they came to destroy our house and kill us?" I couldn't return home, I couldn't run to my parents to help me. I was on my own with a commitment to learn to be something I was not prepared for. Then I realized I had no place to stay.

As if reading my mind, Caterous said, "Henry, you will be staying here. While you are here, you will remain on the grounds. You will not venture into the woods or go anywhere near Dayok or the elf village." His tone left no room for argument. "The same rules apply to you, young lady." His attention was now squarely on his daughter, his eyebrow raised questioningly. Thorn let go of me and quickly took a step away. His piercing eyes bore into mine now. "Your room is in the wing opposite Thorn's. I will know if there are any late-night wanderings. You have been warned." He swept from the room before I could ask any more questions.

My mind was reeling from the day's events, and I barely noticed as Thorn showed me to my room. When she opened the door, I was again stunned at the proportions. The room was larger than the entire downstairs of my house. My bags lay at the foot of a massive four-poster bed in the middle of the room. Heavy crimson curtains hung around the mattress. There was a large wardrobe, a desk on one wall, and a door leading to a bathroom on the other. Thorn showed me a bookshelf that currently held only a few old elven history books.

I sat on the edge of the huge bed, trying to come to terms with all that just happened. Thorn sat next to me, not saying a word. I turned to say something, couldn't decide what it was, and just stared at her. She smiled and nodded and took my hand, reassuring me without a word. I knew I could cry, scream, yell, throw things, and she would understand. She was with me and would be by my side when I needed her.

Thorn stayed with me until she thought I was okay. When she left, I couldn't help myself. I lay facedown on that huge bed, feeling alone and scared in a way I hadn't felt since I was a small child and got lost at the market. Finally, after several minutes of sobbing, I decided I was done with crying.

I looked around the room again. Besides the bed, the most prominent item in the room was a portrait of my benefactors. The cold stare of Thorn's mother sent a chill up my spine. Caterous stared down with contempt, causing even more discomfort, but the younger version of Thorn smiled at me with that sly grin that made me feel like we were getting away with something. I covered the two adult faces with a sheet that night, leaving only that smiling girl watching me.

It was the genuine smile that got me through the next few months. At first, Caterous left me alone as I tried to acclimate to my new home. Every day I hoped for some news from my parents. Two weeks passed before the first brief note arrived, informing me that they were safe and well. But, unfortunately, they couldn't tell me where they were. After that, Caterous pushed me to learn. I don't know if it was to distract me so I wouldn't be overcome with worry or if he wanted to continue what we had started.

Every day there was more and more reading. We translated ancient texts, learned elder chants, studied herbology, and demonstrated our understanding in front of Caterous's stern face at the end of every day. Then Thorn and I had sparring matches. This didn't go well since I had trained in Dad's combat style while Thorn was versed in several different styles. However, Caterous said it was good that we had learned to adapt the way my parents had. Naturally, something demanded his attention when I asked him to explain, and he left.

CHAPTER 22

The first week I lived at the manor, I wanted desperately to talk to my parents. I wanted to know if they were safe and what was going on. I had never been away from home, and I missed them so much it hurt. I hated the idea that I couldn't go home. Thorn was awesome, and Caterous tried, but it wasn't my home. It was too big, too cold, and too full of sadness and anger from the past.

Once my parents were safe, they wrote to me. Their letters were a bright spot in my darkness. Their words felt like a return to normalcy. However, my feelings toward these brief correspondences changed as weeks turned to months. Once, they tore at my heart. Then they infuriated and frustrated me. Now, they stirred only a tiny hint of longing.

I thought about all these things as I read through a note from Mom. The missive contained no new information. It was simple and inane. I folded it and put it away in a box in my room. Even when I was furious at my parents, I kept every letter, no matter how short.

For the past year, I had amassed a total of twenty-one. I no longer hoped to see the arrival of parchment on the table at breakfast. I no longer wondered how the letters arrived. If I didn't hope, I couldn't be disappointed. That was the attitude I adopted.

I hadn't left the grounds since arriving that first night. Other than some hinted information in my parents' letters, I had no idea what was happening outside the manor walls. Serina would give Thorn some news, but she only traveled at night and stayed away from most settlements. When Scratch came to see me, he had more news. However, his visits were less frequent than the correspondence from my parents, and the information he relayed was never comforting. The entire elf village had been cleared out. The same type of thing was happening all across Notelek. Rumors of an impending elf revolt spread faster than wildfire.

"Why now?" Thorn asked after reading a letter from my dad. He was trying to be reassuring but failing miserably. Dad said elves were only banding together for protection. I always let Thorn read my letters, and she always shared what Serina told her.

We were our only sources of information.

"If they band together and fight, won't that just make matters worse?" Thorn questioned.

"That is what is most disconcerting," Caterous muttered. He must have overheard our discussion when he silently entered the room. "They are leaderless and scattered." Suddenly a look of panic flickered in the wizard's eyes. Then, before Thorn or I could ask, all we saw was the hem of his cloak disappearing through the door. Several minutes later, he returned, looking relieved. However, he continued muttering under his breath. I only caught the words "how" and "couldn't," but I could tell Caterous was trying to convince himself of something which wasn't working.

So when I received yet another letter from my mother telling me everything was fine, I didn't believe her. The number of letters I received was still far more significant than what I felt I was learning at the manor. Thorn seemed to master every lesson with ease. At the end of each day, it seemed I was getting further and further behind. Thorn eventually spent more time with her father after our lessons. Then, in the evenings, she was learning Magic and combat from Serina. Caterous also spent more and more time alone in his study. As the messages from my family dwindled, the correspondence with the mage tripled.

Mixed with my loneliness was an ever-increasing feeling of tension. Finally, something broke in me. It was after a rather disastrous lesson. We were supposed to make an invigorating draft. "*Not the desired effect*? Could he have been any more condescending?"

"The rabbit fell asleep." Thorn laughed.

"Naturally, the queen of the manor had no trouble. It must be nice to have the extra lessons so you can laugh at the stupid elf," I spat.

"Wait, hold on." Thorn grabbed my sleeve as I stormed down the hall. "What's that supposed to mean?"

"You're so smart. Figure it out!" I wrenched my arm free. All I wanted to do was get out of the house, maybe even finally leave the grounds. But instead, I glanced up at another portrait of Thorn's mother. The woman stared down at me. Her glare was venomous. I spun to point accusingly at Thorn. "Why the hell are there so many portraits of your evil mother!" I shouted. "I can't go two feet in this cold, dark prison without her hateful gaze on my back."

Thorn's face was unreadable.

My rant continued unabated. "Do you and your father get some sick, twisted joy from having someone glare at you with smoldering hate in her eyes?" I stormed up to the nearest frame, intent on knocking that glaring bitch off the wall.

"No, don't, please!" Thorn cried.

My hand froze on the frame. I glared back at those disapproving eyes. "Fine!" I turned back to shout at Thorn. "If you like the constant reminder of your mother, fine! I hate her! I hate this house! I hate not knowing where my parents are!"

I realized I still held the books and papers from our lesson. Disgusted, I threw them across the floor at Thorn. They skidded to a halt directly at her and her father's feet. He had come out to see what the shouting was all about.

Before he could open his mouth, I held my hand to quiet him. "Don't worry, I'm leaving!"

I marched to the front door and flung it wide. I wanted Thorn to stop me from leaving. I wanted her to yell at me, to tell me to calm down. Instead, when I glanced back, she was where I'd left her. I exhaled in disgust as I slowly pulled the door shut behind me. I glanced back in time to see her books and papers hit the floor next to mine. She spun and disappeared up the stairs. I decided against slamming the door. Instead, I quietly pulled it shut. The last image I saw before closing the door was Caterous staring at the disheveled books and papers. I rested my head against the massive door for a moment. I hated myself for acting out, but I had no idea what to do, so I ran off.

I reached the furthest part of the wall from the house. My stomach squirmed as my thoughts swirled. I had no right to yell at Thorn like that. I saw the confusion, anger, and hurt in her eyes as the door closed. *Good*, I thought savagely. Then I chastised myself for lying. Trying to keep my anger from turning into embarrassment, I blindly kept walking.

I left the cover of the trees to an open area with a bench and a small fish pond. The sun felt warm and pleasant after the cold chill of the manor. Sitting on the bench, I tried to calm down. "Why does it always have to be so dark and cold?" I growled. The tranquil setting wasn't helping to calm me. I wandered as far away as I could to sit with my back against the wall.

I thought about my parents. How much different our house was. It was small but always warm, not in the sense of heat, just with love. My parents loved each other, and they loved me. Thorn's father always felt like a teacher. I didn't expect anything different, but he treated Thorn with the same cold detachment. I was tired of the cold.

The cold house.

The cold interactions.

Even Thorn had turned cold.

"I just want to go home," I whined.

"Stupid elf should go back to the village to die." Serina's voice scared me. She was sitting on top of the wall, glaring down at me. "Today, I witnessed one of the nastiest interactions since Thorn's mother spat contempt at her daughter." She jumped down to face me.

I scrambled to my feet. I opened my mouth to argue until she snarled.

"You think either of them wants to have that old hag's face peering down at them?" Serina jabbed a finger into my chest. It hurt a lot. "Every time they tear one down, three more appear. You think they want more of that bitch in their house?" She was so angry her canine teeth elongated. I tried to ease along the wall as horns sprouted on her head. Serina stepped back. She was breathing heavily. "I can't believe you would treat Thorn like that. I can't believe you!"

I was terrified. Serina's demon side was coming out, and she didn't seem to care.

Suddenly Thorn's hand shot up between us. A dangerous ball of fire ignited in her grip. Serina cackled, slowly raising her hand. "What? Are you going to protect this little brat? After what he said to you?"

"Are you ready to face me in a fight?" Thorn's glare was terrifying. I held my breath, but nothing happened. Instead, the two women stared daggers at each other.

I had to do something. There was no reason for these two to fight. Especially since my tantrum caused the problem in the first place.

"Thorn, Serina, stop it," I called weakly as I pushed between them.

Serina's face contorted into absolute fury. She flexed her fingers as if she would like nothing more than to rip me apart with them. "You have no right to say anything. You hurt her."

"What's the matter?" Thorn taunted. "You think I need a champion? I don't need you or him!" She ended by yelling the word *him* while pointing but not looking at me.

"You horrid little bitch!" Serina flew at Thorn. "I'm going to kill you like I should have done when we first met!"

Thorn cried out in fear while falling backward. Without thinking, I tried to capture the rampaging vampire demon. Her small stature hid a strength not to be believed. Her terrible gaze turned to me the instant I got a hand on her arm. I was flying for a moment, then my surprise ended in pain as I smashed against a wall. The demon woman was almost upon Thorn. Suddenly she stopped to hold a hand out to her. Serina quickly morphed back into her usual self. "I told you he would still do something stupid to defend you. Didn't I?"

Thorn was on her feet in a second, rushing to my side. "You jerk," she said to Serina, "you could have really hurt him!"

Serina shrugged, then swore. In a flash, she was gone. Where she'd been, I could see Caterous striding toward us.

He pulled Thorn to her feet. "I used to know you." Caterous lowered his head. "How could you do this to your friend?"

"What? I didn't! You see, he—" Thorn stammered.

A fire ignited in Caterous's eyes: "Was it your vampire friend? I will not tolerate this!"

"No!" I shouted, getting unsteadily to my feet. Caterous turned slowly to face me. My mind went blank, "I-I-I . . ." *I what? What can I tell him?* I winced under his glare, and my back hurt a lot.

"The thing is," Thorn waved vaguely at the wall, "Henry was upset."

"I gathered that by the shouting in the hall," Caterous replied dryly.

"Yes, I was really, um, upset." My mind still wouldn't think of a reason I had been on the ground in pain.

"Pathetic and overly emotional," Thorn hissed.

I limped over, not wanting to hear Thorn's taunting. No matter how much I might deserve it.

"I, um, I tried to climb over the wall, and I fell." I smiled at Thorn. I was proud of my lie. She, however, rolled her eyes and slapped my arm.

Caterous pretended not to notice. "You should be more careful and more *agile*."

The way he said agile cemented my feeling that he didn't believe me.

"How was Serina even out here?" I demanded as soon as Caterous was gone.

"You chose the darkest part of the wall at this time of day," Thorn explained like it was obvious.

"But it's daylight," I protested.

"Daylight is painful, not fatal," Serina replied. She was back on top of the wall. I nearly fell over in fright when I saw her.

Thorn looked at me questioningly.

"She was going to kill me before you showed up!" I pointed at Serina, who wore an innocent expression. "I've seen what she can do! She was losing control and—"

"And you still jumped between us." Serina shrugged. "You're an idiot."

Thorn was shaking her head. "She wouldn't have killed you." Thorn turned her attention to Serina. "You didn't have to throw him so hard, you know." Thorn's voice held a hint of anger.

"I was annoyed with how he treated you." Serina didn't seem to care about the pain she caused me.

"I need to talk to my father. Can I trust you two to get along?" Thorn asked.

I whimpered slightly in response.

Serina laughed and threw her arm around my shoulder, making me flinch. "I will make sure he lives."

"Thorn?" I reached out to her. "Thorn, wait. I'm sorry."

"I know," Thorn turned her back to me. "Have fun with Serina."

"Thorn," I called, trying to follow her.

Serina blocked my path. "Listen," she huffed. "Sorry about the throw—really hurt her and me—but you need to know how things were when her mother was here." She sat beside me against the wall and began telling me some things I needed to hear.

"I know how Thorn got her name and what that awful Debkohr does," I replied, wincing as I tried to get comfortable. My back was bruised. I knew it.

"I was here when that witch disappeared." Serina stared off as if looking back in time. "Thorn wasn't an unhappy child; however, she *was* unwanted."

I already knew this. "Why did Caterous marry her mother to begin with?" I asked, disgusted.

"They were never married," Serina replied. She seemed shocked that I didn't know. "She was a prisoner here. I don't know how it happened, and I'm not sure even Caterous knows how. But," Serina shrugged, "Althea became pregnant.

"Okay, so how could he not know how it happened?" I was annoyed with her now.

"What I mean is he has no memory of *being with her*." She seemed to be thinking it over. Suddenly she shuddered as if she wanted to shake the images from her mind. "Anyway, one day, she announced she would have his child. Since there had been no visitors to the manor, there was no other person it could have been. So Caterous did everything he could to ensure she was comfortable and cared for."

"He was sure she didn't get out, and . . . ya know," I demonstrated with my hands.

Serina slapped them, then glared at me. "Gross."

I shrugged. *Better than saying it.*

Serina inhaled her annoyance. "If he thought it, it didn't change how he treated her. Apparently, she acted very loving toward Caterous, and he was happy, I guess."

I waited. "So what happened?" I prompted.

"Thorn arrived." She sighed. "That's when everything changed. Althea had some expectations that Thorn didn't fulfill."

"What expectations could a baby possibly fulfill besides being a child?" I demanded.

"You're asking me like I know." Serina's scowl turned darker. "All I know is parents tend to have unrealistic expectations." We sat in uncomfortable silence for a bit before she continued the story. "Caterous loved Thorn immediately and unconditionally. However, no matter what kindness he would give his little girl, Althea would do double the evil to undo whatever happiness Thorn had."

"What the hell?" I gasped.

"No matter how Thorn tried to please her mother, it was never enough. Caterous became cold to her so Althea wouldn't torment Thorn." Serina blew out a long breath. "This went on for years."

"So long that Caterous got used to being cold? Is that why he can't be good to her now?" I jumped to my feet, ready to tell Caterous exactly what I thought of his treatment of Thorn.

Serina's strong hand pulled me back down. "She won't let him get close now. I think she's scared to let him get close. But, since her mother was so awful, she felt she'd have nothing if he stopped showing what little affection she got from him."

"So, when did her mother leave?" I felt an ache in my heart for Thorn. I couldn't let myself feel guilty for having loving parents. All I could do was share that same loving feeling with Thorn and Serina.

"I'm not sure she did." Serina watched some bats flutter in the dusk light. I know she could feel me staring at her. "I think Caterous got sick of the constant berating and finally did as he had been asked from the beginning and had Althea locked away somewhere."

Panic brewed in my chest. "If Caterous couldn't keep her from doing . . . ya know . . . *things*, how did he expect someone else to hold her?" I asked, then something jumped into my mind. "You don't think he killed her, do you?" Then another just as bad thought hit. "Did *you* kill her?"

"Unfortunately, neither Caterous nor I did." It was Serina's turn to glare at me. "I'm not as bloodthirsty and violent as you think, jerk!" Without another word, Serina took flight.

"Well, I guess we'll talk later," I growled. But then I felt the simmering fury only Caterous could express. Thorn's calm voice disconcerted me more than anything Serina had told me about Thorn's mother.

"Serina has been telling too many stories about the past, hasn't she?" Thorn's eyes searched mine.

I stuttered in shock at the true accusation.

"Come on!" Thorn pulled me by the back toward the house.

"Thorn, your mother was—is—crazy," I tried to say.

"Yeah, I know that. I don't care what that woman has ever said or done." She scowled. "I wish Father would have killed her." Thorn shook away her disappointment. "Don't try to change the subject." Then her eyebrows disappeared into her fringe. "Hey, are you okay?" She was staring at me with concern. "You got thrown pretty hard."

"I'll probably be bruised in the morning, but I'm fine," I grumbled. "You're welcome, by the way, for getting between you two."

"That was pretty stupid, you know." She frowned at me. "If she had been really angry, you would be dead. *Spleew*, remember?"

I rubbed my back. "Yeah."

"Thank you, though." She smiled and punched my arm. However, her smile didn't last long. "So, what were you two talking about?"

"What do you mean, me and who?"

"You know what I mean, you dummy. Serina!" Her eyes were hard as she glared at me. "What were you and Serina talking about all afternoon?"

We reached the house. I was surprised to see many of the shutters were no longer shut. When we walked in the door, I saw many of the portraits had been covered.

"Well?" Thorn demanded, bringing my attention back to her.

"Nothing really." My voice broke. "No, really!" I threw up my hands in defense.

"Thorn?" Caterous called. "Sume?"

Before I could speak, Thorn pushed me through a door into complete darkness while she went to talk to her father. I heard snatches of the conversation.

"I know Henry did not fall off that wall." Caterous's voice didn't sound angry, but . . . "Did you do something to him?"

"What?!" Thorn shouted. "No, I would never hurt Henry! You know that."

"He was correct. We—well, I—let your mother haunt this house far too long. You must never believe what she said. You were and always have been wanted."

I heard some muttered words from Thorn. I imagined her being held, but not really. They didn't seem like the hugging type of family. I was suddenly aware again of how much I missed my parents. They were huggers.

"Thank you, Tosan." It was Thorn's voice, then silence.

I wondered how long I should wait before emerging. My hand searched for a latch.

Thorn wrenched the door open and slammed into me.

"Hey, watch out!" I cried.

Thorn's hand clamped over my mouth. We waited in silence until she was sure her father wasn't coming back. Then, a blue flame ignited on Thorn's fingertips, giving us faint light. I could at least see we were at the top of a set of stone stairs leading down into blackness.

"Brilliant—leave me alone in the dark at the top of a staircase," I growled, still annoyed at being left alone, slammed into, and hushed. "How did you do that?" I demanded, pointing at her fingers. "Also, what is Tosan and Sume?"

"What? You can't?" I could just make out her face. She somehow held contempt with a smirk. "After all that reading, what Magic do you know?" she asked innocently.

"I can make potions, hear the trees, and make something fly or change shape," I defended. "What did your father have to say? Sume?" I asked, deflecting, as she pulled me into the dimly lit hallway. Finally, we reached a closed door.

"Just what you heard—my mother is horrid, and he loves me. Sume is a pet name for me. It means daughter. Tosan is mine for him. It means Dad." She shrugged. "Nothing new and nothing you will use when referring to me." Then, she opened the door and extinguished the flame. "Or my father, for that matter." She then led me to the library. We spent the rest of the evening speaking very little. I did, however, catch her looking at me several times throughout dinner and across our study table.

CHAPTER 23

That night I snuck out of my room. In reality, I didn't have to sneak. I had no restrictions as long as I stayed away from Thorn's room. So I sought out Serina. After about an hour, I was ready to call it a night.

"Are you coming to apologize?" Serina's voice asked from the darkness.

"Thorn has forgiven me, and she's the only one I need to say I'm sorry to," I responded, immediately on the defensive.

"Then don't come looking for me." I could tell she moved since her voice came from above me.

"Wait, please," I called, trying to follow the sound of her movement.

"Why should I?" Her voice was directly behind me, causing me to jump.

"Listen . . ." I had to swallow my pride for this. "I need your help."

Her harsh laugh made me cringe. "Why would I help you?" She was above me again. I still hadn't seen her.

"Because I didn't mean to hurt either of you." I tried to sound remorseful.

"Well, you did." This time, when I turned around, I jumped back. She was standing right there, frowning, but there was something playful in her eyes. She had me and knew it. "Well, what do you want from me?"

"I thought maybe you could help me. You know, learn Magic and maybe improve my sword skills?" I replied hopefully. "Please?"

Serina stepped back into the shadows and sighed. "Fine, but not tonight." I knew I was alone right after she agreed. I was nervous about my decision, but I had to find a way to keep up with Thorn and hopefully impress her.

———⚬⁓⚬———

"Very good, Henry," Caterous praised, sounding pleased for the first time I could recall.

I had completed a rather difficult incantation. I smiled, then tried to quell a yawn as soon as his back was turned. Thorn glared at me. It had been a week since I had asked Serina for help.

Thorn pounced as soon as our lessons had ended for the day, and we began heading downstairs. "Why are you tired all the time? How did you learn that spell so quickly? What's going on?" she asked. "Why is Serina coming to see you every night?"

I didn't think she knew Serina was coming to see me. I also didn't want to tell her why. I didn't want her to judge me for having Serina help me with my spell work.

"What? She hasn't." The squeak in my voice gave me away.

"I saw her—don't deny it!" Thorn's eyes flashed threateningly.

I knew I had to come clean. "She's been helping me," I admitted. "I have trouble with the ancient words and inflections."

"I thought an elf your age would know more than that," Thorn grumbled.

"You know, sometimes you really live up to your name," I growled. "A real pain." I immediately regretted saying it. I was about to apologize.

"I'll take that as a compliment coming from someone who can't seem to hear how to recite spells even with those long ears."

My hand reflexively flew to rub the point of my left ear. "My ears are normal. Yours are too long," was my pathetic retort.

"The better to hear the inflections and your sad attempts at them."

I so wanted to have a witty comeback to that, although it was the truth. I hadn't noticed. When we reached the bottom of the stairs, I saw someone was waiting to make things even worse.

"Oh gods, if you two are going to flirt, you can head back upstairs right now," Serina groaned. She waved us into a room from the doorway. A torch burst to life, illuminating the space. My mouth fell open. The walls were adorned with various weapons and targets.

"Welcome to the training room." Serina held out her arms, spinning on the spot as a fireball ignited in her hand.

The fire entranced me. I tried to comment, but it came out as an *eep*. Serina hurled the ball at a dummy wearing armor. The *eep* turned into a cry of fear. I jumped back as it burst into flame. Blue energy crackled behind me as Thorn threw her own ball of magic.

I stood there watching the two friends attempt to outdo each other with larger and more explosive Magic. They seemed friendly enough, but something felt off. Thorn and Serina seemed to be having a silent argument with their spells.

I looked down at the weak spark I was able to conjure. Compared to the morphing and intricate spellwork around me, my attempt was embarrassing. Moreover, I found concentrating hard when spellwork around me transformed and expanded, becoming more violent with each cast.

"Um, I think you're getting carried away," I shouted over the explosions. I barely heard my own voice, so I doubted they heard me. Even if they did, I don't think they would have stopped. I watched two spells collide to become an orb that continued to gain size and power.

"What do we do?" Serina called.

Thorn looked stunned, "I-I don't know. Was there something in our books?" she demanded of me.

"I have no clue," I yelled. The electricity in the air made our hair stand on end. The light coming off the orb was beginning to affect Serina. Her skin was turning as red as her hair.

"Serina," I yelled. Thorn noticed too. "Go!" I yelled. "We'll handle this."

Serina refused. Seeing her curled up whimpering, even with her trying to hide it, told me she was in excruciating pain. Thorn tried to push Serina to the far side of the hall toward a door.

Then the orb grew very small, its light intensifying as it did so.

I had read about this phenomenon. The spell was feeding on its own energy and was about to explode. I knew neither Thorn nor Serina would get through the door in time. I didn't know if they'd be safe if even they did. My mind flew through all the lessons I had read. It only seemed to find one spell. Naturally, it was one I'd never tried before.

I closed my eyes and began to chant. "*Ha ali bin for he. Ha ali bin for he.*" The room went silent except for Serina's crying. I concentrated on the chant. "*Ha ali bin for he, Ha ali bin for he.*" As my knees shook, I tried to ignore the physical and metal strain, but my head was starting to hurt.

"Whoa," Thorn exclaimed, forcing me to open my eyes. What I saw made me say the same thing, or something similar. I was stunned.

In the middle of the room, surrounded by the same kind of blue barrier my mother had used back in our kitchen, was a massive ball of fire. I slowly imagined the ball getting smaller and smaller until it ended in a poof and a whiff of burnt sulfur.

"Did you see that!" I shouted, hopping around. "Did you see what I just did!"

"Yes, yes, I did," Caterous stated calmly from the stairs. Only then did Thorn force Serina through the door. I tried to keep Caterous's attention on me.

"Yeah, I thought I should try to . . . you know . . . test a few spells out, and um . . . Thorn said this would be a good place, so I, um . . ."

"Enough." Caterous rubbed the bridge of his nose and sighed as if exhausted. "Thorn, where are you?"

She appeared from behind a column.

"Were you going to let Henry take all the responsibility for your mistake?"

"What? No!" she yelled. "I made the fireball like he said so we could, um, practice."

"Yeah, and look what I did, sir." I faltered under his gaze. We were in trouble, and we knew it. "It's just . . . we wanted to try something practical," I mumbled.

It wasn't that *I* wanted to—Thorn had been desperate to practice for weeks.

"Well, now you see how badly it can go wrong," Caterous explained seriously. "You will both take over the cleaning duties for a month."

"Father, no," Thorn protested.

I realized I'd never seen anyone cleaning despite the manor always being in order.

"Henry, you will not find this pleasant."

I was stunned.

Caterous continued as if Thorn hadn't protested. "What disturbs me most is not that you came down here to play. Or that you let things get out of hand." His face showed utter disappointment. "No, it is the fact that you seem oblivious to your friend's pain." He held a stack of clean cloths, a bowl, and a flask. Sheepishly, I accepted them.

"I may not want her here, but that is no reason to let her suffer." He shook his head sadly, then turned his back on us and left.

The shame I felt was overwhelming.

Thorn swiped a tear from her face as she pulled me to the door.

We found Serina lying on a stone slab, trying to roll unto the cool surface to calm her burns.

"I'm so sorry," Thorn whispered as she poured the liquid from the flask into the bowl. We spent several hours applying and re-applying the cloths. It was the early morning hours when Serina had had enough of our ministrations. She looked and felt much better. No matter his feelings about Serina, Thorn's father made sure the medicine he had provided was extremely well made and healed her completely.

Soon I found Caterous's comment about the cleaning not being pleasant extremely truthful. The mage, it turned out, employed several small creatures similar to faeries known as Brownies. They were incredibly proud of how well maintained they kept the house. Because of their pride, if they felt the job Thorn and I did was not up to their standards, we would find ourselves redoing the same thing for hours. While I felt the punishment wasn't as bad as it could have been, Thorn became increasingly disgruntled. While I had experience cleaning, Thorn had none. Our supervisors seemed to take great pleasure in making her redo tasks.

⸱ঌ⸱

I'm guessing the Brownies were unhappy with our work since Thorn convinced her father to end our suspension a week early.

He conceded, "The complaints about your cleaning skills are more of a headache for me, so please, take the lessons seriously." It was, however, explained exceptionally clearly that if we did anything that caused harm to ourselves or others, our training would be at an end—permanently.

I promised myself that I'd never put myself in a position that would allow others to get hurt. But, more importantly, I never wanted to have those Brownies overseeing my work ever again.

"You know, Thorn," I said, slightly giddy at being released from our custodial tasks, "let's get a smaller house when the time comes." My eyes shut tight while my fists balled up. I couldn't believe I had just voiced one of my fantasies.

Thorn didn't seem to notice at first, then she rubbed her shoulder as she rolled her arm. "Yeah, something closer to your house would be perfect."

I might have imagined Serina, now back to normal, making a gagging noise. Even if I had, nothing could remove the smile from my face.

CHAPTER 24

I wondered if I would ever see my parents again. What little news made it through the walls was all bad. With each passing month, the world seemed to get darker and more dangerous. After the incident in the practice room, an understanding seemed to have formed between Serina and Caterous. Serina became our combat trainer. She was a true task master, so time passed quickly between the studying and the more intense practical magic. Before I knew it, Thorn and I turned seventeen. My birthday happened when I was busy training. I didn't even realize it until a week after it happened. Thorn's birthday, which took place a couple months after mine, was a quiet affair with barely a mention. I decided it was best not to mention we missed mine. So instead, I was in the library, bent over a book taking copious notes.

"*Oh*, come *on*," Thorn shouted from the doorway. "All you ever do is study. Let's go have some fun." She crossed the room to stand behind me when I didn't respond. She grabbed my shoulders as she crouched to inspect what I was reading.

After all this time, her touch still affected me. I could feel her Magic, but it didn't have the same impact since mine had grown so much. Nevertheless, it was still there, that thrill of extreme power coursing into me.

"When did you get to be so boring?" she grumbled, bringing me back from my thoughts. I felt the warmth from her face right next to mine. It felt like the sun on a warm spring morning. Now I was distracted. Having her this close to me always had a distinct effect. I couldn't concentrate. My blush crept from my neck up to my face.

"Come on, let's go do something," she whispered, her breath teasing the tip of my ear.

"Stop it," I grunted.

Laughing, she pulled up a chair to sit behind me. "You know, if you only read about things, you'll never know how to react."

I shivered as her slender fingers combed through my long hair and began to braid it. I had let it grow long in the tradition of elves as they grew older.

"Yeah, yeah, when the time comes, I won't have the experience to do the spell." I tried to sound annoyed. I knew she was right. I pretended to keep reading, like what she was doing had no effect on me. In reality, I thoroughly enjoyed her fingers in my hair and her presence so close to me. It was a trick. We both knew it. When she wanted me to do something, she only had to braid my hair and *accidentally* brush her fingers against my ears.

"More than that, your sword skills are still lacking." She laughed, tying the end of the braid. "So I called someone in to help."

There it was. I had been manipulated again.

I knew she had called Scratch, who had completed his training with the garrison even though rumors about why his parents fled still swirled. He had proven his loyalty to the kingdom and was now stationed in Dayok. Every time he visited, he brought news about the goings-on in the outside world. Things never got better, only continually worse.

I was always happy to see my friend. However, I always felt panic in the pit of my stomach when he arrived. What information would he bring this time? During his last visit, he brought news of another elf village that had been destroyed.

Another issue I had with Scratch was that he had grown strong and handsome since joining the guard and had become an adept swordsman. Thorn, on the other hand, seemed to find these attributes a bonus. Her excitement only tempered mine.

Thorn started pulling me from my chair. I resisted since now I *really* didn't want to go. Scratch was still my friend, but I hated training with him. I missed the sessions with my parents. Even though they flirted way too much.

The sun hurt my eyes after spending the entire day in the library. There stood my friend and rival, if only in my mind, Scratch. He was now a lieutenant in the Lord of Dayok's Guard. He was destined to be a captain and had the skills to prove it. Rumor was the Grand Army of the Capital was interested in him.

My displeasure only increased as Thorn ran up to Scratch and threw her arms around him in an embrace. Scratch pulled her off her feet to twirl her in the air. I tried to force the jealousy from my face. I was pouting, and I knew it.

"Henry could use some help with his offensive attacks," Thorn explained.

"I'm your defender," I replied sullenly. I know it wasn't my best trait. "I'm to keep you safe while you're doing the fighting." I frowned, knowing I would never be the hero. But then again, I had no idea what event would warrant this much training. Grudgingly I nodded a greeting to Scratch. He pulled me into a one-armed hug. An action that only emphasized how much taller and stronger he had become.

"How's the spellwork going?" Scratch asked me as we followed Thorn into the house.

"Spells won't always be the way to keep me safe. You need to be able to defend both of us and eliminate an enemy," Thorn explained, opening the door to the armory. Although, again, it was easy for her to say she knew what she was doing.

The light of the room shone on Thorn when she entered, highlighting the few light purples still in from her youth. She swept it aside to hang her sword on her back, exposing the light skin of her neck for the briefest of moments. Next, she pulled on a belt holding her short sword. Finally, she gathered her long tunic, pulling it tight around her slim waist. She turned to face me, smoothing the tunic over her modest chest.

When had she become so pretty? *She's always been pretty.*

Today I thought she was beautiful. Her face held a serene kindness that was magical to behold. Then she broke the spell.

"Hey, Elf Boy, heads up!"

I barely caught my sword. "Don't throw swords at people," I admonished.

"Oh, come on." She laughed, tossing my crossbow to me. "Where is your sense of adventure?"

"Back in the library," I muttered, following Thorn and Scratch. They happily chatted about strategies and techniques. We were on our way back outside when we found our path blocked. "Lord Caterous," I bowed. Thorn addressed her father with the same deference, albeit with a hint of humor, as if mocking me.

He barely acknowledged us. "Henry, Sume, Sebastian," he nodded. His attention was fully on a scroll he was reading.

"Father, the time has come for me to kill Henry," Thorn explained. "I'm going to bury him in the garden."

"That sounds nice, Sume." Caterous nodded, still intent on the parchment.

"It was nice living here." I smirked, catching Thorn's eye. "I like living, so I think I'll kill Thorn and take her place as your son."

"Excellent idea, Henry." He patted Thorn on the head while he moved down the hall, wholly absorbed in the scroll.

"These father-daughter talks are always so heartfelt." Thorn laughed. "I guess we should try to kill each other."

"What if we do? Will Scratch bury us both in the garden?"

"Maybe." She threw open the door. "Then Scratch can take our place as the great mage's offspring."

"Maybe we should just run away and let Scratch have that honor without the bloodshed," I suggested.

Thorn turned to face me. Her smile was more radiant than the sun. "That would be so nice," she said, taking my hands in hers, "but what fun would there be without bloodshed?"

"You always say the most wonderful things to me," I smiled.

Scratch laughed at us as he asked, "But what makes you think I want to take your places?" He then adopted a thoughtful look. "Although I might put these swords to better use than I've seen so far."

"You'll pay for that insult," Thorn growled in mock anger at him. She pulled the sword from her back and leveled it at him. "Prepare to defend yourself, knave."

"Hey, I just got back from the Imperial Academy," he said, pulling his sword. "They were teaching a new sword technique." He did some fancy flourish with his blade. I smirked at his confidence. Although, this conversation reminded me painfully of my parents flirting, making my heart ache. I began trying to recall the stances and techniques they taught me.

Thorn began her warm-up as she always did. Even though I saw it daily, I had to ask, "Does that really help in combat?" I hoped Scratch would back my complaint about Thorn's showy movements. Her blade blurred, crossing from left to right behind her back, flipping high before being caught, a cheeky grin on Thorn's face the entire time.

"Interesting," Scratch said, in a tone that would make any imperial captain envious. He hefted his long sword, giving one swipe through the air. "It's distracting, I'll grant you that." He smirked in a way that even I thought was pompous. But, if it bothered Thorn, she didn't show it.

"Okay, before you two kill each other. . . ." I held up my hands, reciting a spell that would keep their swords from causing damage to each other. I wished the magic could be used in wars. However, the combatants had to agree to allow it to be cast to use it, and they had to recite an agreement spell. After ensuring it was effective, I sat on a bench and watched them do the dance they did so well.

Scratch took the formal fighting stance, squaring his shoulders and holding his sword in both hands directly in front of him. His wide shoulders and armor presented an intimidating figure of a warrior. Thorn, in contrast, turned sideways to present as small a target as possible. Her eyes turned steely as she took a fighting stance, drawing her slim one-handed sword held parallel to the ground. Her left arm was straight in front as the sword point was held at about half her arm's length.

While Scratch's sword was a five-foot-long double-edged deadly steel war sword, Thorn held a blade as contrasting as her stature to his. It was only about three feet long with a single-edged, slightly curved blade. She looked more like an assassin than a warrior.

They slowly stepped sideways, one foot crossing in front of the other as they moved in a large circle. They would feint and retreat, feeling each other out for an opportunity. Then, without warning, Scratch committed to a full-frontal assault. Thorn blocked and parried. The flash of blades and the clang of steel filled the courtyard.

I watched, jealous and annoyed, as their swords sang their beautiful, deadly song. I smirked. Scratch actually still believed he was doing well against Thorn. She was far better and faster. Right now, out in the sun, he was the only person who could give her anything close to a challenge. The fact he was holding back pissed me off. I had drawn my sword, using its tip to draw sigils in the dirt. Scratch whooped. He had got a lucky counter that set Thorn on defense.

The furrow of Thorn's brow told me she found his overconfidence more than a bit annoying. Thorn changed tactics and used flipping and spinning acrobatics to keep Scratch at a distance. She had just done a flip during which she tossed her sword from one hand to the other, landing behind Scratch, who spun to meet her blade.

"Oh, for the gods' sake!" I shouted in annoyance. She pulled me out of my studies, and now she was just playing with Scratch. She said she had asked him to come to help me. I didn't need his help, and I would prove it. "She's just humoring you," I shouted. I was on my feet, standing in front of Scratch.

"You think you can do better?" Scratch laughed. I was thin and pale. I spent too much time reading and not enough time outdoors—that's what he thought about me. I glared at him. I would show him he was in for a surprise. Serina still came by to help me even after our formal practices. When you learn combat under a vampire, you learn to fight while having all your energy sucked out of you.

I didn't answer his challenge. Instead, I faced Thorn.

Her face held a smirk. "Come on, Henry—as you said, this isn't your forte."

We began moving in a circle, waiting for an opportunity.

"I told your father I would bury you in the garden." I jumped forward—a feint. "I may just do that." But I wasn't going to play fair either. I did a quick sidestep, jumped back, and flipped over her head. I then tossed an energy ball at her. Thorn blocked it quickly, as I knew she would, but my attack was fast. Unfortunately for me, her defense was just as quick.

She laughed. "Sneaky . . ." I saw her fingers moving and her lips trying not to betray the spell she was forming. "Not enough, though. What?" Her eyes widened with surprise as I nullified her spell and pressed an attack.

My blade sang out against hers. Her smile had been replaced with a grimace. We fired spells at each other, dodging and deflecting with magic and swords. At first, Scratch had been enthusiastically cheering us on. Now he was silent. There was no one else in the world, just her and me. I struck and spun, pushing her back. I had to dive away. She sent fireballs from the end of her sword, ten of them. Scratch yelped, diving for cover. I was on my feet, returning her fire with energy bolts as several planters exploded.

Our combat returned to close quarters. Our blades crossed, and we glared into each other's eyes. Thorn's deep, piercing blue eyes turned fiery red as they stared into me. Her pupils held flame. Though her brows were creased and her arms were taut, I could see it in her face and those fiery eyes. She was enjoying this. "You fight like a human girl," she taunted.

"So, as bad as half of you?" I responded.

"Not nice." She smirked. I threw her back with a blast of magic. Thorn was on her feet in a blink, coming at me, sword flashing. I dodged her attack and spun my sword in a wide arc. Time stopped. Thorn let out a cry of surprise and pain. I watched in horror as red blossomed on her tunic from her arm.

"Oh, gods!" I cried. Terror and panic gripped my heart as I dropped my blade. Rushing to her side, I tried to apologize. "I forgot. I'm so sorry I forgot to put the charm on my blade."

Suddenly my whole body vibrated. My head stung where her sword rested. Blocked by the charm I forgot to add to my weapon.

"You can't let your guard down, dummy." She smiled. Instantly her smile turned to a grimace as she dropped her sword and grabbed at her wound. I pulled her hand away and chanted a healing spell. I was better at them than she was.

"See, I told you he was getting excellent with a sword," Thorn called over my head.

Scratch approached, clapping slowly. "Nice work. You must ensure you're completely prepared for battle, though." He pointed to Thorn's now healed arm. "Just think—if you had forgotten a spell that would keep her safe in actual combat."

I looked down at my hands, red with her blood, and my face burned with embarrassment. I was supposed to keep her from harm, but instead, I was the one who injured her.

"It's okay—it wasn't bad, and you healed it perfectly," Thorn whispered. "I'm not hurt or mad." She tried to hug me, but I pulled away.

I tried to apologize but couldn't form words. I pushed past her, heading into the woods. Some would say fleeing. I sat alone at the base of a large tree, my stomach clenched in anxiety.

"Wallowing in self-pity and hatred?" A heavily cloaked figure spoke from the shadows. I ignored her. "She pushed you. You fought back. I told you this was coming." Serina's red hair fell loose and extended from her hood. "You aren't a fool. You know what was going on."

I turned my back on her as I felt my frown deepening.

"You tricked me too," I growled at her.

"That's true," she conceded. "Scratch and I have been training together. I've shared that training with you." Fluttering and falling leaves told me she was above me in the trees. "Training you asked me for, if you remember."

"I just wanted to show her." I didn't know what I wanted to show her, though. Confusion and frustration fought for dominance over my guilt.

"You wanted her to see you were capable and just as good as Scratch? Or as good as she is?"

"No, I'm not good enough for her." I felt my toes curl as I grimaced. It was not what I wanted to say.

"You're an idiot, you know that, right?" Serina frowned down at me.

"I have some Magic power. Even with my teachings, my mother is still more powerful than I am. I train night and day, and Scratch can beat me easily." I wish my mouth would just stop. My eyes closed tight as my fists clenched and unclenched.

"Scratch can't fight either of you." Serina floated down to sit beside me as shadow crept over the area I sat. "He knows he can't beat either of you." She sighed. "Still, he worries."

"Well, he isn't the one who ended up hurting her, is he?"

Serina's hand impacted the back of my head painfully.

"What the hell was that for?"

"Because you're an idiot," she growled. "I know you. When you got into trouble with Caterous, you made sure you never did anything to anger him again." She stood, holding out her hand to me. "So now that you've hurt her, I know you'll never let it happen again." She was right, as much as I hated to admit it. Taking her hand, she pulled me to my feet. "This day is too bright for me." Her smile was all I could see of her face. "Tell Scratch to come see me." Then, she was gone with a flutter and a breeze that made me instinctively close my eyes.

"You done being upset?" Thorn's voice was cautious.

My back was turned to her. A smile fought to chase away my scowl. "No," I said as harshly as I could.

"I had to show you." Her hands tentatively brushed my shoulders, then gripped them. "You're better than you pretend. Stronger."

Unconsciously, I lay my face against her hand.

"Something is happening, and I need you to believe in yourself. Believe in yourself the way I believe in you."

I stood up straighter. "What's happening?" I asked.

Thorn's chin rested on my back. "I don't know. I just know something is about to happen." She sighed, her arms encircling me. "I just know I'll need my defender."

My hands shook as I covered her hands with mine.

"I'll need my best friend."

Best friend . . . I guess that's good enough for now. "I'll be with you forever—I promise." My heart tightened painfully.

"As my defender?" she whispered.

"Always."

"As my friend?" She let me go to stand in front of me.

"Forever," I breathed, looking into those eyes. The fire still burned deep in Thorn's pupils.

"As anything more?" She looked down, then glanced up.

That look—what was it? My heart, a moment ago, so tight and constricted, now beat faster and harder than I thought possible. Was she really asking me this? I knew my answer. I knew it from the first day we met. Could I tell her—is that what she wanted to hear?

The moment was broken when Scratch burst through the bushes. Thorn quickly stepped away. Her face was filled with concern that matched Scratch's worry and fear. "Lord Caterous wants to see us immediately." There it was—that terror in the pit of my stomach. I had allowed his daughter to be injured again.

My feet turned to lead. As I slowly followed, Scratch and Thorn debated what had happened to cause our being summoned.

"He was distracted by a letter this morning."

"There have been rumors of trouble at the Notelek imperial court," Scratch whispered. "They say a mage caused it."

"I allowed you to get hurt again after I promised I never would," I mumbled. Neither Scratch nor Thorn acted like they heard me.

"What has that got to do with Father?" Thorn glanced at me, shook her head slightly, then continued, "He's been here with us." She stopped so suddenly I ran into her. I'd been staring down at my feet too intently. "Mother . . ." she breathed, dashing away.

Scratch and I had to run to catch up to her. She was through the front door, down the hall, and in the library before we could reach the front steps.

Rushing to catch up, I sped toward the library. I ran into Thorn's back for the second time in about five minutes. She stood just inside the library door. On the desk lay three scrolls.

CHAPTER 25

No, no." Shaking her head and ignoring the scrolls, Thorn ran through the house, calling for her father. When she finally returned to the library, I tried to point out the scrolls. Thorn steadfastly ignored them, pacing the floor in front of the desk. A thought paused her pacing. I called out to her, but Thorn disappeared through the door. I could see my name on one of the scrolls, Thorn's was on another, and to my shock, a third was addressed to Serina. I had a moment's hesitation, wanting to reach for my scroll. I decided against it and instead followed after Thorn.

Before I got three steps, I smashed into Scratch, standing in the hall. "I'm going to see what I can find out," he explained. Then he touched my shoulder. "You need to get her to accept this and get ready."

I nodded my agreement without actually knowing what I agreed to. Scratch nodded and left. I stood in the hall for several moments. I had to find Thorn and Serina so we could read the messages together. I looked left, then right, only to realize I had no idea where Serina lived after all this time. That made the decision for me. I had to find Thorn. Together we'd get Serina, read the scrolls, and find out there was nothing to worry about. I knew I was lying to myself, but I kept trying to keep my mind from going to the darkest places.

After twenty minutes, I was at a loss. I had been all over the house from top to bottom. I spent twenty minutes searching the grounds. I had no idea where Thorn was. I tried several locating spells to no avail. Finally, running out of ideas while the growing concern ate at my stomach, I returned to the library. If nothing else, I could read the scroll. That way, when she did return, I could reassure her that all was well.

I walked into the room with my head down, lost in my thoughts as to where Thorn could be.

"She's one of the strongest people I know." Serina's voice startled me. "But she's avoiding an important truth." She was reading the scroll addressed to her. "We need to get her together. Too much time has passed already."

"I've looked everywhere," I defended.

"Everywhere?" Serina asked.

"Yes!"

"Even outside the grounds?" She looked over the top of the scroll at me.

I swore. Turning, I sprinted to the door. I was out of the house, across the grounds, and into the forest. My feet seemed to know where to go. It was a guess, and I wasn't even sure if I remembered how to get there. However, I felt like I was being guided. As soon as I passed the beautifully carved statues and entered the cave, I knew she was there.

"Thorn, we need to return to the house," I called.

Her back was to me. She held a blue flame in her hand. The light flickered against the pictures on the wall, making them appear to move. "I'm not ready for this." Thorn's voice was quiet.

"We don't even know what *this* is," I countered.

"Come on, Henry." Her voice was suddenly angry. "You know just as well as I do, nothing good can come of my father disappearing. Do you think he would leave you and me and Serina scrolls if he was popping out to visit a neighboring town?" Thorn took several deep breaths, sat down, got up, sat back down again. She was on her feet instantly, grabbing my shoulders. "Your parents had to go into hiding. Elf villages are being cleared out. There's been talk of war and a mage stirring up trouble, and now my father has left."

"Then what the hell are we doing out here?" I argued back. "If there's something to know, then let's find out. Hiding from it will not make it go away."

"I know that!" she shouted. "That doesn't mean I don't want to try."

A ringing silence hung in the air until I couldn't help myself. "Do you know how stupid that sounded?"

"Yes!" she countered grumpily before she started to laugh. I couldn't help but join in.

Cautiously I approached as she stood up. However, she remained with her back to me. Carefully I put my arms around her. "We'll face whatever this is together," I whispered.

Thorn nodded her thanks. "We need to get back," she said, extricating herself from my embrace. She was correct. We'd been away far too long, as Serina had mentioned. Together we hurried through the woods. The closer we got, the tighter my stomach grew. As we climbed the stairs to the front door, the light began fading toward dusk. Serina was lounging on the couch in the library when we walked in. She briefly nodded to Thorn before returning to reading a book I had never seen before in the library. It looked to be a work of fiction. I was about to ask about the book until Serina gave me a look. My questions could wait.

Thorn slowly approached the two remaining scrolls. The tension grew heavier on my shoulders. The sound of heavy boots thundering down the hall caused my current dread to chew a bit further into my stomach.

"We have to go!" Scratch burst through the door. "That inspector that tried to kill you is back. He's leading a battalion to arrest Caterous."

"After all this time?" I couldn't believe he still held such a grudge.

I saw something in Scratch's eyes I had never seen before—*fear*.

His long strides brought him right to me. He lay a hand on my shoulder. His face was serious. "They're looking for you and Thorn."

My mouth dropped open as my heart froze.

Scratch ran a hand through his hair. "They think you or your families have something to do with a nearby village getting wiped out."

My hands curled into his lapels. "How do they even know Thorn exists or where we are?"

"The inspector has been promoted to inquisitor captain and brought troops. I was told he's here to put down an elven uprising."

My hands dropped to my sides as he began to pace.

"I was supposed to report to round up the elves. The thing is, I think the captain suspects me." He paused. His thoughts were scattered and building on each other. "I wouldn't be surprised if he had me followed. I was careful, but they have ways of finding people." His hand flew to the hilt of his sword. I hadn't even noticed that Serina had left until she dropped several bags in the hall.

Scratched nodded his thanks. "As far as how they know about you and Thorn . . ." He took a deep breath. "The rumor is a witch attacked the destroyed village. She had several elves with her. One was captured. He told the inspector about the mage, this house, and you. He claimed you three planned the attack."

I had no idea what to say or do. Thorn's father had disappeared, and we were accused of killing an entire village. Thorn grabbed my arm. I could feel her shaking. Whether it was fear or anger, I couldn't tell.

"Thorn, pull yourself together and grow up." Serina's tone was harsh and tinged with anger. "Your father has left. Your mother is behind the attack." She pushed past Thorn, grabbed a scroll from the desk, and thrust it at Thorn's chest. "Your father is missing, correct?"

Thorn nodded meekly.

"So I believe it's safe to say your mother has betrayed you."

"She's gone to the elves?" I asked, pleading silently for the answer to be no.

"I don't know. I don't think so. Last time Thorn's mother used other creatures. We might know something if Thorn would read this." She pushed the scroll harder into Thorn's chest. "I read what was left for me, now it's your turn to learn some hard truths." She let the scroll fall and Thorn caught it.

Serina's glare of disgust softened as she turned her back on her friend. It seemed I wasn't the only one that she could manipulate. However, this fact didn't make me happy.

I watched Thorn's eyes as she read her scroll. Her emotions ran the gambit of anger, amusement, and finally, sadness. "Father has gone after my mother. He's contacted the council of elders." Thorn's voice was thin. "I don't think he knows she's framed us for the village." Her eyes scanned the page, and her brows creased deeper as she read. "This makes no sense." I saw the flames beginning to burn in her stare. "Father says something else is going on, though." Finally, recognition lit her face, and she ran from the library. Her hand caught my arm as she passed, pulling me stumbling after her.

I recognized where she was taking me. We stopped for a breath outside Caterous's private study, a room I had never entered. Thorn threw the door open and skidded to a halt, knocking her father's chair out of the way. She nearly fell as I staggered into her. She had to hold herself up with the desk but didn't complain. I was just gaining my feet when Scratch and Serina arrived. Two drawers had been thrown from the desk already.

"Got it!" Thorn shouted, pulling a scroll from the desk. She began reading with the same intensity her father had earlier. "Oh, this is bad," she hissed. "There have been rumors of massing troops along the borderlands." She kept reading, as her frown grew. "Some mages have disappeared." She began pacing around the room. "No, not disappeared," she paused. "They left their positions." Her pacing stopped, but her mouth kept moving. "War is coming. Mother's starting it. That's why the mages are leaving. They're going to remain neutral."

I joined Scratch and Serina as we watched Thorn read. "Is she trying to get the elves to revolt?" I asked. "Why else would the Capital send the army to subjugate the village?" My anger bubbled up. It tasted awful.

"No." Thorn turned her eyes to me, sadness darkening the deep blue. "She hates all elves and humans." A tear escaped her eye. "She especially hates half-breeds."

"What the hell?" Scratch demanded.

Thorn stared down at the scroll and cursed. We were running again, back to where she dropped her scroll. Scooping it up, she swore. "Father left more. He says Mother has been trying to regain her old allies in the north." She cocked her head in confusion. "Serina, there's something for you here. I can't read it, though." She handed the scroll over.

Scratch and I gaped at each other. Thorn's father had never acknowledged Serina. Now he was leaving her multiple messages.

"This is old writing—ancient." Serina grimaced as she deciphered the text.

Thorn and I exchanged an anxious glance.

"That bastard," Serina growled. Thorn cringed.

"What?" we all demanded.

"Caterous wants me to take you to my people." She threw the scroll back to Thorn. "He knows how I feel about them. He *knows*!" she shouted. Thorn tentatively reached out to comfort her, but Serina brushed off her hand. "He's right, though, damn him. They would never follow you there."

"No, you left for a reason. We'll go somewhere else. But wait. Why are we going anywhere?" Thorn asked, grabbing the scroll again.

"That's what I've been saying," Scratch shouted angrily. "Haven't you been paying attention? The city guard is coming to take you into custody."

"No, I've been paying attention," Thorn stated dryly.

"Obviously," I muttered.

Scratch gaped at Thorn. "The city guard will find this place. They want both of you in jail or worse." He gestured to Thorn and me. "You're the children of the people heading the insurrection."

"But they aren't!" I protested. "We aren't." I was confusing myself. "You know what I mean, damn it."

"Doesn't matter. You'll be used as leverage against your parents or killed as an example. I don't know."

Thorn ignored his response. "What evidence do they have?"

Scratch paced in frustration. "I don't know, but we have to go."

"What insurrection? We know who attacked the village. So why don't they?" I protested.

"Collect what you need, and bring warm clothes," Serina commanded, flinching at the thought. Then, shaking off her annoyance, she continued. "No matter the weather, you'll be cold where we're going."

"Wherever that is, we need to get going now," Scratch ordered. "It won't be long before they find us. They know you're somewhere in this forest."

"What about the spell your mother used to hide us?" Thorn grabbed my shoulders, forcing me to face her.

"I . . . we . . . I-I'm not sure," I stuttered. Her face fought with disappointment and anger. "Your father told me never to use it." I hung my head. "He took it away and hid it."

Before Thorn could say anything, Serina was barking orders again. "Pack what you can. Then seal the house." She was intently drawing something on the back of the scroll. "Follow these directions." She thrust the map into Scratch's chest.

"Where the hell are you going?" he demanded.

"To slow them down and scout ahead." She took flight the second she was out the door. Thorn and I nodded to each other. We ran in different directions, her to the armory, me to the library. I heard Scratch heading into the kitchen.

"Wait!" I shouted, running to stop him from wasting time. He had a bag out with food strewn across the wide prep space. I grabbed the bag, recited a quick chant, then threw the bag back to him. "Now you can carry three times as much as before."

He gazed in amazement at the bag, then at me. A smirk curled the corner of his mouth. Then, he turned to the spread-out food and shoved it all into the bag. I charmed two more bags before heading back to the library.

I looked with longing at the shelves and shelves of dusty, musty, beautiful books. So much knowledge and valuable information, and I had to choose. It felt like choosing a child to be left behind to slaughter. The sound of clanging swords and armor behind me announced Thorn's arrival.

"Move it," Thorn cursed. "I wasted too much time already."

"What if they burn our house?" I swallowed painfully at the thought. Thorn's hand lay gently on my shoulder.

"You have no idea how much having you calling it *our* house means to me." She said it so sweetly, but then it warped into steel. "But grab what you need and let's go."

I made a noise that landed between affirmation and whimpering.

Thorn pushed me toward the desk. "Don't worry, the house will be protected—I promise—now move!"

I charmed a chest with the same spell I used on Scratch's bags and began throwing all the defensive, healing, and combat Magic books I could remember inside, then scanned the room in a panic. Did I get everything we needed? I knew I'd forgotten something important when Scratch called me.

"I think Serina is hindering their progress." He ran by the room. I heard the clattering of cookware. "The fire isn't too far away. It's time to go." His voice grew distant.

"Damn it." I slammed the lid shut. Then I ran as fast as possible with the heavy trunk out the front door. Thorn had transfigured several logs and a bench into a wagon. Scratch was finishing hitching up two of the horses he'd brought. His own was tied to the back. Apparently, a knight's horse was not to pull a wagon. I loaded in my trunk next to the food bags and weapons. Then it was my turn to be amazed.

Blue light spread from Thorn's hands. She made deliberate movements, like someone folding clothes or paper. I was too distracted to really pay attention. The house demanded all that I had. The roofs flattened, folding over each other. In fact, the entire structure folded in on itself. Windows shrunk, doors became diminutive, and the multiple chimneys stacked themselves neatly against each other and blended seamlessly into the roof. Ultimately, we stood in front of a small shed.

"Why didn't we just hide in the house?" Scratch complained.

"That would have been a horrible idea," Thorn explained as she opened the shed door. I could see why. Furniture, books, shelves, and everything condensed into a tiny area. "If we hid in there, we would be crushed."

I whistled in appreciation. I suddenly remembered the Brownies. I grabbed Thorn by the shoulders. "What about the—"

"They're fine," she replied calmly. "I warned them. They can change their bodies to conform to any space they want. I told them they could leave. They wanted to stay to keep the house clean." She shrugged then moved out of my grasp as an evil grin spread across her face. "The Debkohr wasn't so lucky." The demise of a creature that had made Thorn's life hell had been banished. I couldn't help but feel a bit of shared satisfaction at its demise.

"What if they try to knock it over?" Scratch asked, scratching his stubble as he looked closely at the brick shed.

"They would have to bring a battering ram." Thorn shrugged climbing into the wagon's back. She held out a hand to help me up. "If they did try, it would be like trying to smash a granite mountain." She laughed, throwing out some clothes to Scratch. He pulled them on over his leather armor, then climbed onto the driver's seat once he hid all evidence of his training and station.

"Head west," Thorn instructed. "We'll go through the other gate."

"What other gate?" I asked, thinking back to the first time I came here. "We've walked the entire estate. There's only one gate."

"It's hidden. Obviously, very well hidden."

Her pitying smile annoyed me.

"Oh, don't pout." She laughed as I turned my back to her.

I couldn't stay that way because I wanted to see where this hidden gate was. Scratch kept heading west through the woods.

After several minutes, Scratch called over his shoulder nervously. "Um, I'm not one to doubt you, but I'm heading straight for the wall."

Thorn sat up to look over his shoulder, then her hands glowed a pale green. An area to our left burned the same color. "Over there." She pointed to the dim light.

"So, you want me to run into the glowing wall?" Scratch shrugged. "Why not?" Our pace never wavered. Scratch turned his head slightly and shut his eyes tight while I braced, ready to grab Thorn, who was staring intently at the wall. Cringing, I prepared for the impact, instinctively closing my eyes as he hit the wall.

Except we didn't.

In a blink, we were galloping outside the walls. I spun to see where we'd come through. There was no glow, just a blank section of stacked stones staring back at me. Then, in the distance, something exploded. A fireball rose in the sky. Silhouetted against the red-orange glow, I saw Serina's bat-like wings.

"She really is something," Scratch declared in appreciation.

I turned to see Scratch looking past me to the fading flames. I thought back to the night she saved me at my house. I could only imagine what a full frontal assault bearing the brunt of her anger would bring to the soldiers following us. I couldn't suppress a shudder.

"Pay attention to the road ahead," Thorn admonished. Scratch pulled hard on the reins, keeping the horses from running into a tree. Annoyed, she asked, "So, where are we heading now?"

Scratch searched his shirt. He produced the map Serina had made. "Looks like the mountains." He passed the map back. "Not too far up, though." He didn't seem too happy. "Just to the dark pass, which will be fun."

I detected a nervous determination in his voice.

CHAPTER 26

After the excitement of leaving the place I had called home for the last two years subsided, I took stock of our supplies. We had spellbooks and weapons in abundance. We had water and food, and the cooking utensils were all accounted for. Even Thorn's traveling clothing and extras were present. Suddenly I felt a sinking feeling hit my stomach. I looked around again at our supplies. Scratch had a bundle on his horse that I assumed would be his necessities as a soldier. Serina had a satchel. I realized all I had with me were the clothes I was wearing. Thorn's soft laugh came from behind me as she thrust something against my back.

"I knew you wouldn't think about it," Thorn teased, tossing me a small pouch filled with clothes. "I thought about forcing you to wear some of my clothes since you didn't think to pack any."

"I could have borrowed some from Scratch," I countered.

"He's twice your size!"

"He's not twice my size," I grumbled.

"Oh, don't pout."

After an hour of traveling, the adrenaline wore off, completely replaced by exhaustion. I stretched out on the wagon floor and let the rhythmic rocking lull me to sleep. Unfortunately, it wasn't a restful sleep. Between the increasingly bumpy road and the waves of anxiety, I barely slept for more than a couple of hours.

It was midday after we left the manor, and I was in a foul mood. The sky seemed to agree. Even though the sun was at its highest, the day darkened. Thorn handed me a coat as the temperature continued to drop.

"Serina said it would be cold." I shrugged, nodded my thanks, and pulled the coat on.

"Yeah, but it's too soon for what she described," Scratch responded. "We must be near a lake or something." He pointed to low fog moving in. The fog increased in density until it felt like we were traveling in a cloud. "I can't even see the horses' rears," Scratch grumbled as he pulled back on the reins.

"We could stumble into a bog or off a cliff," I agreed, moving to sit next to Scratch.

Thorn poked her head between us. "Look, is that a sign?" She pointed up to where the fog was thinner. We could just make out arched lettering over an open town gate.

Thorn read the rune-like symbols on the sign. "Ritalinford. . . . That sounds familiar."

"As long as it has an inn," Scratch eagerly said, although his smile faltered the closer we came to the center of town. While the buildings were well maintained, there wasn't a soul in sight. Instead, I could see movement in the shadows. Scratch pulled the horses to a halt next to a merrily splashing fountain.

"I think maybe we should keep going," I suggested. A memory itched in my mind causing my unease to rise by the second. The soft thump of boots on the ground made me jump. Thorn appeared around the front of the wagon, heading toward a building that appeared to be a pub. Before I could protest, Scratch jumped down to secure the horses to a hitching post. Cursing, I scrambled to catch up with them.

Thorn pulled on the door to no avail. "That's odd."

Scratch tried to look through the window. "Looks ready for business, but no one's in there."

We checked several other buildings. Each was locked, their windows dark. However, there were signs that people had been there recently. In the window of the bakery, fresh bread was on display. Meat hung at the butchers, clean and ready to sell.

"Where is everyone?" Thorn asked.

A cold wind swept through the square as a chill ran up my spine that had little to do with the cold. I stood next to the butcher shop when the breeze cleared the fog for an instant. The stench of rot was overwhelming, filling my nose and making my eyes water. It may have been a trick of the light, but the whole building seemed to change. The window was shattered, and the front door smashed in. Dried gore and rotten meat covered the floor and walls. Then, in a blink of an eye, the fog returned, as did the previous scene of serenity.

"Something is very wrong here," Thorn whispered.

I was about to tell her what I had just witnessed when someone spoke.

"You are quite perceptive." A young woman stepped out of the shadows. She looked to be a couple of years older than we were. Her movements were catlike and fluid. It was captivating to watch her move. I felt a strange but familiar tingle at the base of my skull—the feeling of a spell being cast on me. Immediately I began to steel my mind against the encroaching Magic. I was about to warn Thorn but should have known better. The faint glow surrounding her told me she was already defending her mind. Scratch was another story.

"Do you live here?" Scratch asked in an almost dreamlike manner. "It's a charming village, and the people . . ." He was watching something Thorn and I couldn't see. "They seem so happy and, thank you, generous." Scratch held out his hand as if receiving something. Then, he moved to place the invisible item into the closure of his cloak.

Thorn and I called out to him, but if he heard us, he didn't acknowledge.

The woman took Scratch by the arm. "We are a very peaceful village," she said sweetly. "You should stay with us."

I was shocked when Scratch readily agreed.

"Oh *hell* no," Thorn growled. I nodded my agreement. Before we could take more than a few steps, I let out a cry I'm not proud to admit I could make. Out of the fog shambled several walking corpses, blocking our advancement. In an instant, we were surrounded. Scratch, completely oblivious, followed the strange woman. She glanced back at us, a look of victory in her smile.

Thorn pressed her back to mine, sword drawn and ready. I conjured a shield charm around us, knowing it wouldn't be much good against physical attacks. I cast the few combat spells I knew. The undead I hit crumpled to dust, instantly replaced as more emerged from the fog. Thorn threw her spells, more powerful than mine, but the result ultimately was the same. The dead she destroyed were replaced in moments. The circle around us grew ever smaller. Scratch and his guide had almost reached a house that shimmered in the fog.

Thorn cried out, throwing her arms up to cover her face. Intense heat and light blinded me as I pulled Thorn to the ground. Fire surrounded us, held at bay only by the shield spell I had cast earlier. The flames died, leaving scorched buildings and smoldering corpses. The fog was gone, but the area was still shrouded in dusk-like light. I looked to where Scratch had been. He stood unscathed yet swaying slightly, a vacant smile plastered to his face.

The sounds of large wings descending announced the arrival of Serina. "Hello, Kerrin. It's been a long time," Serina called to the woman holding Scratch by the arm. Then, Serina pointed at him. "That's a friend of mine. I would appreciate you letting him go."

"You have been away a long time, Serina." Kerrin's face held an ugly grin. All her features seemed sharper, harsher. Her movements became stuttered and jittery. "I don't think my new defender wants to leave, do you, my dear?"

The woman took Scratch by the arm. "No, I like it here, with you."

"That creature . . ." Kerrin pointed at Serina. I felt the term *creature* was hypocritical as Kerrin looked less and less human by the moment. "That thing wants to take you away from me."

"I shall not let that happen, my love," Scratch announced, drawing his blade. Kerrin's wicked grin oozed contempt.

"Oh, my dear Serina," Kerrin spoke in mock concern. "How will you fight your friend?"

Thorn and I had taken up positions on either side of Serina. I glanced over at her. I thought I would catch her eye, letting her know we were there to support her. Serina, however, rolled her eyes. Then, sweeping her hand through the air, Scratch flew into the fountain. The old cracked stone was covered in weeds and thick slime. Scratch emerged, swearing and covered in green disgustingness.

"What the hell's going on?" he demanded, climbing out of the foul water. "Whoa!" He pointd at Kerrin, whose appearance had taken on the distinct impression of a hag. "What the hell is that?"

"You always were an annoying little girl," Kerrin spat.

"Well, you're a hag, so there's that." Serina shrugged, unconcerned.

Without warning, Kerrin let loose a cry of fury, throwing lightning at Serina. I was taken off guard and didn't have time to throw up a barrier. I needn't have worried. Serina held out her hand, catching the hag's spell. Balling up the energy, she threw it back to Kerrin, who barely managed to dodge it. Thorn threw a fireball at her next. I worked quickly to create a barrier. Serina began throwing spells one after another at Kerrin. Her attempts were clumsy and erratic. The movements worried me until I saw she was distracting Kerrin.

The sound of spells exploding ended as the silver tip of Scratch's sword broke through Kerrin's chest. Eyes wide in pain and shock, she turned her head to see Scratch behind her. The surprise never left her face as he pulled the blade free. Kerrin turned around to grab Scratch's shoulders for support, opening her mouth to say something, but nothing coming out. Only the gurgle of death escaped the hag's throat as she sank to the ground.

"No one forces me to hurt my friends," he growled. He marched up to Serina as he cleaned off the sludgy black blood from his sword. "What the hell was that all about?"

"Old acquaintance." Serina shrugged. "We're bound to meet a few more the further we go." Then, unfurling her wings, Serina flew off into the darkening sky.

"Well, there's something to look forward to." Thorn sighed. "Let's get out of here and find a nice bog or swamp to camp in." All around us, the village showed its true self—dilapidated buildings filled with rot and gore surrounding a filthy stagnant fountain.

Finally, I remembered why Ritalinford was familiar. "This place is cursed," I shouted, covering my mouth. Thorn and Scratch both looked at me with expressions of, *well, duh*. "Okay, let's find that bog or a nice haunted forest." I tried to laugh it off.

CHAPTER 27

Scratch hurried the horses to put as much space between us and the ruined village as possible. He kept muttering angrily as he drove. It took quite a while before we found a decent place to camp. When we finally stopped, the flood gates opened. "I can't believe I was enchanted so easily," Scratch growled, punching the side of the wagon. He then mumbled something, that sounded suspiciously like, *And right in front of her.*

"Oh, let it go. Kerrin was a powerful magical being. Besides Serina knows it wasn't your fault." Thorn's words were placating, but her tone was harsh.

"Easy for you to say, you weren't taken in."

"We all saw the prsitine village," Thorn argued.

"She was in complete control over me," Scratch shouted.

"How is this my fault?" Thorn demanded.

I sat listening to them over a rather tasteless meal.

"I could teach you some defensive Magic," I offered, but Scratch only glared at me in answer.

"He's angry at himself," Thorn explained when she saw the look on my face. She was right—I was hurt, but I understood Scratch's feeling of helplessness. After a restless night camping, Scratch was still in a foul mood in the morning. My greeting was met with a grunt as he abused the breakfast with unnecessary roughness. Each sausage was slammed over, as the coffee cup must have offended Scratch somehow by how he served them with extreme force.

"At least we know the sausages are dead," I joked as I tried to keep my spirits up. Thorn did not need both of us to be unhappy simultaneously. Unfortunately, my attempt at humor only seemed to annoy Scratch and Thorn even more. So we spent the rest of the day in grumpy silence. The next morning didn't improve matters. At least it was my turn to make breakfast, so no food or dishes were abused. This was for the best, as Thorn had not been kind to our place settings the previous evening.

It was the end of the second annoying day when we finally reached the foothills. Scratch jumped from the driver's seat to angrily begin setting up camp. I had just finished getting the fire going and was setting up the cooking pot when Thorn exploded.

"Enough!" She pointed accusingly at Scratch. "Get over it. She was a strong magical creature!"

I nodded my agreement until Thorn turned her anger on me.

"And you." She glared at me. "Give the fake cheeriness a rest. You were never this cheerful the entire time I've known you."

"Sorry," Scratch and I muttered in unison. Scratch hastily warmed some soup to avoid Thorn's continued wrath.

She sat muttering to herself for a short time. Then, suddenly, she was on her feet again, pacing, which is never a good sign. "We need to figure out what's happening and how to deal with it."

"Well . . ." I sipped my soup. "One of us really needs to learn to cook."

"You're not wrong, but you're also not helping," Thorn huffed. She stared down the road we had just traveled. "Why isn't anyone after us? I thought we were running away from danger."

"We *are* running away. However, annoying as that would be, it sure doesn't feel like we're being pursued." Scratch angrily threw a log into our fire, sending sparks into the air.

I had to agree. "It feels quite the opposite." I watched the flames. "I mean, after the hag encounter, nothing has happened."

"That was enough, if you ask me," Scratch grunted.

"I thought an army would be after us." Thorn looked back down the road. "We've had nothing to do except watch the same scenery pass by hour after hour."

She was right. There was nothing but the mundane road to distract us. I tried to read, but the wagon's motion made my stomach churn. We couldn't practice spells in the extremely confined space; worst of all, we felt we couldn't show ourselves.

"I don't know what's worse," Thorn growled. "Not being pursued or the fact that they expect us to act like fools."

What Thorn meant was that we were being *hunted*. We found that out at the first hag-free town we visited. It was early when we arrived at a village, and the townsfolk were just waking up. It was a small town, maybe sixty inhabitants in total, a tiny farming community with one main building in the square for meetings. I was looking forward to getting out and stretching my legs. Our horses clopped along the hard-packed dirt ever slower. I had just readied myself to jump down when we sped up. Scratch waved to some older men as they came out of their houses.

"Stay down and stay silent," he hissed over his shoulder.

A bumpy hour later, we were well off the road, sitting around a fire cooking lunch. Scratch had just finished explaining. "There was a poster in town." He reached into his shirt. Pulling out a crumpled parchment, he handed it to Thorn.

She bit back a laugh.

"Seems like word is out about you two."

I tried to wrestle the poster out of Thorn's hands. We struggled with it. I couldn't imagine why she didn't want me to see it. I won our battle and saw why she fought so hard. Two faces stared up at me. The picture of Thorn was pretty accurate, but the description was not so much.

"Evil Temptress," I read, looking over the paper at her. "*Purple hair*, hmm, got that right. *Elven ears*." I put the poster down and looked sternly at her. "I guess they could pass for elven."

"Hey!" Thorn tried to grab the poster.

"Oh, here we go," I announced as I retrieved the poster, "wicked eyes that will entrance a man." I laughed. "Yes, those entrancing eyes." I tried to sound like I was falling under a spell. I quickly altered my commentary when I saw the look she threw my way. "Those charming eyes that will now shoot flame and turn me into a cinder." I rolled away, laughing as she snatched the parchment from me.

"Well, since you were so intrigued by my picture and description . . ." She cleared her throat. Snapping the parchment straight, she began to read. "*This vile half-breed witch* . . ." She frowned. "That is just insulting. I'm not a witch."

She let the paper hang loose momentarily as her head shook in disappointment. She resumed reading. "*The witch is traveling with a criminal elf*." She looked pointedly at me. "*The public is warned not to underestimate her power and cunning*. Okay, I can accept that."

I snatched at the paper but danced out of reach.

"*This elf, although quite dim, is responsible for several deaths, theft, and unearthly acts*." I was aghast.

She turned the picture around, and that's when I saw it. Her picture was much larger, while mine was much crueler. My face was depicted in an expression of a half-wit, while my ears appeared more batlike than elven. I held a knife I assumed was covered in blood in the picture.

"*If seen, report them to the local inspector immediately.*" Thorn let the poster hang loose as she looked at Scratch. "Since when do we have local inspectors? I thought they were only territorial?"

"Since the day before we left," Scratch explained, getting to his feet. "They took over the barracks at Dayok and either conscripted or dismissed the rest of the town guard."

"Dismissed?" I couldn't believe it.

"Me included. That's why I'm not on the posters yet." It was after this he became sullen again.

Scratch finished packing up our pots and pans. "Time to get moving." The wanted poster, bland meal, frustrated companions, and inspector news put a damper on an already somber mood.

Another day of travel brought us to the head of the Dark Pass. "Why do you humans insist on naming things that look slightly foreboding as 'Dark' this or 'Haunted' that?" I asked.

"I think it was meant to be ironic or funny." Serina's voice startled me so much that I thought my heart had jumped out of my chest and kept running. "See that bunny?" She pointed at a cute little rabbit not too far away. "It's a were-rabbit. It will kill you." Then, as if to prove the point, the were-rabbit exposed huge teeth and growled in a way that would terrify the fiercest warrior.

"And over there, that fox?" Serina continued in a bored voice. "It spits acid and will kill you." She continued to point out various animals, birds, mice, snakes, voles, mountain lions, and no matter what she pointed to, said, "spits lava, exudes poison, razor-sharp teeth," and it was always finished with, "it will kill you."

Thorn anxiously watched a butterfly as it landed next to Scratch's seat.

Serina also watched it. "That's the death's head reaper scourge," she explained.

"What does it do?" I asked fearfully. "Explode into thousands of carnivorous smaller butterflies?" I edged away, as did Thorn and Scratch.

"No," Serina held out a finger. The butterfly flew onto it, slowly flapping its wings. "It's just a butterfly." She watched the insect ascend into the sky. "The pollen it collects will kill you."

"I hate this place," I whispered to Thorn. She nodded emphatically in agreement.

We traveled in silence for a while. The deeper into the pass, the more desolate it became. Serina flew off to scout ahead. Even though it was just after mid-afternoon, the sun barely shone in this place. Thorn and I sat close together, studying one of the books from the chest. She bumped into me as we traversed some rough terrain, so I bumped her back. Then, we started playfully pushing each other. I was beginning to relax and just enjoy some shred of normalcy.

Suddenly Thorn stopped messing around and grabbed my hands, presenting a shy smile. My cheeks warmed when the wagon abruptly stopped. Thorn fell on top of me. Her forehead collided with mine, sending the back of my head smashing into the wagon's bed. My world spun. Thorn scrambled over me to get to Scratch. In her haste, I took a knee to the face as I tried to right myself. I rolled over in an attempt not to pass out. It didn't work. I heard Scratch's fearful voice as the blackness closed in.

"That is a Dullahan. That isn't a good sign."

I was comfortable with my head lying on something warm and soft. Someone was stroking my head and whispering something. Then, my mind and the world returned to me. My head rested on Thorn's lap as her fingers traced patterns on my forehead and cheek. I was aware we weren't moving. "What's going on?" I mumbled. I was still a bit dizzy.

"Sorry about your head," Thorn failed to look sincere. "How's your face?" She traced the same pattern on my bruised cheek. A smile fought to emerge.

"Fine. I guess it hurts a little," I lied. I was enjoying the feeling of Thorn so close to me.

"Good." She snorted. "Because it's killing me."

The pain was gone, as was my enjoyment. So I brushed her hand away. Then, sitting up, I glared at her. "Ha ha," I said sarcastically.

Scratch was still in the driver's seat with his sword out. His shoulders betrayed his tension. "Why aren't we moving?" I asked. The memory of Scratch mentioning the Dullahan came back to me. Looking past Scratch, I saw a Dullahan blocking the passage. He sat astride a huge black horse. In the crook of the rider's arm was the pale staring face of the rider's head. A blue flame burned where his head should have been.

"Isn't he the messenger of death?" Scratch whispered to us, not taking his eyes off the dark figure.

"Death's collector, I believe." I tried to remember something I had read about them. "They appear when someone is close to dying, then take the soul to meet death."

"Some believe they're the worldly personification of death," Thorn explained. "Once they pass into the world of the fae, they become death."

"It matters not what you believe," the Dullahan's voice echoed off the rocky walls. "Mortals shall not pass. You must face me to continue." He drew a long broadsword, but then something distracted the guardian.

"Oh, look!" Thorn pointed unnecessarily at the Dullahan. Serina landed right in front of him. They stared at each other for what felt like an eternity. Finally, Serina cocked her head to the side as she stepped closer.

"Colin, that can't be you, can it?" Serina asked. The Dullahan and its horse, who seconds before, stood ready for battle, suddenly relaxed. Then, hastily putting away the sword, he jumped down.

"No way, Serina. Wow." He hugged her. "What has it been? A hu—"

"It has been a while," Serina interrupted.

Suddenly he held her at arm's length. Colin moved his head close to her face. "Do your parents know you are back?" His eyes were serious and even a little concerned.

"No," she grumbled. "Believe me—if I didn't need to be here, I wouldn't be."

"Serina," Colin admonished. "They have missed you."

"Ha," Serina scoffed.

Colin's shoulders hunched as he sighed.

"I need you to let my friends through."

Colin took a step back. His eyes blinked several times. "But they are mortals." He backed further away from her as if to avoid whatever insanity afflicted her. "My job as guardian is to keep them out."

"Colin . . ." We couldn't see her face, but Serina's voice held something I'd never heard before. "You know me." Her hand caressed the cheek of the severed head.

Scratch's grip on the reins tightened.

I looked at Thorn. A blush crept up her face.

"You could let this pass." Serina was now holding the head with both hands.

Colin's arm hung out in the air, still reaching for his head. There was no panic or opposition to taking his head further from the body.

The reins twisted in Scratch's hands.

Serina's lips moved closer to Colin's ear. Colin's hair moved as her breath blew it from his ear.

We couldn't hear what she said, but it was something like *do it for me* from what I could read on her lips. She then kissed Colin on the cheek before returning Colin's head to his body. Scratch made a weird noise in his throat while Thorn gasped. Serina sauntered over to us. Her walk was, well, there's no other way to describe it other than alluring. She didn't look at Scratch. Her eyes were looking past us. "Colin will let us through." Her shoulders rose as she sighed. "This is not going to be pretty."

"It's already been extremely uncomfortable," Scratch grumbled. Serina ignored him.

Thorn watched her friend apprehensively.

"Maybe we should reconsider," Thorn suggested.

Serina waved her statement away. "This day was coming one way or another." Serina's face was set with determination.

"Do you know what we're walking into?" I whispered to Scratch.

Shrugging, he spoke out of the corner of his mouth. "All I know is Serina and her mother had a rather nasty falling out."

CHAPTER 28

S cratch kept his head down, trying to avoid looking at the Dullahan. I, however, was intrigued by what I saw. From the majestic black stallion to the blue flames where the head should be, this was an experience few could say they'd ever had. Then, I saw the head held under his arm. Next, I was struck by the Dullahan named Colin, who looked apprehensive as we passed. Serina gave him a girly wave, something I thought I would never see from her. Once we were well past the Dullahan, she turned to us. "Not a word about this." Her glare held an intensity that could melt armor. "Ever."

"Which part?" Scratch's grumpy question received a venomous reply.

"Anything from when we met Colin until after we were on our way." Her canine teeth grew to become the fangs of her kind. There was also the fact that her eyes had become entirely black while her flaming red hair was blowing and swirling even though there was no wind. I was ready to pretend I was never here. Thorn's smirk did nothing to help Serina's mood.

Scratch, on the other hand, stared at her. His eyes seemed unfocused as his mouth hung open. "Wow, amazing," he whispered, then I was sure I heard him say something that sounded like *gorgeous*.

"Ugh." Serina's annoyance peaked. "Just follow me," she growled, taking flight.

"Wow." Scratch shook his head like he had just woken up. I turned to ask Thorn what had happened. To my surprise, she was forcing a pillow over her face. The tips of her ears were bright red, and her shoulders shook while the pillow muffled her laughter.

Her mirth ended as the cold seeped into the wagon. We entered a cave or a tunnel so long I couldn't see the other side. Serina lit a flame in her hand, thankfully. Even though the light from the fire was strong, it couldn't dispel the darkness. We passed several passages branching off from the main path we were on. A tingle crept slowly from the base of my skull as I caught the red reflection of eyes in the dark, like a hundred cats all about six feet tall. I turned to say something to Thorn when I saw she was busy going through the books I'd brought.

"What are you looking for?" I asked through chattering teeth as I shivered. The cold had become piercing now. At least it *felt* cold. I found it strange I couldn't see my breath or feel any warmth from the blanket I wrapped around myself. Thorn's fingers shook with the chill. I threw the blanket over her and pulled the lantern closer, but I couldn't get any warmth from the flame.

"You're sweet," Thorn muttered, shrugging off the blanket. "Ah, got it." She recited a spell. The bitter cold disappeared, so now all I felt was the cool dampness of the surrounding rocks. "I never thought to use this spell." In the book, she pointed to it. "This spell blocks the draining effect. Serina was never a threat, but this many vampires in one place. Wow." She shuddered. Scratch whispered his thanks, also shaking. I decided to join him in the driver's seat, bringing my crossbow with me.

"Other than Serina," I whispered, glancing around to see if Serina was within earshot, "have you ever dealt with a vampire?" From what I could see of his face, he was uncomfortable.

"Yes," he confirmed quietly. "I haven't mentioned it to Serina, though."

"What happened?"

"We got a notice from the council of a rogue vampire in the territory."

"Council?"

"Yeah, you know." Scratch glanced at me.

I shook my head.

"Wow, really?" He whistled. "You're friends with a vampire and don't know about the council? The vampires have a king and queen who rule them, to use the label." He didn't seem to like the taste of the word. "The other dark creatures have their own leaders, but they all send representatives to the council. This council makes laws and keeps track of violations of the treaty."

"Treaty?" I hadn't heard of any of this.

"Seriously?" This time he turned to look me straight in the face.

"We've lived isolated in the forest for the last couple of years," Thorn explained from behind us. I didn't think she'd been listening.

Scratch twisted in his seat to look at both of us in turn. "Wow, okay. this treaty has existed for years." He double-checked our faces as if we would lie about not knowing. "The treaty between the day and the night, as they call it?" His voice held exasperation as he stared, hoping that naming it would jog something in our memory. But, unfortunately, it didn't. "It's meant to keep us from killing them and vice versa. It also keeps them from joining either side during a war. If the . . ." Scratch seemed to search for a better word. ". . . others who prefer not to avoid the sun?" He ran a hand over his face. "If they joined one side, that side would have an enormous advantage."

"What if the orcs decided to side with the humans?" I asked.

"That would go against the council's will," Scratch explained as if it was obvious. He eyed a passage we passed before continuing. "Individuals could go and fight for whoever they like. However, if their leaders committed troops, that would violate the treaty. It would lead to ostracization and even war against their fellow *beings*." He seemed to like that word better.

"We would never side with the humans." Serina landed silently on the footboard. Her eyes had returned to the deep green I was used to seeing. "I doubt we would side with the elves either. But you humans have always been far more hostile toward us."

"Your kind has wreaked enough havoc toward humans to make the distrust even," Scratch replied on the defensive.

"Only when we've had to defend ourselves or our lands." Serina bent forward, getting closer to his face. "Your cowardly attacks during the day when we are defenseless are reprehensible."

Scratch leaned in, his forehead almost touching hers. "We were driven from our homes by your kind." Then, he pointed at her dramatically. "Or killed in our beds!" His voice rose to match his anger.

"You're both right, and you're both at fault. Neither side has clean hands. Hence the treaty," Thorn interrupted, pushing the two apart. "You'd just go on killing each other for real and perceived offenses unless—" Thorn suddenly went quiet.

Confused, I turned from Thorn to the other two. Their glares didn't need the light to glow and bore into Thorn.

"Unless what?" Serina growled.

"Oh, she means unless the all-powerful mages hadn't come to make peace," Scratch sneered.

"Wait, that wasn't—" Thorn stuttered.

"Yes, we children couldn't possibly take care of our own business." Serina spoke in a childlike voice, resting her head on Scratch's shoulder, and wrapped an arm around her back.

"Bad humans and dark creatures too dumb," he said thickly.

"That's not what I said." Thorn's frustration grew. "You're just—Stop it."

"You know," I mumbled. "The mage did get you two to stop arguing."

Suddenly the human and vampire turned their burning glares on me. Thorn grabbed my shoulders, pulling me into the back of the wagon. Serina took my place next to Scratch. They began grumbling to each other.

"Well," I shrugged, "At least they have a common enemy."

"I just wish they'd get on with it already," Thorn hissed.

I felt my brows crease. "Get on with what?"

Thorn sighed, her hand on my cheek. "I'll tell you when you're older."

"Hey," I shouted, "we're the same age."

We were hushed from the front. Something was going on. We returned to the driver's seat to see our path blocked again—this time by armed troops. Troops that held weapons as well as had sharp fangs and wings. We were looking at an army of Royal Vampire Guard. At least, that's what Scratch said as he swore.

"Shit," Serina hissed. Then, she took a deep breath and blew it out in resignation. "This will not be pleasant." She straightened her back, unfurling her wings with a grace and poise I hadn't seen before. She rose in the air, landing a few meters from a vampire that appeared to be in charge, and held her head high. A look of astonishment crossed his face. Then, to the shock of three non-vampires in a battered wagon, the troops knelt on one knee.

"Princess Serina," the leader lowered his head respectfully. "Welcome home."

Scratch swore, my mouth fell open, and Thorn fell back on her butt. She lay back, staring up at the canvas in shock.

CHAPTER 29

S omeone must have seen this coming," Thorn moaned, throwing an arm over her eyes. "Not me, of course, but someone."

"Yeah, the vampire girl living in the catacombs under the scary mage's house would turn out to be a wayward vampire princess. Who'd a thunk it," I grumbled.

Serina walked regally through the soldiers, accompanied by their leader. "It is a pleasure to see you, Zoban." Serina nodded to her escort. "I see you are fulfilling your ambition to become the leader of the royal guard." As they passed, the ranks of his soldiers reformed and drew their swords.

"I hope she remembers us," I hissed, watching the vampires fanning out to surround us.

"Daywalkers." A mountain of a vampire stood directly in front of our wagon. His sword wasn't drawn as he ordered, "You will vacate the wagon immediately. You will lay down your arms and prepare to be searched upon doing so."

"I don't like this," Scratch hissed to us. Jumping down from the seat, he pulled his sword. I held my breath. By his stance, I thought he wouldn't relinquish his weapon. A tense moment passed. Scratch changed his grip so he was holding it by the blade. "If I die, I'm so going to haunt her," he grumbled as he set it down.

Thorn jumped out next, also pulling her sword. I took a deep breath and followed. A laugh ran through the vampires when I pulled out my dagger and lay it on the ground.

"I am Lieutenant Hume," the large vampire announced.

It was our turn to snicker. At least Thorn and I snickered. "More like huge," she joked.

Ignoring us, he continued, "Daywalkers are not welcome here. You will leave now."

"What do we do?" I hissed to Thorn out of the corner of my mouth. All humor evaporated from the moment. Scratch made a move to retrieve his sword. Then, with impressive unison, all the soldiers took a step toward us. They held swords at the ready. Scratch backed away with his hands up.

"You will leave as you are," Hume instructed.

Thorn stepped forward to face the lieutenant. "If we leave without our weapons and wagon, we won't reach the entrance."

He shrugged at her. "Your fate is not our concern."

"But Serina brought us here," I stammered.

Thorn motioned for me to be quiet. "We don't wish to have a confrontation," Thorn announced, "but we *will* defend ourselves." A ball of light erupted in her hand. The vampires closest to it recoiled, hissing. "I'm the daughter of Mage Caterous. I demand an audience with the King of the Vampires." The ball of light intensified in her hand.

Hume watched her hands warily. "You are the young mage Thorn Caterous?" he asked.

"That's my name, yes," she announced loudly. "I'm sure you're aware of my father and his displeasure if anything happened to my friends or me."

"Mage Caterous would know better than to send you to us," Hume scoffed. "He, above all, knows our rules." His body tensed for battle. "We have defeated mages, so a young and inexperienced one, such as you, will be no problem." He barely made a motion with his head. It was the signal for his soldiers to attack.

I have no idea how, but Scrtach was ready for this. The moment the signal was given he dove for his sword. On instinct I threw out a protection spell. Thorn called out, "*Solaraextre*," sending a wave of light from the ball in her hand. The advancing vampires were thrown back from the expansion of the protective shield and Thorn's magic. Cries of rage and pain filled the cavern. Smoke rose from several vampires as they scuttled away from the light. Arrows and projectile Magic rained down upon us from unseen archers and magic casters. I concentrated on keeping the protection solid. Each bolt that bounced off felt like bees stinging me. Deflected spells exploded against the cave walls and roof, showering our attackers with sharp stones. Thorn focused, her eyes tight in concentration, as another burst of light expanded out in waves from her hand at the vampires.

My own concentration needed rebuffed as my barrier was attacked. I felt every blow and found it hard to keep standing—until a spear was thrust at me.

I screamed, causing Thorn to direct a shaft of intense light that blasted the spear wielder, sending him flying. I watched as he landed, his armor smoking and his skin blistering as he screamed in agony. Thorn threw another blast of light over the heads of the other attackers. They dropped to the ground, giving us a a second of reprieve.

"I don't want to kill you, but I will." Thorn's voice filled the battlefield, causing a few vampires to falter. Hume, however, barked a laugh.

"It is you who will die here." Then, a thousand armored soldiers spilled from the tunnel.

"They will not!" A voice thundered through the cavern. The vampires were parted and thrown against the walls like puppets on strings. My shield evaporated in my shock as Thorn's ball of light extinguished. The only thing that illuminated the room was the burning glow surrounding Serina. "How dare you attack my friends," she demanded of Hume as he struggled to his feet.

He pointed to us accusingly. "These Daywalkers are not welcome here."

"On whose authority did you decide to attack?" She was at least a foot shorter than him and unarmed, yet as she advanced, he backed away. "I have asked you a question. You will answer."

"I-I do not acknowledge your authority." His statement might have been more believable if he wasn't trembling. "Your power ended when you left the community." His voice cracked, but he held his ground now.

"Do the rest of you doubt me?" Serina turned slowly on the spot as she spoke. "Do you doubt I have authority over you?" Several soldiers immediately dropped to a knee and bowed their heads. Many of the others looked a little confused but followed suit. Only four of the ones that attacked us still stood.

"I see," Serina whispered.

Someone shouted, "Death to the traitor witch!"

I immediately moved to protect Thorn. I stared at Hume's smile of defiance and triumph. It felt out of place to me.

Then chaos erupted. The remaining soldiers moved to join a mob that appeared out of nowhere. While this happened, the soldiers Serina had thrown immediately took up arms, guarding the path Serina had just emerged from.

Scratch joined Thorn and me, standing between the two groups. "Looks like we walked into the middle of something," he muttered.

Serina stood alone several feet from us. The air was filled with shouting and hissing. Finally, someone threw a stone. It flew toward Serina, halted, floated in the air momentarily, and landed with a soft thump at Serina's feet. The cavern was silent. Serina kept her head down as she slowly raised an arm to point toward the vampire mob that threw the stone. One of the defiant soldiers stood in front of the others. A creaking sound of metal grinding against metal filled my ears, and I heard Thorn gasp as she grabbed my arm.

The vampire's armor began to cave in as if crushed by an invisible hand. Then, the metal constricted so tightly that blood sprayed out from every gap. Finally, the vampire's screams ended when his helmet crushed his skull like a grape, and his brain and blood poured from the eye holes.

Thorn turned her eyes from the gore, burying her face in my shoulder. Serina was now pointing at another vampire. I watched, transfixed, as unseen forces pulled him to pieces in an instant. The sound was that of wet meat slapping stone mixed with the clatter of a sword. Many in the mob panicked and turned to flee. One of the soldiers who had stayed standing now dropped to a knee and loudly pledged loyalty. The last one dropped his sword and began to run.

I wanted to cover my ears. I tried to cover my eyes. I tried to forget that my friend could cause such violence. Bones shattered. It started in the running vampire's legs. Serina snapped her fingers, and the man turned to jelly. All his organs and blood were now held in a shapeless bag. His eyes stared at me in terror, unable to draw breath, drowning in his own fluids.

I couldn't help myself, "Spleew." Thorn nodded and whimpered.

Hume stood frozen to the spot. His already ashen pallor had become alabaster. "Princess," he pleaded.

"Serina, please stop," Thorn shouted.

Serina spared her a glance before she turned her attention to Hume. "The soldiers of this land swear upon their lives to the royal family." Serina waved her hand, throwing the lieutenant against the wall. His feet were off the ground as he struggled against invisible bonds. "They make an oath with all their heart." She moved closer to him. "Did you forget that oath?"

"No, I-I serve the royal family loyally," Hume gasped.

"Yet you doubt me." She cocked her head to one side. "You sided with those who called me traitor." Her anger grew. "Do you still doubt my power? Do you not believe I am of royal blood?"

Hume flinched as she spoke. Even the vampires that guarded the gate seemed to recoil in fear.

Serina turned, eyes blazing red, and long black horns grew from her hair that danced like a flame around her face.

Terror etched his voice. "I never—*never*—doubted your power." He struggled to get free or just further from the advancing fury of Serina.

"Just my authority, then." Her voice was like ice. It froze the blood in my veins and the air in my lungs. "Or is it the entire royal family?" she hissed.

Hume was begging now. However, Serina wasn't listening to him. Instead, she cocked her head as if listening for something, "I can hear them, you know. Your friends who call for my death." She spat. "I have easily defeated three of your warriors," she shouted, so her voice echoed through the caverns. Then, her venom returned to Hume. "I have killed three royal guards. What is the punishment for that?"

"Vampires who kill a royal soldier are to be put to death," he gasped.

"Unless?" Her face was inches from his. She had levitated to stare him in the eye.

"Unless they break their oath."

"Their oath to the royal family?" she asked. He nodded fervently. "So, am I not a member of the royal family?"

"I did not attack you," he choked as tears ran down his cheeks.

Serina's appearance had returned to her human form. She appeared to be considering this fact as they descended. When their feet touched the floor, the bond holding Hume released. However, before he could get one pace in, Serina grabbed him by the throat, holding him in place with her own strength. "You are correct. You did not attack me. Nor did you do your duty to defend me."

"You have my support as a royal," Hume sobbed.

"Louder!"

"Princess Serina is part of the royal family and heir to the crown," Hume shouted.

"Very good." Serina let go of him. I thought it was over as she turned away from Hume. He stood before her, head bowed. Serina looked sadly at Thorn for the briefest moment.

Before I could call out, Hume pulled a dagger from his belt. It was still raised as Serina's hand flashed into Hume's chest. His look of triumph was replaced with horror. A scream of fear and agony pierced my ears. Serina held out Hume's heart before his eyes. It beat twice before it was still. The life left those shocked eyes as they continued to stare at her as his body crumpled.

Holding Hume's heart up high, she caused it to burst into flame. Serina addressed all those still present and, by the volume of her tone, those we could not see. "Soldiers, you have made an oath with all your heart. I will hold you to that oath. Your heart and lives are pledged to the royal family."

The sound of metal upon metal echoed throughout the chamber. The vampire guard held their swords to their chests in salute.

"Our hearts for the Crown," they all pledged.

Serina walked slowly around the cavern. "Those who oppose the chosen royal family know that I, Serina, the witch, the demon, have returned."

Serina threw the charred heart away. I heard creatures fighting over it. "Know that I will take your hearts if you are disloyal." Next, she rubbed her hands clean with the dead lieutenant's cloak.

"This is one of the reasons I left," she mumbled to us as she moved away from the assembled soldiers. "Rule with absolute authority and absolutely no mercy."

Thorn gaped at her, disbelief, horror, and sympathy all fighting for dominance. I, too, had no way to understand my feelings.

"I'm sorry you had to see that. But, unfortunately, it's just how it is here." A frown of disgust creased her face. "If you don't show this level of brutality, you don't get their respect. Then you have unrest. If you show this level of violence, you gain respect and loyalty. It's crazy and stupid. We don't rule by fear. We do this because that is what the people want." Serina turned from us.

I wanted to say something, but the screams were still fresh in my ears.

Thorn, however, reached out to her friend. "I'm sorry you had to do that. Maybe when you're queen—"

"I never want that." Serina patted Thorn's hand, then turned and addressed the cavern. "If any harm befalls my friends, I will take it as a personal and political offense." She turned to us. "Come along and meet my parents." There was no joy in her voice.

Zoban stood waiting patiently for us. "You know you didn't have to do that," he hissed as Serina approached. "We do not support such brutality."

Serina looked slightly surprised.

"This will be a relations nightmare," he grumbled to himself. "I could have spun the wayward daughter's return, but now?" He looked back at the carnage left in our wake. "Missing princess returns, wreaks havoc on dissidents." He kept muttering as he led the way into the Vampire Fortress.

An odd smile played on Serina's face as she listened to his complaining.

CHAPTER 30

Seventeen years ago, Caterous Manor

Lawrence Caterous held a blue flame in one hand and a sword in the other. He crept slowly through the maze under the manor. Something was here. He felt the presence, and it wasn't a good feeling. It was somewhere between the slow creeping of frustration about to spill into fury and desolate sadness. "Ah," Caterous sucked in a breath. He caught a glimpse of flaming red hair that sent his heart racing. A vampire and a powerful one to be sure. She radiated strength. He was certain she hadn't detected him so close by but knew she could feel his presence as he could hers.

Why would a vampire come here now? he wondered. *What could Althea be planning?* Deciding he didn't want to find out, Caterous pondered the best way to destroy the intruder. "A solaris spell would be the most efficient," he mumbled. "But do I really want to have that smell in the house?" He shook away that option. "Decapitation then. No, that is far too messy. Obliteration, yes, no fuss no muss."

Serina moved silently and quickly. She knew she was playing a dangerous game. However, right now, the home of a powerful mage would be the last place anyone would suspect to look for her. The magical power emanating from this house would cover all traces of her. Serina jumped high into an alcove and listened. She felt his presence but couldn't determine where he was.

Caterous returned to the main floor and headed toward his library. "I remember something that will reduce a vampire to dust—that is the spell to use." Caterous spoke to the darkness. He didn't doubt his abilities, but still, a rogue vampire could be difficult and unpredictable. If it were in league with

Althea, that would be all the worse. His hand reached for the knob when his thoughts were interrupted by thunderous banging on the front door.

Initially, the sound startled him. As it continued, the knocking filled the mage with dread. It was night, and neither of his friends from the village would be out this late, nor would they pound upon his door with such force.

A vampire in the catacombs and pounding on the front door caused Caterous to cast several spells and prepare for a fight as he moved to face his visitor. Retrieving his staff and readying his sword, Caterous braced and magically threw open the door, prepared for a fight that didn't come.

A cloaked figure stood before him. Piercing green eyes glowed from under the hood. *Now I have two vampires at my house.* Caterous's mind grumbled.

"Lord Caterous." The robed figure bowed. "I am Asha, and I have a request of you."

Caterous bowed in return. "Asha, to what do I owe the honor of a visit from the Vampire Queen?"

"I am not here as a queen but as a mother," Asha replied simply.

Caterous found this visit could not be a coincidence, so he bowed again, inviting her in.

"I dare not. My daughter will know I am here. Lord Caterous, I know you are already burdened."

Caterous began to question the queen, who waved off his denial.

"It matters not how we know," Asha sighed. "My daughter is extremely powerful. In fact, she is likely the most extraordinary of our kind to ever exist. Serina's abilities are far beyond my control but not yours—yet."

Caterous's eyebrow disappeared into his fringe. "What are you asking of me?" Trepidation coated his question.

"No, no, please." Asha panicked, "I ask that you allow her to stay here, to hide. Some wish to destroy her. They have tried to use her to start a civil war, and there have been attempts on her life."

"She is a royal. There should be no greater protection."

"She has been accused of crimes. They have built false evidence and killed many in her name. Please, my daughter is not safe at home."

"And you fear what she could do if cornered. What you ask is quite a lot." Caterous replied, exasperated.

"I know it is too much to ask. However, I will forever be in your debt if you can grant me this request. I promise the assistance of the vampires if you or your daughter are ever in need."

"I cannot keep her here if she desires to leave," Caterous began.

"I cannot ask that of you, but I do know my daughter. She may decide it is a game if she thinks you know of her and want her gone." Asha smiled sadly. "After all, she is still a child."

"I will do as you ask," Caterous paused Asha's gratitude, "but conditions do apply. You know who resides here. If I think they are in contact, Serina must leave. If my daughter is ever in danger, Serina will leave—or worse."

Asha seemed to fight the urge to assure Caterous, and in the end, she agreed to his terms. Caterous's cloak rippled in the gust created as the Vampire Queen flew off. With a sigh of resignation, Caterous returned to the catacombs.

"I know you are here, young one. If I ever find you, I will force you out." He called to the darkness. The game was set now. As long as she thought she was tricking him, the easier it would be to keep her hidden.

Serina laughed quietly to herself, thinking she could enjoy a few years of cat and mouse. "If you ever find me? Just try it."

CHAPTER 37

Zoban kept muttering as he led us through a long tunnel away from the open cave. Nervously, we passed a long line of soldiers. Serina occasionally nodded to their salutes, but she mostly kept her eyes straight ahead. Thorn, Scratch, and I anxiously anticipated another attack. Then, suddenly, the tunnel opened to reveal an unbelievable sight.

Carved from the solid rock was a structure unlike any I've ever seen. The building that stood before us wasn't a castle. However, it wasn't quite a palace. It was magnificent and could only be referred to as *power*. Gold and white banners adorned the parapets. Bioluminescent moss cast a blue-green glow over the entire structure. I marveled at the hints of gold and silver intricately inlaid around all the window frames.

The closer we got, the more Thorn tugged on my sleeve and pointed out different examples of ornate craftsmanship. We passed beautiful statues so remarkably done they could have been frozen in time. We gawked at the massive front gate that must have been hewed from the cave's stone walls. It looked like the entire area had been carved out of solid stone. An ancient language twisted and coiled over the arch to the gate. I swore it moved the closer we approached. I was so intrigued by the writing that I wasn't paying attention to where we were going until a voice pulled me out of my trance.

"Halt!" shouted a guard. He struck the hilt of his pike on the ground, sending up sparks as we approached.

Serina's shoulders sagged for a moment. Then, recovering quickly, she stood straight and glared at the soldier.

Holding a hand, he continued, "Sorry, this area is off-limits to non-vampires and annoying little girls."

Wide-eyed in shock, I immediately turned to Thorn, who glared at me contemptuously.

"No, not her," the guard scoffed as he pointed at Thorn. "That one." He gestured dismissively at Serina.

Thorn sucked in a breath in expectation of more violence. But instead, Serina, taken aback, stuttered, "D-do you know who I am?"

I cringed as she said it. Nothing good ever came from that question.

"Oh, you did not just say that." The guard laughed at Serina's stunned expression. "I know exactly who you are, Rina," he continued.

Serina straightened to her full height. Holding her head regally, she opened her mouth to say something, but the words escaped her, leaving her deflated. In a flash, she grabbed his helmet. Terrified, Thorn screamed for her to stop. The helmet flew off, revealing a handsome vampire, a huge smile on his face. Serina stumbled backward in shock.

"Jamie!" she shouted, jumping into his arms. They laughed together as he swung her around. "Oh, gods!" Back on her feet, she looked him over. "You look good." Her hand twirled the end of his long black hair. "Your hair is a bit longer."

"You do not look much different. Lots of Magic, I guess." Jamie smiled. "Who are your friends?" he asked, easily looking over the top of her head at us.

"Thorn, Henry, Scratch, this is my little brother, Jamie." We stood dumbfounded. He looked around thirty, whereas Serina appeared to be in her late teens, closer to our age.

"Jamie?" Thorn asked, approaching, "Serina told me about you. I thought you would . . . um . . ."

"Be younger?" He laughed. "I am—by six years."

Serina looked embarrassed, not meeting our questioning eyes. The sheepish and amused smiles disappeared from the siblings' faces as another voice joined our conversation.

"Yes, even at two hundred and nineteen, my daughter has not grown up in the slightest." A stunningly beautiful woman dressed impeccably floated toward us. Scratch, Thorn, and I bowed despite ourselves. It was apparent we were in the presence of royalty and someone who wielded great power. A thin, elegant hand lifted Thorn's chin. "Daughter of Mage Caterous, welcome. It is a pleasure to meet you finally."

Thorn thanked her in a quiet and respectful voice I'd never heard her use.

"I must thank your father for taking in my wayward daughter."

I stole a glance at Thorn. She also was confused. Her father had constantly threatened to have Serina expelled if he found her.

"Yes, his animosity was only to make her feel she was getting away with something. He knew."

Thorn's attention turned to the very unhappy Serina.

Serina's mother continued. "When he discovered you were in his house, I believe he was not pleased." Something caused her to smile at the memory. "His only concern was for his daughter's safety." Serina's mother beckoned us to follow her through the gate as Jamie and Serina pushed each other like kids at play.

The Vampire Queen ignored her children. Then, taking on the airs of her station, she continued to explain. "When we realized the vampire hiding in his home was none other than our daughter, we paid him a visit."

We passed into a vast entrance hall. The carpet was rich and luxurious, the tapestries exquisite. Between the opulence and the story, I felt like I was in a dream.

The queen continued. "Mage Caterous is a long friend of the vampires, so I asked him to look after you. He was happy to do so and keep up our ruse."

"That must be when he started treating me, not exactly kindly, but without malice." Serina frowned. "He knew who I was all this time." Serina grabbed Thorn's arm. "I'll have something to say to him when we find him."

"Wait . . ." I was confused. "When did you arrive at the house?" Serina had frequently told me about when Thorn was very young.

"She was there about a a decade before Thorn was born. Serina, I believe a thank-you would be in order." The mother turned to face her daughter. "As I must thank you. That Lieutenant Hume was starting to become a problem." The queen's glare turned stern. "Although we rarely destroy enemies now, although his attack on you justified your response, I would rather have seen him exiled with his followers. Oh well, too late now." She shrugged.

Serina stood stupefied until her brother pushed her to keep her moving.

"You would have known if you had been home," Jamie whispered.

Serina glared at him.

"Just saying . . ." He shrugged.

We stood outside two highly ornate doors flanked by royal guards. Serina's mother turned to her daughter. Though she was smiling, there were tears in her eyes. "I have missed you so much." She hugged Serina. Once she released her daughter, she pulled Thorn close. "I am so sorry about your father."

Thorn looked surprised.

"I know he must be in trouble if he sent you to us for safety." She cupped Thorn's face in her hands. "We will do what we can to help." A cloud descended over her face as she spoke. "No matter what my fool of a husband says."

Serina seemed to have recovered from the shock of being hugged. "Um . . . uh . . . thank you." She seemed confused, and for the first time I could recall, Serina didn't to know what to do. Queen Asha acted as if she hadn't noticed as we continued deeper into the fortress.

The guards nodded to the queen. I saw a look pass between them when they saw us, but they pushed open the heavy double doors in silence. Gazing up at the ornate ceiling and the beautifully carved woodwork, we slowly entered a long hall with a raised dais at the end. That was when I realized we had entered the grand throne room. I saw two vampires at the end of a long blood-red carpet leading up to two large thrones of different sizes and heights. Both thrones were covered in rich midnight-blue fabric.

The vampire named Zoban stood stooped, whispering into the ear of a regally dressed vampire seated in the smaller of the two ornate chairs. I assumed the seated vampire was the king and Serina's father. He waved away Zoban, who stood, bowed, then waited. The queen gave a subtle nod, which he returned and then left the throne room through a door to the right.

I swallowed my fear as Serina's father glared down at us. He had the face of a warrior and leader. His eyes were red and angry. When he opened his mouth to say something, I flinched instinctively. However, before he could get a word out, Serina's mother drifted past us to take the larger seat next to her husband. Her throne was actually above his, so she looked down at him disapprovingly.

"Serina, my darling daughter! You are home," Asha announced happily. "It has been too long since this chamber was filled with your smile."

"Serina's smile? Our Serina?" I whispered to Thorn, who replied by slapping my arm.

"I have missed you as well." Serina smiled uncertainly as she spoke.

"I see," her father grumbled. I felt his annoyance in the air. "And the first thing your daughter does when she returns is kill four royal guards." His voice grew in intensity as he glared at Serina.

"Quiet, Nicodemus." Asha dismissed her husband's anger as if she was waving away a wisp of smoke.

"You still defend her." King Nicodemus was on his feet now. But then, his full attention was on his wife. "Nothing has changed! She is still killing indiscriminately, and you still treat her like a naughty child."

"What the hell happened?" Thorn whispered to me. I could only shrug, being as clueless as she was. It was then I felt a presence behind us. Jamie ushered us close.

"My sister and mother were always very close." He glanced up. Serina stood with her head bowed as her father continued to berate her.

"Father used to dote on Serina." Something dark crossed Jamie's face. "She has always been strong with her Magic and weapons skills. She was always far ahead of anyone her age. However, her control over her Magic needed some attention."

"Jamie," Serina's mother interrupted. "Would you please see our guests are comfortable."

"Yes, My Queen." Jamie bowed as he beckoned to us.

We followed him to a table off to the side of the hall. He gestured, so we took seats. A servant arrived with several goblets, and Jamie whispered something to her. She placed one in front of Jamie and then disappeared with the rest. "You have to understand." He sipped from the cup. "The vampire clans have only been united for a few centuries. When our family came to power, the laws of domination still held sway."

The servant returned with wine, bread, and cheese for us. Scratch eyed Jamie's drink warily.

"Yes," Jamie held up the vessel. "This is blood. I did not think you would wish to partake."

"I thank you," Thorn replied, holding her glass in a toast. He inclined his head in response.

"When my parents became the rulers, it was through a vicious conflict. At the time, we ruled the Northlands Vampires." A visible shiver ran through him. "The Varato have always been *different*. They have a much more difficult time passing in the human realm. They are generally very tall and extremely gaunt. Their hands and feet are also very long and thin. Most have no hair—or very little—while their faces are gray and sallow."

He opened his mouth to show us his canine teeth. They elongated as we watched. "You see our teeth? We can hide them, but the Varato have sharp protruding front fangs." He tapped his front teeth as his fangs retracted to normal size. Then, he stared off, lost in a distant memory. "While the four points, if you will, began to tire of the constant bloodshed to end disagreements, the Varato reveled in it." He paused to take a sip. "It was this bloodlust that led to Serina running away."

"Jamie! We do not spread such prejudice." Asha's stern voice from behind caused me to jump so hard I banged into the table, sending our drinks teetering. Thorn recited a quick spell setting everything back to normal. I thanked her as I stood quickly, as did Scratch.

"Your Highness," I bowed.

"Please." She waved dismissively. "Sit." A regal chair was brought to the queen, and she took her place at the head of our table. "It was a dark time for the confederation. Our family was named ruler, but there is also the council. We sit at the head of the council, but more as referees and tiebreakers." She sighed. "Serina's father was always the more . . . *cultured* of us. My family is from the western warrior clan that fought against vampires, humans, elves, and other creatures. Our lands were hard-won and defended. We have a long distrust of the Southern Clans. They have cooperated with some of our enemies." She sighed. "The usual political intrigue and mistrust you find in all councils."

"Father is from the Northern Clans. While more interested in art, literature, and music, they are not to be underestimated in ferocity," Jamie interrupted. "I take after Father." He smiled proudly.

To my surprise, his mother also smiled happily and patted his hand. "Yes, you do." Then, her smile faded. "While Serina took after me. As the daughter of the Western Clans, I was brought up to be fearless and ruthless to our enemies."

"No disrespect," Thorn interrupted to ask the question. I desperately wanted to know the answer as well. "But, um, your highness, how did you and the king . . . um . . . was it arranged?"

The queen laughed. The effect was amazing. Her eyes lit up, and her smile was wide and genuine. When she spoke, the ice melted from her voice. "Oh no, not at all." She looked down at her steepled fingers, still smiling wistfully. "If you want the overly romantic version, we can call it forbidden love, and please, call me Asha."

Jamie threw up his hands. "Believe me. You do not want to hear it. So let us just leave it as opposites attract."

"Fortunately, it worked out." Asha smiled at her son. "Can you imagine if we had broken up?"

Jamie shuddered dramatically.

Again, the queen's smile faded. "Then again, the trouble it caused." Regret stole the warmth from her eyes. She was silent and still.

Jamie squeezed his mother's hand. "With their marriage, the Northern and Western Clans were united—at least it had the *appearance* of unity. However, our cousins can be a real pain in the ass."

Asha made a noise between disapproving and a stifled laugh.

"Mother, please, I am a hundred and sixteen. The Eastern Clan has always stayed out of sight and out of everyone's business. They are council members and highly respected. They value knowledge over interaction. Their knowledge of magic also makes them extremely capable of defending themselves. Although they prefer to hide their existence and live a simple life."

"They generally will remain neutral in any conflict between clans," Asha explained with a mixture of annoyance and respect in her tone. "However if our people are threatened, they will help defend us." She directed her gaze pointedly at Scratch.

"I was with the guard at Dayok, Ma'am. I have never sought to engage in combat with any vampires—or any non-humans, for that matter," Scratch replied nervously.

"It seems you hold no prejudice." Asha smiled at Scratch. "However, you should be warned. Not all inter-species relationships produce such results as this young beauty." She patted Thorn's arm. "Or last long enough to reach that stage."

Scratch did not react, yet it seemed he wanted to say something. I could only look between Thorn and Scratch. I was confused about what Asha was insinuating. Unfortunately, raised voices caused the queen to sigh heavily before I could ask what she meant. Serina had finally started to argue with her father. It was then that Thorn did something I could and would never do.

"That doesn't explain why Serina left," Thorn inquired, "or her deception." She finished a little bitterly.

"As I explained, my daughter was, and apparently still is, a fierce and talented warrior and Magic wielder." She glanced at the throne just in time to catch Serina's eye. I wondered how much she had heard. "What you are about to hear is not one of our—or *my*—finest hours. What you must understand . . ." She inhaled deeply. "Serina was acting out of loyalty to the kingdom and her family. It was not her fault what happened, nor were her parents' actions, who should have known better."

That's when I learned of Serina's past. The destruction of the Varato village, her time as a bounty hunter, and how she was used as a catalyst for war. The tale was long and, at times, painful for the queen to tell. However, Asha didn't deny details of how her reactions hurt Serina or her responsibility for her daughter's exile.

"I spent a long time trying to figure out what I did wrong," Serina mumbled behind her mother. "How you could think I would do something so horrid."

Asha exhaled as she slowly closed her eyes. "I was wrong," she whispered. "I do not know why I doubted you."

Thorn nudged me hard in the ribs. Scratch had already stood and was being led away by Jamie. They spoke loudly about an armory. Confused, I looked to Thorn. Her eyes told me to get up, but the queen began to speak again. "There were so many calling for war. After what had happened, I just wasn't sure you disagreed."

Serina stood rigidly behind her mother.

Asha opened her eyes. She studied her steepled fingers as she spoke. "I thought, either way, it was safer with you out of the Capital. I know how strong you are, and you were willing to do anything to win and prove we were not to be underestimated." Her head slowly shook. "I was so scared for you. What would happen if you stayed and they killed you?" Asha's hands trembled. "What if you stayed and argued for war? Either way, you would be used as a symbol, a rallying point."

"I did what you wanted. I ran away, and I stayed away," Serina lashed out. "All I ever wanted was to make you proud," she ended quietly.

"I have always been proud of you," her mother admitted. Silence ensued. I held my breath, waiting to see who would speak first. Another painful hit to my ribs made me grunt.

I glared at Thorn who returned it with vigor. "What?" I hissed.

"We should take a walk." She inclined her head toward the pair. I half rose from my seat when they spoke again.

"I envied you a little as well." Asha shrugged. "You were free."

"I was alone." Serina's head was bowed, and her voice was quiet. "I thought you were scared of me because of what I can do. I can kill so *easily*. I don't even have to touch someone." Serina was crying. "I thought you abandoned me."

"I did not have time to explain properly," Asha lamented.

"You sent me away." Serina's voice was barely a whisper. "It took me years to understand why. To understand that you were trying to protect me—at least, that's what I told myself, but . . ." Serina was breathing heavily as her mother stood before her. "Well, it didn't work! I became more powerful, and I learned to kill easily." She was shouting now. "I hate what I just did, I hate what I have done, I hate killing. I have killed so many, seen so much death."

"Yes, that first few months as a mercenary was brutal," the queen acknowledged. "I saw what I forced upon you. I am so sorry."

"If it weren't for you, I would have been here. I would have—wait, what?"

"I was wrong. I should never have forced you to such extremes. I should never have doubted you. I should have supported you then."

"Everyone thought I massacred a village."

"Yes, and I should never have let that happen. I was wrong." A tear formed in the queen's eye. "I caused you to leave and to feel like you could never return. I thought I was saving you from all of that pain and suspicion. I could not believe what I had done." Asha rose slowly, turning to face Serina and taking a single step toward her daughter, only stopping as Serina recoiled. "I wish I had never put you through that."

"If you knew where I was, why didn't you try to contact me?"

"I was afraid," Asha replied, barely above a whisper.

"Of me?" Serina asked, anger etched on her face.

"No, of this." She held her arms wide. "Of the fact that I did this to you. I made you hate me."

"I did, and I do," Serina announced, tears in her eyes. "I hate what you made me do. I had to live among those who hated us. I was never safe."

"I hate that too. I lost you, and I hated myself for it."

Finally, they hugged and cried.

"What the hell just happened?" I whispered.

"Family." Thorn shrugged.

"My family isn't like this," I mumbled. I regretted saying it. Thorn's mother had been absent for most of her life. "Sorry," I muttered, but Thorn waved away my apology.

"It could have been worse." She indicated the mother and daughter. "I don't think they ever really stopped loving each other." Thorn pulled me to my feet. "I doubt my mother ever loved my father or me."

I could only stand and watch her walk away.

"Go after her, you dummy," Serina said from her mother's shoulder.

By the time I reached her, Thorn had wiped away the tears. I could only see the redness left in her eyes.

"How long do you think we should wait here?" I asked because I couldn't think of anything better to say.

"Father sent us here." Thorn looked around at the darkness. Torchlight barely made a dent in the gloom. She moved closer. "I miss our house and the woods. I don't want to stay here."

"And no human or elf would blame you," King Nicodemus announced as he materialized from the darkness. "Your father left something in our care."

He grimaced before finishing his thought. "In case he needed it." Serina and the queen approached. Both faces held a look of confusion. "That is a private matter. Bring the human male. Scratch, is it?"

Serina nodded.

"We will meet in my private study." As the king left, I noted suspicion in Asha's eyes. The appearance of two guards only increased the ball of foreboding in my stomach.

CHAPTER 32

We were led deeper into the fortress, down several flights of stairs, and through several corridors. My paranoia kept my brain thinking we were being led to the dungeons or our death. Finally, we reached a door and entered the king's study. The room was smaller than I expected. Our escort indicated we sit at a table and wait. Scratch and I exchanged nervous glances. Serina whispered something to him. Instantly the tension left his shoulders, and a relieved smile crept up his face. I waited, but she didn't share with Thorn and me. I was about to voice my annoyance when Thorn gasped, rising to her feet. The king entered the room carrying an ancient book. It was huge, covered in deep red leather binding. The pages were composed of thick parchment. I remembered moving similar books in Caterous's library when I was younger and struggling under the weight. Tears appeared on Thorn's cheeks as the king handed her the tome. I half expected her to drop it. Instead, silently, Thorn returned to her seat. Her hands shook as she traced the sigil on the cover.

"H-how did you come to have this?" Thorn's voice was barely a whisper.

I felt more than saw the queen ushering Serina and Scratch to follow her. I wondered why they had called us all here in the first place. King Nicodemus seemed to hesitate. I slowly pushed my chair back, but Thorn's hand found my forearm. Her touch was light but held me firmly at her side. With a nod from the king, the others left the room.

"Your father left this in my care when he came through recently." Nicodemus remained standing. "I have not opened it. That is only for you." He backed slowly into the shadows. "I will leave you now."

I heard a door click shut but couldn't stop looking at Thorn. Her head was down, one hand on my arm, the other caressing the rich embossed leather cover.

"What was that all about?" I whispered, not expecting an answer.

"This is Father's Grimoire." Her voice felt small and frightened.

I know my gasp didn't help. A Grimoire is not something a mage would easily be parted from. I had assumed it was back at the house. That's where mine was. But, of course, my few years as a mage's apprentice cumulated in barely a pamphlet. I'd seen Thorn's once, which was the size of a novel. Lord Caterous's was huge.

Grimoires are made of enchanted parchment that chronicled the deeds and achievements of the mage. It also contained the research and discoveries written down by the mage themselves. Mine was primarily handwritten.

I felt the warmth of Thorn's hand leave my arm. Sitting up while pulling the book toward her, she exhaled. I thought it best to leave her alone. I had barely moved when she spoke.

"Stay." It wasn't an order or a request. She needed someone to share this with her, yet I was surprised it was me. Still, I moved my chair closer to hers. The thick leather binding creaked as she opened the cover to reveal an envelope on the first page. Elegant handwriting told us it was addressed to Thorn. That didn't surprise me. However, when she retrieved her note, there was another folded piece of parchment. Both notes were closed with a black wax seal.

The second note was addressed to me.

Each of us held our envelopes, the quizzical look on her was mirrored in my own. Flipping the envelopes over, we both saw the words, *For you only.* We exchanged apologetic smiles as we opened our letters.

Henry,

I have always been proud to have you as an apprentice. You have more power than you allow yourself to be aware of. It is time you embrace your abilities, as you will need them for the road ahead. Thorn, my precious daughter, will require you, and I trust you to help and protect her. I know she is dear to you as well. You must step out of her shadow. She is quite capable. Stay with the vampires as long as you need to. Practice your Magic and learn theirs. You will need all the power and knowledge you can gather for what lies ahead.

Your Teacher and Friend,
Lawrence Caterous

I looked at Thorn, my mouth hanging open. I immediately held my letter out to her, accepting hers in exchange. We smiled, knowing we would always show each other.

My Dearest Sume,

I know you will share this with Henry, even though this is for you only. At one time, that might have dissuaded me from writing what I felt. That time has passed, and I am sorry. Your mother disapproved of affection. She thought it would make you soft. I see now it only made you sad. I should have hugged you every day. I should have always encouraged you, helped you, and told you how proud of you I have always been. I am leaving my Grimoire with you for safekeeping. I fully expect to reclaim it. For now, please work with Henry.

You must continue to learn from each other and your friends. Nicodemus, the Vampire King, has agreed to keep you safe until you are ready to come find me. I am going to stop your mother. I hoped she had changed. But, alas, I was deceived. She is not who you think she is. She is something far worse. I wish I could curse the day I agreed to be her guardian, but I cannot. If I had not, then you would never have come into being. I will never regret a moment you have been with me.

I know you and Henry have grown close. Please know that I trust you both to focus on the task ahead. We will need to have a long talk when we see each other again. For now, trust and look after each other. You will need to work together. When you are ready, head north to the Capital. You will find it unwelcoming, so you will need to disguise yourself. Go to the Inn of the Cyclops. I will leave further instructions there.

Your loving Father.

I handed back the letter. The question formed on my lips and escaped before I could entirely compose it. "Your dad is giving us a quest." I thought for a second. "Why does he need us to find him?"

Thorn shook her head at me. "Because he believes someone will try to stop him." She grabbed my hand, the note crumpling, as she said, "We need to go now."

"No, wait a second." I couldn't believe what I was saying, "We need to prepare first. He said to train, to learn the vampires' Magic."

"Serina can train us on the way."

"He said to *practice*," I argued.

"Scratch can help you with your sword training. Even though you could best him if you just let yourself believe it." She was up, pacing.

"No." I stood. I rarely challenged her. It was clear from the beginning that she was the leader. We all followed her. Serina was the only one who ever called Thorn's ideas into question. Even then, it was rare her mind could be changed.

"No, I mean it. You need to get over your insecurities."

"That isn't what I'm saying. You aren't thinking this through," I said in a voice I hoped held some conviction. "We're just going to march across the lands of Notelek? An elf, a half-elf, a vampire, and a human? What are we going to say when we run into soldiers? We're his prisoners?"

"Not all humans hate elves."

"No, just most," I argued. "How many came to help us when the inspector beat us? You may be a half-elf, but that doesn't help anything. I guess it's good you look more elf than human, but . . ." I looked her over. It isn't like I'd looked at her closely every day, but this time I tried to appraise her appearance as others would see her. "Yes, you could pass as one of us."

"It would be easy to act like an elf," she growled at me. "Oh, peace and harmony with nature, please dominate us," she said in a wispy laid-back voice. "We would totally not care if you grind us into the dirt."

Her words hurt. I knew there were warriors among us—my parents, for instance. Thorn knew not all elves were so subdued.

"Oh, look at me, even though I have pointy ears and purple hair, I'm human, yay, money and war. I hope I can dominate the whole world." I shot back at her. "Good luck being accepted by the superior race."

She looked shocked.

I don't know why, but I kept going, "Or is it because you're a mage? Fear me, oh weak mortals."

"You know you're a jerk, right?" She glared at me with hands on her hips. "The Capital is full of all kinds of creatures. The further you travel from the city, the more ignorant the people become. We'll be fine."

"The emperor is the one who controls the army. Remember that guy who tried to kill us, oh, and destroyed my house and came to take us away?"

Thorn unconsciously rubbed her head just above the hairline. "They all can't be like that."

"I heard the Capital is more accepting, but it still isn't welcoming." I couldn't believe I had to explain this to her. "Don't you remember what I told you the last time I went home? About my cousin from one of the Dagar? How you never travel alone?" I frowned at her. "You could be stopped and searched for just being non-human."

"There are so many non-humans in the Capital. It would be difficult to stop all of them," she countered.

"We need to prepare." I wanted to stop going down this road. I hated the way we were treated. I was grateful she hadn't been exposed to that kind of hate, and I would be there when it finally reared its ignorant head. "I want you to realize that people are going to hate you. For being an elf, not being an elf, for being a mage." I took her hand. "Thorn, they won't see who you are or your beauty. They'll only see your differences." I know my eyes went wide as I dropped her hand and the blush burned my face.

A look of shock was there and gone instantly from Thorn's features. "You're sweet, but I understand the danger." Thorn's hand cupped my face for a second. "We have to find my father." Then, before she could leave me with my embarrassment, the door swung open.

"We'll go after Lord Caterous," Serina explained, "only after we prepare."

"How did you know?" Thorn asked. A frown crossed her face. "Oh, right, your damned batlike ears."

"They aren't as pointy as yours." Serina laughed, pushing Thorn's shoulder. She glanced at me. I felt my face go red again.

"Hey," Scratch pushed into the room. "Serina says we're going to learn some vampire combat skills." He could barely hide his excitement. "You know, before we go save Thorn's dad."

Frustration brewed in Thorn's eyes. Her shoulders slumped in defeat as she faced a united front. "Fine, I'll give it a week." She turned to glare at me. "After that, I'm leaving with or without you—all of you." Her attention fell on Serina and Scratch, who had been quietly celebrating.

"I'm not saying we won't go with you," I protested, "I just think we need to be prepared. Also, your dad *did* say to take the time we need."

"So?" Thorn demanded.

"So . . ." I tried to use a soothing tone, "he must be safe. He wanted us ready to take on whatever danger we'll face."

"We will be." The statement held finality. "So let's get started." I was startled, while Scratch and Serina seemed thrilled. After hearing about Serina's training, I was concerned for our well-being. It seemed like we might not survive the rigors of Serina's instruction.

CHAPTER 33

O ur stay with the vampires was longer than Thorn wanted but less time than I'd have preferred. It turned out to be three weeks of intensive combat and magic training, nothing like I learned from Mom, Dad, Scratch, Thorn, or Caterous—combined. Serina's training was intense and overbearing, if I'm being truthful. She was the harshest taskmaster I could ever have anticipated. I assume the gleam in her eyes only hinted at the fire that had been there when she was with the guard. Her brother, Jamie, would laugh at our complaints and sympathize with our failures.

"This is nothing. My sister is seriously going easy on you," he liked to say.

Scratch took extra lessons from both of the siblings, and he spent an extra two hours per day working privately with Jamie. For some reason, that time annoyed Serina. I preferred the Magic lessons I got from Asha and a vampire named Lydia. However, my private lessons with Lydia caused some trouble for me.

"You're spending a lot of extra time with—what's her name, Lydia?" Thorn said one afternoon.

"Yeah, she's a great teacher," I explained, not realizing I'd just stepped into a hornet's nest.

"That's great. I'm glad you found someone you can so easily learn from." But unfortunately, Thorn's tone didn't match her words.

"Well, you seem to enjoy the private lessons from the guard captain," I retorted. It was a pathetic attempt to show her hypocrisy. The captain was obviously much older and far too grizzled. Lydia, however, was attractive and free with hugs and touching my shoulders and hands. I can't say I didn't enjoy the attention, but I knew there was nothing behind it.

Thorn didn't see it the same way. "Be careful. Lydia might be after your life force." She turned her back on me. "Although you might like that."

I tried to call after Thorn, but she disappeared through a hidden passage.

During our brief stay with the vampires, Thorn learned to be extremely stealthy and hard to follow. I found myself growling at a blank wall more than once while trying to have a conversation with her.

After our disagreement about the Capital and forcing her to stay longer than she wanted, Thorn had been hard to talk to. On top of that, we spent so much time training, I barely saw my friends except when our training schedules overlapped or at mealtime. When we ate, we were all too tired to talk.

Thorn reached the end of her patience after a month, and announced she was ready to leave alone if she had to. It might have been a coincidence or my imagination. Still, her announcement came after a successful spell attempt by me that ended with a rather tight hug from Lydia.

We said our goodbyes to the royal family and thanked them for their hospitality. Serina and her father spent several minutes in hushed conversation before we left. Scratch watched with a tense hand upon the pommel of his sword. Jamie placed a cautioning hand on Scratch's shoulder. A collective exhale spread through our group when Serina and Nicodemus briefly hugged.

"Not what I hoped for," Asha sighed, "but it could have been worse." Then, to my surprise, she hugged Thorn, shook my hand, and, shockingly, kissed Scratch on the cheek. "Take care of each other." Asha smiled as Serina joined us. "I look forward to seeing you again." We bowed and turned to leave.

"A word, Master Heraldry," Nicodemus called. Asha gave Scratch's shoulder a reassuring squeeze before she pushed him forward. Then she held Serina back to allow the two men to talk.

"Will he be okay?" Serina questioned.

"Which one?" Asha shrugged.

Whatever the Vampire King said to Scratch, he didn't seem concerned, more embarrassed. Scratch wouldn't tell us what was said, no matter how much Serina pestered him. So, we left feeling ready and excited to continue our journey. Unfortunately, the feeling didn't last. Now we were too cold to speak.

"I never thought I would miss the dark of the vampire kingdom," Thorn complained, "but I would trade the darkness of that place over the cold and dark out here." Snow fell heavily over the trail and on our carriage. Thorn was bundled under blankets while Scratch was driving under several coats and wrapped in a scarf. Serina had disappeared again. I didn't say anything. I shivered under as many coats or blankets as I could find. I swear it wouldn't have been as cold in the wagon if Lydia hadn't kissed me on the cheek when we left. I swear she looked right at Thorn when she did it. When I tried to explain to Thorn that it was nothing, the temperature dropped about a hundred degrees.

I stayed silent as Thorn tried to create an element to keep us warm. The canvas covering of the wagon barely kept the wind out. Thorn was becoming extremely frustrated, so I decided to join Scratch. I sat huddled deep in my blankets and jackets beside Scratch in the driver's seat. The cold didn't seem to bother him as much.

"I bet you wouldn't shiver as much if Lydia were here," Scratch teased.

Thorn swore loudly behind us. She tried to play it off as frustration with the spell.

Ignoring his teasing, I asked Scratch how he wasn't freezing. He shrugged and said, "I spent so many cold nights on guard duty. I guess you get used to it." I didn't think I'd ever get used to it as my teeth chattered. Then he said something that added a shudder to my shivering. "You know, the higher we go in these mountains, the colder it'll get."

This information didn't improve my already gloomy mood. I grumbled an apology and went into the back to see if I could help Thorn with the incantations. She grudgingly allowed my assistance.

I'd only been back there about half an hour before we were thrown forward in a tangle of limbs and blankets. Extricating ourselves from the covers and each other, Thorn and I exchanged an embarrassed glance, which quickly turned to concern. Something wasn't right. Cursing at Scratch to watch the road, I opened the flap to see what was happening.

"Where's Scratch?" Thorn asked over my shoulder.

The driver's seat was empty. Snow quickly filled in the place where our friend had been. The confused horses stamped in the snow as they looked for something to eat. I crawled onto the driver's seat while Thorn jumped out the back. The snow had been disturbed on the canvas, and there were signs of a struggle.

"Thorn," I shouted, "did you find anything? Did he fall off?"

"No, I think he was lifted off." She shouted as she ran toward the front. "Where's that damn vampire when I need her!"

"I don't see any blood." I noticed something as I investigated. "Hey, what do you think made this?" I pointed to four long scratches on the wood of the driver's seat.

"Just a second." Thorn disappeared into the wagon momentarily. I heard her rummaging through our bags. When she returned, she held a crystal on a string and chanted. Silently I cursed myself for not thinking of this. The crystal would show us the aura of the person or creature that had left the marks. Slowly it grew blue. That indicated a human. Then it faded to all red. "Vampire." Thorn cocked her head to the side. I shared her confusion.

"Maybe . . . you know . . ." I started awkwardly. I wasn't sure how or if I wanted to voice my thought. I plowed on without looking at Thorn's face. "Maybe Serina just wanted to be alone with Scratch . . . um . . . you know."

"And leave us without a driver on a mountain road that could have bandits?" She frowned at me. "I don't believe she'd do that just for a little alone time with him."

"So, you think something is going on between them too?" I was surprised.

"Is now really the time? Grab our weapons while I see if I can figure out where he was taken." She rummaged in her pocket for a moment, pulling out a different crystal. She hung it from another string and tied a few pine twigs onto it. It was a locating charm. She looked back at me. "Just in case."

I knew what she meant. It was in case she couldn't find the wagon tracks in the ever-deepening snow.

I groaned as I pulled out the weapons. Thorn's sword felt heavier than mine. I struggled with my crossbow, short sword, and both her blades. Although I awkwardly held my staff with my elbow and tried my best, one of her scabbards was inevitably dragged through the snow. Thorn spared me a look of disapproval at my care of her weapons. It lasted an instant. I followed her footprints and the disappearing wagon tracks back along the road. I barely saw the horses and wagon through the falling snow when I reached her. Thron held a blue orb that levitated above her palm.

"This is where he was taken," Thorn explained as she pulled her swords onto her back.

"Are we sure it was a vampire?" I asked. "The light is weak, but it's still daylight."

"I think it was a harpy." I had to shield my face from the added wind of Serina's wingbeats. I couldn't see her face as she was covered from head to toe in a long robe. Some smoke rose from her wings as she pulled them under the cloak. Thorn pulled a small vial out of her bag, handing it to Serina. After drinking it, Serina exhaled in relief. "Thank you, I *hate* burning."

"Yes!" Thorn yelled, slamming a fist into her open palm. "I should have seen. The red was less fire, more sunset." I, of course, had just thought it was red. Nuance in color wasn't one of my strong points. Then, as if she read my mind, Thorn turned to me. "There are various hues, you know." I threw my hands up in surrender.

I thought for a moment, puzzled. Then, the question came out before I could think it through. "Why didn't he kill it?" I cringed. It was wrong to call the Harpy an *it*. She had as much right to live as I did. But, my speciesism aside, Serina questioned the same thing.

"Maybe he thought she was someone else," Thorn offered. Immediately she continued, catching the glare from under Serina's hood. "Damn it. I'm not saying all fanged flying women look alike!" she shouted at Serina. "It's snowing, he's tired, and maybe he was just hoping to see a familiar face."

"So, this is my fault?"

"Wait, what?" Thorn demanded.

"I'm sorry." Serina threw her hands up in frustration. She quickly withdrew them, leaving smoke trails in the air. Thorn handed her another vial. "I just—it's my fault." Then, her shoulders slumped. "They took him to get back at me for killing that bastard Smith."

"Who did?" I asked.

"The vampires who want a war—the ones who tried to frame Serina twice," Thorn answered for me.

"Okay," I said, clapping my hands together. "Let's go and get our boy back. Thoughts on where they'd take him?"

"There is no need to hurt your puny brains," a rough cackling female voice called. "I will let you know exactly where I took him." A blue-gray harpy hovered above us, her wings barely making a sound over the blowing snow.

On instinct, I raised my crossbow. Thorn pushed it down.

"Good girl," the harpy laughed harshly. "If the dumb elf kills me, you'll never find your precious human."

CHAPTER 34

"Oh great, we're back in a cave," Thorn growled as we were led into yet another cold dark recess in the mountains. Thorn's and Serina's anger emanated through the chill. I wondered if the harpy had any idea how much trouble she was in. I was also angry and scared for Scratch and myself. I wasn't concerned for the women's safety—only for the damage and death they might cause.

"At least we're out of the snow," I offered lamely, trying to ease some tension.

"I see your choice of companions has not improved with age." The harpy laughed sharply as she waved vaguely in my direction. "This one seems very dim."

"I hope you're close enough to your friends, as you'll share their death," Serina threatened. The harpy laughed. I was aware of watching eyes and several pairs of hurried feet heading back the way we came.

"I think some of these vampires may be aware of who they're dealing with," Thorn smirked.

"Or," the harpy turned in midair to glare at her, "they are cutting off your escape. Elves and humans are cowards. So I can only imagine how terrified a half-breed like you must be."

"Of a stupid talking bird and some long-toothed cave dwellers? Oooh ahh, so scary." Thorn hugged herself theatrically. "Oh, no offense."

"You called me a talking bird! I take offense."

"I wasn't talking to you." Thorn turned her attention to Serina, whose grim expression hinted at a smile.

"None taken."

"Enough!" Exposing her sharp teeth, the harpy landed in front of Thorn, her talons scraping loudly on the stone floor. "I was tasked with bringing the princess to the leader. That means I do not have to keep *you* alive." She screeched as she sprang into the air, then straight at Thorn.

I dove to the floor as a torrent of flame shot toward Thorn's attacker. I threw my hands over my head to block out the heat, roaring fire, and agonized screaming. When silence settled in the room, my nose was filled with the stench of burnt flesh. Slowly, I opened my eyes and yelped, jumping away from a blackened, smoldering skull and bones, all that was left of the harpy. From my knees, I looked up at Thorn. She held an orb of burning energy that reminded me of the sun.

"I am Thorn Caterous," Thorn announced. I stared in awe at the authority in her voice. "I am the daughter of the Grand Mage Caterous." She paused as a ripple of whispers ran through the shadows. "You have one of my companions and are threatening another." The orb grew slightly more prominent. I heard hisses from the darkness like a thousand angry snakes. Serina slipped on her gloves as she pulled her cloak over her head. "You have interrupted my journey." When Thorn made this announcement, a blast of light flew out in a circle from the orb. The flash illuminated the cave and the hundreds of vampires hiding in the blackness.

Gasps of pain and surprise followed the light. "I demand to speak to the one in charge." A brighter, longer blast of light pulsed out. Screams of agony and fear filled the cavern. "I demand the return of our companion!" Now the orb began to expand. A vampire caught in an outcropping could not escape the growing sun. Forever in my mind, I will see that creature thrashing. I still hear the cries of fear and agony sometimes late at night.

"Stop! Stop!" a voice called. "Our quarrel is not with the House of Caterous."

The expanding circle of light paused. "You have made it a quarrel with me by taking my friend and attacking me." Thorn sent a ray of light high above us to where we thought the voice emanated. The ray lit up the cave wall. Rock exploded, raining down over the stone floor. Silence followed, pierced only by the whimpering smoldering of the vampire Thorn burned on the ledge.

"Chivred attacked of her own accord. For that, I apologize." A tall gaunt creature emerged into the pool of light emanating from the globe in Thorn's hand. From the flinch of his cheeks and the clench of his jaw, I could tell the solaris spell hurt him. The bone-white skin, long fingers, and overall pallor of death told me he was a Varatu. "I am Orloc. I shall return your companion unharmed." Scratch stumbled out of the darkness, nearly falling. Orloc chuckled. "Well, mostly unharmed. He seemed a bit too tempting for some of my followers."

A hiss from under Serina's hood removed the smirk from Orloc's face. I
rushed to my friend's aid, pulling him deeper into the safety of the light. Scratch
leaned heavily against me. Serina's thick glove gripped his shoulder lightly. His
shaking hand moved to squeeze hers reassuringly.

"Prince Orloc," Serina spoke, her voice quivering with anger. "I understand
your anger toward my family and me."

"Do you?" he spat, his eyes glowing red in the darkness. "That village was
where my son lived. They wanted nothing but peace. They wanted to live and
let live, and you *murdered* them." He pointed a long ghostly white finger at
her.

"What happened there was not my doing!" Serina spat angrily. Then her
voice softened. "I am, however, to blame." Serina bowed to Orloc. His hand,
still pointing accusingly, shook. A look of confusion crossed his face. Serina
continued, "I must live with what happened to those innocents. I know that
comes as little comfort for you." As she spoke, her body bowed lower, but her
voice remained firm. "Why should you care what I live with as your child is
dead? I cannot undo the evil done in my name and as a means to start a war."

"Y-you admit your actions were evil!" Orloc countered uncertainly.

"Yes, I do. I should have seen the traitors in my midst. I should have acted
before so many had to die. I was warned to avoid the expedition." Serina seemed
to struggle momentarily. "It cost me, my friend, my family. . . ." She whispered
in pain, barely audible in the cave. Then she spoke clearly. "I understand you
have the right to end my life."

Scratch and Thorn immediately protested.

Serina quieted them with a wave. "I accept this. I know it makes nothing
better, nor will it make you whole, but know I am truly sorry for what happened." Serina dropped her hood. Her pain must have been excruciating. Thorn
pulled the light back to decrease Serina's discomfort. Serina didn't react. Instead,
she kept her eyes on Orloc's. "I failed to stop the violence, and I failed you and
your son." She pulled her sword from its scabbard.

Panicked movement and gasps erupted around us until Serina lay the blade
in front of her, bowing. Then, ignoring the protests of Thorn, Scratch, and
me, Serina got down on her knees and bowed her head, exposing her neck. I
shouted as she held the weapon by the blade, presenting it to Orloc. Her grip
was so tight, blood dripped from the tip. Her shoulders shook.

Orloc's fingers closed on the hilt as he looked down at her. When she felt
his grasp on the weapon, she let go, letting her hands fall palm up onto the
floor. Deep cuts bled freely on her hands. An angry-looking female vampire

rushed out to pull Serina's hood further away, then pushed Serina's flaming hair aside to expose her pale neck.

"No, no, not happening," Thorn began muttering.

Scratch pushed off me to grab Thorn's arms, keeping her from casting her Sunfire.

"This is her choice," he hissed. I heard the pain and sadness in his voice. "She has to make amends."

"I hope, one day, you can forgive me," Serina said to Orloc and us. "Please, please let my friends continue on their journey. Their only crime was being in my company."

"They die," the vampire that had removed her hood spat. "They killed our harpy and one of us. A death for a death. That is the way of things as it always shall be." Her words abruptly halted in a gurgle of blood, a look of surprise and confusion on her face. Her eyes flew back and forth as her mouth opened and closed for a second. Then, slowly her head slipped off her neck. It hit the ground with the sound of a pumpkin dropping from the roof. I looked from the severed head to Orloc. He held Serina's sword slightly behind him at the end of the follow-through. His face was filled with disgust.

"I have waited years for vengeance." He looked down at Serina, who remained bowed, waiting for her fate. "I wanted to hear you beg me. I wanted to see you understand you were wrong." The blade clanged on the ground. "You realized it on your own."

"Our clan has treated you poorly in the past. My family does not wish to have you as adversaries. They were not behind the attack." Serina's head came up just a bit. "However, I fear we took something I can never replace from you."

"That is something I will never forget." He held out a hand to her. "I will forgive and maybe even begin to believe it was not on your orders." Hisses of dissent filled the cavern. Orloc pulled Serina to her feet. "I do not wish to continue our fight." He bowed to Thorn. Something passed between them. If you were to ask, I'd say it was understanding. Not forgiveness or friendship, but perhaps the beginning of healing. Orloc looked up and announced, "They are free to leave."

Cries erupted in the darkness.

"No!"

"You promised us death to their rule."

"Traitor!"

"I have what I wanted," Orloc shouted to his followers. "Do what you wish, but they will not be harmed."

The sound of rushing feet and wings told us they weren't likely to listen. I pulled Scratch along as Thorn burned a path to the entrance. I glanced back to see Serina bow once more to Orloc, who returned it. He then disappeared as a sword swung through the empty air where he had been. Serina's wings expanded as she flew backward, the leathery skin of her wing slapping lightly on my head as her arms encircled Scratch, flying him to safety. Unencumbered, I ran to catch up to Thorn.

Pain blossomed between my shoulders, and I fell hard to my knees, throwing my arms out to catch myself. Unfortunately, my face still slapped painfully against the stone.

"You die now, elf," a voice rasped above me. I turned my head to see a spear being raised above me. Hatred and ruthless determination marred the face of the vampire holding the weapon.

"NO!" Thorn screamed.

The weight on my back lightened but didn't completely disappear. I rolled over and cried out as I saw nothing but the vampire's leg from the knee down. Thorn had incinerated the rest of him. She pulled me, dazed and stumbling, to my feet, and we broke out of the cave entrance. I moaned in despair as we realized night was falling.

"We'll never get away!" I accepted defeat.

I heard the clattering of hooves announcing the approach of our wagon. Serina drove like the devil toward us.

"Help me," Thorn shouted, spinning me around and pointing at the cave entrance. I could have slapped myself, except she'd done it for me.

I sent several spells against the roof of the cave. The stone exploded, sending rocks tumbling, sealing the entrance, then Thorn used her sun blast to melt the stones into a thick wall.

The wagon wasn't slowing. We would have to catch it as Serina sped past. I was still unsteady from my fall, and panic burned in my chest. Thorn grabbed my arm as my feet left the ground. She must have used a levitation spell on me. I flew around to land next to Scratch in the back of the wagon.

Groggily, he looked up at me. "I didn't know she could fly too," he exclaimed, wide-eyed. Then he shrugged. "Maybe she can just jump really well." He ended up mumbling the last words as he lay back down.

I looked at the opening to see Thorn hanging desperately onto the back of the wagon. I hurried to help her get inside, throwing my hands around her shoulders and pulling her into the wagon. She landed on top of me, and her arms still held me tightly. My heart pounded as she slowly raised her head. I swallowed. Our lips were inches apart, and her eyes searched mine.

"Are you guys going to kiss?" Scratch laughed, his eyes unfocused. His face held a foolish grin.

"Sorry, I tried to sedate him so he'd recover faster," Serina called from the driver's seat.

The moment gone, Thorn pushed herself upright. I took her hand as she pulled me up next to her. "I'll take care of him. Just get us out of these mountains," Thorn called.

Together we brewed a potion to help Scratch sleep and one to help heal the burns Serina had sustained. Serina must have used some of her power on the horses as they thundered along untiring. Their eyes glowed red and it seemed as if their hooves didn't touch the ground. We reached the other side of the mountain in roughly two hours. It should have taken at least another two days.

Once we were below the snow line, Serina called me. "Take . . . take over the reins." She slumped against me as soon as I sat beside her. The horses had slowed to a canter, breathing heavily. "I need to rest," she muttered.

I caught her before she fell, and Thorn pulled her into the back to lay next to Scratch.

After fleeing the vampires at breakneck speed, we found a place to camp. It was late into the night as I sat gazing into the fire, stiff and sore from the fight. Thorn had applied a healing balm to my back where the vampire's armor had gouged into me.

I glanced back at the wagon where Scratch had been asleep for hours. Serina was still resting as well. I thought Thorn had fallen asleep until her hand lightly touched my arm.

"It's okay—you can rest now," she whispered.

I just shook my head.

"Please," she said, slipping a small vial into my hand. "This will help."

CHAPTER 35

It had been a week since we escaped the mountains. I still wasn't sleeping well, and it was starting to show. I nodded off while driving and ended up off the road, deep in the woods. We lost half a day trying to navigate back. Once we were back on the path, it was another day before we discovered it wasn't the correct one. Between Serina's flight to escape the vampires, my exhaustion, and the fact that none of us knew exactly where we were going, we had become increasingly lost.

"Where the hell are we?" Scratch grumbled as he rummaged through a pile of maps. "And where the hell is Serina when we need her?"

I had to agree with his annoyance. Even though it was my fault, we were lost, a fact Thorn reminded me of several times a day. The lack of progress to the Capital was starting to wear on her. The problem was that Serina received a message asking her to return home.

Orloc had appeared at the vampire council and requested Serina as his advocate. When he left the separatist vampires, they decided to attack the other Varatos. The attack led to more vampires joining the separatist. We couldn't fault her for returning with the vampire nation on the brink of an all-out civil war, but it did mean we lost our scout and navigator.

"We're starting to run low on supplies, it's cold, and I haven't slept in a bed in weeks," Scratch grumbled.

"Nor have you had a bath in that same amount of time," Thorn muttered. "You either."

"Yet you still smell like a summer rose," I replied facetiously.

"A summer rose left out in the rain under a pile of hot garbage, maybe." Scratch's lack of subtlety cost him several well-placed punches and a few slaps. "Hey, hey, ow! Hold on, does this look familiar?"

Thorn stopped the onslaught long enough to look over his shoulder. He was pointing to an area on a tattered old map.

"That could be the tri-fork we passed." Thorn moved to get a better look, pulling the map toward her.

"Always has to be in charge," I whispered to Scratch, earning a second of scornful glare.

"If it wasn't for you," Thorn growled, "we wouldn't be lost in the first place."

I'd had enough of the blame. I ignored Thorn and her lack of including Serina. I pointed at the map. "That's definitely the mountain we passed." I studied the crude drawing. "I don't recall that large tree, though."

"This map is over two hundred years old." Thorn traced the road. "Things might have changed in that time." Her finger stopped on drawings of several buildings. Under them was some Old Elvish I couldn't read. "I think this is Low Elvish." Thorn chewed on the inside of her cheek. "If my translation is correct, it reads, Haven."

"It's not that far. Assuming it's still inhabited, we might be able to get resupplied there," Scratch pondered aloud. "And our faces aren't posted on wanted posters all over town."

"I don't know . . ." I frowned. "Two centuries ago, the elves were still fighting in some places." My finger traced the Low Elvish. "Low elves were disagreeable even in times of peace."

"Haven," Scratch pointed out.

"Maybe," Thorn looked nervous. "It might mean Hellmouth. My ancient Low Elvish is rusty."

"That's surprising," I said sarcastically.

"Why?" Scratch asked.

"Because the low elves were almost entirely wiped out," Thorn replied. She pulled the map entirely away from us now. "Okay, this might be a warning." She held out part of the map with something scrawled along the edge. This elvish I could read.

Some of the words were blotted and torn. "*All*, something, *welcome at the* . . . I can't make it out, but then it reads, *price of life*."

"Okay, that doesn't sound ominous. . . ." Scratch rubbed the scruff on his chin. Thorn opened a cask to show us the meager contents. "Well, maybe it's gotten better in the last century."

The discussion ended with us silently agreeing to visit the place marked on the map.

The sun was already setting when we saw the first evidence of a town. "Can't say much for the suburbs," Scratch joked. We passed several houses that were falling in on themselves. Broken and scattered furniture and a few wagons littered the front gardens. Occasionally we'd see scrawny wild dogs running behind the houses or across the rough pocked road. "Not much upkeep on a road to abandoned houses," he noted.

"This area might be abandoned, but look." Thorn pointed to just above the trees ahead. Darkness was falling fast, but above the outline of the swaying trees, we could see the orange flicker of a fire.

"Let's hope that's a warm, welcoming glow." I tried to sound cheerful as discomfort crawled up my spine. Not much was said as we drew closer to the light. We passed through a tree line to a large clearing where a cliff face rose from the flat plain as if the side of a mountain had been cut away. Running straight out from the cliff stood a high wooden and stone wall. It was at least twenty feet tall. We could see places where archers or other defenders could attack enemies all along its length.

"I'm starting to think it isn't all that welcoming." I pointed to the gate ahead.

Two massive doors showed evidence of withstanding onslaught. One huge door was shut as if it no longer moved. The other door was only open wide enough for one person at a time to enter.

"Doesn't look like we can get the wagon in there," Scratch pointed out. "Hey, why don't we use that place for tonight." He pointed to a house far less dilapidated than most we'd seen. Thorn made a noncommital noise as the building leaned so precariously that a strong wind would blow it over.

"I don't see anyone on the walls or the gate," Thorn remarked nervously.

"See that mark?" Scratch pointed to something carved on the closed door. A brassier's light flickered below it, making it visible in the gathering gloom. "That's a mercenary guild mark."

"A guild is reassuring," Thorn exhaled relief.

"Not necessarily. Mercenaries aren't above being bounty hunters." Scratch guided our wagon to the wreck of a house. A falling-down barn quickly concealed all our meager earthly possessions.

"So either of you could be worth something to them," Thorn laughed, "while I would only be worth half either way."

"You're a mage," Scratch pointed out.

"You're also a beautiful woman," I said before I could stop myself. "There's no telling what those ruffians would do to you."

Scratch looked Thorn over as if he'd just realized she was female. "You think she's pretty?" Scratch asked. "She's all right—a bit on the skinny side."

I was again shocked by his obliviousness. He was shocked at how hard Thorn could hit. "Ow, what was that for?"

"Gods, you're an idiot," I said, pushing him before us as we left the barn. Then, standing out in the night, the three of us pulled our cloaks up to cover our heads. "This is a bad idea," I breathed.

"Starving is also a bad idea," Thorn informed me as she passed. Scratch and I had to hurry to catch up before she reached the gate.

"Either this place is so peaceful they don't need guards or," Scratch adjusted his cloak for easier access to his sword, "it's so bad, they don't care who enters."

"Sure would be nice if we had someone who could fly to check it out for us," I grumbled. Scratch paused as if he wanted to say something but thought better. I realized I'd annoyed him and didn't push the matter. Instead, I silently followed him as we passed through the opening between the doors. It didn't look as if they'd been moved in years.

The first thing to hit us was the smell. It was a mixture of an open sewer, field workers at the end of a summer day, and stale spilled beer. Thorn's hand came up to cover her nose. I wasn't sure which was worse: the smell or the fact that I could taste the foulness if I breathed through my mouth. Even Scratch seemed to have an issue with the stench.

"Gods, it smells like—" Scratch began.

"An ogre," Thorn hissed. I nearly fell backward into her. Walking past us was a green-gray creature around eight feet tall with a pair of battle-axes on his back. His muddy brown eyes glanced at us but didn't linger. He grunted and kept on his way. He was the first of many sights that I'll never be able to forget. An extremely drunk elf weaved toward us, hanging heavily on an equally intoxicated goblin. I tried to avoid them. Unfortunately, their unpredictable swerving put me directly in their path.

The goblin tried to stand up straight, swaying on the spot. Instinctively I almost reached out to steady him.

"Extremely sorry, scuse ush." He tried to bow. Losing his balance, he smashed headfirst into my stomach. It was my turn to lose my balance. I reached out, only grabbing air and the goblin's cloak. Between the goblin's head to the gut and hitting the ground, I could only gasp as the breath was knocked out of me.

"What the hells ya doing!" the elf yelled.

I tried to explain as the goblin attempted to regain his feet by putting his weight on his hand on my stomach. He slipped, fell over, and began an epic battle with his cloak.

"You fool!" the elf stood above me.

I couldn't move, trying to catch my breath. I saw Scratch moving quickly to intervene. Thorn was starting to draw energy into her hands. I braced as the elf leaned over, nearly toppling over onto me. He grabbed my cloak, trying to lift me but only crashed down on top of me.

"Shit, damn, son of a bish," he shouted.

The goblin rolled in the street laughing, extricating himself from his cloak. The weight moved off me as the elf joined his friend, laughing and rolling around. Again, I was left gasping for air.

"Sorry, mate, you're on your own," the goblin said, trying to stand but falling over onto the elf, who only laughed harder. Thorn and Scratch pulled me to my feet.

We'd drawn a crowd by this time, including the ogre we saw earlier. He looked us over as if to ensure we were okay. Then, he quickly picked up the laughing pair. Carrying one under each arm, he disappeared into the crowd.

I watched as the ogre's head bobbed above the slowly dispersing townsfolk.

"No worries, mate," a squeaky voice explained. "Tal will get them home."

"Tal?"

"New in town, eh?"

I looked down to see a goblin leaning heavily on a crutch. He was missing a leg and an eye. "Name's Rollins." He smiled with a grin missing several teeth. "If you be looking for work, I suggest Wolf's Tooth Tavern right down the street. Can't miss it." He pointed down the muddy street ahead.

I thanked him and looked at my companions. Their faces said *it's a start*. So, I motioned for Thorn and Scratch to head down the street. As Thorn passed by, Rollins caught her hand. I reached for my dagger and tensed as the goblin cocked his head at Thorn. He either ignored me or didn't notice my actions.

"You, my dear . . ." His eye seemed to look through her. "You are a flower with a sting." He released her hand. His gaze was unfocused as he continued, "A proud father he is." Thorn stood motionless as Rollins blinked a few times. "I'm sorry, did you say something?" he asked.

Thorn shook her head.

He glanced at the three of us standing around him. "Oh, dear me. Must have happened again," he muttered. "Sorry to bother you." He gave an awkward bow before moving faster than I thought was possible with a crutch. Before we could ask him anything, he was gone.

"What was that about?" Scratch asked. Thorn shrugged slowly.

"Come on." I reached for her hand. "Let's find this tavern. If nothing else, we can get something to eat."

Scratch and Thorn seemed to doubt this, as the both stared at me. "Have you seen all the um, different . . . beings around us?" Scratch hissed.

Thorn seemed to agree. "I . . ." She bit her lower lip. "I have no idea what these . . . people eat."

"If there's an elf in this town, then they have to have food that elves eat, which means humans can eat it too," I explained. Neither of them seemed to be able to find an argument, but neither moved. "What?" I glanced around, trying to understand what was holding them in place.

"Who is that?" Scratch asked, pointing past me. I spun to look, but I could only see a filthy building. Its windows were smeared with what I hoped was mud.

"I really don't know," Thorn replied, also looking past me. No, not past me. She walked up to me, her face inches from mine. I could feel my blush beginning to creep up my neck. "It looks like Henry."

"It does." Scratch was now right behind her, inspecting my face. "But this one is making sense and leading the way."

Thorn turned to face Scratch. "Doppelganger?"

He nodded his agreement. "Doppelganger."

"Shut up, and come on," I growled, stomping away from my two friends as they giggled at my annoyance.

Rollins was right. We couldn't miss the tavern as a huge carved wolf's head baring giant fangs glared down at us. Sounds of a crowd and music drifted out the open door. The smell of delicious meat cooking over an open fire. The mixture of spices and the comfort of baking bread caused my mouth to water. A moan of longing erupted from the three of us. We looked at each other and hurried toward the door. I hadn't realized how hungry I was until then. The three of us shared a glance and pulled our hoods over our heads, thinking this was the best way to avoid attention.

We found a table out of the way. Our server was a gruff dwarf with a wispy gray beard.

"Thank you, miss," Thorn said when our drinks arrived.

Scratch coughed the foam off his beer. The dwarf's demeanor improved slightly after that.

"That was a *woman*?" Scratch hissed, hurriedly wiping the spilled beer from the table and his cloak.

Thorn looked at me for backup, but I pretended to be interested in a horrid painting behind the bar. It was a depiction of a scantly clad female ogre. She had lank, greasy hair that fell—alluringly?—over half her face and one shoulder.

What I could only assume was an enticing smile formed around her two lower tusks. I was repulsed but couldn't really look away, either.

"You're both idiots," she grunted.

Scratch took some offense at this. "How is it you can tell, yet you never left your house your entire life?"

"I *read*," Thorn replied as if this settled the matter.

I was still pretending to be interested in the décor when movement near the door caught my eye. Someone had shouted "Tal!" when the blue-gray ogre from earlier entered. He briefly surveyed the room before heading to a figure half-hidden in shadows. I was pretty sure it was a man, whether human or elf I couldn't tell. He was too small for an orc but too big for a goblin. I watched Tal speak to the shadowy form. This was someone who knew how to not to draw attention. Then, the shadow man leaned into the light. He was older than I expected and built like a warrior, with a scar running from under his shaggy mop of hair down his face to his cheek. I couldn't see clearly, but I was sure the eye was milky white and blind.

Tal and the man spoke for a moment. When the ogre pointed directly at our table, it felt like the air was sucked out of the room. All sound ceased as every eye turned to stare. The only one who didn't seem to care was our server. She deposited our food, looked at our faces, then scanned around the tavern. Putting down her tray, she grabbed a chair to stand on. All eyes were now on her.

"An elf," the dwarf said so everyone could hear, "a human, and a halfling walk into a bar." You could have heard a pin drop. "Get over it." She jumped from the chair, grabbed her tray, and returned to the kitchen. Tal stood straight up and stared, then broke out in a deep, hearty laugh that shook the room. As if nothing had happened, the tavern returned to music and laughter. Nervously we began to eat.

"I think we might be getting too much attention," I whispered to my companions.

"Let's just eat and leave, okay?" Scratch glanced around nervously.

We were just finishing our meal when Tal approached our table, unnoticed by us. "Wolf would like to meet you." His deep voice vibrated our chairs. My heart felt like it had jumped out of my chest and kept running. The wide-eyed look on Scratch's face told me his heart might be racing mine for the door. Thorn began rummaging for coins to pay.

"Do not worry. Your meal and lodgings are already handled."

The three of us exchanged nervous glances as Tal waited for us to follow.

CHAPTER 36

We passed by the empty table where Tal had been speaking with, who I guess was, our host. As we were escorted through the bar, I quickly surveyed the room but didn't spy a trace of the grizzled figure. Instead, Tal led us through a barely noticeable door into a gloomy hallway. Darkness shrouded the end of the corridor. Nervously, I fingered the handle of my dagger. Behind me, I felt the electricity of Thorn prepping her magic.

"How long is this hallway?" Scratch muttered.

I nodded my understanding. It felt like we were walking too far to be in the same building. I got the sense we were being led underground. The slope was subtle, deceptively so, but the smell of earth around me was unmistakable. Images of barred doors and chains on the wall filled my mind. We stopped before the vision of our skeletal remains, chained and forgotten in the darkness, sent me running. Before anything more ghastly entered my imagination, Tal knocked on a door that seamlessly blended into the wall.

"Enter," growled an unseen voice. Tal held open the door as he bowed with an arm extended, telling us to enter. Scratch went in first, followed by Thorn. I brought up the rear, quickly taking in my surroundings. It was a cavernous, windowless room. Every wall was covered with shelves containing books, small chests, or weapons. Several oversized caskets sat open, overflowing with beautiful fabrics. Others remained closed, held tight with large locks without keyholes. A gentle push forced me forward. I turned to see Tal bending over to fit himself and his axes through the door. My attention returned to the room. Near the back wall was a large desk, and behind it was our host, Wolf.

"Welcome, welcome." Wolf stood holding his arms wide. "Come in," he replied to another knock at the door. I thought it opened of its own accord as three chairs floated in. I then noticed three diminutive goblins were carrying them. "Tundra goblins."

I turned to face Wolf.

He gestured to the tiny creatures. "They're tundra goblins. You seemed interested."

I could only nod. I'd never heard of their kind before. Then, seeming to understand my thoughts, he explained.

"They aren't seen very often. Thank you, gentlemen—oh, and lady."

The tundra goblins bowed and left silently. However, I saw one pause at the door to wave at Tal. To my surprise, he smiled and returned the wave by raising his hand chest high and moving his fingers up and down quickly. He caught me looking, and his face returned to its stony mask.

Thorn and Scratch were busy investigating the furnishings of the room. Thorn at the books while Scratch inspected the weapons.

"Thank you," I said, aware of my companions' rudeness. "Should I assume you paid for our meal and arranged lodging for us?"

"Very astute, as I would expect from a Dreamweaver." Wolf laughed. "Henry—is it okay that I call you Henry?"

I nodded. Before I could ask how he knew my name, his attention turned to Scratch.

"Ah, you have a good eye, Sebastian. That's an imperial knight's sword."

"Y-y-yessir, but . . ." Scratch turned confused. "Why is my family name on it?"

"I see both your fathers in your faces," Wolf laughed. "As I see, they've never mentioned me." Coming around the desk, Wolf motioned to the chairs again. "Please have a seat." He took a step toward Thorn.

She didn't turn to look at him. Instead, she held out her hand, and it crackled with energy. A loud *shwing* of a battle-ax told us it had been removed from Tal's back. The heavy blade sent the chair I was about to sit in toppling.

Wolf held his own hands out to quell the potential conflict. I reacted with my own Magic. I held crackling lightning in my hand while Scratch drew the imperial sword he held a third of the way out of the sheath.

"Young lady, you are a guest here." Wolf's smile evaporated, replaced with an intensity you could feel. His commanding voice rose as he spoke. "I will tolerate many things." His eyes glowed an eerie green. "However, I will not tolerate threats of violence in my personal study."

"These aren't the books of a good man." Thorn slowly turned to face him. Her face held no fear, simply distaste.

"I never claimed to be a good man," Wolf growled, "just a better man than the one I took those from."

"So you're keeping them safe? Not using them?" Thorn asked, her mouth showing her disbelief.

"I never said that either."

"I see." Thorn shook her hands, letting the energy dissipate.

Wolf's eyes returned to a piercing green. I was wrong about the vision in the eye that sat in the path of the scar. The scar was familiar in the way it seemed serrated on one side.

"Morax war blade." Wolf pointed to his face. "I assume you recognize it from the one your father has on his chest."

My mouth fell open. "He said it was a threshing accident," I stuttered.

Wolf barked out a laugh. "And you, Sebastian—what was the explanation for the scars that cover your father's arms and back?"

Scratch met Wolf's eyes for a moment. His gaze fell. "He always hid them. I saw them once and asked my mother," Scratch muttered. "She wouldn't tell me. I just assumed he got them from helping Henry's father."

Wolf clapped his hands as he leaned against the desk. "You're quite intuitive," he said happily, pointing at Scratch. "Your fathers did receive their wounds at about the same time. Thick as thieves, those two. Also, the most undisciplined soldiers I've ever had the pleasure to command." He returned to his seat behind the desk.

Scratch and I took the remaining chairs as Thorn skulked along the shelves.

Wolf continued, ignoring Thorn's disapproving tuts. "In the camp, they were constantly up to something." His shaggy hair fell across his wide shoulders as he shook his head. "But there was no one you wanted more to have your back in combat. They rarely lost a man or failed a mission."

Wolf leaned back, seemingly lost in memories. "That also had a lot to do with your mother. Finest commander you could ask for and brilliant with Magic." Suddenly he sat forward. Scratch and I both jumped back. Neither of us had known we'd been on the edge of our seats. "Well, what did you expect?" He clapped his hands. "Your fathers and mother were the highest decorated and capable of any."

"Of any who?" Thorn asked.

It was a question Scratch and I both wanted an answer to, but we didn't understand what was happening. We'd only learned recently of our parents' previous lives as soldiers.

"What do you mean?" Wolf roared. He was on his feet now and pacing. "You, Dreamweaver." He pointed accusingly at me. "You know nothing of the great battles won by your mother and father, of your parents' heroics to save the students of Fluxx Academy?"

He turned almost pleadingly to Scratch. "You don't know what the master spy did for the Grand Army?" He looked desperately from one to the other before collapsing onto his chair. "I don't believe this," he muttered, holding his head. Tal moved to pat his shoulder awkwardly. Wolf frowned as he continued to speak without raising his head. "So if you don't know about their service to me, then why are you here?"

"We were lost and running low on supplies," Thorn explained. "We had an old map with this town on it."

"So you don't even know where you are!" Wolf's hands slammed the desk as he stood glaring. "No knowledge of history, no idea who you are." He paced again, anger rising as he did. "You just blundered in here for what? *Supplies?*" He turned to a shelf behind him. "Lies!" he roared.

Thorn let out a shout of surprise. The tundra goblins had returned unnoticed. They threw ropes around her, tying her tight and toppling her to the floor, where she was quickly gagged.

I tried to help her, but heavy hands grabbed me, forcing me back to my seat. Ropes flew over me from the industrious goblins. Naturally, the binding was magic, and I felt my power being blocked. I hit the ground hard next to Thorn. She was extremely pale.

"Stop. We aren't here to harm anyone. We need help," I shouted before a gag was forced into my mouth.

Thorn's eyes had gone unfocused. I was terrified for her.

The clang of swords above me sounded like lightning striking. Scratch used his sword to parry Tal's battle-axes while a short sword he had grabbed from a shelf deflected Wolf's cleaver.

"You didn't think I knew who you were, girl?" Wolf screamed. "Althea, you foul witch! I will end you this time. How dare you, using the faces of my friends to assassinate me?" His swings were heavy and accurate, and Scratch's sword skills were incredible but barely keeping up. Nevertheless, nothing could beat Wolf's power and experience.

Tal's giant foot got tangled in my chair, and his ax blade fell close to my face. I screamed into the gag, fighting against the ropes, trying to get closer to Thorn. Her eyes had rolled back so I could only see the whites. I had no idea what the ropes might be doing to her. Splinters showered my face as Tal retrieved his ax, only to have the other one end up buried deep into the desk. A well-placed kick sent Tal to the floor. The ogre's hand flew out to his side, colliding painfully with my face. I tasted blood while light exploded behind my eyes.

Well, I *thought* the flashing was behind my eyes. I was wrong. Thorn's bonds blew to threads, and the bookshelf next to her to matchsticks. She floated above the floor, white light pulsing from her. Tal moaned in agony, covering his eyes. Wolf dropped his sword as he threw his arms over his face. The very air in the room felt heavy while gravity seemed to double. Wolf and Scratch were forced to their knees.

"We aren't here to harm you. I am not my mother," Thorn's voice boomed. "We don't even know who you are."

Black tunnels closed slowly at the corners of my vision. I couldn't catch my breath as the darkness closed to a pinprick of light.

CHAPTER 37

My world was shrouded in darkness and the voices I heard were miles away. I became aware of tugging on my hands and chest. Slowly the room came back into focus.

"Can't we go anywhere without getting into a fight?" I grumbled as Scratch removed the ropes binding me to the chair. Once he had me free, he handed the frayed rope to a tundra goblin who bowed and quickly left without a word. Thorn was tending to a wound on Tal's head.

"Where's Wolf?" I didn't see our host through the broken chairs and toppled books. One of Tal's axes was still half-buried in the large desk.

"He went to get something for Tal and Thorn," Scratch explained, wiping blood from his face. I immediately treated Scratch's many wounds, mostly from shattered glass and broken wood. Several dwarves appeared, carrying trays of drinks and a few potions. I was wary of the brews. However, Thorn didn't have the same hesitation. After she drank one, I also did. It was highly and shockingly restorative.

The door had barely shut when it was thrown open again. I felt disappointment as a surly-looking goblin entered. "Wolf has requested you, Tal." As he spoke, he jumped up on the desk. With Tal's help, he pulled the ax free. "Here, learn something." The dwarf jumped onto a bookshelf to send down a massive tome. It landed with a thud on the ruins of the desk. "Damn, kids." He clicked his tongue in disgust as he hopped down, opened the cover, and flipped through several pages. Then, jabbing a spindly finger at a picture, he said, "Educate yourselves." He began to leave but paused to look up at Thorn. "Uncanny, how alike you are to Althea the Evil." Then he spat on the floor at her feet. Instinctively I grabbed for him to force an apology.

Thorn stopped me. "We've done enough damage for one day." She shook her head. I protested, but she smiled sadly as she squeezed my arm reassuringly.

"You won't believe this," Scratch called from the book, oblivious to what happened. "We've been lied to all our lives." Thorn and I joined him as his eyes flew across the words. I couldn't help but stare at the drawing at the top of the page.

Younger versions of Wolf, my parents, and Scratch's father stared back at me. All in armor, standing proudly in front of hundreds of soldiers under a banner I didn't recognize. A bold heading at the top of a paragraph exclaimed:

The Grand Army generals and their troops, again victorious in battle. Finally, after five years of war, the Grand Coalition Army won its freedom. Men, elves, goblins, ogres, and dwarves joined forces against the evil mage Althea.

"Mother," Thorn gasped.

"Yes, I'm afraid so." Wolf re-entered the room, looking leery and a bit on edge. "I wasn't sure at first. There's something of her in your face, but you have more of your father's bearing."

"The hair tends to throw people off," I offered.

"It's naturally this color," she gruffly replied.

"Nothing natural about it," Scratch teased.

"You're correct, young Heraldry," Wolf interjected before a fight could start. "Her eyes and hair result from her use of Magic. Apparently, extremely powerful Magic." He rubbed his temples as he looked at the book before us. A crooked smile graced his face as he ran his fingers along the picture. Finally, he stopped, pointing out four distinct and easily recognized figures. "Caterous, the Dreamweavers—I think they had married by this time—and Heraldry . . . Never have I seen better friends—inseparable they were." Wolf looked over his shoulder at us. "They were the best team of fighters I ever knew until that last battle." He grumbled an obscenity. "No offense, young mage, but you should never have existed."

Wolf stepped back, seemingly lost in his memories. I wanted to scream at him for saying such a thing.

Thorn, however, calmed me with a touch to the arm. "How did they end up together? My father and the most reviled witch of an age?" she asked.

Wolf stared at her a long time before he spoke. "No one knows for sure." He began to pace. "Caterous entered the room alone while the Dreamweavers were still holding off Althea's minions. By the time we'd dealt with them, Caterous had the witch subdued. He led her out, restrained in a Magic field." Wolf's frown deepened. "We should have destroyed her right then."

"Why didn't you?" Thorn's question was barely a whisper.

Wolf looked shocked. "Because of your father," he choked. "He insisted she stand trial. Soon after, she was remanded to his care."

"Why!" Thorn demanded. "Why did he save her? Why wasn't she found guilty and put to death?"

Wolf looked at Thorn with pity and resignation. "There was much debate about that. Many thought your father had been bewitched. They believed Althea had been in control the entire time so she could escape death in battle." Wolf glared at Scratch and me. "That's why their families followed him to that village. To make sure he was okay and that she didn't escape."

"Why didn't they tell us?" I demanded, my anger getting the better of me. I didn't expect an answer, but Wolf had one.

"Because they wanted to protect you." He paused to look between Thorn and me. "You don't remember, do you?" I guess the questioning looks he received answered that question. "I'm not really sure exactly what happened. I got a letter from your mother." He nodded toward me. "Well, you and Thorn used to play together when you were young."

I staggered back at this revelation, and my hand caught Thorn's arm. We stared at each other, our eyes wide in shock. Then, the world disappeared, and I was three years old. I was playing with my imaginary friend in the front yard— except she wasn't imaginary.

Thorn broke the silence first. "You were *real*!"

"So were you!" I replied. How could I have forgotten her? Her light purple hair and the different colored eyes had always seemed so familiar. Now I knew why as the memories flooded back. Thorn held my hands in hers. Our broad, happy smiles faded simultaneously as if we were sharing the same mind. We remembered our fathers fighting, then the words of a spell.

"They made us forget each other!" we shouted in unison.

I'd never felt such anger against my father in my entire life. I couldn't understand how he could make me forget my best friend. But the flames of my rage were doused by the soft words from Thorn.

Dropping my hands, Thorn slowly stepped away. "I hurt you." A tear raced down her cheek as she kept her head bowed when she spoke. "I used a spell. It was something my mother taught me in secret." Hate hardened her eyes when she looked up. "She told me it was a tickle spell. As soon as I used it, you were screaming." A look of disgust curled her upper lip. "I didn't know how to counter the spell. Your mother saved you. I remember now."

Wolf made a noise in his throat. Then, he nodded. "That was a spell she used to torture her enemies during the war. She didn't use it to get information because the person could only scream in agony."

Thorn looked at me. "That's when your parents knew my mother was still a threat."

Her eyes were wide as she stared down at her feet. She couldn't or wouldn't look me in the eyes. When I reached out to her, she recoiled. It was the same guilt and shame I'd experienced when I hurt her during our duel. It was different, though, as she'd been tricked. I tried to speak up. I wanted to tell her it wasn't her fault. But, before the words could form, she talked over me.

"I know it wasn't my fault," she shouted angrily at me.

I threw up my hands in defense, stepping away from her.

"My mother has been ruining my life since it began!" Thorn slammed the book shut. "I hate her," she mumbled as she wiped a tear away.

"I don't," I said without thinking.

Thorn rounded on me. "Why not?! She used me to hurt you! She used my father to hide. I don't know what her purpose was for having me, but it was something to control my father, no doubt. She's the perfect bitch! She's done nothing but lie and hurt people."

"She made you," I muttered.

Thorn's glare softened a little.

"Well," Scratch spoke, "I guess nobody's perfect." He shrugged. I'd forgotten he was even with us. The silence that followed his statement ended with Thorn and me laughing until we couldn't breathe.

Regaining our composure, we heard a slight cough behind us. I know my face turned red. I'd forgotten Wolf was also still in the room.

"This has been a long, tiring, and"—he looked at the scattered broken chairs and the considerable ax hole in his desk and sighed—"expensive day. Why don't we all start fresh in the morning." Then he whistled. Another dwarf grumpily entered the room. "Would you please show our guests to their room?"

The dwarf rolled his eyes and grunted at us to follow.

"I need to ask you more about my mother and father," Thorn protested.

"It will have to wait until morning," Wolf replied. Tal got up to help Wolf clean up the room. We heard them arguing as we were led out of the room. Wolf wouldn't accept Tal's help, as he kept telling him to relax. I smiled at this. I could tell Wolf cared about the ogre.

Our guide led us back to the bar and up a steep flight of stairs. "Imagine having a few and trying to make it up these," Scratch chuckled.

"It's not a pretty sight," the dwarf grumbled. "Usually ends with me having to clean something liquid up."

Scratch and I silently agreed not to ask for any additional information.

Finally, we reached a long hall with several doors. The dwarf let out a long-suffering sigh as he pulled out a clattering ring of keys. It took him a few minutes to find the one to our room. Finally, he pushed the creaking door open and stood impatiently, holding the key out.

"Is there only one room?" I asked nervously.

"You've been traveling together for a while, right?" the dwarf grumbled. I nodded. "Then you should be used to this." He slapped the key into my hand, leaving us standing uncomfortably in the hall.

"Oh, for crying out loud! Come on—I'm tired," Thorn whined.

Entering the darkened room, I stumbled over a chair, searching for a lamp. Once it was lit, the awkwardness only intensified. There was one bed, a chair, a desk, and a lumpy couch. There was also a small lavatory with an ugly copper tub. The sight elicited something close to bliss from Thorn. "I don't care who's sleeping in the bed with me, but I'm getting a bath first," she explained. "Whoever it is will take a bath second. I won't continue sleeping beside your unholy stenches tonight!"

The lavatory door shut with finality.

Scratch gave me a weird smirk. "Better make sure to clean behind those big ears, elf boy," he laughed, jabbing me in the ribs.

I hit him back, to which he hit me back. We were just starting to get into a tussle when we were interrupted. "Boys, knock it off."

"Yes, Mom," we replied in unison. Then, wet purple hair and a scowl appeared at the door. We acted innocent and confused at her admonishment. With a growl, Thorn disappeared back into the bathroom while Scratch and I laughed.

Then I asked, "Why do you get to sleep in the bed?"

When she reappeared, she didn't say anything. She pointed to the tub and kept me at a distance.

"Oh, please," I grumbled. "You aren't going to catch dirty."

Still no answer. She just stomped her foot and pointed to the tub. Thorn had cast a scouring charm on the bath. The water was perfect—another spell from Thorn, no doubt. I couldn't help but get lost in the comfort.

———∞———

I knew it was late and I'd been in the tub too long. However, this was the first time I didn't feel disgusting in days. I finished washing my clothes and drying them. I was just opening the door when I heard Thorn and Scratch talking.

"I think we can learn much about who we're going up against here," Scratch was saying.

"Maybe, but I need to get moving. Father's been gone too long now."

"Are we not going to talk about how Wolf went nuts and tried to kill us?" I asked as casually as I could.

"Oh, thank the gods. How long can one tiny elf take?" Scratch exclaimed upon seeing me.

"I'm serious! He was so happy to see us then—" My fist smashed into my palm. "He's tying us up and trying to kill us!"

"You were still unconscious," Scratch nodded sagely. Sometimes he was infuriating.

"*Obviously*. How did he explain himself?" I turned to a surprised Thorn. "And what the hell kind of spell did you use?"

"Wolf is a little high-strung," Thorn replied calmly.

"High-strung and nutty as a squirrel turd." Scratch laughed.

"Be that as it may . . ." Thorn frowned as she pushed Scratch toward the bathroom. "There have been many attempts on his life. So he tends to be a bit paranoid at times." Thorn looked from Scratch to me. "Tal told me." She shrugged. "Wolf suffers from terrible memories from the war as well. He's seen horrible things. So, apparently, sometimes he just snaps."

Scratch and I shared a glance, and something my mother had told us came to mind.

"Our dads sometimes had what Mom called 'episodes.' She usually made a calming drought for them." Suddenly I remembered something else. "Mom used to partake as well." I was shocked at the realization.

"Wolf said she was one of the best fighters as well," Thorn whispered. "She must have seen things too."

I nodded. There was so much coming out today. My head felt too full and too empty all at once.

"Well, this has been fun, but . . ." Scratch seemed at a loss.

"But you smell," Thorn replied with a laugh, pushing him toward the bath.

"Couldn't even bring yourself to touch me," I muttered.

"What did you say?" Thorn asked as the door snapped shut.

I shook my head in reply.

When Scratch closed the door, I realized it was the first time Thorn and I had been alone in days. I watched her brush her hair. She was dressed in a light tunic and loose short pants that came down just below her knees. What caught my attention were her feet. I'd never seen them outside of shoes before. They were small and, in my opinion, cute. Thorn realized I was staring and hid them under the rough wool blanket. A blanket we'd be sharing shortly. When I realized this fact, I felt my face go red. I quickly became interested in the worn table in the corner.

"Don't be so embarrassed. You're making me self-conscious," Thorn muttered. I sat on the opposite side of the bed, trying not to hyperventilate. Then, without looking, I lay back on the straw-filled mattress. It was lumpy, and the pillow smelled musty. It was heaven after sleeping on the ground or the back of the wagon for the last few weeks.

I rolled over on my side, expecting Thorn to want to talk. Instead, she was wrapped in the blanket, so all I could see was her face. Her lips were slightly parted as she began the rhythmic breathing of sleep. She looked so peaceful and pretty. I just kept staring at those light pink lips. I was only a few inches away. Shaking my head, I rolled over onto my back, feeling my heart pounding. The bathroom door opened slightly. I saw Scratch peeking through the gap. Satisfied nothing was happening, he blew out the candle in the bathroom and closed the door.

"What are you doing?" Scratch mouthed at me.

"Nothing, she's asleep! What would I be doing anyway?" I hissed.

"I gave you two some alone time!" He pointed furiously at Thorn. "Did you, ya know. . . ."

"Do *what*?" I demanded silently.

He glared at me. "Did you kiss her?" As he made a kissing face and held out his arms like he was holding an invisible lover. "What were you waiting for?"

"She. Is. A. Sleep!" I breathed, stabbing my finger toward Thorn.

"And I want to stay that way," Thorn grumbled, rolling away from me, "so can you two wrap up whatever this is?"

I wouldn't have doubted if my eyes were half as huge as Scratch's. Without another word, Scratch extinguished the lantern quickly. I heard him shuffling around for a bit until something landed on my chest. It was a cloak.

"Thanks," I whispered. I received a grunt in return.

I lay in the darkness for the next few minutes, listening to Scratch settle on the couch. Finally, I was left with the sounds of the building settling and my heart pounding. After an hour, I listened to the strangest call and response that ever could have been. Scratch would make a sound like *Geeehaaa*, and Thorn would answer with a *Weehoo* sort of whistle. I rolled onto my side with my hand under the pillow, listening. The sound and repetition were both soothing and annoying.

I was just at the cusp of sleep when Thorn started moving around. I held my breath as she settled back into sleep. I was shocked when her hand found mine. Her breathing told me she was asleep as her hand lightly gripped mine. It wasn't long after that I finally found sleep. That night, my dreams weren't filled with horrible memories for the first time in days.

I awoke with the early morning sunlight filling my eyes while snickers filled my ears. Scratch stood at the foot of the bed, beet red, trying to cover his laughter. I looked down at myself and gasped. I was on my back, Thorn's head was on my shoulder, her hand was on my chest, and her knee was on my leg.

"I wish I could capture this moment for all time," Scratch stilfled a laugh. Smiling, I couldn't help but agree. Then, to my amazement, Thorn lifted her hand from my chest and made an obscene gesture at Scratch. She then rolled off me to the gales of laughter coming from him. I immediately missed her warmth.

CHAPTER 38

Notelek Capital

First Lieutenant Oxbow rushed as fast as his heavy armor and swaying long sword would allow. He ignored the raised eyebrows and scandalized looks of the courtiers. Oxbow nearly fell, skidding to a halt in front of the two white and gold doors flanked by guards. Regaining his composure, he addressed one of the sentries.

"I have urgent news from Hoont!"

Nodding understanding, the guards pulled open the doors to reveal chaos. Several large tables stood in the center of the room, each surrounded by men in uniforms, all pointing and arguing over small models atop of maps.

A prematurely graying man in the only white uniform in the room noticed the new arrival. "Lieutenant, what news from Hoont?" he called hopefully.

"Emperor," Oxbow bowed, inwardly cringing as he saw the hope die in the emperor's countenance. "Hoont is lost. Althea now holds almost half of the farming communities."

Emperor Maximillian von Itey allowed himself a second of disappointment before asking his follow-up. "What of the old alliance? Will they come to our aid?" He stared down at the map as several models moved to show the taking of Hoont Valley.

"Sir, their response was . . ." Oxbow shifted from foot to foot. "Well, sir . . ."

"Did they side with Althea?" Maximillian demanded in a panic.

"Report what happened," a general ordered.

"Sir, I spoke with General Amelia Dreamweaver." A ripple of recognition spread through the older military men. Oxbow felt their trepidation and strained hope.

"If she's with us, we have a chance. If she's against us . . ." someone called.

"What of her husband and Heraldry?" another general demanded of Oxbow.

"Was the Mage Caterous there? What did he have to say?" a grim-faced commander cried, slamming a fist onto a table, scattering some tiny models.

"Gentlemen, please!" Maximillian silenced the shouting. "Lieutenant, what was her answer?"

Swallowing his nerves, Oxbow reached into his traveling cloak. He pulled out a large folded parchment. "Sir, she demands we honor our promises." The room erupted in cries of treason and blackmail. It took several minutes for Maximillian to regain order.

He crossed the room to accept the parchment held out in Oxbow's shaking hand. Before he released the document, the lieutenant whispered to the emperor, "It's what's right, sir."

Maximillian showed slight surprise at being addressed by such a low officer of his army. Oxbow couldn't believe he'd said it either. He might have just signed his own death warrant. Maximillian's father was the one to break the original treaty. Maximillian and Oxbow stared at each other. Both had a hand on the parchment. The emperor squeezed the lieutenant's shoulder with his free hand and whispered, "You are correct."

Oxbow relaxed, having fulfilled his duty to the emperor and to himself.

"Gentlemen," Maximilian raised the treaty above his head, "today, we right a wrong. Today we honor the pledge we made." The room exploded in arguments.

Three hours later, the now Captain Oxbow set out with the signed promise of equality for the camp of General Dreamweaver. He urged his horse faster in hopes of catching the army. He knew that no matter the outcome of his mission to the Capital, the Dreamweavers and their allies would march against Althea. They had hoped for equality but would settle for reinforcements. Oxbow knew his mission was dangerous. He would have to avoid Althea's spies and assassins, but he counted himself lucky as the young man sent to Haven might be killed as he entered the gate if they didn't believe his copy of the treaty was real.

CHAPTER 39

If Thorn was embarrassed by how we woke up that morning, it didn't show. Instead, she enjoyed a hearty breakfast that I could only pick at. Unfortunately, I only ate about half. At first, my stomach clenched at the thought of what Thorn's father would do to me if he had seen us. Then, however, my mind wandered back to being in bed. Although Scratch wasn't there then—it was just Thorn and me. Her pale pink lips glistened as she drew closer to me. Then, sudden pain in the back of my head brought my consciousness to the breakfast table.

"Pay attention," Thorn chastised between mouthfuls of bacon. "This is important." Scratch was with Tal, going over a map of a mountain.

"As I was saying," Wolf cleared his throat, "I don't believe your coming here was a coincidence. I had some of my associates look into rumors, and what they found isn't good. I don't think your father made it to the Capital. From what little information I gathered, he went missing somewhere in this area." He tapped a different map. I could tell it was a larger area of the same mountain as the one on Tal's and Scratch's maps.

"Which would make sense since that's where my mother's old stronghold was, correct?" Thorn poured her and me some more coffee. "Do you think she took him back there? Why?" Thorn wondered as she grabbed a couple of slices of toast, dropping one of them on my already crowded plate. She jabbed me in the shoulder. "Eat."

I couldn't believe her appetite. "I'd have guessed she'd just kill him. So, why take him there?"

"I believe she'd be looking for revenge." Tal's deep voice caused me to jump. "She most likely will contact your fathers, and in your case, young elf, your mother as well, in the hopes they will come to rescue him." He rubbed his bald head, thinking. "Or maybe, she hopes you'll try." His gaze fell on Thorn.

"That would be just like her," Thorn growled. "She wouldn't be happy just to take on the ones that beat her." Thorn finally seemed to have had enough to eat. Tossing down the bit of bacon she had been using as a pointer, Thorn continued as she paced. "No, no, she would want to use us to hurt them. Sick bitch." Thorn glared at my toast as if it had personally offended her. "How did you beat the witch before?"

"It took an army last time," Wolf sighed. The battle still burned in his eyes. "An army that fought bravely. It cost us many lives."

Thorn took the toast from my plate and added jam with wholly unnecessary violence.

"Yeah, but she had an army then as well," Scratch added hopefully. "She's alone this time."

"If the rumors are true, many of Althea's followers have returned. We believe she has an army again." Wolf slumped down into a chair opposite me. He began taking bacon from my plate and eating it slowly. I admit I wasn't very hungry, but that didn't make it okay for everyone to keep taking my food.

"Tell me more about the people of this town," Scratch said.

"Veterans of the last war established this village. Creatures and people who fought hard for everyone's freedom only to be shunned by those in power." Wolf dropped my bacon as if it had turned into a slug.

"So a village full of experienced fighters then?"

Thorn looked up at Scratch's question.

"Oh yes, highly experienced—and worn out." Wolf leaned forward, dropping his voice. "This is where you go when you have no place left to go. We've all lost almost everything. Some lost their homes or their livelihoods, limbs, and loved ones. Although you can easily see the scars that battle gave us, you cannot see the wounds we carry deep in our hearts." He leaned back, scowling. "I could not and never would ask more of these people than they have already given."

Scratch stepped forward, about to speak, when Tal touched his shoulder and shook his head. Tal leaned forward, whispering something I couldn't hear. Scratch nodded solemnly, then returned to studying the map.

"I'm sure some of them would help us," Thorn suggested. "I don't suggest we try to recruit anyone, but we should at least share what we're planning." As she spoke, she didn't look at Tal or Wolf. Instead, she paused, took a breath, and marshaled on. "So they can make their own decision." Now she held Wolf's gaze. "There's no shame in having fought in a war and sitting out the next one. That, however, is a choice a warrior can make for themselves."

Wolf slowly rubbed his chin. I was amazed at Thorn's ability to understand the man before her.

"True, true," Wolf mumbled, still rubbing his chin. "Some warriors would still have the fire of battle in their hearts." Behind Wolf, Tal elbowed Scratch, knocking him off balance. Wolf suddenly shook his scruffy head. "You'd have a hundred lions with no leader." He leaned back, looking passively at Thorn as she sat.

"I highly doubt that," Thorn said, meeting his gaze.

"Oh?" Wolf's eyebrows rose, disappearing into his gray locks. "You have someone in mind to lead troops?" He rested his hands on his stomach.

"Well . . ." Thorn was now staring up at the ceiling, leaning her chair back onto two legs to match Wolf's. "If no one in town can do the job, I have someone in mind. She's a highly volatile vampire princess, but I think that might work to her advantage."

Wolf's chair hit the floor at the exact moment his fists slammed onto the table. "There is no way in hell I am allowing a vampire to lead my troops!" Aghast, Wolf turned to Tal for support. "A vampire!" He shouted, pointing at Thorn.

Tal shrugged. "I had a good vampire friend—couldn't ask for a better fighter."

"That is because they are born killers!" Wolf shouted. "Right after they help win the battle, they are off eating your troops!" He glared at Thorn. "I will command this expedition, which is final." Wolf stormed out of the room, followed by Tal.

The ogre smiled at Thorn as he passed. "Great job!" He gave a thumbs-up before disappearing through the door.

"If it weren't so manipulative and scary, I would say I was impressed." Scratch frowned.

"Oh please, he wanted to be in charge." Thorn waved off the pseudo-compliment. "He just needed an excuse."

Not long after this exchange, we were summoned to the town square where a large crowd had gathered. Eager energy rippled through the different species as they waited for Wolf to appear. We heard our names mentioned, Dreamweaver, Heraldry, and even Caterous. Some with a tone of respect, others in anger or suspicion.

We stood a little way from the crowd with our backs to a wall. That is until Thorn positioned me in front of her. I was about to ask why when I noticed her ears elongating and becoming fox-like. Her ears twitched and oscillated, taking in the murmurs and whispers around us.

"What do you hear?" I asked nervously. "Are they going to throw us out?"

"Several of the townsfolks would like nothing better," she responded. "However, most are just interested in what Wolf has to say." Cocking her head to one side, she listened intently. "They know who you two are." Her face betrayed disgust. "They don't know who I am. Their opinion of me isn't great." Suddenly she was angry, glaring at me. "Not that I want to, but why wouldn't I be a good barmaid?" she demanded.

"I . . . well . . . I . . . um," I stuttered as her eyebrows rose in annoyance. Thankfully Wolf joined us, taking her attention away from me.

I blew out a breath of relief, thinking I'd dodged that arrow. That was until Thorn hissed at me, "We're not done talking." She shook her head, returning her ears to their normal size and shape.

"My friends," Wolf spoke with authority, "you probably recognize our old comrades of Dreamweaver and Heraldry in the youths you see here." Wolf had us step forward.

Nervously, the three of us assembled before the meeting. Scratch stood straight and proud while Thorn shifted uncomfortably next to me. Wolf raised his hands to quiet the muttering. "I know their appearance is highly coincidental to the rumors we've been hearing."

Shouts and demands erupted around us.

"I see the witch in the half-elf!"

"Who is she?"

"Why is the witch still alive?"

Wolf tried to calm the potential mob. "Friends, please, I shall explain." However, he could barely be heard over the protests and demands.

"I am Thorn Caterous, daughter of Althea and Lawrence Caterous!" The crowd stood silenced by Thorn's statement. Tal and Scratch tensed for battle. I swear the blood drained from Wolf's face the instant she said her name. It took only a beat before the uproar started. The insults were the first things thrown at Thorn, followed by stones and calls for her death.

A rage I had never felt before overtook me. Someone had thrown a dagger that barely missed my closest friend. I watched as Thorn allowed herself to be pelted with insults and debris. Finally, I heard myself scream, "Enough!" I felt the power flow through me. Reaching up, I pulled the energy from the sky. It flowed into my soul, and I coiled it, amplified it, then slammed my fist on the wooden stage we stood on. A shockwave shot outward from my hand, knocking the crowd off their feet.

"This is not the evil witch you fought!" I screamed with trembling rage. "This is Thorn, who was born through no fault of her own!" I glared around at the stunned faces. "She is kind, loyal, and my friend. She's absolutely nothing like her wretched mother, and you will *not* harm her!" My voice boomed so loud that everyone covered their ears. Their eyes now glared their hate and distrust at me.

"Well, you heard young Dreamweaver. So there is that," Wolf spoke to the stunned crowd. "Also, she could have killed all of you when she arrived." He eyed me warily. "So I suggest you listen to what I have to say."

CHAPTER 40

After my outburst, the town meeting went slightly smoother, but I felt pretty embarrassed. As soon as the townfolk began to discuss options, Thorn and I decided the best course of action for us was to make ourselves scarce. The looks of hatred and fear had not completely subsided and followed us as we walked back to the tavern, receiving a wide berth the entire way.

Before entering, Thorn touched my arm. "That was very sweet." She smiled at me. Then anger flashed in her eyes as she slapped me on the back of the head. "Don't let your anger get the better of you! Your outburst could have done much more harm than good."

"You could have been hurt," I protested angrily. "Someone threw a *knife* at you, along with all those rocks and garbage! How could you just stand there and—and—" As I spoke, I realized what had happened.

"Got there finally, have you?" she smirked.

"The knife didn't miss you," I grumbled. "You had a protection spell."

"Henry, I'm not helpless."

"Yeah, I know, it's just when they were saying all that stuff . . ." I whined, and I knew it.

"Listen." She grabbed my shoulders, turning me to face her. "I know you want to protect me—"

"It's my job!" I protested. "Your father made it clear that I should protect you at all costs."

Her grip on my arms tightened to the point of pain. "That was *his* job, and he failed. He failed the day he saved that woman." I tried to argue, but Thorn overrode me. "I know you care about me a lot, but I won't change my mind on this." Then, letting go of me, she stomped her foot. "I don't understand how I came to be."

"Well, I would have expected you to understand by this age," I ventured. She cocked an eyebrow at me, waiting for me to continue. "Um, you see . . . when a mommy and daddy love each other very much—"

"Dammit, Henry, that's not funny. I mean it. I don't understand how my father could be with her." Then, balling up her fists, she let out a frustrated growl. "You have no idea what she's like!" Finally, she was so angry she couldn't find an appropriate outlet to vent on. "You don't know what it's like to grow up knowing your mother hates you, and there's nothing you can do to change that." When she turned to face me, my heart broke. The pain and anger on her face was excruciating. "To think that somehow my father forced her . . ." She couldn't even finish. "I can't see her inviting him to her bed."

"What if," I said, carefully reaching out to her, "she seduced your father in an attempt to control him." She allowed me to hold onto her upper arms, though her face was full of extreme doubt. "You're just the happy accident that came from that."

"I'm sure I was an accident, but I doubt I was a happy one." She sniffed but allowed me to pull her into a hug.

"You make me happy," I said softly.

"Yeah, but you're a dork," she muttered. All I could do was hold her and agree.

"Hey, guys!" Scratch slid to a halt. "Oh, hey, sorry. I can come back."

"No, it's fine," Thorn said, pulling away from me. "What's going on?"

"Apparently, between your contrition and Henry's little outburst, we've convinced several townsfolk to come with us!" He whooped and jumped in the air.

"Scratch, Scratch, *Sebastian*!" Thorn shouted to calm him. "That's great, but I have a favor to ask you."

———

Several minutes later, I had to run to catch up with Thorn. I was still attempting to process what I'd just witnessed. After Thorn made her request, Scratch readily agreed and I could only stand in shock. Finally reaching Thorn, I caught her arm. "How could you do that!" I demanded. "We need him with us, not going off alone. What if the others find him first? What happens then?"

"I understand your concerns, but we need her." Thorn shook her head wearily. "Twenty beings in our expedition are not enough to face my mother. Even if they're hardened veterans."

"You think Serina can take her on?"

"I'm hoping she'll bring some help." Thorn bit her bottom lip nervously. Then, she shrugged. "Henry, if my mother can capture or control my father, we're outmatched."

I followed Thorn into the tavern and my frustration matched the rising voices as we ventured further into the bar.

Finally, I was sitting across from Thorn. "If that's the case, what the hell are we doing?" I demanded. "If you don't think we can beat her, why did we come all this way? Why did you ask for help?"

"We're going to investigate the rumors and free Caterous if need be," Wolf stated as he slammed a battle-ax down on the table next to us. "But we do it without vampires."

I swear my heart was halfway across the bar and still running, again. Thorn, however, just seemed tired and annoyed.

"I will not have those demons around my people." Wolf glared at Thorn.

"I understand you're the leader of this little expedition." Thorn stood up to glare back at Wolf. But even though she barely came up to his chest, he took a step back. "These are my parents, and I'll bring in any allies I deem necessary to defeat them."

"Them?" Wolf and I asked in unison.

"I don't know what happened before," Thorn sighed. "I don't know if he took her in willingly or was bewitched. But, unfortunately, we can't assume my father will be on our side when we face Althea."

"I still do not like dealing with those bloodsuckers," Wolf growled. "However, I do see your point." Wolf shook off the idea. Anger returned to his features. "Your father is extremely powerful. If he does team up with your mother, though, it will not matter who is on our side. We have already lost."

"You may not think we have a chance, but I assure you, I'm up to the task!" Thorn announced before she stormed off.

Wolf's attention was now on me. I had no idea if she was up to the task. So I nodded my assertion and then hurriedly followed in her wake.

Naturally, her statement didn't inspire much confidence in me. When I found her, I tried to ask about her plan. But unfortunately, she only patted my shoulder and told me she needed to do some research. So I was left not knowing what I should be doing to prepare.

Thorn, however, was a whirlwind of activity. Unlike when we were with the vampires, she took her time to prepare. She met with the volunteers, discussed tactics with Wolf and Tal, spent time picking the best weapons in the armory, and studied magic in Wolf's library.

I don't know if I ever felt so distant from her. She spent all of her time running between things. She ate alone in the library and had little to no time to talk to me. When we returned to the room, she was so exhausted that she'd be asleep almost the minute she lay down. With Scratch gone, I slept on the lumpy couch.

It was late on the fourth day since Scratch departed. I tried in vain to talk to Thorn or help organize our party. Instead, I found I was always more in the way than helpful. Finally, I decided to see what I could learn, so I wandered into the library. I always did well back home with the reading.

Back home, I thought. Which one? The manor or the house I lived in with my parents? Both felt so long ago. I shook my head as I sat in the large comfortable chair. The room was in familiar disarray. Although I smiled slightly, this is how she tended to leave the library back in the manor.

On the desk, Thorn had left out several books. Intrigued, I opened one. What I found disturbed me. Thorn was learning some arcane and extremely dangerous magic. These spells had only one purpose—to kill. But, unfortunately, that wasn't the only frightening part. Depending on which spell they used, the caster sacrificed power, vitality, and even years of their life. I had to talk Thorn out of this course of action, but when I returned to our room I found her asleep. I would catch her when she awoke and force her to talk to me. That was my plan.

I lay on that uncomfortable couch, staring out into the darkened room. Thorn whimpered something in her sleep. I kept thinking about what I'd discovered. I had to find another way if I couldn't change her mind. There had to be a way to counter the spells to not harm the caster.

I kicked off the blanket and quietly made my way to the door. I tripped over one of Thorn's boots, catching myself before I fell onto the bed. Again, she muttered something incoherent before returning to the regular breathing of sleep. Using two fingers to be as silent as possible, I opened the door and slipped silently into the empty hall.

I was proud of my stealth until my light footfalls sounded like thunder in my ears in the silence of the night. I'm not sure who I was concerned about waking. Fortunately, I met no one on my way back to the library. I lit a lamp and started my research. I have no idea how long I sat there until sleep overtook me. When I woke, I had a moment of triumph before everything came crashing down.

I'd found a way to keep Thorn from casting any spell that would cause her harm. My finger still rested on the words that would save her when I noticed someone standing before me.

"Just what do you think you're doing?" Thorn demanded.

"I—" *I what? Was I looking for a way to keep you from using the research you've been doing for the last few days?* That was the answer. It was obviously *not* the answer she wanted to hear. I don't think there was an appropriate answer to the question. So, I asked my question in return. "You aren't considering using one of these spells on your mother, are you?"

"My mother, father, anyone who gets in my way." Her conviction frightened me. "*Anyone* who gets in my way." She glared at me. "Anyone!"

"You can't be serious. That's something your mother—"

"Something my mother would do?" Thorn demanded, "Yes, it is. That's how you beat someone like her."

"This is dangerous." I tried to calm the escalating tension. "Using these spells will hurt you. I can't allow that." The instant the words left my mouth, I knew I'd made an error in judgment.

"You can't *allow* it?" She glared at me. "Listen here, elf—I've put up with your arrogance long enough!"

I was shocked.

"I've been putting up with this nonsense for years."

"What are you talking about?" I demanded.

"Oh, here it comes. The wounded little boy is about to start pouting because I hurt his feelings." She made a gagging noise. "I have no idea why my father took you on, but I have hated every boring moment of it. There it is." She pointed at me and laughed. "The confused, stupid elf face I have come to loathe."

"Why are you acting like this?" I was on my feet now. I couldn't understand the source of her venom against me. I tried to grab one of the books. She must have read something that altered her memory or changed all her feelings to negative thoughts. "Hold on." I hurriedly tried to figure out which volume. "Let me find out what you might have read."

Snatching the book from my hand, Thorn glared at me. Her face contorted in disgust. "It has been so easy to manipulate you." Her laugh was harsh. "Show you a little affection, lead you on a bit like there was some chance I'd be interested in you. Ha! Disgusting. Serina, Sebastian, and I would laugh at your pathetic, awkward attempts to show me, what? That you're useless as a suitor as well as a wizard?"

My legs had given out at some point. I sat in Wolf's colossal leather chair, feeling like a tiny boy.

"I have what I need. Fighters, warriors, mages. I have true strength, and *we* will face my mother. Your tag-along days are over." She picked up the rest of the books from the table. "I expect you to be out of my room in an hour. Oh, and when Sebastian returns, maybe I can tell him how I feel about him. Especially since we don't need you around anymore. Oh, wait . . ." She turned, her eyes holding a meaningful glint. "He already knows—*intimately.*" An evil giggle escaped her lips as she swung around me and out the door.

I was alone, in shock. Thorn had just taken every fear I'd buried deep down and hoped to keep secret and threw them in my face. She'd taken a dagger to my heart, pierced it, twisted the blade, and then tried to rip open my chest from my throat to my stomach. Slowly I stood up, determined to understand what had caused this change in my closest friend.

I threw open the door only to be met by one of the dwarves. He thrust my belongings into my stomach. "They're already gone. I don't suggest you follow."

Ignoring his curses, I pushed past him. I ran out into the street, where several townsfolk gawked at me. The horses and wagons were all gone. Everything we'd been preparing for the journey was gone.

She'd left me behind.

CHAPTER 47

My head buzzed, and my vision blurred. My legs quivered as I stumbled blindly through town. My stomach clenched, and I was sure I'd be sick at any moment. I couldn't believe the events of the last hour. My shoulders bounced off angry creatures, until I finally fell into a filthy puddle. At that point, I couldn't even move. I just sat in that fetid water, trying to understand where I'd gotten everything so wrong.

"Master Henry," someone called me. "Master Henry, why are you sitting there?" It was Rollins, the goblin we'd met when we arrived.

After blinking several times, I was finally able to see him. I hadn't even realized I'd been crying until then.

"Master Henry needs to get up. They're looking for you."

"Who's looking for me," I asked, trying to get to my feet. My limbs refused to respond properly. I slipped and fell over. Rollins's thin arm was under mine, trying to help me. For a second, I didn't remember what was going on. "Who did you say is coming?"

"Everyone! You aren't well. You need to hurry!" The urgency in his tone sent off a warning in my mind. "They're coming for you!" He was pointing frantically the way I'd come. Fear gripped my chest. I had to get out of here.

Once on my feet, I could see the looks I was receiving. Even Rollins could barely contain his evil smirk. Panic took over as I pushed him away. "Help! I found him! I found him!" Rollins cried.

I ran to the only escape I could think of, back to the wagon we'd hidden days ago. Suddenly, it felt like the entire town was trying to grab me. I twisted out of one grip only to be clawed at from the other side. I blindly threw spells over the curses and cries of my pursuers. Finally, I crashed into the gate as several what appeared to be trolls attempted to close it. I was out, running to the barn. The trolls were now struggling to open the door wide enough to allow the others to chase me.

Ducking behind the dilapidated houses, I crouched in the wild bushes and tall grass. Several pairs of running feet passed my hiding place. Taunting voices called my name, saying things like they wouldn't hurt me. They insisted they only wanted to help me. I'd have laughed if I wasn't so terrified. Slowly I made my way to where the horse and wagon should have been. I snuck under the collapsed door and stood triumphantly in the gloom of the empty barn. But, unfortunately, they had already taken the wagon.

Frozen lead hit my stomach. So many questions ran through my mind. What had Thorn told the villagers?

She didn't need to tell them anything, my mind responded. *You alienated the townsfolk at the meeting.*

At the meeting where I'd defended Thorn. But why had she turned on me? Again my mind had an answer.

She didn't need you anymore. You're always been a tag-along—second-rate.

"Shut up!" I shouted. Movement outside sent me scurrying into the darkest corner. I pulled a moth-eaten horse blanket over myself.

I heard two gruff voices complaining,

"We don't have time for this."

"I know, but she wants to take him."

"Seems like a coward to me, running off like that."

"Doesn't matter what we think, do it?"

"Nah, but I'm getting bored and hungry."

"Well, the little elfling isn't in here. Come on, let's head back to the tavern."

"Finally, something I can enjoy."

I breathed a sigh of relief, yet I was slightly annoyed. That was a lazy search. Cautiously I crept along the wall, listening for any more visitors. I was alone. Sitting back, I held my head, trying to figure out my next move. Suddenly, the boards of the wall shattered behind me. Four firm hands grabbed me, pulling me through the hole. No matter how I struggled, I wasn't getting away. Before I could shout a spell, a coarse cloth was shoved in my mouth.

"You are the worst at hiding we have ever seen." An ogre with a scar on his cheek grinned menacingly at me.

"I thought we were going back to the tavern because we couldn't find him. How did you know he was there?" The speaker must have been half-troll.

"It was a ruse," the ogre sighed.

"I'm not wearing rouge," the half-troll said as he rubbed his face with one hand. The other still held me tightly.

"Nevermind, Duane—I'll buy you a drink when we get this little guy back to the lady."

"Lady? What lady?" I demanded although all they heard was, "MMM-MMPHH WHMMMMPH."

Duane chuckled as his friend tied my hands and feet. Then with little effort, Duane picked me up and carried me under his arm toward the gate. I hadn't noticed all the bones, broken weapons, and bloodstains covering the walls when we arrived. How did we not notice this den of horror?

No matter how hard I struggled, Duane would adjust his hold and grip me tighter. I was starting to have trouble breathing. Between the gag in my mouth and the constriction of my chest, I was beginning to feel lightheaded.

Passing through the gate, I could barely focus. Duane stumbled to a stop in front of an ancient hag. "You fool," she rasped. "He was to be unharmed. Drop him this instant." Duane, however, carefully lowered me to the ground. My feet were unbound, but my hands remained tied tight. "Let this stupid creature speak," the hag ordered. Rough, nasty fingers were forced into my mouth. The gag was removed so I could at least spit out whatever had been on those fingers.

"Listen, you old hag," I said in a tone that sounded braver than I felt, "I don't know what you were told to do to me, but you won't succeed." Instead, I focused on an incantation to burn through my bindings. My hands were free, unnoticed by anyone. The hag was talking to a grisly-looking Bearman and a cruel-looking troll.

Now was my chance. "I told you, you wouldn't succeed," I shouted, casting several spells at my captors. Unfortunately, I was outmatched and didn't even realize it. A shield surrounded me, so my Magic and I couldn't escape. No matter how hard I threw myself or destructive spells at the barrier, I couldn't make a dent in my cage.

Out of frustration, I pounded on the invisible blockade. The field shimmered. I jumped back, not believing my eyes. I thought for an instant that the hag and the others were Thorn, Wolf, and Tal. Cautiously I approached, reaching out to find the border. When my hand could move no further, I flicked the barrier. There was no change to my captors.

The old crone approached me. "Little elf will stay safe and quiet in his little bubble," she cackled.

Furious, I punched the invisible wall. The hag was Thorn again. "Please stop. We'll figure this out," she said before reverting to her ancient form. "That's right, you can do nothing."

My head began to hurt. "None of this makes sense," I screamed.

"Of course, it doesn't. You're too stupid to understand," the Bearman heckled.

I had to think to clear my head even as the pain was starting to pound. I forced a few calming breaths as I sat on the ground. Then, putting my elbows on my knees, I rested my forehead on my palms. How did this all start? I woke up and snuck out of my room to go to the library. The library, the books Thorn was reading. I was looking for a reversal spell. Then what happened.

"What *happened*?" I demanded, forcing my fists against my eyes.

"You were meddling in things you don't understand," the hag said.

"No, I was trying to keep Thorn safe. I didn't want her to use spells that would hurt her."

"Do you think I'm stupid?" she asked, but the tone was soft, almost gentle.

"Then she came in and, and . . ." The memories of what she'd said still tore at my heart. "She said she was only using me."

"Would I say that, though?" Her voice was rough but familiar. "Think! Think hard. What did I say?"

I was confused and angry, "I don't even know who you are!" I shouted.

"Yes, you do—think. Henry, look at me." I looked up at her heavily lined face.

Her eyes—I recognized those eyes. The crystal clear blue next to the crimson laced. I could see Thorn's face under the wrinkles and leathery skin.

"Thorn?" I shook my head. This was trickery. "Stop messing with my head!" I shouted, instantly regretting it. The pain felt like my skull was splitting open, and my brain was trying to escape.

"Yes, yes, we're tricking you," the Bearman confirmed. "If you tell us what spell you were reading, we'll make the pain stop."

"No!" Hag-Thorn shouted. "Let him suffer!"

"It hurts!" The pain was becoming unbearable. I could barely think. My head was on fire. I needed it to stop. I was going to die. I knew it.

"We can make the pain cease," the troll spoke softly, "just tell us the spell, and it will stop."

What did I care if they knew? Thorn had deserted me. Scratch had betrayed me. All I wanted was for the pain to stop. What did I owe anyone? My parents hated me. I was sure of that now. I had never been loved. "*Palendromiabifor-cate*," I muttered through the agony.

Through the burning pain and my streaming eyes, I saw the hag run off at a rate that was surprisingly spry. I curled into a ball to fight the burning as my skin cracked from the heat.

Someone was chanting.

My eyes were going to burst as flames surrounded my body. My bones began to splinter.

Someone was holding me. Whoever was chanting was moving around me. The pressure behind my eyes began to subside while the flames consuming my body were slowly extinguished. Soft hands cradled my head while a sweet voice called my name. More muscular arms lifted me gently. As I was taken inside, someone put cool water on my lips. I could only drink a little. I felt exhausted and was still in agony. Someone told me to sleep, so I did.

———⋯———

When I woke, I was back in the somewhat lumpy bed in my room. It was dark out, and a candle was burning. I realized I wasn't alone. Thorn was curled, fully clothed, next to me. A bowl of water was tipping precariously toward her. She held a damp cloth in her hand. I had no idea how to react, so I carefully attempted to move the bowl. However, this action didn't have the desired outcome. Thorn woke with a shout, covered in icy water from half her head to midway across her stomach, and her hair was plastered across her face. Her blue eye blinked at me as she realized what had happened.

"Oh, thank the gods, you're awake!" Her relief was apparent, but I was still confused.

"You," I swallowed painfully. My throat felt raw. I remembered screaming a lot. Thorn handed me a cup of cool water with a hint of mint. "You left me," I croaked.

"Drink. It contains a soothing ointment for your throat," Thorn whispered.

"You said . . ." I had to force myself to continue through the pain. "You said you were in love with Scratch, and you only used me!" The memories came crashing back. The look of disgust on her face and her words stabbed my heart.

Thorn's face turned from concern to annoyed anger. "You're an idiot Henry Dreamweaver!" She leapt from the bed and began using a drying spell. When she turned back to glare at me, the red-tinged eye bored into me. "When and where did I make this declaration of love?" Her tone made it clear that I was going to answer.

"In the library, after I-I—" I swallowed more of the water, more to give myself time to think than due to thirst. "I told you I wouldn't allow you to use the spells you were researching." Her glare told me she wasn't pleased with my choice of words.

"You don't get to make decisions for me. That's a well-established rule." Her hands had found her hips, and I knew I was in for a lecture. "There are so many things I want to say to you right now." She was pacing. It was definitely angry pacing. "You had everyone worried, running off like that! Where did you think you were going?" She shook her head. "No, that doesn't matter! You're an idiot!"

Finally, she shouted. "Do you know how worried I was? I woke up, and you were gone. I had no idea where you were, and then you were running through town causing trouble!"

"Like I said, I went to the library."

"Yes, and we'll get to that in a second!" she said, cutting me off. "I didn't make it to the library until after Rollins tried to stop you. Not until you ran out of town, throwing spells at people as they were just going about their business. Not until you tried to hide and Duane and Steve, the two excellent trolls, found you and tied you up so they could bring you back." She was back to glaring at me. I was about to say something, except she raised a finger to silence me. "No, you are *not* talking." She stood before me like a disappointed parent, shaking her head and muttering. "Damn it, Henry! First rule! It's the first rule my father taught us." Again, she glared expectantly at me.

"Are you waiting for an answer?" For my comment, I got the, you've-got-to-be-kidding-me look. So I searched my fuzzy mind for the first rule. "No spell casting in the house?"

Her red-tinged eye became frighteningly menacing. "No joking,"

I tried to think.

"Gods, Henry!" She stamped her foot. "*Never read a spell aloud if you don't know the effects!*"

"Ooohhh, yeah." I smiled at the memory, but it quickly faded.

"Oh, got there at last, did you?" Her arms folded tightly across her chest. "So, we're, one: going into other people's business without asking anything." She counted off one finger. "Two: being overly protective and demanding without discussing things rationally." Another finger went down. "Three: reading spells out loud with no knowledge of what they might do." Another finger down. "Four: running around like a crazy person, scaring everyone, and making them worry." She was now making a fist, balling it tightly. "Five: believing that I would leave you behind, use you, and, for the love of the earth, tell you that I'm in love with *Scratch*! You . . ." She punched me in the arm. "Complete . . ." A hit to the shoulder.

I covered my head in self-defense.

"IDIOT!" She smacked my hands that I held over my head.

I didn't let down my guard until I heard the door slam. "That spell," I groaned, flopping back onto the bed, pushing my palms into my eyes. "I remember now. It was a reversal spell. I thought it could keep her from getting hurt." I moaned.

"It didn't work, MORON!" I heard Thorn's muffled shout from behind the door.

"Damn bat ears," I muttered.

"You're not making it better!" she yelled and hit the wall for emphasis.

"I'm sorry!" Silence followed. "Thorn, I'm really sorry."

The door creaked open enough for me to see her blue eye. "I thought we knew each other better than that." Her voice sounded hurt.

"I'm really sorry." I meant it too. "I should have talked to you about what was going on. But, it was just like, you were on a mission."

"I *am*." she said with some force, bursting into the room. "I need to find my father. I'm worried sick about him, and now I have to worry about you." She closed her eyes, attempting to find some calm. "Henry, I need to be able to trust you." She held her hands over her heart. "I need you to trust *me*."

"I'm sorry—it was just like every fear I keep tucked away came out," I admitted, then felt horrid.

Thorn closed the door and slowly approached the bed, sitting with her knees tucked under her. Then, taking both my hands in hers, she looked into my eyes. "Henry, there's something between us, something I want to explore."

My heart, which only moments before had been torn to pieces, suddenly pounded in hope.

"However, right now, I can't think about that. I'm already terrified of something happening to my best friend. I don't want you to come with me, but I can't stand the thought of going without you." She bowed her head, touching her forehead to my fingertips. "When this is done, we'll talk, and then we'll, hopefully, move forward." She looked into my eyes again. "Please remember that you're the world to me, so be careful and continue to watch out for me."

"I'm sorry I worried you." I wiped a tear from her face. I was surprised when she wiped one from my cheek. "I don't have any right to ask . . ." I swallowed. "But could I sleep here tonight?" She smiled and nodded. She began to pull away, but I held her hands. "Um, next to you—just sleep. I'm not asking for anything else. I just want you here beside me."

She smiled at me. Then she pulled her hands out of mine and slapped me on the head. I threw my arms up for cover. "You dummy—I had no plans to sleep on that lumpy ass couch." She slid off the bed. "I'm going to change into something to sleep in, and you're right. You keep them grabby little elf hands to yourself." She paused at the bathroom door. "You're not off the hook. I'm still furious at you."

The night wasn't restful. My dreams were a tormenting series of visions of Thorn's hatred for me. However, each time I woke in fear, she was beside me. Just having her within reach allowed me to sleep. Then, I reached for her early in the morning only to find I was alone.

CHAPTER 42

I woke confused from another horrible dream. In the dream, Scratch held me back while Thorn taunted me. "You're weak," she laughed, pulling one of her swords out. "I think it's time we cut out some dead weight." Her blade sliced through the air to clang loudly against the wall, then she slashed again, causing another loud clang. As the blade inched closer to my throat, I struggled against Scratch's grip. Suddenly, I was wide awake, sitting up in bed. Someone was calling my name.

Reality came into focus. The clanging turned out to be the city's warning bells, while the grip on my arms turned out to be Tal's. However, waking to his face did cause me to scream. But if he was offended, he didn't show it.

"Wake up, Master Dreamweaver." The urgency in Tal's voice chased away any lingering sleep. "You're needed on the rampart." Then, when he was sure I was awake and understood what was happening, Tal left me to prepare.

I hurriedly dressed and rushed to the city walls. It took me a few moments to get my bearings. Thankfully I could easily find Tal. After moving through the crowded walkway, I finally joined Wolf, Thorn, and a couple of archers. I followed their gaze into the distance. "What is that?" I asked, seeing a dark mass undulating as it entered the narrow passage at the beginning of the abandoned outskirts.

"That, my dear elf, is an army," Wolf growled. "Although, *whose* army remains to be seen."

"I can't see any banners yet," Thorn added. Nevertheless, there was a buzz of activity all around us. The front gate was closed and heavily barred. Along the entire length of the top of the wall, creatures of all sorts readied weapons. A fire was being stoked under a cauldron that I assumed held oil. Several small fires were lit next to archers who added oil-soaked cloth to the tip of their arrows.

The squeaking of wheels and the groan of wood announced the arrival of several trebuchets. "Where the hell were they hiding those?" I asked. No one answered me. "Maybe it's Serina and Scratch?" I announced. Again, no one seemed to hear me.

"Henry, you aren't going to believe this," Thorn said, swatting my arm as she looked through a telescope. "If I'm not mistaken, that's your family crest." I took the telescope she offered.

"Th-that *is* our crest and that of Scratch's family," I confirmed.

"I see three knights at the lead, followed by the standard-bearers," Tal informed Wolf.

"Why are they marching on us?" Wolf asked, deep concern lacing his words.

"Maybe they've come to help us," Thorn offered, hopefully. Her face told me her words lacked conviction.

I shook my head. My stomach twisted with anxiety. "They have no idea where we are," I explained. "I didn't know where our parents were, so no, I didn't tell them we were here." More for Wolf's benefit than mine.

"So, they are coming to see me." Wolf nodded. "Well, old friends, I have an appropriate greeting for you." He signaled a goblin who shot an arrow high into the air. Wolf gripped the low stone wall and waited. After what felt like an eternity, I heard a thump on the protective wood barrier that stood ten feet tall, crowned with spikes.

Frowning, Wolf reached through an opening in the wall to retrieve an arrow. Unscrolling the attached message, his frown deepened. "They are riding under a banner of truce."

"Well, that's good," I suggested. "That means they haven't come to fight."

Wolf scowled as he crumpled the message and spit out the opening in the wall. "If that was your father's command, he would be approaching under the banner of friendship."

"Banner of friendship?" Thorn asked before I could.

"When we fought your mother, there was a high risk of infiltration. So we came up with a way to differentiate friendly armies." Wolf kept his eye attached to the telescope. "Your father would know the correct banner to ride under."

"But that's Henry's father at the head of the army!" Thorn protested.

"That may be, however, if he's coming to attack, his mind is not his own," Wolf growled before shouting orders. Pausing momentarily, he glanced at me. "Your mother would be in the lead, not your father."

"Wait, wait, wait!" I finally shouted. "My father is leading them!"

"That just makes this more dire," Wolf shouted back. "Your parents and Heraldry by themselves are extremely dangerous. Give them an army . . ." Wolf shook his head, unable to finish the statement.

I turned to Thorn. "Tell me this is just another dream!" I grabbed her shoulders, shaking her roughly.

"Ow, Henry! Let go!" Thorn pushed me away, "Get a hold of yourself. You're no good to us in a panic."

I backed away from her.

"I understand, you're upset, please, try to—"

I didn't catch the rest of her plea. I grabbed two arrows from the quiver beside Wolf and leapt through the opening. I spun, jamming an arrow into the wood. I used the other one to lower myself down to the stone portion. Thorn was shouting at me from above. It took only one slip of my foot for my brain to finally kick in.

"What the hell am I doing?!" I screamed. I looked back up only to be smacked in the face by a heavy rope. I almost fell right then. Grabbing the rope, I clung to it like my life depended on it because it did. I flew up back onto the top of the wall. Tal was shaking his massive head at me. I bent over, hands on my knees, trying to catch my breath. Thorn's familiar boots appeared close to me. I stood up, about to apologize, when she slapped me harder than I'd ever been hit. I saw stars, and my face stung. In the next instant, I was enveloped in an extremely tight embrace.

"Henry Tano Dreamweaver," Thorn used all three names. I was in it deep. "How could you scare me like that?" She held me at arm's length. Her concern melted into anger. "You do something idiotic like that again, and I'll kill you myself." She pushed me away and stalked back to the opening to watch the approaching army.

I looked to my other companions for help. Tal shook his head slowly, holding up his massive hands. The look on his face said he wasn't getting involved.

Wolf tried to hide his laughter. "That is twice in two days you have set her off," he snickered. "I would watch your ass for a while."

"Okay, I messed up. I'm sorry." I tried to sound as if I wasn't wholly mortified by my actions. "That doesn't change the fact that my father is leading an attacking army."

"That is true," Wolf's expression hardened. "I hate fighting against my friends, and that bitch knows it."

Thorn turned her blazing anger back on me. "One more stunt, outburst, or even bad joke, and I will have you bound and gagged and thrown into the deepest dungeon this town has!" Then, turning her back on me, I saw the shudder. "You're not well enough to be out here." She muttered, barely loud enough for me to hear. "I can't trust you."

I couldn't think of any way to contradict her. On the other hand, I didn't completely trust my mind. So all I could do was stare out past the ramparts as my parents' army advanced through the abandoned houses outside the gate. My parents and Scratch's father sat tall on warhorses. Two elf lieutenants flanked each of them. My mom was waving a large parchment with a huge smile.

"Wolf," Mom called, "we did it finally. We have a treaty from the emperor giving us equal rights."

I observed the elves next to my parents. Something about them felt off. The army behind them also seemed to be elves, but there was a shimmer around them. "There's a spell on them," I said in surprise.

Thorn was already chanting the beginnings of a disillusionment spell.

"Hello, Wolf," my father's voice reached us from below. "I will say I expected a bit more of a welcome from an old friend."

At the opening in the wall, I joined Wolf. "Oh, I see you've met my son." Mom shifted in the saddle. "Tell me, is that charming Ms. Caterous with him?"

Thorn finished her spell. It looked like a strong wind blew through the soldiers. To my relief, about half of them disappeared. But, to my horror, the remaining army were some of the vilest dark creatures I've ever seen.

My dad looked back at the beasts behind him, then up to us. "I see she's here. So much for the ruse, and so much the better."

My mom pulled out the paper she'd been waving. "You know, Wolf, it's a shame. This is real. This treaty, it's the one we fought for. We received one before we met Althea."

My dad took up the narrative. "We weren't sure you were still here until we caught the courier bringing you a copy. Althea was insistent we should visit our old commander." Then, without any other warning, he called for the attack. A hellish roar filled the air, followed by thousands of arrows.

Wolf called upon our archers, who added to the shadow in the sky as it was filled with deadly projectiles. I leapt behind cover as thousands of thuds hit the wood at my back.

"Swordsmen to the wall!" Wolf cried. Our archers already up here began firing into the approaching horde. Thorn threw spell after spell, carving huge craters into the earth. But no matter how many fell, they were replaced almost immediately. I was casting protection around our fighters. So far, none of our people had been injured. However, this was a fact that I knew wouldn't hold.

"Tal, NOW!" Wolf ordered. Thorn gasped as the wall shook. The abandoned house exploded, sending dark creatures and splintered wood high into the air. Silence followed. The small spark of hope in my chest died as the smoke cleared.

While hundreds of our attackers lay dead, scattered through the detritus of the village, a thousand more were regrouping for another charge. My parents had split to take command of two separate groups, with Mr. Heraldry commanding a third.

Huge stones flew overhead, launched from our catapults. Our enemy seemed to have brought their own heavy artillery. However, between myself and a few other magic users, we could deflect the enemy missiles against the stone wall.

Little Rollins limped speedily along the wall, bringing water and aid to the fighters. He turned to me with a smile and a thumbs up. Suddenly the sky darkened. Spells, stones, and arrows assaulted our defenses. Screams of fear and agony rose all along the barricade. Blood and bodies covered the stone. I searched for any sign of Rollins. The place he'd been was now a smoking gouge in the wall. His crutch lay unneeded next to a dead archer. My heart ached.

Smoke and chaos enveloped me. I had no idea where Thorn or Wolf were fighting. I only hoped they were safe. I threw out defensive spells, trying keep our fighters safe.

"Ladders!" someone shouted.

I realized I didn't have a weapon. My sword was back in the room, I think. So I ran toward the armory, being jostled and pushed by fighters heading to defend the wall. Then, ahead, I saw Tal. Thorn had to be near him. Forgetting my need for a weapon, I sprinted toward the huge ogre.

I watched in amazement as Tal leapt from the wall. Landing lightly, he ran to the gate, throwing his weight against the undulating doors and holding fast as others threw crates and wagons against the barrier. A spearpoint broke through the door slicing into Tal's arm. His howl of pain and fury sent me into a crouch. A knee hit me in the back, sending me sprawling across the stones.

A hideous face hit the floor right next to mine. I recognized the owner—a grumpy dwarf who worked at the tavern. I thought she was dead until she rolled over, pressing a sword hilt into my hand. I recited a quick healing spell. I had barely finished when she was swept away by some tiny mountain goblins

Groups of the small creatures ran through the forest of legs, picking up the injured to ferry them to safety.

I barely had time to marvel at their swiftness. I was grabbed by the back of the shirt and lifted to my feet. An ancient spriggan nodded to me and then disappeared to fight one of the invaders.

"There is a sword in your hand. Use it, boy!" Wolf shouted at me.

I was back where I started. However, Thorn wasn't there. So I ducked and rolled away from a battle-ax, parried and slashed a goblin sword, and stabbed a gray-green thing with sharp teeth. I knew I'd killed that creature. I most likely had killed more than one of the enemies. I tried not to think about that. I was defending myself and my friends. I couldn't think about the families and loved ones my victims had.

I never realized how blood could be slick and sticky at the same time until my hands were covered in it. I was hurt. I could feel cuts and bruises but couldn't tell my own blood from the rest that covered me. My appearance was nothing compared to the horror spectacle that was Wolf.

The man was covered in gore and dirt. His two-handed bastard sword sliced through attackers like they were nothing. Blood sprayed from his victims and blade, painting the walls crimson, and ran from his lips into his beard. I wasn't sure if he was injured or had ripped out someone's throat. The look on his face told me I was seeing someone I had never met. This was a warrior with brutality unseen by his attackers. I saw their fear as he unleashed his attacks.

A sword swooshed by my ear. Then, as I turned to face my assailant, he was blasted off his feet and over the wall. With his scream echoing in my ears, I saw the face of beauty and terrifying power.

Thorn ran along the wall, blasting climbers off their ladders as archers shot flaming arrows at the attackers. She jumped high into the air, spinning while sending fire out in a wide circle. Landing, she threw one hand out to balance as she crouched. A cheer rose from our fighters as all the attackers within the circle were destroyed. We had time to share a glance, saying we were okay, before she was off again. I treated as many of the injured as I could. While I had a moment, I took a second to glance over the wall at my father.

He sat on his mount, watching his army being decimated. I lost track of my mother while Scratch's father tried to flank us. I observed that both commanders still had their lieutenants close by their sides. That's when I noticed the elf guards were holding staves with glowing crystals. It clicked in my brain.

"Thorn! I need you!" I shouted. She was at my side in an instant. I picked up a bow and nocked an arrow. "I need to kill the beasts on either side of my father." She nodded without question. She cast a spell on my arrow as I let it fly. I didn't watch its flight, trusting my aim and Thorn's Magic. Instead, I prepared my second volley. She released the same spell as I let the second arrow fly. This time I watched it find its mark.

Light exploded from the crystal, burning away the top half of the being holding the staff. My father remained seated on the horse. However, his head was down like he was asleep. My heart stopped as he slowly slid from the saddle to crumple on the ground. I either saved or killed him. The creatures under my father's command faltered.

Thorn was back to immolating our enemies. I had a moment's hesitation, torn between my father and keeping our friends safe. I threw a protection spell at my father and returned to protecting the defenders.

"Tell the archers to take out the crystals!" I shouted.

"Tell 'em yourself!" Wolf barked.

Running the length of the wall to where I'd last seen Heraldry, I searched for my mother. I was stunned when I reached the far end where Heraldry was attacking. Without Thorn, Tal, or Wolf, they weren't fairing as well. Intense fighting was happening on the wall, with a steady stream of dark creatures flowing up the ladders.

"Shoot the crystals on the staves!" I shouted at the few remaining archers we had. Behind me, a bright flash and explosion sent us tumbling. I prayed for my friends' safety. Then, regaining my feet, I slashed my way to the front of the wall. Pulling a bow from the death grip of a hobgoblin, I found some arrows. Sweat and blood ran into my eyes. The field below was chaos. "There!" I shouted, pointing to the two elves on either side of Mr. Heraldry.

No one paid attention to me. I pulled a goblin by the neck to my side. Blocking a sword, I shouted, "Take out the crystal bearers!" I could only pray he was on our side. Recognition crossed his face as he nodded. Both our first shots went wide. I tried to remember the spell Thorn had cast. Giving up after a second, I tried one I knew. My fellow archer's bolt hit true, instantly vaporizing the elf and staff. Panic rumbled through the attackers.

Heraldry and his lone guard began to flee. Calls for my head rose from enemy commanders. My comrade became my defender. I blocked out the noise, the smell, and my fear. I took aim, drew my breath, and let loose my arrow. After the green flash, Mr. Heraldry slumped and fell from his galloping horse.

The tide turned as reinforcements from town arrived. The army below in the ruins began a chaotic retreat as we slaughtered their companions on the wall. The ladders fell and were not replaced. Shouts went up and down the defenses as our victory became realized. That could only mean one thing—my mother must have been defeated as well.

Rushing back along the wall, I found a stairway. Jumping down stairs at a time, I landed unsteadily near the gate. One of the huge doors lay broken and burned on the ground. Bodies littered the entry. Tal lay propped against the wall, several mountain goblins attending to his wounds and burns. Stunned, I recognized one of the tundra goblins—the one he had waved at when we first met—administering water to the giant ogre. Upon seeing me, he sent the little goblin over.

I knelt down as she beckoned. "How's Tal?" I asked before she could speak.

I noticed the goblin had a pleasant, cute face. More surprising, however, when the little goblin spoke, her voice was high-pitched, almost tinkling. "Oh, the big galoot will be fine. Come with me." She moved so fast through the crowd, weaving through legs and bodies, I found it hard to keep up. Until, suddenly, I found I couldn't move.

My mother was on the ground, surrounded by many more mountain goblins and several healers. Her eyes were closed, and her face was serene. Her armor, however, was burned and dented. Blood flowed freely from a wound somewhere under the plate armor. A push from around my knees finally sent me to her side. Through tears, I added my own healing spells.

My mother's labored breathing calmed and evened. I held her hand, praying she would be okay. Her eyes fluttered to slits. "Henry," she breathed, but that was all. I let go of her hand as she was bundled away on a stretcher.

"Tal heard your orders to destroy the crystals." Squeaked a voice in my ear. I was still on my knees. "He took out both elves and saved your mother." The small face cringed a little. "She was always a good friend to Tal."

"What's your name?" I asked.

"Dobaker," she replied, somewhat confused.

I looked past her back to Tal. "Dobaker, I think you're his favorite now." An orc was helping Tal over to us. Dobaker scampered up Tal's arm to rub foreheads with him. I smiled at the sight.

"See, Doba—I said I was okay." Watching them twisted a yearning in my stomach. I had to find Thorn and my father.

CHAPTER 43

My heart was shredded between running out the front gate, racing along the wall, and returning to my mom's side. I saw the way out of the gate was nearly blocked with dead invaders and defenders. Along the wall, great sections were missing or damaged. The dead lay strewn about like forgotten toys while blood ran down the broken stone in rivulets. My feet grew roots of indecisiveness while my mind tried to tell them where to run.

Thorn appeared at my side, exhausted, battered, bloody, filthy, and the most beautiful person I could imagine. I knew I likely mirrored her appearance. I didn't care as I pulled her into a hug of relief, fear, exhaustion, and sadness. Unfortunately, our post-battle hug was all too brief. The enemy had retreated, but they had not left the area. Instead, they stayed just out of range.

"What are they doing?" I asked Wolf, who had joined us.

"They are regrouping. Come now, this is not over." Wolf sent Thorn and me to help remove debris from the gate while he sent out a group to retrieve my dad.

"I want to help!" I protested. However, Wolf wouldn't let me go with them. I could tell he still didn't trust my judgment. Thorn could only give me a sympathetic shrug. I knew she agreed with him.

The smell of charred flesh that accosted us when they opened the door was almost toxic. It took several solid trolls and orcs to push the door open against the bodies. Thorn stood beside me as we waited for the two humans and two goblins Wolf sent to retrieve Dad. I didn't know if I was more frightened if he was alive or dead. They had been under a spell—I knew that. I, however, did not know what it had done to their minds. Would they see me the same way I'd seen Thorn recently? Was I an enemy to them?

Thorn gripped my arm as Mr. Heraldry was brought in. "Wait, he was further away. Where's Dad?" I shouted at the man carrying Mr. Heraldry's stretcher. I tried to push past the groups bringing in wounded and rebuilding the gate. However, Thorn held firm.

"Don't," she urged. "Let them do what they need to do." I didn't understand at first. If Dad was still under the spell or had his mind altered, the rescuers would become his executioners. My mind went fuzzy, and my stomach prepared to revolt.

Finally, I saw the team Wolf had sent. I whimpered as I saw they were returning empty-handed until I saw the orc carrying my dad.

"He was buried under several bodies," the orc explained in his deep grunting voice. With his free hand, he patted my shoulder, causing my knees to buckle. "It's lucky he had a protection spell around him." Then he carefully laid my dad on a stretcher.

I watched as healers attended to him. A tear ran down my cheek as he was carried past me. His eyes were barely open, and his face was deathly pale. I was about to turn away, hoping to hide my tears, when my father's hand shot out to grab me. "Your mother can't be trusted." His eyes were wide open, wildly searching. "Sebastian's family." He fought to stay conscious. "They're under her spell." His eye's rolled up as he fell back onto the stretcher.

"Mom and Mr. Heraldry are safe," I explained. "We freed them too." I carefully pried his grip from my arm but held his hand.

The anguish melted from his face as he lay back on the stretcher. I smiled a little at his calm face, then thanked the men carrying my dad as I placed his hand back on his chest.

"He'll be okay," Thorn assured me as she appeared at my side. I looked at her, thankful for her reassurance, when she screamed.

With swiftness and strength I didn't think possible in his condition, Dad leapt to his feet. He grabbed Thorn violently, his fist crumpling her tunic in his tight grip, nearly lifting her off her feet. I grabbed his hands, trying to loosen his painful-looking hold on Thorn.

Although his eyes never looked at her, he knew who he was talking to. "Your mother," he gasped, "she's going to kill you."

Suddenly, Thorn struggled under his dead weight as she tried to hold up his unconscious body. With the help of a few others, I extricated Thorn and wrestled Dad back onto the stretcher. I held out a hand to help Thorn back onto her feet.

"That was unwelcome news," Wolf understated from behind us. "I think we need to act now." He continued. "The witch—no offense." He nodded at Thorn

"None taken," Thorn muttered.

"She is going to use our friends and family against us."

"How do we know who we can trust?" she asked, deep in thought.

"We need to watch for actions out of character. That is the only way we discovered the enchantment last time."

"In times of war, that must be hard to discern," I offered. Wolf and Thorn both stared at me in surprise.

"Again, that was quite perceptive." Thorn laughed. I frowned at her teasing. Then, her face turned serious. "We need to find Scratch's mother, so we can dispel her and anyone else under mother's spell." Thorn frowned. Movement through the crowd caught my attention. One of the dwarves that worked at the tavern hurried toward Wolf.

I watched a brief exchange between Wolf and the dwarf before they both hurried off. I felt something telling me I needed to know what was happening. So, grabbing Thorn's hand, we followed. What we saw was something I wasn't prepared for. My dad thrashed, half-conscious, on the sweat-soaked mattress.

"She was sent to kill Henry," my dad rasped.

"Henry is safe," Wolf soothed. "He is here."

"She's going to the house. You must stop her."

"Who?" I asked.

"Scratch's mother. Althea used her prejudice as a weapon," Dad yelled at the dwarf.

"I will send out riders immediately." Wolf called to an elf, then gave several quick orders. The elf saluted, then hurried from the room. "No need to worry. We will retrieve her."

My dad lay back, momentarily calmed. It lasted long enough for my shoulders to relax. He bolted upright. Again his eyes rolled, unfocused and bewildered. "Caterous is in the dungeon. He fought her."

Thorn stepped closer. "Mr. Dreamweaver, is my father okay?"

Dad focused the second he heard Thorn's voice. "She has bound his magic. He's unhurt but helpless. Sebastian's mother is going to the house to kill him and Henry. His father now leads Althea's third army after Henry's mother." His voice was calm, and his focus on her was intense.

"Where is Althea?" Wolf interrupted.

"Cal Barra Dune," my father whispered before his strength failed him and he collapsed.

"Cal Barra Dune?" I asked, not understanding the words.

Tal's deep voice explained, "Cal Barra Dune means Mountain of Beautiful Flowers in the language of my ogre brethren."

"Not the type of place where I would have expected to find an evil sorceress's stronghold," I said, immediately apologizing to Thorn. She waved off the apology, calling her mother far worse than evil.

"It is a barren, forbidding place," Wolf explained. "The craggy rocks afford us some cover, but they also hide ambushes."

"So why the name?" I couldn't help but ask.

"Because it was ironic," Tal shrugged. "We ogres don't have the best sense of humor."

"Arla!" Wolf shouted. An attractive human female approached. "How are our other guests?"

"Both are sleeping quietly. I've told Dreamweaver and Heraldry that they and their children are safe. I will send an eagle immediately to the vampires to inform the young Heraldry." Arla saluted and left.

"Our task just increased in difficulty tenfold," Wolf sighed, rubbing a hand over his face. "With Caterous trapped . . ." He shook his head. "On the plus side, Althea no longer has your father and mother as generals or Heraldry as a spy." He shuddered, then patted my shoulder as he passed. "That is something."

His words did little in the way of reassurance. I just nodded and followed him to the door. Exiting the tavern, we were met with a buzz of activity. Wagons were being loaded, and the sound of sharpening swords filled the air. I saw all sorts of species trying on armor that was suddenly too small for them. Others were trying to choose between different weapons. The main gate was being reinforced, and other defenses were strengthened.

Noting the astonished look on my face, Wolf smiled. "We may want to live in peace. However, that does not mean our enemies will go unpunished."

The assembly of seven or eight hundred heavily armed and experienced warriors took some of the fear from my heart. I had no idea what the enemy's number would be. However, I felt we might have a chance if Serina could get her people to help.

———⌘———

A quiet tension settled over the town as the day wore on. The enemy army seemed to be setting up camp. I wondered if the battle had become a siege instead.

"How will the rider get through?" I asked Wolf while we watched tents blossom in the enemy camp.

"We know ways off the plain." He laughed, then became solemn. "As long as there are not too many of us using the paths."

"So, evacuation is off the table?" I muttered.

"Damn straight!" Wolf barked. "This is our home, and we will defend it." He left me on the wall, watching as small fires were ignited. All I could do was hope some help would come soon.

Serina's assistance proved to be harder to come by than I thought. Arla's eagle had returned bearing no good news. The vampire civil war seemed to be about to break. Rumor was that Althea's influence was behind it all. We couldn't count on the vampire reinforcements. Although Wolf seemed fine with the knowledge, his town would be free of *those life-sucking bastards,* as he put it. Many found the news less than reassuring.

My father hadn't regained consciousness since his warning about Scratch's mother. The local healer told me his condition was due to mental exhaustion from fighting Althea's control. I was assured he would recover in a week or two. Unfortunately, Mr. Heraldry and my mom had only woken up briefly. While they gave us some useful information about Althea's army, they were incapable of much else.

"We could definitely use their skills," Wolf grumbled. I agreed as we looked out from the ramparts to the enemy fires burning in the distance.

"The healers said they'll all be fine, " I muttered, thinking my parents would die in their beds if we were attacked by an army led by Thorn's mother.

My concern was at least constant. First, Thorn alternated between guilt and anger at her mother. Then, she would suddenly hiss a curse on her mother for using our family and friends against us. I had no idea what to say to soothe her. Finally, we received a message that Scratch's mother had been found and released from her spell. I could take some solace from that as I looked out at the orange glow of the enemy camp.

Sometime during the long night, I got used to the random twang of bow-strings and the screams of night beasts. Althea's army would send creatures to us. We didn't understand why, as they never made it over the wall. Some would catch fire when they hit the ground. We assumed they were carrying incendiaries in hopes of burning us out. Others simply died in the dark.

Patrols roamed the town, but that didn't seem to alter how the inhabitants lived. The taverns were full, and the wild escapades continued. However, Wolf assured us that banning this behavior would be detrimental to our cause. I could only trust his judgment.

A bright spot had appeared earlier in the day in the form of Tal. He returned to Wolf's side, healed and ready for battle. Thorn jabbed me in the ribs when we saw him. A thin gold ring now encircled his left ring finger.

"Dobaker?" I asked, nodding to the ring. He smiled in return. If you've never seen an ogre blush, I will tell you, it's a sight to see.

It was just past dusk when Wolf and I stood silently along the wall—we'd been watching the enemy practice marching—when I became aware of Thorn's presence. I felt my face break into a smile. My family was safe, and Thorn was with me. I barely noticed the twang of a bow until I heard the bowman scream.

Flames incinerated an arrow midflight, then a ball of fire hit the rampart close to where the shot had originated. Warning shouts rose along the wall. Wolf's sword was drawn. Using the blade as a pointer and a conductor's baton, he ordered the archers to fire. I saw the shadow of a winged creature with weirdly long legs cross the moon. Flaming red eyes burned like embers from the shadow.

"Wait!" Thorn shouted, then ran along the wall. "Don't shoot, don't shoot!" I recognized those eyes as well.

Hesitantly, Wolf ordered the archers to stand by. The flapping of huge, leathery wings on the wind passed overhead. A terrifying demon dropped a man lightly on the ground before setting down herself. Serina's wings sent smaller villagers tumbling while the larger soldiers ran in fear or prepared for battle. By the time Thorn and I reached the ground, Serina was back to normal. Scratch seemed a bit shaken by the flight but roused quickly. Thorn flew into Serina's embrace while I hugged my friend.

CHAPTER 44

e stood surrounded by some of the most feared creatures in the entire world. I saw orcs, ogres, goblins, sprites, spriggans, minotaurs, and creatures I couldn't even name that I'd only seen in nightmares. There were also men, dwarves, and elves. All these creatures were united as they stood staring at us, silently agreeing to avoid Serina. For her part, Serina seemed just as happy to be avoided, while Scratch seemed anxious to talk to Wolf, Tal, Thorn, and me.

Wolf eyed Serina with annoyance as he barked to the crowd to disperse. We quickly returned to the tavern as the townsfolk parted for Serina, allowing us to pass unencumbered. A fact I believe she secretly enjoyed.

We were ushered into a back room as soon as we arrived at the tavern. We sat around a table cluttered with maps, goblets, and small plates of food. Neither Wolf nor Serina had acknowledged each other. It didn't matter too much since Scratch seemed willing to do all the talking.

"You've got a highly defendable town here," Scratch complimented. "On two sides, you have high mountain walls, then a sheer cliff drop on another. The main wall is stone and wood, sturdy and thick." Nodding approvingly at Wolf's confident smirk. "However, there's no way to escape, no way to get supplies or freshwater." Scratch glowered.

Wolf, however, continued to smirk. Then, calmly, he placed a hand on Scratch's forearm. "We can withstand what, two, maybe three?" He said, looking at Tal.

Scratch's hand slammed the table. "Days? Weeks? That army has the entire valley blocked."

"Years," Tal's deep voice reverberated in my chest.

Scratch slowly sank into his chair. "Years?"

"Maybe longer, if need be." Wolf shrugged.

"How?" My astonished question was met with Scratch's enthusiastic nodding.

"Oh, these two with their secrets," our dwarf server grumbled. "You take a hidden path to a hidden tunnel through a hidden door and use the secret knock." She shrugged. "We get almost all our supplies that way." Wolf growled in annoyance, and the dwarf's face turned, if possible, sourer. "Okay, okay, I get it."

Wolf's glare followed her out of the room.

"That *is* how we do it." Tal seemed abashed, while Wolf looked like we'd taken away his favorite toy.

"Okay, so that problem is sort of solved," Thorn interjected, "assuming no one finds the secret passage."

"Only three of us know it. Tal, myself, and that grumpy dwarf." Wolf hooked a thumb over his shoulder. "She would never betray us," he stated emphatically.

Nodding her understanding, Serina continued, "We have food and water and a high wall."

"A high wall that was almost overrun," I noted.

"That was before," Wolf shouted. "We were lazy." He was on his feet, glaring. "That wall has repelled many invaders, numerous bombardments, and fire. It will hold firm, as will the people who defend it." Proudly he stood tall as if daring us to contradict him.

"I've seen how fiercely your people fight," Thorn agreed. "I'm confident in the wall's increased defenses." Then, she began to pace. "I do, however, fear the overwhelming force we face."

"We turned them back once, and they no longer have their strongest fighters," Wolf reiterated. "It matters not how many they throw against our spears." His confidence was absolute.

Scratch exhaled his frustration. "You don't see the extent of what you're up against."

"Althea could not raise such a force that could take this town."

"Her forces cover several leagues." Serina stepped out of the darkness. "She'll simply overwhelm you with numbers. You'll run out of arrows and spears long before she runs out of fodder."

"You children forget yourselves!" Anger boiled over into Wolf's tone. "I fought her before, and we won!"

"We have some preparations in place," Tal replied calmly. "Are your people coming to help us?" Wolf began to protest until Tal lay a hand on his shoulder.

My heart fell at the apology on Serina's face. Her look turned to stone as she addressed Wolf.

"It's with great regret I've even entertained Sebastian's request to return," Serina stated.

Wolf didn't attempt to hide his disdain. "It is with great regret that I allow filth like your kind into my town."

Wolf and Serina stared daggers at each other.

"I would prefer to remove my friends from danger and leave you to your fate," she said.

Wolf was on his feet again, hand on the hilt of his sword. Serina's hands glowed and crackled. Thorn and Tal rushed between them.

"I will not stand for this insolence!" Wolf roared.

"Bellow your lungs out, you insignificant butcher!"

"Butcher! Is that the lie they tell back in your cave?" Wolf barked a mirthless laugh. "I guess they leave out the part where we came to you for help." He drew a breath, then shouted at Serina. "And your dishonorable assassins attacked us!"

Serina tried to push past Thorn and Scratch as she screamed at Wolf, "Liar! We offered you shelter and aid. But instead of thanking us, you attacked us in our homes at daybreak."

"What homes!" Wolf managed to push past Tal. "We met you at Red Bounty Cave, as you requested, where you attacked!"

Serina and Wolf were now glaring at each other, their faces mere millimeters apart.

"We took you in at Vandergrart. A village in the north."

"We were never at Vandergrart," Tal spoke over the angry breathing of Serina and Wolf. He was calm as he moved between them. Easily, he steered both combatants to chairs on opposite sides of a table. "Is it possible that neither side was at the place the other holds as the point of betrayal?"

Serina and Wolf steadfastly stared in different directions. Finally, Tal sighed. "Could it be someone who desired you to be enemies was the one who betrayed you both?"

"You were not there!" Wolf shot back at his friend.

"No, I was not," Tal turned his attention to Serina. "Were you, Princess?"

"Princess?" Wolf was halfway to standing but faltered under Tal's glare.

"Yes, this is Princess Serina." Tal shrugged. "I am on friendly terms with her brother, Jamie. He is also of the opinion there was a third party responsible."

"Why has no one mentioned this before?" Serina and Wolf demanded simultaneously. Tal shrugged his answer.

"Well," Thorn offered, "maybe if we survive, we can find out what happened." She frowned. "It sounds like something my mother would come up with. Make enemies of potential allies so they wouldn't join against her."

Both Serina and Wolf grudgingly grunted their agreement.

Suddenly Serina sprang up. "It doesn't matter who was at fault! My people couldn't help you now even if we wanted to." She looked at Scratch imploringly. "I've already been gone too long." Then, her attention turned to Thorn and me. "I can get you to safety, but I have to leave."

I looked from Thorn to Serina. Serina read the same thing I did in Thorn's expression. Serina pulled Thorn into a tight embrace, then, to my surprise, she hugged me as well. "Watch over her," Serina whispered in my ear. Releasing me, Serina touched Tal's arm and smiled at him. "I will tell Jamie."

"Do not worry, Princess. I will see you and the prince again." Tal smiled confidently. I'm not sure either Serina or Tal believed that to be true.

"General Wolf." Serina spoke as if the words caused her discomfort. "May the battle see you victorious. Please watch over my friends." She finished with a bow.

Wolf stumbled to his feet to return the bow. "Um . . . uh . . . thanks?"

Serina didn't meet Scratch's eyes as she turned to him. "Please," she breathed.

"I can't leave them," he whispered.

Serina nodded as she placed a hand gently on the side of his face. "You be careful." She closed her eyes and a tear left a trail down her cheek as Scratch whispered something that sounded very much like a declaration to her.

Suddenly no one in the room knew where to look. We were all reluctant witnesses to the painful parting kiss of two lovers who may never be together again. Slowly Serina turned from Scratch. Her hand lingered in his as she began to leave.

My heart broke as his hand fell limply to his side when Serina disappeared through the door.

CHAPTER 45

Two days after Serina left, I questioned if we were actually in danger. Small attacks tested our defenses but nothing like the first assault. I also wondered if any mountains were anything but dreary and foreboding. A cold drizzle started falling an hour after Serina departed and had continued since. As a result, the gloomy gray of the area became that much more damp, miserable, and uncomfortable. Even Wolf, who seemed impervious to the weather, decided to stay indoors that day.

With nothing else happening, I took advantage of Wolf's vast library. I'd been researching spells all morning in Wolf's dimly lit study and decided I needed a break. Something I had promised Thorn I would often do. She still didn't trust me on my own with the spellbooks. Stepping outside, I couldn't tell where we were in the day. I didn't think it was too far into the afternoon, but the gloom made it feel like it was nearing dusk. A cold, damp wind soaked my face and hair. It didn't take long before I'd enjoyed enough of the outdoors.

As I entered the tavern, my stomach made a noise like an angry dragon. I hadn't realized my hunger until I smelled stew bubbling over the fire. Then, hearing my name, I searched the crowd for the voice's owner. Scratch waved me over to a table. "How goes the search?" he asked unenthusiastically.

A bowl of stew appeared before me. I barely thanked the server before delving into the meal. I shrugged noncommittally in response to Scratch.

"That good, huh?" Scratch frowned. I wanted to say something comforting or encouraging, but since Serina left, Scratch hadn't been much for conversation. So, I decided to encourage him to talk.

"So, uh, you and Serina, huh?" I cringed at my lame attempt to communicate and my choice of topic. Scratch didn't offer a response. "I, well, there was this book you might be interested in." I was grasping, and he knew it. Even so, Scratch humored me by feigning interest.

Suddenly, a bell was tolling from the square, and the tavern emptied in seconds. Scratch jumped up, grabbing my shirt to hurry me along. I looked longingly at my half-finished meal and half-ran as Scratch half-dragged me to the street.

I could feel the whole town's tension as they readied for action. My hands instinctively found the daggers at my hips. "Caterous, Dreamweaver, you are needed on the wall," Tal's voice boomed from everywhere. I sprinted to the access stairs with Scratch a step behind. I wasn't sure where Thorn was, but I trusted she'd beat me to the top.

Upon reaching Tal, I wasn't surprised to see Thorn there. They were surrounded by spearmen and archers. Everyone was looking over the wall past the already battle-scarred outskirts. I heard a rhythmic beating when I was about to ask what was happening.

"Damn," Scratch exhaled in astonishment. The valley undulated in a black mass, like waves in a dark ocean about to crash on our defenses. Our enemy had started their advance.

Suddenly, Wolf joined us, his weapon at the ready. "Tal! Send the signal!" The ogre nodded, then a blue sphere shot up into the sky. "Hold, hold," Wolf held his sword high. "Hold."

I had no idea what Tal and Wolf had planned. I could only see a line of heavily armed soldiers getting closer with every step. "What are they waiting for?" I growled.

"The right moment," Scratch replied quietly, his eyes darting between Wolf and the approaching troops.

I could just make out individual soldiers as they entered the furthest area where the abandoned buildings used to be. Their pace slowed slightly as they funneled into an area away from the ruined houses. Wolf smiled and let his arm drop. Tal sent a red globe into the air.

The rhythmic march was instantly drowned out by the rumble of falling boulders. It looked like the entire face of the cliff had broken free. Stones and boulders rained lethally onto the advancing army, throwing it into disarray. Their ranks dissolved into chaos as death crashed down. Enemy soldiers fleeing for cover ran to the few buildings remaining on the plain. Their relief, if there was any, was short-lived.

It wasn't but an instant after the first soldier entered till the structures exploded. Bodies and debris flew high into the air before being pummeled by the rock avalanche.

Scratch swore as more explosions rocked the ground, sending us staggering. Boulders continued to fall from the high cliffs. The dust began to settle while the crashing of stones quieted to the sound of gravel trickling to a stop. The survivors had pulled back a safe distance to regroup with a second wave of attackers. It would be slow moving over the debris-strewn field. I wondered why the archers weren't notching their arrows. I watched as the enemy approached the rock-strewn, cratered land where their comrades had just died. Several meters from the destruction, the thunderous sound of a second avalanche announced the death of the second wave. When the dust settled, and the sound died down, fewer of our enemies survived.

"That will make them think twice before they try that again!" Wolf shouted, looking at the debris blocking the enemy army's advance. Wolf howled in delight, pounding on Tal's shoulder in triumph. "You see that?" he yelled at Thorn and me. "Before those bastards can reach us, they have to make it over that new barrier. Then they must navigate the large craters left from the explosions." He pulled me along, pointing to the area in front of us. "Then, once they make it over that wall, they have to make it through this area that is also heavily cratered and full of debris and obstacles."

"Clever," Scratch commented.

"Not quite the welcome they had anticipated." Wolf barked out a laugh as he slapped Tal on the back. "Runners!" Wolf shouted.

I had to dodge as several goblins ran past, dropping bushels of arrows along the wall for the archers. "They should be able to pick off a lot of fighters as they reach the top." Scratch pointed to the new barricade to answer the confusion on my face.

"Excellent use of your environment," Mr. Heraldry exclaimed as he joined us on the parapet. He was able to briefly shake Wolf's hand before Scratch hugged him.

"Dad, are you sure you should be up and around?"

"I can't listen to Dreamweaver snore for one more second."

"Hey, I don't snore!" my mom defended from behind me before I was enveloped in a bone-crushing hug. "Your father says to tell you we're very proud of you."

Hugs and handshakes between the old friends took over my reunion with my mother. We discovered that Tal, the seemingly ferocious ogre, was a hugger. "He's the largest of his kind with the biggest heart of anyone," my mom explained. Thorn had begun to melt into the background, not wanting to get between friends and family. However, my mom was having none of it. Grabbing Thorn by the hand, she pulled her to her side. Mom held on loosely but wasn't about to let her leave.

Thorn attempted to excuse herself. "This is a time for family and friends."

"And just what are you if not family?" Mom demanded. "Aren't we at least friends?" Thorn couldn't find an argument. "Come, my husband will have to be restrained if we don't get to him soon."

"Yes, we need to formulate the plan," Mr. Heraldry noted as he descended the stairs with his arm over Scratch's shoulder. My mother had looped her arm through Thorn's.

I had mixed feelings about this as I watched them go. Wolf gave me a little push as I paused. Tal moved past me, a smile on his face. I felt a tap on my shoulder as my vision blurred. I remember my brain felt like it was trying to burst free. Finally, my knees gave out, and I found myself in my mother's arms. Thorn stood behind her with unconcealable concern.

As the waves of pain passed, I was helped to the tavern. To my embarrassment, Thorn explained about the spell I had adversely conjured. I was placed at the foot of my dad's bed.

"What did you see?" my mom demanded as Thorn helped my dad into a seated position. Three pairs of eyes stared intently at me. I found I couldn't meet any of their gazes.

"I saw you and Thorn walking away, arm in arm," I mumbled. "Then . . ." I really didn't want to explain the rest. I knew by the way Mom and Thorn stood. Each had a hand on their hip, giving me that look. It was better to get this over with. "Then, you," I pointed vaguely at Thorn, "turned to glare at me like you won a bet or something."

"So you thought your mother would prefer to see me instead of you?" Thorn frowned at me. "We need to work on your self-esteem issues."

"I'm afraid," my dad began, his words interrupted by a cough, "it's more problematic than simple feelings of self-worth." He reached out to me, but the strain caused his face to turn ashen. My mom helped him lay back.

Taking over the explanation, my mom continued. "How can we trust you in battle if you can't trust your own eyes?"

"It was just for a moment, a small relapse," Thorn defended. "Henry." She turned her eyes to me. "You understand that what you saw wasn't real, right?"

My hesitation, however, confirmed everyone's suspicion.

I could still be a liability.

CHAPTER 46

I stood in the hall on shaking legs. Mom had asked me to get Dad a drink, even though there was a full pitcher right next to the bed. I knew they were going to discuss what to do with me. Even with that knowledge, I didn't expect that what I overheard would affect me so much.

"I don't see how we can bring Henry along," my mom explained.

"He's come too far and been through too much for us to leave him behind," Scratch defended.

My father spoke. His voice was weak, but his conviction was strong. "Henry was an adept fighter when we left, and I know Caterous has taught him well."

"It doesn't matter if he turns those skills against us in the midst of battle," Mr. Heraldry countered. After that, the conversation became cyclical. I began to slide down the wall as doubt crept into my mind.

Was I sure that what I heard was *actually* what was being said? Was this another instance where I heard my fears? Then I heard the voice I most wanted yet feared to hear.

"Henry has fears and many doubts." Thorn's words cut through my heart. "He's easily hurt and doubts his abilities." She sighed.

"This isn't instilling us with confidence," Mom replied.

"I know. It's just that Henry feels inferior to everyone." I could hear Thorn pacing as her description of me cut me like daggers. I prayed that what I was hearing was again just in my mind. However, what she said next struck me harder than anything else. "But you'll never meet anyone more loyal, caring, and loving. He's put himself in danger over and over, for me, Serina, and Scra—um, Sebastian."

"Who's Serina?" Mr. Heraldry asked. I could imagine his eyebrows raised as he addressed his son. But instead, I heard Scratch mumble something similar to the word *friend*. I felt a small smile tug at my lips.

"Friend," I scoffed. If he ever tried to say goodbye to me the way he did with Serina, he and I would have to have a long discussion. The smile that had crept up my face melted as I listened to the others decide my fate. I knew they'd force me to stay out of the battle. Still, Thorn had stood up for me. Okay, she first pointed out a lot of my faults, *however*, in the end, she thought I was all right. I guess.

I sat up straight, listening hard. Thorn was speaking again. "Like I said, Henry has many doubts and fears, but he's aware of how these fears affect him and his perception of reality." I could hear the plea for understanding in her voice. "He'll fight even harder for those he loves. I'm certain he'll ignore the false images and know we'd never betray him."

"That is not what we have witnessed thus far." Wolf's voice held a tenderness, but his statement couldn't be disputed.

"That was under the full effect of the spell and without his knowledge of what was happening," Thorn protested.

"So, you maintain that, in the thick of battle, Henry will have the presence of mind to understand what he may be seeing? He'll know it's just a flashback?" Mr. Heraldry's scorn was palpable. "Are you positive he won't act on his perception in a way that could harm us? Or, you specifically?"

"No matter what Henry might perceive, Thorn is the last person he'd harm." My heart leapt to hear Scratch join the conversation.

Wolf growled, "How can you be so certain?"

"He loves her too much." Scratch's explanation was stated matter of factly. My face burned and I knew Thorn's would be bright red.

"That—that's true," Thorn stammered, "and that's why I trust him to join us." Her voice grew quieter as she spoke. I couldn't listen anymore. I had to participate in the conversation and in the planning. I also had to see Thorn.

I walked into the room and froze. All eyes were on me as I gulped at the air, trying to make my brain and mouth work together. "I-I-I do love her." My throat was too dry and my tongue was too big. Thorn glanced at me. Her red face clashed horribly with her purple hair. I couldn't help but smile at her embarrassment.

Calming my shaking hands, I continued. "However, she isn't the only one here that I love." I drew a deep breath. This would be awkward, yet it needed to be said. "I love my parents. I love you." I lay my hand on Scratch's shoulder. "I love your dad, who has always been there for me." I turned to Wolf, whose face was the textbook description of surprise. "I even like you." I smiled. "I also love Serina." Scratch's attention flicked to me. "Not the way you do. I love Thorn like you love Serina. I mean, like, she's my friend, and I love her like that. I know Thorn is my friend too, but it's different."

"Henry, you should stop talking now," Mom said gently as she suppressed a laugh.

"Dude . . ." Scratch muttered.

"You're such an idiot," Thorn hissed, yet a smile was behind her scowl. My parents were failing at trying not to laugh. Mr. Heraldry was again staring at his son expectantly as Scratch did everything he could to avoid his father's gaze. Thankfully, Wolf saved me and ended the discomfort.

"Yay love and all that." Wolf's gruff voice didn't match the sentiment. "What we need now is a plan. A plan that will erase hate or, at the very least, evil."

"Yes," Mom said, all sense of mirth gone. "We know they're planning another attack. What other surprises do you have in store?" she asked Wolf.

Wolf described some other horrible devices they could use during the next enemy advance.

It seemed that my participation in the coming fight was settled. We pored over old maps and battle plans for the next couple of hours. Scratch and I had little to contribute, but the things we learned about our parents and their participation in the war were shocking. Stories of battles where the three, well, four friends, including Thorn's father, would cut bloody swaths through enemy forces.

When you learn that your loved ones have seen war and participated in it, you understand something about them. They may have helped save the world, but they still did things they'd rather not remember. I understood only a little of what they'd been through. The times I'd witnessed death and pain already haunted me. The amount of carnage they witnessed was, at the time, unfathomable to me.

The slap of Wolf's hand on the table brought me out of my thoughts. "Then it is decided! We mount a counteroffensive. We take the fight to her!"

"We still have to get through her army on the other side of the barricade," Thorn argued.

"Have you not been listening?" Wolf demanded. "With this group, and your magic, our enemies will fall like wheat before the scythe."

"Twenty years ago, when you were in your prime, maybe." Thorn didn't back down. "You aren't the people you were, and I'm not my father."

"From what I have seen, you are stronger than Caterous. I mean Lawrence—your dad." Wolf laughed.

"I may be. However, I'm not nearly as experienced or ready." Thorn didn't look at Wolf as she finished.

"Ready? You have wanted to go after your mother since you got here!" Wolf shouted, red-faced.

Thorn spun to address him, matching his anger. "Yes, to go against my *mother*! Not to wade into a river of blood and bodies. That's how you described one of your—what was it you said?—your most excellent victories."

It was one of the stories Wolf spoke of in reverence. It was also one of the times I noticed my family's discomfort. The Dreamweavers and Mr. Heraldry remembered that battle differently than Wolf. My parents whispered comforting words to each other as Mr. Heraldry shook his head and muttered a prayer.

"That is what war is, little girl!" Wolf countered in increased volume, completely oblivious to the reactions of his friends. I noticed Tal easing into the room and cautiously watching Wolf as he continued his tirade.

"War is pain! It is death and killing and watching those around you die!" Spittle flew from Wolf's mouth as he shouted. There was a look in his eye now, something leaning beyond reason. "She died so your father could betray us. She should be here, and you should not!"

Thorn sprang back as Wolf lunged at her. His eyes held the unhinged look they held the first time we met him.

"I will avenge her death with yours!" Wolf's fingers tried to grasp Thorn's throat as he reached for his dagger. Tal's strong arms wrapped around Wolf's shoulders. Lifting him like a rag doll, Tal carried a cursing, struggling Wolf out of the room. I could hear Tal's deep voice whispering soothing words over Wolf's shouted curses as they passed. Suddenly, Wolf went limp, the fight in him evaporating in a second.

"I miss her, Tal. I miss her." Wolf, to my surprise, wept as they left.

I realized I was holding Thorn protectively. So I released her and asked, "What the hell was that about? You say you can't trust *me* in battle, but he's okay?" I didn't mean to say it out loud, but the looks of embarrassment told me they might feel the same.

My mom tried to explain how the loss of Ursula, the second in command yet first in his heart, affected Wolf.

Tal returned as she finished her explanation. He stood quietly for a moment before he clarified. "Sometimes, the war comes back to us. It returns as vividly as if we are again in the middle of the fight."

My dad looked far older as he stared off into the corner. His eyes were watching something I couldn't see. "You can smell the blood, feel the grime and sweat of the battle . . ." He covered his ears. "Hear the screams."

"See their faces," Mr. Heraldry whispered, "the pain, the hate, the fear."

"Watch friends and foes repeatedly die in your dreams," Mom joined in, "sometimes even in your waking hours."

My dad's attention turned to me. He held out his hands. I took them. "We never wanted you to experience any of that."

"We fought so hard so you could live without that pain." Scratch's father embraced his son.

My mom brought Thorn into a hug with me and Dad. "We're so sorry you have to finish what we couldn't."

"You will have some terrible times ahead," Tal explained. "Remember, you will have us, and we understand."

"Even if we sometimes lose sight of who is in front of us." Wolf stepped into the room, his eyes puffy. "I am sorry, Ms. Caterous."

Thorn stepped out of our embrace. Walking up to Wolf, she stood as tall as her five-foot stature allowed. "I'm not my mother. Your hatred of her is well deserved, but please remember . . ." She held out her hand. "I'm your friend, as you're my trusted ally."

The burly, scarred warrior deflated in relief as he took her hand.

Relaxed smiles spread around the room. We began to discuss our next move when the door was flung open. A young boy with cat eyes and ears stood holding the doorframe, trying to catch his breath. "You," he gasped. "You're needed on the wall." Thorn hurriedly gave him some water. He coughed, gulping it down, letting the water run over his chin and onto his shirt. "Please hurry. Something's happening to the barricade."

CHAPTER 47

Dad yelled for Mom to be careful as she sprinted from the room. Thorn, Scratch, and I rushed after her to the wall. Lightning danced along the top of the recently created embankment. We watched as unnatural darkness crept along the horizon like death extending its wings. My mom's grip tightened on my shoulder as the midday sun disappeared behind the rolling clouds, casting the world into muted twilight colors interrupted by the lightning's electric blue. Each flash revealed another part of the barricade being blown apart.

"I don't think she will let us take the fight to her," Wolf growled behind me.

"What about those other surprises you had ready?" Thorn asked hopefully.

Tal sadly shook his head. "It looks like they have already been destroyed." He pointed to various small craters showing where the last of the booby traps had been.

My mom edged past me. "We need to take out the magicians working on the barricade." I saw the general in the woman who raised me surface as she pointed to the lightning. "Gather a small raiding party to infiltrate their lines undetected and take them out."

"Scratch and I will go." I volunteered my friend without hesitation. To his credit, he agreed without complaint. Then to my surprise, my mom didn't protest. Then, as an added shock, neither did Thorn.

Tal's wife appeared at my side. "I'll show you the way." She smiled happily. "We've been scouting a path." Doba said a brief goodbye to Tal and led us along the bottom of the wall, away from the great doors. Finally, we arrived at a sort of pen holding some scraggy chickens. Doba walked toward a small sty, then suddenly disappeared.

I rushed to where I saw her last and only found myself looking into a deep hole. I called out to Doba, and a second later, I saw her eyes reflected in the torchlight.

"I don't know if I can make it." Scratch frowned at the hole.

"It's larger on the inside," Doba laughed.

"Come on. We've squeezed through tighter," I encouraged.

"When I was young and scrawny, like you," my dear friend protested. I admit I may have called him several choice names as I slithered into the opening.

Doba and I waited as Scratch grunted and swore, pushing his broad shoulders into the tunnel. I had to turn away to stifle my laughter as Scratch got stuck. His butt and hips were lodged at an odd angle. As if that wasn't enough, to see the tiny mountain goblin trying to pull him by the arms was almost too much to bear.

"Thanks for the help, you pointy-eared idiot!" Scratch stormed at me. Doba rushed between us. Her thin arms held out to keep us apart. Scratch scowled as he turned away. "Don't worry. I'm not going to kill him—*yet*."

I just laughed as we followed the long, dark tunnel. The further we went, the more room we had. "We may use this as a staging area or create another trap," Doba suggested.

Finally, I felt fresh air moving in from somewhere nearby. Doba urged us to be silent. Slowly we crept forward. From this point on, all communication was done through hand signals.

Doba held up her tiny hand, telling us to stop. I shrugged at Scratch's poking, questioning why our progress was halted. I almost cried out when Tal's wife's head disappeared. Relieved, I finally noticed the hole she'd poked her head through. Then, popping back down, she gave us the signal to follow. I drew my short sword, nodded to Scratch, then followed out of the tunnel.

Keeping low, I ran from cover to cover. I spied Scratch not too far away. Doba was nowhere to be seen. Then, a sound caught my attention. I turned to see Doba beckoning me. I signaled Scratch, then followed her. We were on the other side of the barricade from the town, shouting reaching us from the distance. At my feet were bodies. That's when I noticed there was no lightning hitting the barrier.

"Dear gods, what did this?" Scratch gasped.

I had my suspicions but wasn't willing to voice them just yet. The bodies were, for lack of a better term, shredded. Distant screams told me whatever happened here was still going on. But then, I felt a tug on my sleeve.

"This must be reported," Doba squeaked. Scratch nodded as he followed her. I only hesitated a moment before realizing I might not be able to find the tunnel back. I rushed after them, slipped through the hole, and landed next to Scratch. The sound of small feet running through the tunnel told us we'd been left behind. Following our guide's lead, Scratch and I flew through the passage.

I scrambled out of the tunnel and turned to help my friend. Pulling Scratch free of the opening created none of the humor it held previously. By the time I extricated Scratch, pikemen had surrounded us.

"Whoa, hey, what the hell?" Scratch yelled. The pikemen looked embarrassed as they slowly lowered their weapons.

"When the bombardment stopped, we became concerned," one of the soldiers explained.

"So, you point spears at us instead of congratulating us?" Scratch growled.

"The carnage young Doba reported was worse than anything an elf or man could bring," a pikeman who hadn't completely lowered his weapon growled.

"That's because we didn't do it!" My irritation forced me to push my way between Scratch and the guard. "Something else is going on." Then, turning to Scratch, I said, "We need to tell Wolf and Thorn." My argument was interrupted by screams of fear from several people who had come to see what all the shouting was about.

The sound of heavy wings above us brought a smile to Scratch's face. "I knew it." His face glowed with joy. I understood how he felt and shared in his relief, as I knew what those wings would bring us.

Serina landed softly between Scratch and the soldiers. Her appearance sent the pikemen into nervous caution. They couldn't decide who should be on the receiving end of their spears.

"Oh, put down your weapons before you hurt yourselves." Serina's eyes glowed red with impatience.

My smile faltered at the rumble of hurried boots. Wolf jumped down the small depression to where we stood. Landing lightly despite his size, his hand flew to his sword.

"Your presence is not welcome, Vampire," Wolf announced. Now it was Thorn's turn to roll her eyes.

"And I told you," Thorn interrupted, "that she's my friend and will be welcome by me." Thorn faltered briefly as several vampires landed around us.

"You brought some friends," Scratch yelled.

"Obviously," I muttered, noting the five vampires accompanying her. "Although not as many as I had hoped."

Serina glared at me. "We were enough to take out all those magicians trying to bring down the mess you made out there." Damn her bat-like ears. Her attention snapped to me. "I heard that too."

Embarrassed, I apologized. I hadn't realized I'd said it aloud.

Thorn pushed between Serina and me, releasing an agitated huff. Taking Serina's hands in hers, Thorn smiled. "We're just happy you came to give us any assistance." Thorn turned her glare back on me. "One vampire is worth twenty elves in battle."

I held up my hands in surrender. However, I felt she was being unfair.

"Sebastian Heraldry came to ask for assistance," a tall, serious-looking vampire explained. "We are here to offer that aid."

Wolf spared him a snort of disdain. "Vampires do not help anyone without cost," he shouted.

"Do you believe Althea will leave us in peace?" Serina asked. Crossing her arms over her chest, she tapped her foot impatiently, waiting for an answer.

"I do not answer the foolish questions of children," Wolf growled. "Especially vampire children."

"Wolf, I don't think you remember who you're talking to." I tried to calm the situation. Thorn, however, rushed to embrace Serina. A hurried discussion between them ended with Thorn waving away the grateful pikemen.

"It's okay. No one interfered with them." Thorn spun, smiling at me. "I told you Mother never knew she was there."

Scratch hesitated, stealing glances to catch Serina's gaze. Finally, she rolled her eyes and nodded to him. He rushed to embrace her, and my chest tightened watching them. The visions from the spell came crashing back on me. Shaking off the feeling, I approached my friend.

Serina turned to smile at me, and I had the urge to attack her until Thorn wrapped her arm around me. My vision cleared. I realized Serina had her hand out to me but faltered a little seeing the flash of hatred cross my face.

"I'll explain later," Thorn promised.

Serina shrugged it off, but I knew my reaction hurt her. As I cursed my foolishness, Thorn gave my shoulder a reassuring squeeze. She smiled and whispered, "It's okay. We're here for you." I returned her smile, feeling a little more comfortable.

My relief warmed my chest until I turned around to see that everything wasn't settled. Serina glared at Wolf who returned it with intensity. By now, many of our companions had arrived from town. They looked upon the vampires with apprehension, though several seemed either unperturbed or even friendly toward them.

Tal noticed my surprise and explained, "Ghouls and vampires have always had a decent relationship." He shrugged. "They both tend to enjoy the same dark places and—"

"When one would finish a meal," Wolf interrupted with a nasty grin, "the other would get the leftovers."

"What do you mean?" I asked innocently.

"What he means is they eat the dead. The ghouls eat the dead." Serina looked annoyed. While Tal shrugged, Serina continued. "He means we kill people, and they eat the evidence." Wolf held her gaze.

"While trolls and ogres just kill indiscriminately," a female vampire interjected angrily.

"Trolls, maybe," Tal replied calmly. "We ogres are a proud people. We simply defend ourselves and our land."

"Maybe." The vampire turned her back on Tal. "But you are still ugly."

I cringed, expecting Tal to be furious. Instead, he seemed to ponder her statement for a moment.

"To your eyes, perhaps," he stated, "but to me, *you* are not attractive." The vampire spun to face him. To my surprise, he raised his hands in defense. "You are not wholly unattractive, just so small and thin."

Thorn and I held our breath. We couldn't afford fighting in our ranks. The vampire looked Tal over once. "Well, you are not that bad." She held out her hand. "My name is Arrabetta, and you are?"

What happened next surprised Thorn, Serina, and me.

"Not Arrabetta of the deep hall?" Tal asked, horror-stricken.

She nodded, confused.

"Oh, my deepest apologies." Tal knelt on one knee, took Arrabetta's hand, and kissed it. "It is a pleasure to meet you, Duchess. I am Tal."

The change in Arrabetta was instantaneous. "Oh, please, Lord Tal, rise. There is no call to kneel on my account." Then, releasing her hand, he stood. I couldn't be sure, but there seemed to be a slight blush on both cheeks.

A small, tutting voice near my knees caused Tal to jump like he'd been shocked. Dobaker eyed Arrabetta suspiciously, while Scratch, on the other hand, seemed to be annoyed. Serina's companion's status seemed to have little affect on Wolf's attitude.

"Just what this campaign needs, another vampire royal. What does your father say to you running off to help us non-immortals?" Wolf growled.

Serina sighed. "He says to remind you we aren't immortal. We just live longer." Casually, she took Scratch's arm in hers. "Thank you for your kind welcome to my cousin." Serina smiled at Tal.

Wolf appeared to want to continue his protests until an elf ran up to us. "Sir, we've taken some prisoners."

"What? How?" Thorn demanded.

"They were skulking around the south end of the wall," the elf smiled. Behind him, our three prisoners were being led to Wolf by a nasty-looking ogre. Immediately, Thorn insisted she be present during the interrogation. I was volunteered to come along for some reason, a development I wasn't thrilled to be a part of. Upon seeing our captives, I was even less enthused. Our prisoners were two humans and a goblin. While all three showed signs of a fight, one of the humans definitely had been a light snack for a vampire.

Tal brought in some bread and stew. The vampire victim didn't even look at it. His companions, however, displayed no hesitation in greedily eating as much as they could. "It's like they haven't eaten in days," Scratch whispered over my shoulder, "but don't let that fool you."

Confused, I turned to ask what he meant. Unfortunately, I was shushed before I could get a word out.

"Would your companion like something to eat?" Tal asked in a deep, growling voice.

"Nah," the human said, wiping his mouth as he reached for his companion's bowl. "He's not long for this world." The goblin smashed the human's hand with his empty bowl at these words.

"Shaddup, you fool," hissed the goblin.

"Oh, did my brothers drain him too far?" Serina asked as she emerged from the shadows. Her appearance had the effect of abject terror on our captives.

"Keep that monster away from me!" the human yelled, food flying free of his mouth in his panic. Behind me, Thorn stifled a laugh as the human and goblin kept trying to push the other in front as a shield. "I mean, look what those demons did to Yacheck." He was pointing at the dazed man.

Serina frowned as she approached Yacheck. Then, sitting in front of him, she looked deep into his eyes. As Serina did this, the human began hissing something to the goblin that sounded like *she'll know* before the goblin punched him. Then, a moment later, Serina stared at them as they began fighting. Her intense glare stopped them mid-punches.

"They look like little boys caught by their mother," Thorn said as she stepped forward. Both captives turned to the new voice. Their faces turned from scorn to a more profound fear than they had for Serina.

"You're . . . you're . . ." The goblin pointed as he shrunk back as far as he could.

"You're as good as dead," the human laughed, pushing past the goblin. Then, several things happened at once. First, Scratch grabbed Tal, trying to push him toward the entrance as he yelled for Serina. Next, Yacheck's eyes began to bleed as his body expanded. I screamed for Thorn over the cackle of the goblin.

"Even if you survive, we have the plague," the human shouted as Yacheck exploded. Whatever spell had been cast on him was horrifying. His body erupted into a fireball, sending boiling hot entrails everywhere. The man's bones shattered into knife-sharp projectiles. Serina threw out a hand that sent a shockwave out behind her. The wave caught Scratch and Tal, sending them flying out of the tent to safety. Instinctively I cast a protection spell over Thorn and me as I threw my arms around her, trying to shield her from the blast.

When I turned around, I was horrified. Yacheck's parts were everywhere. Serina had been covered in broiling viscera and pierced with splintered bone. The human was in several pieces. What was left of his face gaped as it tried to scream without a lower jaw. The head's one good eye swiveled in its socket for a few seconds before the light left it. The goblin, however, was unharmed. Thorn had cast her own protection around it.

I rushed to Serina, who had fallen to one knee. "That was highly unpleasant," she grunted as the burns healed and the bone pieces fell out of her wounds. In seconds, the only evidence on her of the explosion was the holes in her clothes. "Damn it, I liked this shirt," she growled, observing the damage.

"I, uh, we still have brought the plague," the goblin stated, his tone unsure, Then he suddenly shouted, "You should let me go and run away. Yes, that is what you should do."

Thorn sighed as she recited an incantation. A warm glow filled the tattered gore-strewn tent and through my chest. "There, now, no one here is infected with the plague."

The goblin stared at Thorn. Disbelief covered his face. "She said it could not be cured, not even with magic."

"I just did," Thorn explained. "You should never trust a word my mother says."

"Then, my friends . . ." Tears welled up in his eyes. "My friends need not have died?"

"No," Thorn stated simply.

CHAPTER 48

"My name is Bolguris," the goblin explained. "We were told our families would be spared if we spread the plague in the town." A tear slipped from his eye.

"We can't trust this guy," Scratch whispered. Wolf's hand gripped the hilt of his sword.

Bolguris bowed his head in shame. "I was also sent to kill your companions," he muttered, glancing at Thorn.

"My companions, but not me?" Thorn questioned.

Bolguris shook his head. "You are not to be harmed."

I doubted their families were still alive, but I didn't want to destroy the hopes of Bolguris. However, nothing I'd learned about the dark sorceress led me to believe she kept promises.

"Althea's forces are strong," Bolguris explained without prompting. "They are well equipped, but they are not many." He glanced up at Thorn. Something in Bolguris's eyes seemed to both fear and adore her. "You are not like your mother at all," he stated. A small smile graced Thorn's face at this statement. "She is far more beautiful, yet you are far more kind."

What he said next was surprising to all of us. "You are also more powerful. That is why Her Highness fears you."

"She fears *me*?"

"Well, that is the rumor anyway." Suddenly, Bolguris looked slightly worried. "Perhaps I should not have said that." A second later, his eyes bulged, and he fell to the ground writhing in agony.

"What's happening to him?" Thorn yelled. Scratch leaped on the goblin, forcing Bolguris's arms tight to his sides.

"Hold him!" Scratch commanded. I jumped to help. Then Scratch drew his dagger.

"What are you doing?" I cried, letting go of the struggling goblin. I attempted to push Scratch away from the writhing Bolguris, but I wasn't fast enough. Scratch evaded me, then thrust his dagger into the goblin's skull. Bolguris went limp.

"Why did you do that?" I demanded.

To answer me, Scratch held up his dagger. Speared on the end was a nasty-looking insect that let out a horrid screech as it died. Flicking away the creature, Scratch looked down at Bolguris. "When he wakes up, we'll find out if he knew he was also a spy."

That was when I noticed Bolguris was still breathing.

"Althea was listening?" Thorn gasped.

"She probably didn't like him saying you're more powerful," Serina suggested as she looked over my shoulder.

"Enough!" Althea's voice boomed as if she were everywhere.

"Something is happening!" Tal called from on the wall.

A guard began binding Bolguris's hands as another wrapped his wound.

"Make sure he's locked up!" Scratch called as we raced to join Tal.

The sight before us was something truly bizarre to behold. All the land in front of the wall seemed to quiver. My eyes and ears were instantly assaulted by a wave of power. The entire area before the wall rippled, then flattened, as if it was a giant rug that was aired out to lay flat.

The wave of magic crested upon the wall like a gigantic swell reaching the shore. Thankfully Thorn and some of our magic users had conjured a barrier to ward off any magic attacks. When the wave hit the town's barrier, it shuddered with brilliant light. Blinking away the spots from my vision, I was relieved to see the barrier held. Then, however, I returned to rubbing my eyes to clear the vision or block out what I didn't wish to see.

Slowly opening my eyes, I took in the truth of the matter. Nothing stood between Althea's army and our defenses. Although, Althea didn't exactly level the playing field as it were—the ground rose to meet the enemy. If we were to attack, we would literally have an uphill battle.

I also saw the enemy army. Either Bolguris hadn't seen the entire army, or he lied. On the other hand, he simply might not be able to count. I estimated we were outnumbered by something like one hundred to one.

My despair must have been evident. Wolf's hand slammed my shoulder. "Cheer up, boy." The force of the blow nearly buckled my knees. He threw his arms wide. "Between our mages and the veterans in this town that rabble does not stand a chance against us!"

I tried to look reassured, and I prayed he was right. Yet, at that moment, a cry rose from Althea's forces, sending a wave of terror down my spine. I wanted to run and hide until I felt Thorn's reassuring presence by my side. That is, until she grabbed my arm and pulled me down the stairs toward the open door to the plain.

"Come on, we have to help," Thorn yelled. Confused, I allowed myself to be pulled toward the great gate.

As soon as I saw the wide, flat land outside the door, I hesitated. "What? Why?" was all I could muster before Thorn pulled me out onto the clear plain that was soon to be a field of battle. I instantly felt exposed and vulnerable. Up ahead was a thin line of our troops. They looked like reeds about to be trampled. Then I heard the sound of wings. I glanced up to see our few vampire allies soaring above us. They looked too small and too few to make a difference.

Thorn grabbed my hand, bringing me out of my thoughts. She stared at me. "Henry, are you with me?" she shouted over the din of the opposing army rousing itself for battle.

My confusion at her question must have shown clearly since she grabbed my shoulders, pulling me close, forcing me to meet her steady gaze.

Again she asked, her eyes searching mine, "Henry, are you with me?"

"Yeah, of course," I replied as realization slowly dawned. I finally understood what she was asking me. "Yes! I'm here," I vehemently asserted.

"Good!" Thorn punched me in the arm. "Then get yourself together and help me." She turned to face the enemy. Again, Thorn held out her hand to me. This time I took it confidently.

Thorn and I shared our power, letting it combine and grow between us. I wasn't sure which spell we would cast. I hoped for something defensive yet steeled my mind for destruction. Like it or not, I was about to fight for my life. I breathed out relief as Thorn cast a spell of protection. I watched the magic shimmer as it spread across the field before our allies.

Thorn dropped my hand and ran off to answer someone's call. I stood, feeling drained and missing the feel of her hand in mine and our combined magic. Again, I was alone, vulnerable and exposed right as the battle was about to start, or maybe already had.

Further up the hill, Serina and her friends were already in the midst of mayhem. I watched as large chunks of dirt and rock flew into the air. A cheer rose from soldiers near me as they pointed at the detritus in the air. That's when I noticed the bodies and parts of bodies mixed in with the rocks and dirt.

Scratch slapped me on the back as he ran toward the battle. With a huge smile, he glanced at me. "She's amazing!" He beamed with pride.

I agreed that I was impressed with the carnage, but I didn't tell him it wasn't in the same way he was.

"Well, I gotta get to it!" Scratch called as he ran off, followed by a large group of mixed, heavily armored creatures. With one final glance, he yelled, "I gotta get this lot into position." He gestured to his troops. "See you when it's over!" His voice was cheerful, and I returned his wave and watched him lead his group away in a quick march. I wondered if I'd ever see him alive again. How many of those brave souls would meet their end today?

I was surrounded by a cacophony of noise and action. Terror rooted me to the spot. Serina and her vampires were doing heavy damage to our enemy. Thorn was off somewhere setting up defenses or traps. Scratch had led his troops to their position.

Further away, I saw my mom. She rode a magnificent steed as she rallied troops. Also, on horseback, I watched Mr. Heraldry shout orders while Wolf indicated areas around the field. Tal led a group of ogres marching in perfect precision. They were the most disciplined group on the field. So many things were going on, and I had no idea where I should go or what to do.

"Henry! Get moving!" a familiar voice shouted at me. Although, through the sounds of the burgeoning battle, I couldn't tell who or where it came from. My sword felt like lead in my hand. I slowly wandered toward the line of our troops.

"I said *enough*!"

I crouched when Althea's voice exploded in the air around me. Light burst from behind the enemy lines. The sky dazzled in the brilliant glow of what felt like the midday sun. Illuminated by the bright light were the silhouettes of the vampires in the sky. From this distance, I couldn't see clearly, but I knew they were in trouble. The way the vampires tumbled and fell, I imagined their wings burning as their bodies became engulfed in flame.

My mind immediately brought out the smile of pride on Scratch's face, and my stomach twisted and my heart ached. Then, a single word escaped my throat.

"Serina."

I could only imagine what Scratch must feel at this second. Then, I swore I heard my friend's agonizing cry of Serina's name to answer my unspoken fear.

I wanted to be there to support and help Scratch, but I couldn't see him or Thorn. Then, before I could decide which way to run, the dam burst. Althea's forces unleashed a howl of fury that shook the ground. The sound became amplified to the point of pain in my ears. Their battle cry had the desired effect, as I wanted nothing more than to run in terror. Before my panicked legs could take flight, our forces replied with battle horns and a ferocious battle call of our own. The cacophony was accompanied by thudding arrows, crashing boulders, and exploding spells. If I ran now, nowhere would be safe.

The magic barrier Thorn and I created deflected the first volley of arrows and spells. However, it wouldn't hold for long. So I began casting a reinforcing spell when I was roughly pushed from behind.

"Stupid elf, get in line!" an angry goblin shouted as he thrust me into a group of soldiers marching quickly up the incline. I stumbled along, getting pushed and cursed by my fellow troops. The reality of the situation hit me hard. I wasn't a soldier, yet I was about to fight for my life. My friends and family were somewhere on this battlefield. Maybe they were already fighting. The truth my mind kept trying not to realize was that I might never see them again.

Wait, don't we have a plan? I thought.

Then Wolf's voice came to mind. "The best-laid plans fall apart as soon as the first arrow is let fly."

Ignoring the complaints, I allowed myself to be pushed along. *No,* I thought. *This isn't what's supposed to happen.* We had a plan. Thorn and I were to meet up with Serina. Then the three of us would regroup and use our Magic to defend and assist our fighters. I tried to move out of line but was shoved back in step while being called a coward, traitor, and other vile epithets.

Angry Magic crackled in my hands. I was about to force my way free when we were suddenly engaged in the fight. "Fight, boy! Kill them!" someone shouted in my face. The next few minutes were a blur of mud, clashing steel, blood, and screaming. Battle cries mixed with the moans of the dying. In an instant, I decided I wouldn't die here.

I heard my battle cry erupt from my throat. My blade flashed with the colors of the spells I cast. I saw hatred turn to fear as my blade sliced through flesh. I heard the abrupt end of a cry of fear as my spell exploded a foe. The soldiers who, moments before, were cursing me, now shouted my praises. I cut a swath through the enemy that dared to stand before me. Covered in sweat and gods knew what else, I stood breathing heavily, surrounded by corpses and celebrating comrades. I felt pain and knew I had wounds. Yet, even as those around me cheered our small victory, I had taken the lives of strangers who hated me for no reason. I maimed creatures with desires similar to mine: freedom, acceptance, a safe place to call home.

I couldn't help but notice many of those I had marched with now lay on the ground. The elf with a red sash who laughed a lot while marching, the angry goblin who pulled me into line, lay side by side. Their eyes stared lifelessly up at me, their faces contorted in death. The elf found fear and sadness while the goblin looked as if he had found peace at last.

I will never understand war.

Realizing that many of the dead had become so at my hand, I shook. I wanted to scream at the goblin. Shove a spear into wounded enemy soldiers. They were done fighting. Why did we have to kill them?

"Henry! Thank the gods. Thorn is on the other flank!" Mom called from atop her horse. Then, pointing with her sword to show me the direction, she said, "Go help her! Riders, with me!" My comrades shouted for blood and then ran to follow the cavalry. I turned in the direction Mom indicated. Two soldiers stood in front of me: a goblin and a human.

"We're here to help you," the goblin announced as the human nodded. I returned the nod, acknowledging our fellowship.

"This way." I pointed. The three of us began to run. I tripped and stumbled over bodies and debris. We ducked around and fought through several clusters of battle. Suddenly the ground flew up to meet me. A hand gripped my leg as evil eyes glared hate at me. I saw the silver of his dagger swing toward me. My human companion appeared from above, and his boot connected with my attacker's face in a sickening crunch.

"That's right!" howled the goblin. "Trample the living and hurtle the dead!"

I nodded at his assessment even as the bile of disgust threatened to escape my throat. So, although I hated the thought, the three of us did just that as we ran. I stopped hearing the cries of pain as I trampled on the wounded. At some point, the goblin was killed. Even though I wouldn't let anything stop me from finding Thorn, the agonizing scream of the human broke my heart and made me pause.

The man cradled the goblin's body, begging him to come back to him. Before I could say a comforting word or scream a warning, a spear impaled the man. In a rage, I dispatched the spearbearer.

Next to the man, I dropped to my knees. "I'm so sorry," I moaned.

"Thank you," he gasped. "It's okay. My husband and I will be together forever now." He gently leaned his forehead against the goblin's. A tear dripped from the end of his nose onto his lover's cheek. Together, they left the world and pain behind. I stared at the couple, my mind spinning.

"What the hell are we doing this for?" I screamed. No one answered, so I shouted to the sky. "We all want the same things! Why must we die?" My knees hit the blood-soaked ground. I asked the dead, "Why did you have to die?" They didn't answer, but I already knew the answer. It was because of Althea— because she wanted something. I still had no idea what it was.

The anger I had never felt before brought me to my feet. I had to find Thorn, and we had to end this before any more loves were lost to this insanity.

CHAPTER 49

Battle teaches you many lessons you'll hopefully never need for the rest of your life. You'll never wonder just how heavy a head is, but you'll realize it when a severed one slams you in the back. The bodiless head stared stupidly at me as we lay beside each other. I was amazed at how undisturbed I was by what I saw. I pushed myself up, regaining my footing.

I turned to see two ogres working together. They'd attack a creature, one swinging an ax to slice the neck, while the other used a war hammer to knock the head off. Following in their wake was a group of creatures I didn't recognize. While they appeared to be on our side, they were some of the foulest beings I'd ever seen. Pale skin and malformed bodies screeched in delight with every kill the ogres made. They'd exchange coins or other items. Once the corpse fell, these creatures swarmed the body, looting everything they could.

Disgusted, I realized they were betting on how far the head would go. The ogres, however, seemed oblivious to the entertainment they were providing. Repulsed, I continued my journey to find Thorn. I could only pray that she and the others I cared for were still alive. I also prayed they didn't witness the callousness toward death I had endured.

Although I couldn't be certain, Wolf might be correct about our forces' abilities to handle our enemies. Our lines seemed intact while the enemy forces appeared to be pushed back. I knew our greatest adversary hadn't appeared in battle yet, but I got the feeling she was merely toying with us. Even as this thought occurred, I couldn't help but feel relief.

I was behind the fighting now, and I could see Thorn.

She was filthy. Blood was smeared across her face, and her hair was matted with mud and gore. Her clothes were torn and covered in signs of battle. However, Thorn was the most beautiful thing I'd ever seen. Even with the knowledge that I wouldn't look much better, I ran to her. At first, she recoiled, then recognition dawned on Thorn's face, and she pulled me into a back-breaking hug. I returned it in kind.

"Where have you been?" Thorn's muffled voice demanded against my chest as her hands gripped the back of my shirt hard. Then, finally, she pushed me away, punched me in the chest, and wiped at her eyes. "You're such an ass, making me worry like that."

Before I could explain, I spun at the sound of running feet. My mother hugged me, pushed me away to hold me at arm's length, then hugged me again. "Where the hell were you?" she asked angrily.

"Where is he?" Scratch pushed through several soldiers, grabbed me by the neck, and hugged me. "What the hell happened?"

I was suddenly facing three sets of angry, worried eyes. Then, finally, Scratch looked me up and down. "Dude, you look like shit."

"Well, I've been in a battle," I replied, annoyed. I looked behind everyone, yet I didn't see Serina or Scratch's father anywhere. I didn't want to know, but I had to ask. "Where . . ." was all I got out before seeing the looks of anguish. Thorn took my hand, leading me to an area where the ground had been carved out by a magic explosion. Several healers moved quickly between injured creatures of every kind.

She took me to the darkest corner section into an area that contained a tunnel. We passed three ash piles containing bits of metal buttons and buckles. When the smell of burnt flesh accosted my nose, I knew what I'd seen were the vampires that didn't make it. My knees nearly gave out when I saw Serina.

Thorn held me upright. "Serina, I found him. Well, he found us."

Serina's red hair was mostly burned away, along with half of the flesh on her face. Blackened charred skin contrasted with the white of her skull. One of her eyes was missing, leaving a gaping black hole. One of her wings had burned away, and the other looked useless. Finally, I noticed her arm below the elbow ended in two bones sticking out of blackened flesh. Serina didn't seem to hear us.

Thorn made a noise to let Serina know we were there. Serina moved slightly, causing her sharp pointed teeth to clench while gurgles and bloody drool spilled out of her mouth as there was no flesh to stop it. Scratch pushed past me to sit next to her. He whispered something and helped her to sit up. Serina raised what was left of her remaining hand to beckon me over. It was painful to see she only had three fingers left.

I tried not to show discomfort at the stench of burned flesh and her ruined visage. Instead, I swallowed my pain and the bile that threatened to escape.

Again, Serina beckoned me to come closer. Scratch gently placed a hand on her back. As he helped her remain upright, the look he gave her was still like he was looking at the most beautiful woman in the world. My tears threatened to fall. I wasn't ready to say goodbye to her.

I approached Serina's bed. I bent down slightly so she wouldn't have to look up. Serina hit me on the top of my head as soon as I was within reach. I was shocked. As damaged as she was, she still hit hard.

"Ow!" I cried, grabbing my head and backing away.

Scratch tried to keep from laughing, and I heard Thorn snicker behind me. Serina, however, glared at me with her remaining eye. "Shtupid ef. Hair er ou?" Serina growled. Scratch handed her a cloth to wipe away the blood and spit. Pulling the cloth away, Serina continued, "Horn oz orried hick."

"I'm sorry. I got separated." I felt the tears threatening again.

"It's okay," Thorn whispered, squeezing my arm. "She wouldn't let them treat her until she knew you were safe."

Serina answered Thorn with a sound of protest. Then, to my astonishment, she let Scratch shush her while gently laying her back down.

"She says she wasn't worried about you," Scratch sighed, giving me a look that told me she'd been concerned. "According to her, it was because I'd be too worried to be effective."

Suddenly, Scratch casually pulled out his dagger. Thorn had to hold my arm for a split second as I thought Scratch would attempt to end Serina's suffering. Instead, he pressed the dagger to his forearm, cutting deep. Then, glancing at us, he explained, "Would you please excuse us?" He looked apologetic. "This is kinda personal."

I saw the embarrassment and hunger in Serina's eye and a tear. I then realized how bad Serina's condition was. Unfortunately, I couldn't turn away before Serina attached her ruined mouth to Scratch's wound. I was pulled away by gentle hands.

Thorn led me back through the beds and healers. Once I thought we were far enough, I had to ask, "Will she be okay?" I pausd to look around. "Wait, where's Scratch's dad? Where's Wolf?" Through the increased pressure she applied to my arm, I knew what the answer was before Thorn could tell me. I hadn't recognized the bloody and bandaged ogre near my feet until I recognized Doba. She fretted and dabbed at Tal's wounds.

Tal had heard my question. Sadness radiated from our friend. "They fought bravely." He paused to compose himself. "Their advance and sacrifice have allowed this brief respite from battle."

I couldn't believe it. "Dead? Both?"

Thorn nodded, her face filled with sorrow.

Thorn swallowed. "We know Wolf was killed. Tal was with him. Since no one survived Mr. Heraldry's charge, we can only assume that he . . ." She couldn't finish the statement. Instead, she explained, "Your mom is in charge now. She's putting the plan together for another attack." Thorn's hand slipped into mine as we headed back toward the battlefield. It was quiet and horrid as we watched healers move through the lines of soldiers lying scattered across the blood-soaked ground. They looked for those they could save and ended the suffering of those they could not.

We crested a hill that hadn't been there at the beginning of the fight. Between explosions and defensive actions, it grew to shelter our makeshift hospital. On the other side was a hive of activity. My mom sat upon her steed, barking orders.

My mom's ferocity and capability in battle was astonishing. She was in her element as she commanded the troops. First, she hurriedly reformed ranks and created units. Then she deployed these new units to take positions along a breastwork of stakes and spears.

"Thorn, Henry!" Mom shouted, calling us over as she dismounted. "Tal, I told you no. Don't give me that look."

"My Tal will not sit out this fight!" Doba chastised my mother.

"Yeah," Mom looked Tal up and down, "I don't want to have to fight him to keep him out of the thick of it. Okay, let's get this done."

I followed the group into a white tent past two guards. I had no idea when they'd had the time to set this up. Inside, there were several creatures I could tell were generals. They stood at attention the minute my mom entered. The situation was so surreal to me. This was the woman who read fairytales to me using squeaky voices for talking squirrels.

"What are our assets?" Mom demanded with no preamble, her sword rattling on the table. A hastily created map had been drawn over the top. The town lay at the end of a funnel of mountains, but the area representing Althea's forces was smaller than I expected and appeared surrounded. I was about to point out that we had them where we wanted them when a woman with cat ears and a tail spoke up.

"We have the enemy surrounded. After that last advance, they have lost almost two-thirds of their strength." Her statements weren't met with the happy looks I expected.

A huge orc stood up. "We have still not seen the witch on the field. This action is a ploy to draw us in and wipe us out."

"I agree." Thorn stood up, addressing the generals. "My mother is far too powerful for our forces to route her so easily." Thorn studied the map for a moment. "No, she's planning something." Murmured agreement filled the room.

"Excuse the intrusion, Generals!" A breathless, pale man entered. "We have an emissary from Althea's army." A glance between Thorn and my mom confirmed that they thought this was a trap before they rushed after the messenger. Outside the tent, we were met by a courteous human. He was unarmed and surrounded by swords.

"Am I addressing the leader of this army?" he asked with a bow.

"You are," Mom answered curtly. "Whom do I have the pleasure of addressing?"

A smug smile spread over the man's face. "I see . . . An elf . . . How progressive."

"Kill him," my mom said, turning her back on the man. The stunned shock turned his face comical in an instant.

"But I'm an emissary! I came under a banner of peace."

Mom turned and marched straight up to the pleading fool. "Your forces are beaten by those you look down on. You are in no position to bargain or speak for those troops." She spat. There was a sudden commotion near the defenses as a goblin in armor bearing the signet of Althea was escorted to my mom.

To my astonishment, this goblin still retained his sword. Even though the weapon was sheathed, I began to protest. I was shushed by my mom with a single hand. The goblin stood up straight and presented a crisp salute to her. Once she returned the salute, he said, "General Dreamweaver, I am General Staggert of the Third Mountain Army. I am here to present my division in surrender." He drew his sword and held it out hilt first.

"I accept your surrender, General. However, I'm curious as to the demands," my mother said as she accepted the sword.

"Only fair treatment and perhaps some food and water?" General Staggart bowed.

"You shall have it. Let us talk." Still holding his sword, Mom led the general into the tent we'd exited. Thorn followed, but I stayed outside, watching the well-disciplined troops file into our base. They deposited their weapons as they entered, each receiving some food and water, and proceeded to assist in creating a stockade to hold them. I shook my head and finally followed the others into the tent.

"I feared for the safety of my troops," General Staggart explained. I found this statement odd. He brought troops to fight, yet he was fearful for their safety? Something in that logic defied my understanding.

Thorn read my expression and explained in a whisper, "He joined my mother's army due to an old obligation, but he respected Wolf and your parents. He fought by their sides in another conflict."

I looked over at Staggert. He was pointing to different parts of the map.

One of our generals muttered, "We would have lost that entire flank had he been allowed to make that advance." Another general nodded his agreement.

"I do not know Althea's plan, but I advise caution," Staggert sighed, accepting a cup of coffee from an imp.

"*Would my daughter be so kind as to speak with me?*" Althea's voice boomed through the valley.

The color drained from Thorn's face.

"I knew I'd have to face her," Thorn's eyes looked past me. "I don't know if I'm ready."

"I'm here with you," was all I could say.

CHAPTER 50

Thorn allowed me to accompany her outside the tent. Slowly, we passed through our troops. At first, we moved unnoticed on our way to the front lines, but then a ripple of activity spread through the assembled creatures. Before I understood what was happening, Thorn and I walked along a parade line of troops standing at attention. Each being held their weapon over their heart in salute as we passed. With each step we took, I could feel the pride and encouragement from everyone on our side.

As we crested the defensive breastworks, I took in the scene before me. If I hadn't known the power of Althea, I would have been put at ease with what I witnessed. Our forces had indeed surrounded Althea's. As we stood at the edge of our defenses, we saw the enemy troops begin to separate. Two figures appeared at the end of the lane of soldiers.

Thorn sucked in a breath. "Dad!"

The terrible judging face I had only ever seen in a painting became clear. The portrait didn't do Althea's beauty justice, nor could it capture the cruelty or coldness that emanated from her.

Althea began a slow, almost lazy stroll toward us as we watched. I recognized the disheveled man stumbling along behind her. I gripped Thorn's hand, trying to be reassuring. The closer they got, the more I could see how abused and beaten my mentor was. Finally, Thorn's father stumbled and lurched forward. He was magically tethered to Althea, who seemed oblivious to his struggles.

Finally, Althea and Caterous stood alone in the open area between the two armies. I wished one side or the other would fire an arrow into that foul woman's heart. Although, I'm not sure she actually had one.

"Daughter," Althea called, "I suggest you come out to speak with me."

"Mistress Caterous, I do not recommend this course of action," one of the troops next to us commented. I was suddenly aware that we were surrounded by the high command of our forces. I also saw Scratch, a hooded figure I could only assume was Serina, my mom, and even General Staggert, who had surrendered. Oddly, his sword had been returned to him, and his troops had joined our ranks. I decided explanations could wait.

Althea sighed. We heard it as if she were next to us. Then, half of her forces suddenly exploded in a shower of blood and gore. At first, there was no reaction. How does anyone process the needless destruction of life on that scale? Then the air filled with agony, fear, and anger. Even though they were our enemy, even though they wanted us dead, even though we would kill them if we had to, their deaths were useless. Althea valued her supporters so little she would destroy them without a second thought. If her desire was to break our resolve, it had the opposite effect. As we rallied, screaming for vengeance, Althea spoke again.

"Thorn, if you don't wish that to happen to your friends, I suggest you join me." What was left of her army stood in stunned silence. Then a roar of outrage swelled from them, quickly joining ours.

"Silence," Althea commanded. Instantly not a sound could be heard. All around, mouths worked furiously yet produced no voice. "Thorn," Althea called with a tone like she was calling a favorite pet.

"Gods, I hate that woman," Thorn said. Her voice sounded loud in the silence.

"Really? Is that any way to talk about your dear mother?" Althea responded like her feelings were hurt.

"Oh, shut up, you old hag!" I shouted and immediately covered my mouth. I didn't think I'd be able to make a sound since, all around me, no one else could even squeak.

"Henry, be careful," Thorn admonished.

"Thorn, why don't you bring your mouthy friend along as well."

"Quiet, Mother—I'm talking," Thorn shouted. I saw my astonished face reflected in Thorn's eyes. I couldn't believe what I'd witnessed. Althea's voice had deserted her.

"Henry? Henry!" Thorn shook me. "I want you to stay here."

"And people in hell want ice water," I answered. Then, crawling up over the defenses, I held my hand to her.

"You're an idiot," she told me as she grabbed my hand, "but I'm glad you're with me."

"Henry Tano Dreamweaver," my mother shouted, "where the hell do you think you're going?" Suddenly the air was filled with noise. I used the return of everyone's voice to pretend I didn't hear my mom. I put a hand to my ear, shrugged, and hurriedly followed Thorn.

The closer we moved toward Althea, the more terrified I became. Thorn kept muttering as we approached. Then, suddenly, the world became muffled. Thorn had cast a wide protective spell creating a dome over the impending family reunion. The closer we got, the more I realized this was a reunion, by all accounts, that I really shouldn't be a part of.

"You're more family than my mother has ever been," Thorn stated as if she'd read my mind.

"Thank you, I think." I tried to sound casual, but my voice cracked, causing Thorn to smile slightly.

Too quickly, we stood facing our adversary. Althea looked bored, while Thorn's father looked terrified. "The first thing that will happen here," Thorn announced as if she were simply commenting on the weather, "is you will release my father."

"Do you think you are in any position to make demands, little girl?" Althea's mood turned from bored to annoyed instantly.

Thorn sighed and waved her hand. Mage Caterous fell to his knees, taking in huge lungfuls of air.

Althea's surprise was covered instantly. "Apparently, this fool was able to impart some training on you."

"Perhaps you should rethink what you hope to accomplish today," Thorn offered.

"Some small show of ability, and it thinks it is a challenge." Althea's anger exploded. "Your insolence will not be tolerated."

I could see what was about to happen. I threw out a protective spell on Thorn's father. Magic exploded over the spell, knocking Mage Caterous to the ground, gasping in pain.

"How dare you!" Althea hissed at me, Magic crackling in her hands.

An intricate shield of sigils and runes appeared before me.

"Don't even try it," Thorn warned.

From behind Althea, Caterous began to laugh. At first, it was a quiet rasping sound, but it grew in strength the longer he laughed. Finally, slowly getting to his feet, he straightened up. His balance was a bit in question, but he steadied quickly. "Looks as though your great plan will not be as easy to claim."

Fury blazed in Althea's eyes.

"What plan is that?" Thorn asked. "Use my father to make a mage you could control?" She laughed. "Like you could ever control me."

"Control you?" Althea scoffed. "I created you as a vessel, a tool. Using material from that simple creature." She waved vaguely at Thorn's father. "I used his Magic, but I never sullied myself with him. That would be disgusting."

"Why did he put up with you then?" I asked. "You're charming personality?"

Althea spared me a look of revulsion. "Caterous never had a choice." She laughed. "I bewitched that fool the second he entered my chambers."

"He beat you, though!" Thorn shouted.

"Oh, please," Althea scoffed, "he had moments where his mind was his own." She looked more annoyed. "Unfortunately, they did become more frequent. Then you reached an age where you became truly annoying." Again, Althea's face was a mask of contempt. "I had what I wanted, so why should I care how you were raised?"

I saw the look of greed spark in the witch's eyes.

"Now that the body and Magic have matured, I will claim my power." She cackled. "I will be unstoppable!" Her endless laugh sent ice racing down my spine.

I wasn't prepared when the first blast hit me like lightning. The second blast felt like I had been cleaved in two, even with Thorn's protection. I had to check to make sure my legs were still attached and functional.

Again, I listened to Althea's cackle as she laughed at my pain. Finally, I glared at her and saw a flicker of fear cross her face. It wasn't because of me, though. I turned to see something terrifying.

Thorn's fury radiated out in waves. "How dare you attack my friends!" Fire lashed out like a whip from Thorn's left hand. "How dare you attack my father!" Lightning flowed out from her right hand. The attack was swift and on target, but Althea's speed was astounding. A blur of movement, and Thorn's Magic hit empty space.

"Pathetic," Althea snarled.

"Your sleeve is on fire," I pointed out mockingly to Althea as if I was concerned. Distracted, she extinguished the smoldering sleeve. While I had a second, I motioned for Lawrence Caterous to join me. He stumbled toward me, then past me.

Althea's attention stayed on her daughter. She growled as her hands began to swirl faster and faster. From behind me, I heard Caterous swear. I stepped toward Thorn only to have Caterous's hands grab my shoulders, dragging me to the ground. An instant later, a wave of fatal Magic passed a hair's breadth above us.

"Thorn!" I shouted as the wall of energy crashed into her small frame. I knew my mouth was hanging open as I could taste dirt. Thorn stood braced against the onslaught. Her boots dug ruts in the soil as she was pushed back several feet.

"That should have killed her," I heard Caterous stammer, wonder in his voice.

"Why didn't she block it?" I questioned.

Caterous had the answer. "She absorbed it." I heard the awe in his voice, and it had to be reflected on my face. Yet, as amazed as I was, I saw the strain it caused Thorn.

"Very good, very good, little girl," Althea's taunting voice called. "Now, let us see how you handle this." I couldn't see Althea's movements as Caterous forced my face down. I threw my arms over my head and clamped my eyes shut. Heat and light exploded all around, along with Althea's mad cackle. However, her laughter died quickly. I cautiously stole a glance.

Thorn stood straight and tall, apparently unscathed by the Magic that left the air around us smoking. Ash fell like snow across the charred and broken ground.

Thorn was frowning. "Just what I would have expected from a useless old hag!" Instantly she began throwing spells at her mother. Althea made a noise between a growl and a cry, then the air was filled with the roar of magic colliding.

I couldn't see the fighters through the colors and smoke. Finally, I felt a tug and allowed Caterous to pull me away toward the safety of Thorn's barrier. At least I hoped the barrier was still intact. We were almost to the line—I was sure of it. As spells impacted and ricocheted off the magical wall, I let out a breath of relief. Keeping low, I chanced a glance back, hoping to see Thorn.

Caterous tugged my arm. "Come on, we must escape."

Something wasn't right. I turned to look at him. I was stunned to see the struggle in his eyes. It was like something trying to regain control. Then, as if through great pain, Caterous gasped, "Henry." His grip tightened painfully on my arm. "You have to help her."

Then the fight was gone from his eyes. "We must go. It is too dangerous."

Almost immediately, his face screwed up in agony. "For . . . her . . ." Suddenly he shoved me roughly back away from the barrier.

My mother burst through the magic the instant Caterous pushed me away. She reached out, trying to grab my arm. Ducking away, I shouted, "Help him. Althea is in control!" I began scrambling away.

"Henry! Get back here this instant!"

"Thorn needs us!" Even as I said it, I knew it was true. I had to help her. That's why Althea wanted me gone. That's why Caterous trained me. That was my purpose. Althea needed Thorn on her own. I couldn't let that happen. I was her protector, so I had to give Thorn everything I had: my Magic, and even my life. If I had to.

CHAPTER 57

K eeping as low as possible, I dodged flames, lightning, and Magic missiles. I couldn't see Thorn or Althea through the aftermath of colliding spells and destroyed terrain. I could only head toward the flashing of spells and where the explosions were most intense.

The landscape had changed dramatically in the few moments I had been pulled away. Huge craters were carved from the ground from explosions. In other areas, huge monoliths stood half-buried as if they'd been scooped from the earth and thrown. I'm pretty sure that's exactly what happened. Using these new features for cover, I scrambled from one to the other.

I slid next to one of the larger stone slabs. Between the smoke-choked air, the mad dashes for cover, and the sheer terror of being obliterated, I was left gasping for breath. Staring up at the top of the stone, I wondered how much further I'd have to run. Suddenly, the top of the slab exploded, showering me with rubble. I bent over as my shoulders and back were pelted with rocks, when pain blossomed in the back of my head.

The world spun and blurred. I staggered to my feet in an attempt to run. In an instant, my knees impacted the ground. Bent over on all fours, the world became muted, as if a pillow covered my ears. My sight was doubled and shimmered. Stones still rained down on my back, yet it felt like it was happening miles away.

Someone was calling my name. I could barely hear them and had no idea where they were. Pushing myself up to answer, I fell back, leaning heavily against the broken slab that still rained dust and pebbles on me. A figure, or maybe three, was approaching. Then they disappeared, then only one would reappear. My vision blurred, and I didn't know how many were there. Every time I blinked, there were different numbers. I tried to shake my head to clear it. That turned out to be a huge mistake. Pain and nausea forced me to shut my eyes for a moment. When I opened them again, the figures coalesced into one person, someone I was happy yet frightened to see.

"Damn it, Henry! What were you thinking?" Mom growled. My vision solidified, and the Magic battle's roar returned to my ears. Mom's healing powers chased most of my pain away. Feeling much improved, I tried to stand, but Mom forced me to sit. "Rest for a second."

"I have to help Thorn," I protested.

"You will, as soon as I fix a few of your wounds. Now sit still." The way Mom spoke made me feel like a little kid being tended to after a fall. My patience was thoroughly tested. I was fine now. I needed to go, so I fidgeted and complained to the point I got scolded like a child. "We will help Thorn, but you'll be no help if you're hurt. Now *stop fussing*."

I hated feeling so childish and useless, but after a few moments, I felt whole again. Sheepishly, I thanked Mom as she pulled me to my feet. I shuddered, looking off to our right. "Thorn's getting tired. She needs us," I explained.

"Yes, I know," Mom agreed. "Reinforcements are coming, but we can assist Thorn until they arrive." We ducked around the stone we'd been sheltering behind. The amount of damage before us was astounding.

"Mom . . ." I cursed how young I felt and sounded, but the question wouldn't go unasked. "Can we beat her?"

"I don't know." Mom scanned the landscape. "Althea feels stronger than before, yet something seems to be missing." She took a deep breath and turned to face me. The look she gave me was more serious than I'd ever seen. "Listen, Henry—this may not end as you hope it will. Thorn may not—"

"I know, I know," I cut across her, shouting. I calmed myself. "I'm sorry." Mom didn't say anything, just nodded. I knew what could happen, but that didn't mean I accepted that outcome as a reality. When I opened my mouth to say something, the person I was addressing had resumed the role she'd taken when Wolf died. She might have been my mother, but right now, she donned the demeanor of the warrior elf general, the leader of our forces.

"This way. Stay close and keep your head down," Mom ordered. I followed, slightly amazed, watching the woman who raised me dart effortlessly across a battlefield. I felt like she was in her element here. She dove into a crater, and I quickly followed.

A thought struck me. "Who's coming?" I made a quick list in my head. Caterous was bewitched. Serina was grievously wounded, as was Tal. Wolf and Mr. Heraldry were dead. My father was in no condition to help. Would Scratch leave Serina? Would Doba allow Tal to come in his condition? Who was left to aid in the battle?

It seemed my mom was making the same list in her head. Finally, frowning, she said, "Only those who can."

"Well, that's helpful," I muttered. Then, stealing a glance over the crater's rim, I saw Thorn, and my pulse quickened. Her clothes were dirty and singed, but otherwise, she seemed okay. She was crouched behind a massive stone, throwing spells from around the side. I couldn't see Althea, but I could see where her Magic was coming from as it ate away at Thorn's protection, little by little.

Before I could move, the sounds of fighting ceased. Thorn hung her head, breathing heavily.

"Thorn, it seems some of your friends want to come out to play," Althea taunted. "I am sure you want to end this before you have to witness me killing them all."

The smoke and dust began to settle. "Thorn, let down the shield!" my mother called. I saw why. All around us were advancing troops of all races and sizes. Magic wielders protected them with barriers and shields. Thorn exhaled wearily and ceased her protection.

"Well, this ought to be fun." Althea laughed. Our troops were still far away, and Thorn was still in trouble. My mom stepped out to face the evil witch.

"Go help Thorn," Mom whispered to me. I glanced at my mom and saw the warning in her eyes, telling me these might be the last words we spoke to each other.

"Thank you for everything," I said, hiding the tears that threatened to fall. I quickly crossed the distance, sliding in next to Thorn.

"Ah, Mrs. Amelia Dreamweaver, is it now? Congratulations, and was that your whelp that just scampered to my daughter's side?" Althea taunted.

"*General* Dreamweaver," my mom corrected, holding her sword at the ready.

"A sword! Oh, Amelia dear, you've been out of the game too long." Althea set about conjuring a spell. I used this distraction to pour healing and stamina into Thorn, silently thanking my mother for doing the same for me earlier.

"You shouldn't be here," Thorn sighed as her body regained some vitality. The moment she felt strong enough, she batted my hands away. Then, stepping out to face Althea, Thorn turned to me. Her eyes thanked me, but they also told me the same thing my mother's had. This might be goodbye. Frustration and anger built, but Thorn decided my mom wouldn't die today.

"Oh, you useless hag. I can't believe you fell for that." Thorn drew Althea's attention to her and away from my mom.

Althea sneered at my mom as she turned her attention back to Thorn, who stood seemingly exhausted in front of her mother. The powerful witch leaned and practically lounged against the wall as she surveyed her daughter. Althea's eyes almost seemed disinterested in what Thorn was doing. I wanted to rush to Thorn's side, to support her however I could, but I stayed when Thorn signalled me to stay back. So instead, I scanned the approaching army for familiar faces.

I knew Serina's wounds were too severe. I wondered if Scratch could keep her alive and what effect that would have on his strength. I had to remind myself that Wolf was dead, as were so many brave souls. All of those deaths were caused by Althea, who was currently inspecting her nails as if all the fighting had nothing to do with her.

I looked at the evil witch and noticed someone sneaking up behind her. Someone let out a battle cry, and an arrow zinged toward Althea's head. She barely flicked one of her fingers, deflecting the projectile into the assassin who was close to slashing Althea with his sword. Thorn used that moment to send several spells at her mother.

"Your feeble attempts are even more disappointing than I thought." Althea yawned as she again deflected another weak attack from Thorn. "I bred you to have such power," Althea sighed and threw another series of spells at Thorn. Thorn's shield barely kept them from hitting her, and she fell to one knee.

I was joined by a heavily cloaked figure. Even though Serina's face was whole again, she was extremely pale. Scratch also arrived looking pale and sick. My mom stood with several elves casting protection spells on our archers and throwing whatever they could at Althea. Thorn fell again under an onslaught by her mother.

I was about to run to her when Serina's weak grip held my arm. "Wait for it," she breathed. Serina's eyes were barely open, and her breathing was shallow, yet power pulsed inside her. "When it happens . . ." Serina's grip tightened.

I glanced at Thorn. Her protection spell was shrinking with every strike.

Serina pulled my arm and I had to lean in close to hear her. "When it happens, you must protect Thorn at all costs." Serina's face screwed up in pain for a moment. Then, she relaxed and pulled me closer. "Even if it costs my life or yours." Before I could demand an explanation, Thorn screamed out my name.

"No, Henry! Don't interfere!" she cried, her face filled with horror. My shock was evident to Thorn and Althea.

While Althea's attention was devoted directly to me, Thorn's was not. A spell crashed through Althea's defense. However, it was only for a moment as I saw the shield immediately start to reform. Suddenly Althea screamed with fury. Thorn cast spell after spell at her mother, and each passed through the shell, hitting their target or bouncing inside the shield until they did.

"Help me," Seriana moaned. I finally realized she was casting a containment spell around Althea. My mind went blank. I couldn't remember the spell. "*Azarath*," Serina began. The word formed in my brain and then in my mouth. Althea was trying to force her way out of Serina's enchantment. I added my Magic in time to keep her there. Thorn fired spell after spell. Each slammed into her mother, knocking her to the ground.

Thorn was doing damage but not enough. Serina passed out from exertion while my body shook with fatigue. Thorn's spells were coming slower now, weaker, and Althea struggled to regain her feet.

"Looks like your little trick will not be enough," she taunted.

It was over. I knew it was. Thorn was spent, and my body was failing. Althea would be free, and we would die. I glanced at Thorn.

"I never did tell you I love you," I muttered.

"You can tell her when we're done," Scratch explained as he grabbed me under my arms to keep me standing. My mom was cradling Serina at my side, speaking in the elder tongue of the vampire. She tried to aid my exhausted, injured friend.

"We'll contain her," a vampire I recognized—Orlof—said, standing next to a badly injured Arrabetta. Before I could ask when he and several other vampires had arrived, their containment spell enveloped Althea.

My mother looked up from attending to Serina. "Take him to Thorn," she ordered Scratch.

"I'm so glad you're alive," I told Scratch as he helped me stumble over to Thorn.

"You want to keep me that way? Then you and Thorn need to work together," he shouted to me over the explosions and screams surrounding Althea.

Upon reaching Thorn, she was barely standing. Scratch grabbed her under her arm and held us both together. The instant my shoulder touched her and my arm encircled her back, I could feel her Magic. It was as strong as ever, yet her body and spirit were exhausted and needed help.

"Use my strength and hers to beat Althea," Scratch instructed.

I wasn't sure how I could fulfill his request, but I had to try. I turned so I could embrace both Thorn and Scratch. I focused on my friends, on their strengths and how much they mattered to me. Then I felt Scratch's energy moving into me, then through me, to Thorn. Her spells became more potent. I felt like we were one being, but something was missing. A part of us was empty. Then suddenly, it wasn't. Through the moving energy and feelings, I was aware of wings descending. Asha arrived with Serina and my mom. As soon as she was on the ground, Serina held tight to Scratch. Her other arm embraced me, her magic adding to Thorn's. My mom joined Serina. Scratch held onto my shoulder, and my mom held me around the waist as Serina hugged my chest. I wrapped both arms around Thorn, pulling her into a tight embrace.

Suddenly my mind seemed to detach as Magic exploded through me. I saw Caterous take Thorn's hand. However, it wasn't just Magic—specifically a certain addition *to* the Magic. I felt Caterous's love for Thorn, Scratch and Serina's love for each other, the love of parents for their children, the love of friends for each other, and the love that Thorn had for me. It was there, always there. It was familiar yet new. I knew it, but it was also unfamiliar. Thorn had finally allowed it to be released.

When I felt Thorn's love, I knew we'd won. I knew Althea would be defeated when Caterous shouted, "Thorn, take her Magic. You can do it."

Brilliant, blinding light flowed out of Althea into Thorn. Althea's scream increased in pitch until a shockwave sent us tumbling.

Scratch groaned as he pushed me off him. Thorn was still held tight in my arms. Serina was swept into her mother's arms as together they took flight. Smoke trailed after them as the sun regained the sky. Scratch crawled toward my unconscious mother, but I could see her breathing.

Althea knelt on the ground. She looked older and somehow lessened.

Lawrence Caterous sighed. "I had hoped you would get better. I hoped you would see a different path, a better life. But I know now there is no saving you."

"Sentimental fool, I never needed your saving," Althea spat. "When I regain my powers—"

Caterous sent a spell that surrounded the deranged woman, blocking her voice with a wave of a hand. We could see her screaming, but no sound escaped. I could only imagine the things she was describing she would do to us.

Thorn took a step toward the furious woman. "I am more powerful than you ever were or ever will be. You are not a sorceress or a witch. You're a pitiful old hag." Thorn spit on the ground next to the bubble.

Apparently, Althea could hear us. First, she looked shocked, then pleased, then that taunting face was laughing at her daughter.

Angrily, Thorn evaporated the shield.

I stepped in front of her. "What is it you wanted to say?" I demanded.

Althea spat contempt at her daughter, then turned to face me. "Stupid elf. You have given up your only hope for freedom. You should have stayed home to die," she snarled.

Thorn's hand shot up, and a dangerous fire ignited in her grip. The older woman cackled, slowly raising her hand.

"What is the little brat going to do? Are you going to kill me?"

I held my breath, but nothing happened. Instead, Althea's face melted from mocking self-assuredness to absolute fury. She flexed her fingers as her face contorted as she strained to conjure a spell. She chanted incantations, but nothing happened, only a faint greenish glow surrounded her.

"What's the matter?" Thorn taunted. "I guess you're just a useless old hag after all!"

"You horrid little bitch!" Althea flew at her daughter. "I will kill you like I should have done when I excreted you!"

Thorn cried out, falling backward. I had stepped between them. Althea's nails dug into my shoulder while her eyes glared at me with shocked fury. She was stronger than I thought she would be. My shoulder stung with pain. Still, my right hand held tight to my dagger even as Althea's weight bore down.

"You bastard!" She stopped fighting to move. I followed her gaze to her chest, where I had embedded my dagger deep.

Twisting the blade caused Althea to gasp in pain.

"You'll never hurt her again," I whispered in her ear.

My stomach clenched as Althea smirked at me. "This isn't over, boy," she hissed as the light left her eyes. Her body slowly sank to the ground. I stood there shaking, watching the blood drip from my dagger. From the corner of my eye I saw a flash of green. Thorn lay staring, shaking in fear or shock.

Caterous pulled Thorn to her feet, and I was suddenly aware that they were beside me. Thorn was saying something to me.

I turned to face her. "I'm sorry." That was all I could say. I had just killed her mother.

"Henry, you did what you had to do. You did the right thing," Caterous soothed. Still, there was pain in his eyes

"Thank you, Henry," Thorn said, staring at the corpse at my feet. "I'm finally free . . . of her." Although she never looked at me before she walked away.

CHAPTER 52

I was in a daze while the world around me seemed to move at the speed of light. Althea's remaining troops either surrendered or ran. The post-battle chaos of saving the wounded and identifying the dead began in earnest. Mom took up her position of general, moving troops to secure prisoners or help with the wounded.

When we were finally back in the village where Tal was elected leader, Scratch's father had been found nearly dead, missing an arm and a leg. He was brought back to be healed. My mom assured Scratch we would help in his recovery. Shortly after his father's arrival, Scratch, Serina, and Asha returned to the vampires. I saw Thorn several times, but we never seemed to have a moment to talk.

"She does not know what to say to you right now," Caterous said kindly. "She feels guilty that you had to be the one to end Althea's evil."

"Thorn defeated her her. I just stabbed her." I shrugged. I felt a bit guilty as well.

Tal and Doba were elected—I guess that's how they did it—to govern Haven. Thorn, Scratch, and I were all considered heroes and were to be welcomed at anytime. Tal also gave us anything we wanted from Wolf's library. One day I may take him up on the offer.

When my father was well enough to travel, I found myself back in the wagon where we had started the journey. Caterous and Thorn had traveled to the Capital to ensure the treaty would be honored. Mom and Dad were cautiously optimistic but still doubted equality was at hand. I found I had no energy to care.

A couple weeks had gone by. I was amazed at how quickly my mom returned to normal life, although there were moments when the general returned. She was more vocal about the treatment of the elves in our village. My dad and I now shared a dread of sleeping. We had nightmares we never discussed, yet we knew they were similar.

Then one evening, I was awakened by one of those nightmares when I heard a tapping at the window. I got up, but the window flew open before I could see if it was Serina. Energy crackled in my hands. It felt like I was always ready for battle. Serina stepped into my room and gave me a look that only she could create.

"For all you've done and seen, you're still the dumbest elf I've met," Serina said, clearly annoyed.

"You look fantastic!" I cried, giving her a hug.

Serina stiffened in my embrace for a moment. She was completely healed. I couldn't see any evidence of the damage from the battle, though I did notice a new addition to her left hand. The ring was small but held more promise than anything a thousand times the size.

Pushing me off, Serina couldn't help her smile as I pointed to the ring. Then her face turned serious. "Why haven't you gone to her?"

"I don't know if she wants to see—" My sentence was interrupted by a painful bonk on the head.

"She's worried you don't *want* to see her. *You're* worried she doesn't want to see *you*. You're both idiots," Serina huffed. "Talk to each other, and you'll see." Her tone turned softer. "Henry, you know you're unhappy without her. I know because she's unhappy without you."

"You're right. I'm just scared."

Again, I received a painful tap on the head. "You helped defeat the most dangerous witch in the world, and your best friend's *love* scares you?" Serina shook her head as she jumped onto the windowsill. "Just go talk to her." I couldn't argue because Serina was gone. But I made up my mind.

I was up early the next morning and back on the familiar path to the Caterous manor. Along the way, my nervousness faded as memories returned. Sticky Bat and hiding out in the woods. Suddenly my feet couldn't move fast enough. I took to the trees, leaping from one to the other in joyous abandon. I should have been paying attention. I leapt out to collide with something mid-air. Landing painfully on my back, I felt a familiar weight and magic on my chest.

I looked into those beautiful eyes I had fallen in love with years ago. Thorn sat on my hips, looking down at me. A small smile tugged at her mouth.

"Were you always such a klutz?" she asked as the smile spread.

"Me? You jumped at me first!" I tried to argue. However, I couldn't resist pulling her close into a hug. "I'm sorry," I mumbled in her ear.

"So am I."

"I should have come to see you sooner," we said in unison.

Before I could say anything else, I felt the softness of her lips on mine. I held her tighter as we kissed.

"We should have done that sooner as well." She smiled, getting up and pulling me to my feet. "Come on—Dad's asking about you." Hand in hand, we walked toward the house.

"Thank you, Serina," I muttered before sneaking another kiss.

ABOUT THE AUTHOR

SHAWN McLAIN started writing short stories in high school to entertain his friends. He used his creativity to entice volunteers at work to participate in extra hours and duties and add humor to memos and performance reviews. During this time, it was suggested he use this creativity to write a book, so he did.

Shawn wrote his first novel, *Respect the Dead*, in response to a popular zombie program. He wanted to see how normal people would react while not having the most disagreeable people always coming out on top. His second book was *Nothing is Certain*, another zombie story. Shortly after finishing his second book and starting work on a potential sequel to *Respect the Dead*, Shawn wrote *The Grey Girl: The Haunting of Sterben House*. The story follows a young woman who dies, then returns as a ghost trapped in a house of horrors. She is helped by a young man and his family to escape the evil and curse that bind her. Shortly after finishing what he thought to be a single story, fans of the story asked for a sequel. Two additional *Grey Girl* novels have also been published: *The Van Tassel Murders* and *The Saint Mary's Horror*, with the final book in the series already in revisions.

In addition to writing fiction, Shawn writes promotional commercials and wording for the Pennsylvania Cable Network.

www.ingramcontent.com/pod-product-compliance
Lightning Source LLC
Chambersburg PA
CBHW030404030726
47497CB00002B/479